P9-DNO-653

Sam Fisher works alone.
But fights for us all.

continued . . .

DEBT OF HONOR

*It begins with the murder of an American woman
in the back streets of Tokyo. It ends in war . . .*

"A SHOCKER."

—*Entertainment Weekly*

THE HUNT FOR RED OCTOBER

*The smash bestseller that launched Clancy's career—
the incredible search for a Soviet defector
and the nuclear submarine he commands . . .*

"BREATHLESSLY EXCITING." —*The Washington Post*

RED STORM RISING

*The ultimate scenario for World War III—
the final battle for global control . . .*

"THE ULTIMATE WAR GAME . . . BRILLIANT."

—*Newsweek*

PATRIOT GAMES

*CIA analyst Jack Ryan stops an assassination—
and incurs the wrath of Irish terrorists . . .*

"A HIGH PITCH OF EXCITEMENT."

—*The Wall Street Journal*

THE CARDINAL OF THE KREMLIN
*The superpowers race for the ultimate Star Wars
missile defense system . . .*

"*CARDINAL* EXCITES, ILLUMINATES . . . A REAL
PAGE-TURNER." —*Los Angeles Daily News*

CLEAR AND PRESENT DANGER
*The killing of three U.S. officials in Colombia ignites the
American government's explosive, and top secret, response . . .*

"A CRACKLING GOOD YARN." —*The Washington Post*

THE SUM OF ALL FEARS
*The disappearance of an Israeli nuclear weapon threatens the
balance of power in the Middle East—and around the world . . .*

"CLANCY AT HIS BEST . . . NOT TO BE MISSED."
—*The Dallas Morning News*

WITHOUT REMORSE
*His code name is Mr. Clark. And his work for the CIA
is brilliant, cold-blooded, and efficient . . . but who is he really?*

"HIGHLY ENTERTAINING." —*The Wall Street Journal*

Tom Clancy's
SPLINTER CELL®

WRITTEN BY
DAVID MICHAELS

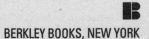
BERKLEY BOOKS, NEW YORK

THE BERKLEY PUBLISHING GROUP
Published by the Penguin Group
Penguin Group (USA) Inc.
375 Hudson Street, New York, New York 10014, USA
Penguin Group (Canada), 10 Alcorn Avenue, Toronto, Ontario M4V 3B2, Canada
(a division of Pearson Penguin Canada Inc.)
Penguin Books Ltd., 80 Strand, London WC2R 0RL, England
Penguin Group Ireland, 25 St. Stephen's Green, Dublin 2, Ireland (a division of Penguin Books Ltd.)
Penguin Group (Australia), 250 Camberwell Road, Camberwell, Victoria 3124, Australia
(a division of Pearson Australia Group Pty. Ltd.)
Penguin Books India Pvt. Ltd., 11 Community Centre, Panchsheel Park, New Delhi—110 017, India
Penguin Group (NZ), Cnr. Airborne and Rosedale Roads, Albany, Auckland 1310, New Zealand
(a division of Pearson New Zealand Ltd.)
Penguin Books (South Africa) (Pty.) Ltd., 24 Sturdee Avenue, Rosebank, Johannesburg 2196,
South Africa

Penguin Books Ltd., Registered Offices: 80 Strand, London WC2R 0RL, England

This is a work of fiction. Names, characters, places, and incidents either are the product of the author's imagination or are used fictitiously, and any resemblance to actual persons, living or dead, business establishments, events, or locales is entirely coincidental.

TOM CLANCY'S SPLINTER CELL®

A Berkley Book / published by arrangement with Rubicon, Inc.

PRINTING HISTORY
Berkley edition / December 2004

ISBN: 0-425-20168-6

BERKLEY®
Berkley Books are published by The Berkley Publishing Group,
a division of Penguin Group (USA) Inc.,
375 Hudson Street, New York, New York 10014.
BERKLEY is a registered trademark of Penguin Group (USA) Inc.
The "B" design is a trademark belonging to Penguin Group (USA) Inc.

PRINTED IN THE UNITED STATES OF AMERICA

10 9 8 7 6 5

ACKNOWLEDGMENTS

The author and publisher wish to acknowledge the work of Raymond Benson, whose invaluable contribution to this novel is immeasurable. Many thanks go to Ubisoft Entertainment personnel Mathieu Ferland, Alexis Nolent, and Olivier Henriot for their cooperation and support. Finally, a big thank-you each goes to Joe Konrath for his input and to James McMahon for his expertise.

1

IT'S like being in a state of nonexistence. A vacuum. Darkness and light at the same time, and no sense of gravity. There's no air, but I know I'm breathing. Certainly no sounds are present. I see and feel nothing. There are no dreams.

That's what sleep is like for me. I'm blessed, I suppose. I can will myself to sleep anywhere, anytime. I didn't train to do it. It's always been that way, ever since I was a kid. I simply tell myself, "It's time to sleep now." And I do it. I'm sure a lot of people in the world would envy this talent. I don't take it for granted because in my business I have to catch sleep in the strangest places and at the oddest times.

I feel the pulsating pressure on my wrist. It gently pulls me out of this dimensionless world, and I slowly regain the use of my senses. I feel the warm metal against my face. I hear far-off nondescript echoes.

The OPSAT attached to my wrist continues to wake me. There's a little T-shaped rod that protrudes from the flexible band when the silent "alarm" goes off. The rod rocks back and forth, nudging my pulse, telling my body that it's time to rouse. When I first saw it demonstrated, it reminded me of a James Coburn spy movie from the sixties in which he played a secret agent who could stop his heart on command. This apparently put him in some kind of hibernation. He had a wristwatch with the same kind of T-shaped rod that poked him until he woke up. I remember laughing in the movie theater when I saw that. It was too ridiculous to take seriously. Now look at me.

I take a few deep breaths. The air is stale and dry inside the ventilation shaft where I spent the last six hours. I flex my hands to get the blood circulating once again. I stretch my feet, even though they're enclosed snugly in my boots.

Then I open my eyes.

There's no more light in the shaft than there was when I first climbed into it.

The OPSAT finishes its duty and the little T-shaped rod retracts. I bring my left hand to my face and press the button to illuminate the OPSAT's screen. There are no new messages from Lambert. No incoming e-mail. All's quiet in the world.

The OPSAT is a handy little device that Third Echelon dreamed up for its agents. It's really called an Operational Satellite Uplink. Primarily a tool for communication, it has many other uses as well. I particularly like the camera capabilities that allow me to snap digital pics of anything I want.

I'm suddenly aware of how hot it is and I remember where I am. The ventilation shaft of the Tropical Casino in Macau. I'm lying horizontally in a space slightly smaller than a phone booth. It's a good thing I'm not claustrophobic or I'd be a basket case by now. Since I had to wait for the right time to make my move, I set the alarm to wake me at four in the morning. I figured that's when activity inside the casino would be at its most muted. It's a twenty-four–hour joint, so there's always going to be someone here.

I'm sweating like a pig inside my custom-made uniform. I forgot to adjust the temperature control before going to sleep. I quickly turn the knob at my belt to make it cooler. Immediately I can feel the cold water flowing through the vessels embedded within the uniform's lining. The military calls it an "Objective Force Warrior" uniform. It's like an astronaut's suit, only sleeker and tighter. I can make it cold or hot, depending on what kind of environment I'm in. It's made of a heavy material with Kevlar sewn into it, yet it's flexible enough for me to perform any gymnastic feat I wish to attempt. I wouldn't call it bullet-proof, but it's close. The tough outer hide feels like elephant skin to the touch, and it goes a long way toward deflecting stuff. I suppose if I were shot at point blank I'd be dead, but bullets fired from a range of fifteen feet or more *might* penetrate the suit but not me. The Kevlar acts as a braking mechanism. Pretty cool stuff. Another interesting feature is that it's got photosensitive threading that reacts when a targeting laser strikes the material. The suit sends a signal to my OPSAT, alerting me that I'm in a sniper's gun sight.

My only beef with the uniform is that it's so tight fitting and neat that it makes me look like a comic book superhero. Even my special headpiece looks like a mask when I have the goggles down.

I pull the straw from the tube in the collar and suck refreshing cold water from the supply stored in the bladders distributed evenly throughout the suit. There's enough water in there to last twelve hours as long as I use it sparingly. It's an odd concept, but I have to "fill up my uniform" every so often.

Time for a little energy. I raise my body enough so I can reach into the Osprey strapped to my back and pull out a ration. The food in those things tastes a lot like the MREs the army gets, so there's a variety of stuff—from Cajun-style rice and beans to spaghetti to grilled chicken breast. Maybe some of that stuff is actually in the recipes. The one I happen to pick resembles trail mix.

As I munch on the delicacy, I recall how I got here and what the hell I'm supposed to be doing.

I had entered the casino during the early evening, just as the big crowds were beginning to populate the place. I wore street clothes and figured I'd be less noticeable when a lot of people were here. Casinos in Macau are different from other ones around the world. The Chinese take their gambling very seriously. There's never any shouting of "Jackpot," much less any hint of smiles from these people. They look as if they'd just as soon shoot you as deal you a card. It's par for the course, I guess. Triads hang out in Macau casinos, and I've never seen a cheerful Triad. Given the fact that since 1999 Macau was no longer a Portuguese colony and was now one of the Special Administrative Regions of China, I could imagine that the inhabitants were not very happy. Like Hong Kong, Macau was now part of Communist China, even though the Chinese government promised that things would remain relatively the same for the next fifty years. It was still unclear what the colony's underworld was doing about the handover. During the twentieth century, Macau had developed a reputation as a hotbed of spies, vice, and intrigue.

I played a few games, lost a little money, gained some of it back, and then went to the washroom across from the broom closet I needed. I had memorized the building plans before the mission commenced. I could make my way around the casino blindfolded if I had to.

I slipped out of the washroom when I sensed no one was in the hallway and moved to the broom closet door. I had to use a lock pick to open it. Luckily, it wasn't a high-tech lock. After all, it really was just a broom closet.

Once I was inside, I locked the door and proceeded to remove the street clothes, revealing my funky superhero uniform underneath. I folded the clothes and tucked them neatly in the Osprey backpack. I donned the headpiece and was set to go. The change from Clark Kent to Superman had taken me about forty seconds.

I climbed a tool shelf to reach the ventilation shaft opening, gently pried off the grill cover, and hung it on a nail on the wall. I tested the strength of the structure to make sure it would hold my weight and then pulled myself in. I could just barely turn myself around to reach out, grab the grill cover, and fasten it back on the shaft from the inside. I did another about-face and crawled silently through the shaft until I came to a spot that was sufficient for a nap. And here I am.

I finish my meal and eat the digestible wrapper so I won't leave any trace of my being here. I doubt anyone is going to look inside the ventilation shaft, but one never knows.

Time to act.

I crawl farther along the shaft, make the left turn I know is coming, go about twenty yards, hook a right, and then shimmy down a vertical drop for ten feet. On the next level the shaft goes in three directions. I tap the OPSAT for the compass mode just to confirm that the tunnel on my left is the westerly direction, and then I crawl that way. One more right turn and I can see the grill at the end of the shaft. The casino president's office.

I peer through the grill to make sure the office is dark and uninhabited. I carefully push the grill off but hold on to it. I don't want a loud clang when I drop it. I worm my upper body out of the shaft and gently place the grill behind a sofa directly beneath me. I then clutch the bottom of the shaft opening, roll my lower back and hips out, and somersault onto the carpeted floor. So far, so good.

I push the goggles over my eyes and switch on the night-vision mode. No need to turn on any lights and attract attention. Being quiet and invisible are the two main rules in my profession. Get the job done without being seen or noticed. If I'm caught, the U.S. government will deny any knowledge of my existence. I'd be on my own, in the hands of a foreign agency with no legal recourse or means of escape except with what I can manage to achieve with my body and mind. It's a test I don't particularly want to take, even though I've studied for it for years. There are always trick questions in that kind of test.

I go straight for the computer on the president's expansive mahogany desk, power it up, and tap my fingers impatiently while I wait for the system to load. When it asks for the password, I type in the one that Carly assured me would work—and sure enough, it does. Carly St. John is a wizard when it comes to technical shit. She can hack into any system, anywhere. And she can do it from her desk in Washington, D.C.

Using the Search function, I quickly find the folders I want. They contain files of payoff records to various organizations and individuals. I have to make sure these are separate from the legitimate casino expenses, and Carly has briefed me on how to tell the difference. Once again, the telltale flags she mentioned are there, so I know I'm in the right place.

I unzip the pouch on my left leg calf and remove a link that I insert into the computer's floppy drive. The other end I plug into my OPSAT. A touch of a few buttons and *voilà*—the files begin to copy onto my portable device. It takes only a minute or so.

As the OPSAT does its work, I think about Dan Lee, the Third Echelon man who was murdered in this casino three months ago. He was tracking illegal arms sales in China, and the trail led him here to Macau. The Shop, of course, are the guys doing the dealing. Before he was killed, Lee had given Lambert proof that the Tropical Casino's accounting department was being used as a front for the illegal transactions. Shutting down the Shop is one of our primary directives, and the only way to do it is to work from the outer ends of the pipelines back to the source. And there are lots of pipelines, all over the globe. Uncovering them is only half the battle. Now, with these files listing the Shop's customers in our possession, other U.S. agencies can act on closing this particular pipeline.

We still don't know exactly what happened to Dan Lee. A Chinese recruit, Lee had worked for the NSA for something like seven years. I never knew him personally—we never meet the other agents in Third Echelon—but I understand he was a stand-up guy. He did his job well and was a good man. Lambert thought that someone in the Shop had learned of his identity and lured him to the casino with information as bait. Lee never left the casino.

The OPSAT finishes the transfer just as I hear noise in the hallway outside. Shit. I pull the link out of the computer. Keys rattle in the door and I hear a voice followed by a laugh. There are two of them. I have no time to shut down the computer, but I hit the monitor's Off button.

I leap away from the desk and eye the distance to the ventilation shaft. The key turns in the lock. There's no time for that route. I scamper up a set of filing cabinets and press myself into the corner, my head against the ceiling. It's a difficult position to hold. I have to use my knee against the top of the filing cabinets to leverage myself while at the same time pushing with my arms on the two walls to anchor my body. It isn't comfortable. Just as I settle myself, the door opens. Maybe they won't notice me since I'm some four or five feet above their heads.

I recognize the first guy, the one with the keys. It's Kim Wei Lo, probably the mastermind behind the Shop's operation in Macau. He's on the wanted lists for all the three-letter agencies—you know, the CIA, the FBI, the NSA . . . When the other guy turns slightly, I make him, too. He's Chen Wong, Lo's bodyguard. Wong is a big guy, but I've seen bigger. If it came down to a face-off, I'm pretty sure I could take him.

Lo hits one of the two light switches on the wall by the door. The fluorescents directly over the desk blink on. Thank God he didn't switch on the other one. My side of the room would've been showered with illumination. At least I'm still in the shadows. If they look up and focus on the back wall, corner and ceiling, they'll see me hanging there like a spider.

The two men go to the desk and Lo says something in Chinese. I catch the word "computer," so I figure he's wondering why someone didn't shut it down for the night. It doesn't bother him too much, though. He sits at the desk and begins to work while Wong paces slowly behind him, gazing out the large glass window that overlooks the main drag cutting through this poor excuse for a city. An *urban area* is a more appropriate term. As it's the middle of the night, there isn't much traffic or neon lights. I hope something will mesmerize him enough that he'll keep his back to me while I wait this out.

As a precaution, though, I mentally practice drawing

my Five-seveN from where I am, but, ultimately, I don't think it's possible without falling to the floor. I have a directive not to kill anyone if I don't have to. Unfortunately, I've had to disobey that directive on numerous occasions. I don't like doing it, but sometimes you gotta do what you gotta do.

It's hot in the room. They must shut off the AC at night. Or maybe it's a ruse to get gamblers to buy more drinks. I'm dying to adjust the temperature in my uniform, but I don't dare move. I can feel the sweat building underneath my headpicce, and it's starting to trickle down my face.

Shit. Wong turns and walks aimlessly around the desk and heads my way. He's drawn his own pistol—it looks like a Smith & Wesson .38 from here—and he's twirling it in his hand, Western-style. He does an abrupt turn and faces a bookshelf. As he continues to twirl the gun, Wong scans the titles of the books. I guess the guy really can read.

Lo says something and Wong grunts in reply. He docsn't walk back to the desk, though, damn it. Instead, he moves away from the books and starts ambling toward the filing cabinets. All he has to do is glance up and he'll see me for sure. The carpet must be awfully interesting, though, because he's keeping his head down. It's as if he's watching his feet as he walks.

Oh, for Christ's sake, he's standing right beneath me now. Most of my body is above the filing cabinet, but my head and shoulders extend away from the wall, flat against the ceiling. Just don't look up, you bastard.

I feel a bead of sweat run down the bridge of my nose. Aw, fuck. I can't wipe it. I can't even move. That little drop of salt water builds up on the very tip of my nose, threatening to fall right on Wong's head. My breathing stops. Time stands still.

And then the drop of sweat falls and hits his square, crew-cut head. He notices it, too. He reaches up, feels the moisture, and slowly arches his head back to look at the ceiling.

I shove off the walls and pile-drive the man to the floor. He drops his Smith & Wesson along the way. For hand-to-hand combat, I exclusively use Krav Maga, an Israeli technique that literally means "contact combat." It's not so much a self-defense martial art as it is a no-holds-barred system for survival in any situation. It combines elements of Eastern disciplines, such as karate, judo, and kung fu, with basic boxing and down-and-dirty maneuvers. It's taught and used by the Israel Defense Forces, the Israeli National and Military Police, and other anti-terror/special forces in Israel. Since its development by Imi Lichtenfeld after World War II, Krav Maga has emigrated all over the world and is now widely taught alongside other martial arts. Krav Maga isn't a competitive sport—it's a fight for your life. The whole idea is not only to defend yourself but also to do as much damage as possible to your opponent as quickly as you can.

So with Wong on the floor beneath me, I ram my forehead, goggles and all, into his face as hard as I can. He screams in agony as the edge of the goggles rips into his skin. I chop him hard in the throat for good measure, but he moves too quickly. My knuckles don't connect with his Adam's apple, so I only succeed in hurting him rather than killing him. The big guy rolls and throws me off as if I'm a blanket. In an instant we're both standing and ready for more.

By now Lo has stood and drawn a gun of his own. It's some kind of semiautomatic—I can't tell for sure what it is because things are moving way too fast. He points it at me and I reach for Wong's shirt collar. I pull him toward me, swinging his body around so he's between the desk and me. Lo's gun fires and Wong jerks as the bullet penetrates his spine and bursts out through his sternum. I feel its heat as the round whizzes past my ear and embeds itself in the wall behind me. The blood follows a split second later, splashing me in the face and chest.

I'm still holding on to Wong, so I shove him backward toward the desk. His body crashes over it and knocks the computer monitor into Lo, who by now realizes he killed the wrong guy. He panics and makes a run for the door. I anticipate this and beat him to it. Lo isn't a fighter—he's more of a brains guy, so he isn't equipped to handle the chokehold I lock around his head. My arm muffles his cries as I pop his head forward, snapping the surprisingly brittle bones in his neck. He collapses to the floor just as the sound of running boots outside grows louder. There's no time to get into the ventilation shaft, so I press myself flat against the wall next to the door.

It bursts open and three armed security guards rush inside to find Lo and Wong dead on the floor. Their shock and dismay give me the opportunity to slip out behind them through the open door. There's no way I can do it without detection, though. One of them shouts something like "There he is!" and the guards are after me.

I run down the corridor to the staircase I know is straight ahead. It's the only way out at this point. Instead of taking the steps, I leap over the rail and land in a crouching position in the middle of the lower flight. I take the remaining steps three at a time and I'm on the ground floor. By now, of course, a few more guards have been alerted to my presence. In fact, one guy is running at me from the direction of the big gaming room. He shouts and

I dart toward him. He pulls a Smith & Wesson out of his holster, but I leap at the corridor wall, bounce off of it by kicking with the soles of my boots, and propel myself into him. He tumbles back as I gracefully land on my finger-tips, do a split-second handstand, and then jackknife in the air to alight on my feet.

The nearest exit is the front door of the building. To get there I have to traverse the gaming room. Unlike many Macau casinos, the Tropical has one big gaming room—much like the casinos in Las Vegas—whereas others in Macau might have separate rooms for different games. Here you have blackjack, roulette, poker, baccarat, slot machines, and a couple of weird Chinese gambling games I've never heard of, all in one big space. At this hour there aren't many patrons, so I decide to give them something to talk about when they go to work the next day. I run into the room and dart through an aisle of blackjack tables.

The place is deadly silent. The fifteen or so gamblers look up from their various games and stare, open-mouthed. The dealers are too shocked to move. Who's this *gweilo* in the funny military costume running through the casino? The two guards at the front of the room, though, react differently. They draw their pistols and aim at me, not bothering to shout to the patrons to drop to the floor. As one guard takes a bead, I leap onto a blackjack table and dodge a bullet. I jump to the next table, spraying a pile of chips in all directions, and then bounce to another one as the second guard's gun erupts. I feel like a frog on lily pads.

Part of my extensive training with Third Echelon involved learning to utilize my surroundings to propel myself quickly. I can use walls, furniture, and human beings as push-off points in order to get across an obstacle course. When I saw other guys doing it, I immediately thought of pinballs doing their thing inside arcade machines—and that's precisely the concept behind the technique. It's especially effective when someone's shooting at you. A moving target that haphazardly changes direction is truly difficult to hit.

Now that the bullets are flying, the casino guests naturally shout in fear and cower. Some are smart enough to fall to the ground as I spring past them. The two guards, now blocking my exit, are firing their weapons indiscriminately, hoping to land a lucky shot. I have no choice but to act offensively. I duck behind a table, draw my Five-seveN and release the safety. It's the Fabrique Nationale Herstal tactical model with a single-action trigger and a twenty-round magazine that holds 5.7×28mm ss190 ammunition. The rounds offer good penetration against modern body armor while keeping the weapon's weight, dimensions, and recoil at reasonable levels. The damage the rounds do to unarmored bodies is something to behold. It's a weapon I don't like to use in full-scale firefights, though. It has a fairly limited range, so I mostly use it in situations where I know I'll have the advantage. Like this one.

I reach around the bottom leg of the table and fire—*one, two*—hitting both guards in the chest. Now the way is clear for me to rush the exit. I stand and move forward, leaping over one of the bodies as I do so.

I hear a shouted command behind me, followed by more gunfire. I glance back and see three more security guards running into the room. Damn, where did all these guys come from at this time of night? You'd think that at four in the morning they'd keep just one or two on duty to save money. I suppose bad guys all over the world retain guards in reserve for that one instance when an American operative barges through HQ in the middle of the night.

I reach for the pocket on my right outer thigh and remove a smoke grenade, one of the more harmless ones. I carry a couple of different types of smoke grenades—one that only produces dark smoke to cover my tracks, and another one filled with CS, or what tongue-twister lovers call O-chlorobenzalmalononitrile gas. That stuff is nasty. Exposure to CS gas causes violent respiratory seizure, and prolonged contact produces unconsciousness. I pull the ring and toss the grenade behind me and wait for the loud pop. The thing works surprisingly fast. Black smoke fills the gaming room in less than five seconds. It's almost as if someone simply turned off the lights. With my goggles on I'm spared the eye irritation and can also see the archway out of the room.

I run into the casino's main lobby and past a couple of frightened patrons. The entrance guards must have left their posts to chase me in the gaming room, because I'm home free. I push the glass doors open and bolt down the steps to the street. It's still dark, of course, but lighting from the street lamps illuminates the area quite well. The few casinos on the street are still open. It will be a matter of minutes, maybe seconds, before more trouble appears on the scene.

I make my way around the building to the small parking lot and go to the first SUV I see. It's a Honda, one of their luxury utility vehicles. I drop to the cement and roll underneath the car. Taking hold of the chassis, I pull myself up and lodge my body into the crevice so I can't be seen from ground level. I spring a hook that's embedded in my belt buckle and latch it on to the chassis to help hold me in place.

Sure enough, I hear running footsteps and shouts. The

guards make it outside and begin to search the parking lot thoroughly. I imagine the looks of bewilderment on their faces. Where the hell did he go? He couldn't have disappeared so quickly!

I see feet run past the SUV. More shouts. More confusion. The guards' boss is yelling at them, cursing in Chinese. It's going to be his head for this! Find that *gweilo* now! More feet patter by as the men search up and down the aisles of cars.

It takes them ten minutes before they give up. They figure the intruder must have gone in another direction. I wait another five minutes to make sure it's completely quiet, and then I lower myself to the cement. I look around for signs of people's feet. Nothing. I roll out from under the Honda, look both ways, and then rise to a crouching position. I slowly lift my head over the hood and survey the parking lot. I'm alone.

I leave the property the way I came, using the shadows to mask my presence. I move like a tomcat, quiet and unobtrusive, sticking to walls and street objects. Stealth is the name of the game and I'm damned good at it.

As missions go, this one went relatively smoothly. No mission is "easy," per se. They all have their challenges. I can't take anything for granted and I must be certain that I do my job invisibly. That's what being a Splinter Cell is all about. Leave no footprints. Get in. Get out. You're done.

A Splinter Cell works alone. A remote team monitors and supports me—professionals that are damned good at their jobs, too—but it's my ass that's out there in the line of fire. Every move must be thought out as if the field were a gigantic chessboard. A single mistake can be fatal.

I like to think I don't make mistakes. I'm Sam Fisher. I am a Splinter Cell.

2

LIEUTENANT Colonel Dirk Verbaken looked at his watch and decided to get going. He had forty minutes before the rendezvous—more than enough time—but he had to allow for unforeseen surprises.

He stood, picked up his briefcase, and walked out of his office. He addressed his personal assistant with a simple "I'll be at lunch." She nodded and noted the time. Verbaken walked down the hall, pausing at the door to the men's room. He nudged the door ajar but didn't go in. Verbaken felt a twinge of trepidation as he looked around to make sure no one was watching. Then he skirted across the hall to the File Room. He knew it would be empty at this time of day.

Rules at the Intelligence and Security Staff Department were very strict, especially when it came to removing files from the building. Anyone wishing to take something from the File Room had to perform a bureaucratic song and dance that involved way too much red tape. A paper trail was kept and the chances of questions coming up were great. It was best for him simply to take what he wanted and smuggle it out. After lunch he could reverse the procedure, replace the file in the cabinet, and no one would be the wiser. After all, he was one of the top-ranking officials in the department, having been with the Belgian Military Intelligence and Security Service for ten years.

Verbaken went to the cabinet marked "B" and used his own key to unlock it. He pulled the drawer out and quickly thumbed through the manila folders until he found the one he wanted. He removed the folder, shut the drawer, and locked the cabinet. He moved to a worktable, and then slipped the folder inside his briefcase. After snapping the case shut, he walked swiftly to the File Room door. Verbaken opened it slightly and peered out. All clear. He moved into the hall and walked toward the elevators, pushing open the men's room door as he passed it. His assistant was most likely paying no attention, but at least he had gone through the motions of using the washroom before going out.

It was a beautiful day in Brussels. Verbaken left his discreetly disguised building, which was located just off the Grand-Place, the magnificent square that was considered the centerpiece of the city. Symbols of Belgium's royal history bordered the Grand-Place on all four sides, and Verbaken, a native Belgian, was usually impressed daily by the marvelous display of ornamental gables, gilded facades, medieval banners, and gold-filigreed rooftop sculptures. Today, however, the dazzling sights of the fifteenth-century Gothic Town Hall, the seventeenth-century neo-Gothic King's House, and the Brewers Guild House meant nothing to him. His mind was elsewhere.

Verbaken walked briskly through the colorful, narrow, cobblestoned streets to the intersection of Rue de Chêne and Rue de L'Etuve. He paid no attention to the tourists who were snapping pictures of the famous statue of the urinating little boy known as *Manneken-Pis*. Verbaken glanced at his watch and noted that he was still on time. There was no need to hurry, so he decided to stop momentarily and stand with the crowd. He was pretty good at spotting a tail, and he carefully scanned the people that had been behind him. He didn't think he had anything to worry about, so he moved on.

Verbaken eventually arrived at the Metropole, the only nineteenth-century hotel in the famed city. Located in the heart of Brussels' historical Place de Brouckère, the Hotel Metropole was more like a palace than a hotel. Verbaken had always wanted to have a second honeymoon there with his wife. She loved the mixture of styles that infused the interior with an air of luxury and richness of materials—paneling, polished teak, Numidian marble, gilded bronze, and forged iron. The place had a decidedly soothing ambience.

Once he was inside the building, Verbaken felt more comfortable with what he was about to do.

ON the sidewalk in front of the hotel, two men dressed in expensive Armani business suits sat at a small round table with cups of coffee. The Metropole Café was a popular spot for lunch on weekdays and today was no different. All the tables were full and businessmen and tourists waited impatiently in line for the next available space. The two men didn't care. They took their time as they sipped their coffees.

One of them, a Russian known only as "Vlad," motioned to the waiter. In French he ordered a dish of ice cream. The waiter looked a bit perturbed, since the two men had been occupying the table for over an hour and hadn't ordered more than coffee—and now ice cream. But the waiter smiled, said, "*Merci*," and walked away to the kitchen. Vlad looked at his companion and shrugged.

The other man, a Georgian who went by the name of "Yuri," started to say there wasn't enough time for dessert but decided instead to stay silent.

Yuri checked his pocket to make sure the passkey was still there. The Metropole still used old-fashioned skeleton keys for the rooms, and it had been a simple matter to steal a master from one of the maids earlier that morning.

Several minutes went by and still neither man said a word to the other. The waiter brought the ice cream and, as a hint, laid the bill on the table. Vlad almost complained that they weren't ready to leave yet, but Yuri gave him a look. Vlad thanked the waiter and smiled.

As Vlad scooped the dessert into his mouth, Yuri continued to scan the pedestrians on the sidewalk. It was the usual midday crowd—businessmen, tourists, beautiful women, not-so-beautiful women . . . and then he spotted the mark.

Yuri nudged Vlad with his foot. Vlad looked up and saw a man carrying a briefcase make his way through the café to the front doors of the hotel.

Dirk Verbaken.

Vlad quickly put money on the table, took one last spoonful of ice cream, and stood with Yuri. They both adjusted their neckties and then discreetly followed the lieutenant colonel inside.

An objective observer might guess that the two Russians were bankers, for they appeared to be men that worked with money. Perhaps they were lawyers. Or maybe they were corporate executives from very large firms. They exuded an air of sophistication, worldliness, and wealth, and that was precisely the image they wanted to project.

None of it, of course, was true.

VERBAKEN knocked on the door and noticed movement in the peephole. After a moment the door opened to reveal a stocky American in his thirties. He was dressed in a T-shirt and sweatpants with a wet towel hung around his neck. Beside his left leg he carried a .22 caliber Beretta Bobcat.

"Lieutenant Colonel Verbaken," the man said.

"Hello." The Belgian spoke fluent English.

"Come in." The man held the door open and Verbaken stepped into the room. The man shut the door and locked it, then turned to Verbaken with his hand out. "It's good to finally meet you in person. Rick Benton."

Verbaken shook Benton's hand and said, "I think I pictured you older."

"I'll take that as a compliment," Benton said. "Please sit down. Can I get you something to drink?" He led Verbaken into the suite's sitting room, which was equipped with a large wooden desk, a minibar, a television, a glass-top coffee table, green chairs and a sofa, a cupboard with a full-length mirror, potted plants, and a large window that opened onto a terrace.

"Some water is fine if you have it. You know, I've lived in Brussels all my life, but I've never been in a room in the Metropole," Verbaken said.

"It's a very nice place," Benton said. He went to the minibar, fetched two bottles of springwater, and joined

Verbaken. He looked at the Belgian and asked, "I assume you brought it?"

Verbaken nodded. He set his briefcase on his lap, opened it, and handed the file to Benton. "I've got a little less than an hour," he said.

Benton glanced at the number of pages in the folder and said, "Shouldn't be a problem. I can snap pictures of each page with this." He showed Verbaken the Operational Satellite Uplink that the NSA provided to him.

"I don't suppose you ever met the subject in question?" Benton asked.

Verbaken shook his head. "No, no, that was before my time. I joined the service a couple of years after the man was killed. There may be one or two of the senior staff who knew him. Very interesting guy."

Benton nodded and snapped a shot of the first page. "Have you heard any more about our friends in the Middle East?"

"No more than what you already have. I'm still looking into it, though. You might say it's a pet project of mine," Verbaken answered. "Have you been to Belgium before?"

"Yes, a while back. I wouldn't mind being stationed in Europe instead of in that cesspool over in the Middle East," Benton said. "Believe me, this is a *vacation* coming here." He continued snapping pictures of the file's pages with the OPSAT.

Verbaken chuckled. "I can imagine."

"Have you ever been to the States?"

"Three times. My wife and I—" Verbaken was interrupted by a knock at the door. The man froze and his eyes widened.

Benton held up his hands. "Don't worry. I ordered myself some lunch. That's room service." He grabbed the small Beretta and went to the door. After looking through the peephole, Benton opened the door to a small man in a white coat.

"Room service," the man said in English.

"Bring it right in," Benton said, holding the door open. The waiter rolled in a cart that held three covered dishes. "Put it over there by the window." Benton looked at Verbaken and asked, "Would you like to order some lunch?"

"No, no thank you," Verbaken replied. "I'm not very hungry."

"Suit yourself." After the waiter placed the cart, Benton tipped him and showed him out the door. Once again he locked the door and resumed his position over the file. "You were saying?"

"Hmm? Oh, yes. America." Verbaken took a sip of water. "My wife and I went on our honeymoon there. New York City. Fascinating place."

Benton took another shot and then took the time to examine the contents of his meal. He laid the pistol on the bed and lifted the lids on the food. "Mmm. Looks pretty good. Creamed potato soup with smoked eel, salmon flaky pastry with Sevruga caviar, asparagus, and a bottle of Duvel beer. Can't beat that, eh?"

"I'm sure it's delicious."

"Sure you don't want anything?"

"I'm fine, thank you."

Benton frowned. "Wait a second. I asked for a basket of bread. And butter. Damn." He went to the phone, picked up the receiver, and punched the button for room service.

"Yeah, this is Mr. Benton in 505. I ordered some bread and butter with my lunch. It's not on the tray. Uh-huh. Okay, thanks." He hung up and moved back to the file to snap another photo. "They're sending it up."

"Go ahead and eat," Verbaken said. "I don't mind."

Benton smiled and left the OPSAT on the table with the file. He moved to the cart but was stopped by the sound of a key in the door.

"That was fast," Verbaken said.

"A little too fast if you ask me." Benton leaped for the Beretta, but the door exploded inward before he could reach it. Yuri thrust the suppressor-fitted barrel of a Heckler & Koch VP70 in Benton's face, preventing him from reacting.

"Don't move, gentlemen," Yuri said, keeping the gun trained on Benton. "Back up, please, and raise your hands high above your head." With his other hand he placed the hotel's master passkey back into his pocket.

Benton did as he was told. Verbaken went pale.

Vlad drew a gun of his own, a Glock, and pointed it at the Belgian. "Don't get up on our account," the Russian said.

"Who are you? What do you want?" Verbaken whispered.

Vlad struck the man across the face with the Glock. "I didn't say to talk," he said.

Verbaken held his hands to his cheek and bent forward.

"Keep your hands in the air, please," Vlad ordered.

The Belgian complied, revealing an ugly scrape on the left side of his face.

Yuri motioned to the sofa. "Sit down over there, please," he said to Benton. "Keep your hands up."

Benton moved slowly around the coffee table, next to the food cart. With the speed of a cat he grabbed a knife from the cart and threw it at Yuri. The Russian, however, was faster. He snapped his body sideways as the knife flew past him and hit the wall. The Heckler & Koch recoiled twice—*thwack thwack*. Benton jerked backward and crashed into the food cart, creating a sickening cacophony of breaking glass and clanging pans. The American eventually rolled off the cart and fell to the floor, facedown.

In a panic Verbaken jumped to his feet and ran toward the door. *Thwack thwack*. This time Vlad's silenced Glock performed the dirty work. The Belgian slammed into the door and slid down slowly, leaving a bloody smear.

After a few silent seconds, Yuri observed, "Well, that didn't go very well."

"Not too smooth," Vlad agreed. "Messy."

"We'd better hurry. That made a lot of noise."

Vlad nodded and went to the copier. He took the sheets of paper from the table—the stack that had already been photographed and the pages that hadn't. He put the paper back in the manila folder, picked up Benton's OPSAT, and dropped it on the carpet. He then lifted his hard-heeled shoe and brought it down forcefully, smashing the device.

"Do we need anything else?" he asked his partner.

"Look in the bedroom. See if his laptop is there. Bring the American's weapon if you can find it quickly," Yuri answered. Vlad grunted and went into the bedroom. Yuri walked over to Benton's corpse and kicked the man's head.

"Fuck you," he muttered.

Vlad returned with a laptop and a Five-seveN, the weapon of choice for NSA intelligence officers. "Look what I found."

"Good. Now let's get out of here."

After cracking the door open, Yuri made a quick check of the hallway. He nodded to his partner and they left, shutting the door behind them.

Three minutes went by before there was a knock at the door again. The silence prompted another knock.

"Room service." It was a woman's voice this time.

Knock knock. "Hello?"

The waitress used a passkey and pushed the door open a bit. "Room service. Hello?" She swung the door wider and saw Verbaken's bloody body on the floor. The waitress gasped, took in the sight of the other corpse on the far side of the room, and ran from the suite screaming.

3

I live in a townhouse inside the triangle formed by I-695, York Road, and Dulaney Valley Road in Towson, Maryland. This suburb of Baltimore has a reputation for being "hip" since Towson University is located here. I guess it's hip. I don't know. Maybe I'm just not very hip. I'm not a social guy. I don't date, I don't go out, and I stay pretty much to myself. When I'm not on an assignment for Third Echelon, I lead a relatively boring existence. I have no friends to speak of, my neighbors probably think I'm some kind of recluse, and the only shops I frequent are the nearby grocery store, a liquor store, and the dry cleaners in the strip mall over on York Road.

I like it that way.

The townhouse is much too large for a single man in his forties. I have three floors in which to spread out. I indulge myself in simple pleasures such as a supersize flatscreen television, DVD player, and a surround-sound system. I keep a library of reference material in the lower floor, and that's also where my home office is. If someone were to look at the books in my library, they'd think I was a geography professor or maybe a history lecturer. For my work I study the countries of the world. I try to keep abreast of everything that's happening politically and economically, especially in the so-called hot spots. Sometimes a single bit of knowledge about an unusual item that exists only in a given country can save your life. Knowing who's really on your side and who's not is of primary importance when you're in the field. So every day I try to learn something new about a place. It keeps me sharp.

I live near Towson Town Center, a huge indoor mall that attracts all the beautiful people in the area. I avoid it like the plague. I detest shopping malls because they're all the same. Same shops, same franchises, and the same ignorant people going about their daily business of spending money—usually someone else's. When I need something, I go to out-of-the-way mom-and-pop shops. I can find clothes anywhere. If I want DVDs or CDs, I buy them online and get them mailed to me. In fact, I do an awful lot of online shopping. It keeps my personal interactions to a minimum.

I want to remain as anonymous as possible.

I cook my own meals. I'm pretty good at it, too. That's one of the things that Sarah appreciates about me. She visits infrequently, but when she does she always wants me to cook for her instead of going out to a restaurant. That's fine by me. Being able to cook is yet another valuable skill that's helpful in my profession. You wouldn't believe the number of strange and inhospitable places I've been where I've had to whip up a meal from whatever I could find around me. I've learned to eat some pretty disgusting stuff in my time, so being able to cook a decent gourmet meal on my own is a gift.

Although I don't go out much, there are a couple of

places I frequent. One is a gym that's farther south on York, past the university. It's actually just over the line separating Towson with Baltimore. It's a funky little gym that appeals to minority toughs. Only a few white guys go there. It's mostly Hispanics and African-Americans who are into boxing or weight lifting. I imagine a lot of them are in gangs, but they don't bother me.

The other place I go, and on a much more regular basis, is the Krav Maga studio that's in the same strip mall as my dry cleaners. It's close enough that I walk there from the townhouse. And that's where I go today after breakfast.

I put on my workout clothes—a jumpsuit, really—and make sure the security system is on. I leave the house and begin the ten-minute walk to the strip mall. It's a fine day outside—spring has come early this year and we didn't have a bad winter. Of course, I was gone most of the winter, so it didn't matter. The assignment in the Far East took nearly three months. I was in Hong Kong for most of that time doing the preparation for the job in Macau. The assignment also involved a couple of trips to Singapore. Tracing the Shop's arms pipeline in that area turned out to be more difficult than was originally predicted.

I received mixed reviews for the Macau job. Lambert was pleased with all the stuff I got out of the casino's computer, but he wasn't happy about the killings. Kim Wei Lo was indeed a very bad man and probably deserved to die, but Lambert felt we could have gotten more information out of him later. He would have gone down in the subsequent arrests that the Chinese government will surely initiate once the NSA provides them with the proof of the Shop's existence in their country and territories. Hell, I didn't set out to kill him, it just happened that way. It was either him or me. Lambert understands that, but he was still perturbed. He'll get over it, though.

As Splinter Cells go, I'm pretty lucky that I'm not assigned to a static location. Dan Lee, the agent who was killed in Macau, lived and worked in the Far East territory. Of course, the guy was Chinese, so that made sense. But there are other Splinter Cells stationed in parts of the world where I certainly wouldn't want to stay all the time. I like coming back to the States between jobs, even if it's only to *hip* Towson, Maryland. I guess I have a special designation within Third Echelon. Being the first Splinter Cell and an agent who can adapt easily to just about any place they send me, I'm more useful as a "contractor." In the old days, spies were often diplomats or embassy intelligence officers stationed in the country where they did the spying. I guess that still goes on. With Third Echelon, though, the Splinter Cells are guys that have no affiliation with the U.S. government—at least, they don't in a public sense. I've used numerous cover identities when I'm on a job and I have to sometimes learn trades and skills to make the cover more legitimate.

I was in the CIA before I became a Splinter Cell. I hated it. Too much bureaucracy. Too much in-fighting and not enough cooperation between the other big agencies. In the CIA I had to spy in the traditional way—usually posing as a diplomat or someone in an official capacity. I had to be in more social situations than I cared for. I'm not good at entertaining some prime minister and his wife and talking about the local politics. Later on I moved to a stateside job in weapons development. I thought I came up with some pretty good theoretical work on information warfare, but the bureaucratic machine hampered my creativity. It was extremely frustrating. I'm a man of action and that's why I left the CIA when Colonel Irving Lambert asked me to join Third Echelon.

I was reluctant at first, but Lambert did a pretty good

job of flattering me. He told me I was the only man for the job. I was a "rare specimen," he said. I was a spy who had never come close to being caught. I had a lifetime's worth of espionage experience (I'm four years older than Lambert!), but I haven't left any fingerprints on the intelligence community. He told me I knew how to survive and stay invisible. He knew I could keep a secret. So I joined.

The Macau job was pretty typical of what I do. My cover in Hong Kong was that of a journalist, which is something I've been on several occasions. I was supposedly working on a book about the changes in Hong Kong since the handover in 1997. To tell the truth, I didn't see that many changes. I'd been to Hong Kong many times before 1997 and a couple of times since, and I can't tell much difference other than the fact that there are fewer Brits now.

Still, there are some British government agencies left in Hong Kong. They provided the private boat that got me to Macau and back. The rest of it I had to do alone, though. I motored around the peninsula at night and moored a couple of miles from the main port. Like the Americans, the Brits supposedly had no knowledge of my presence or actions in the area, although the U.K. is just as interested in closing down the Shop as we are. That's why they helped.

I get to the strip mall and walk inside KM Studio, early as usual. I'm always the first one there. The instructor is an Israeli woman named Katia Loenstern. She's thirty-something and extremely attractive. Very buff and strong, too. I think she likes me, but I can't reciprocate. It's just too dangerous in my business to get involved with someone. Besides, I never know when I have to leave the country, and I can't talk about what I'm doing. It's not the best set of circumstances upon which to build a relationship. I don't particularly *enjoy* being celibate, but I've trained myself not to think about it. I can appreciate looking at a beautiful woman, but that's as far as my thought process goes. I've been able to find the discipline to stymie it there before I allow the desire mechanism to kick in.

Katia is in the studio, limbering up on a ballet rail. I think she rents the studio to a ballet class on some days. I can't imagine that Krav Maga classes alone pay the rent.

"Sam!" she says, obviously surprised to see me.

"Hi, Katia," I reply.

"Where the heck you been? I thought you'd disappeared off the face of the earth."

That's right. I was in the Far East. I hadn't been to class in three months even though I had paid for the whole year in advance.

"I've been away on business," I said. At least it was the truth. "Sorry. I should have told you I'd be gone a while."

She straightens out and faces me. As usual, she's dressed in a leotard and tights for the warm-up. She'd put on a little more clothing later for the sparring portion of the class. Katia is tall, muscular, and has a nice, natural body. Her black hair comes down just past her shoulders. She has brown eyes, a long nose, and a rather pouty mouth. Yep, I would certainly jump her bones in another life.

"Just what kind of business are you in?"

"Sales. Overseas sales. I was in the Far East for three months."

She eyes me skeptically. "You don't look like a salesman."

I put down my gym bag that contains a towel and an extra T-shirt and sit on the mat. I begin my own warm-up stretches and ask, "I don't? What does a salesman look like?"

She gets on the mat near me and continues calisthenics. "I don't know. Just not like you."

"What do I look like?"

"You look like a soldier. Like a career soldier. Someone who's been in the army for thirty years."

"*Thirty* years? I'm not *that* old!"

"No, I guess you're not. Okay, twenty years. How old are you, anyway? I forgot."

"It's on my application for the class, isn't it?"

"Yeah, I could go look it up, but I'm too busy right this second."

"I'm forty-seven."

She makes a face that indicates she's impressed. "Sam, you don't look a day over forty. Maybe even thirty-eight. And that's getting pretty close to *me*."

I look at her and she smiles at me. Is she flirting? Was that a come-on?

"Why, how old are you?" I ask.

"You know it's impolite to ask a woman her age."

"Aw, geez, Katia. Come on, I fessed up."

"Guess."

I'm pretty sure what the answer is, but I pretend to think about it. "Thirty-five?"

She raises her eyebrows. "Very good."

Two more students enter the studio. Josh and Brian are orthodox Jews who believe that "the war" will come to their neighborhood someday, and they want to be able to defend themselves. They're big guys. I don't think they'd have any problem defending themselves, with or without Krav Maga.

"Anyway, welcome back," Katia says to me, ending our conversation.

"Thanks," I say.

Over the next ten minutes the other students arrive. Out of twelve people, nine are men ranging from age sixteen to forty-something. I think I'm the oldest guy in the class. The three women are relatively young, between eighteen and thirty, I think. Katia's a very good instructor. She starts each class with a basic warm-up that includes some kind of aerobic activity, strength conditioning with push-ups and sit-ups, and stretching. Warm-ups are usually different in each class to keep things interesting and to ensure that each student leaves with a variety of exercises that can be used to keep fit outside of class. Following warm-up, Katia leads us in hand techniques for fifteen minutes. This time is devoted to hand strikes such as punches, elbows, and hammerfists, and associated defenses. The next fifteen minutes focus on leg techniques—kicks, knees, and their defenses. The final quarter hour is spent on self-defenses, and in Krav Maga there's a lot to learn. Katia goes through each self-defense move thoroughly, step-by-step to ensure maximum understanding. Then we practice live, with partners. The entire hour includes drills to enhance muscle strength and cardiovascular conditioning, as well as drills to teach students how to operate under pressure or fatigue, defend against multiple attackers, and keep fighting spirit high for the entire duration of a defense or fight.

Unlike the color belt system used by other martial arts systems, Krav Maga is broken down into levels. When you progress through the system, you move up in level until you reach 3B, the most advanced class that Katia teaches. That's the one I'm in, as well as "Fight Class," where we have the opportunity to spar while wearing protective gear. In 3B we work on weapons defenses, grappling, joint locks, spinning heel, and slap kicks, and other advanced combatives.

When the hour's up, everyone is in a major sweat. I can't wait to get home and hit the shower. As folks are leaving, I wipe my face and neck with a towel and catch my breath. Katia comes over to me and says, "Sam, you should be teaching this class, not me."

"You do a great job, Katia," I say.

"I'm serious. You've been doing this a long time, haven't you? I mean, I knew you were good, but today you showed me a thing or two. Where did you study before? Are you from Israel?"

I shake my head. "Nope. Born and raised here in the States."

"You're not Jewish, are you?"

I smile. "Charlie Chaplin was once asked that question," I say. "He replied, 'I don't have that honor, sorry.'"

She laughs. "Well, you're damned good. I'd really hate to fight you for real."

I don't know what to say, so I shrug and mumble, "Thanks."

"You have to rush off?" she asks. "You want to go get a coffee? Or something cold to drink? We can go to the little diner next door."

Oh, brother. This is all I need. Damn. Part of me wants to go with her and the rest of me wants to run like hell. I just can't get close to a woman. I know it doesn't work. I've been there, done that.

"I don't know. . . ." I start to say.

"Oh, come on. I'm not going to bite you. I might kick you in the groin if you don't, but I won't bite."

"We're all sweaty."

She rolls her eyes. "What is this? You looking for every excuse you can think of? We'll sit in the corner and no one will smell us."

Damn, she is cute.

"All right," I say.

She shakes her head as if to say, "I just don't get you." She grabs her stuff, I take mine, and we go out the door to the diner.

Katia buys a medium coffee, black. I opt for decaf. I don't like to have to depend on stuff like caffeine. If you get too used to coffee to keep you alert, you have no business being a Splinter Cell.

Now comes the hard part. She's probably going to ask me a lot of personal questions and I'm going to have to lie. I keep a catalog of cover stories for situations like this. The usual "What do you do for a living?" and "Where did you go to school?" and "Have you ever been married?" questions.

We sit at a table and she grins at me. "So. Here we are. See, this isn't so bad."

"Nope," I reply. Maybe if I keep my end of the conversation monosyllabic, she'll get bored.

"Now tell me again about your business. You get to travel a lot?"

"It's nothing cool," I say. "I sell ball bearings. I travel to other countries and sell ball bearings. It's *real* exciting."

She laughs. "I'll bet it's better than you say. Just the traveling part would interest me."

"It's all right at first, but you soon get tired of the early mornings, the crowded airports, the hassles of security these days, and the jet lag. Believe me, it's not as exotic as it seems."

"All right, what do you do for fun?"

"When I'm in another country?"

"No, here, silly. What do you do besides take Krav Maga classes?"

I look away. Sometimes the shy act turns off women and sometimes it makes them more interested. I'm hoping it'll discourage her since she's such an outgoing lass. "I don't know," I mutter. "Nothing much. I live alone. I'm not much of a socialite."

"Oh, sure," she counters. "A great-looking guy like you? You must have a dozen girlfriends."

I shake my head. "I'm afraid not."

"Really?"

"Really."

Uh-oh. She looks heartened. Maybe I should have told her I had six girlfriends that live with me. Damn, this is hard.

"Well, I know you're not gay, so what is it? Bad marriage or something?"

"How do you know I'm not gay?"

She smirks. "Come on, a girl can tell."

"What about you? You're not married, are you?"

"I asked you first. But no, I'm not. I was married for four years when I was just out of college. Big mistake. Haven't looked back. You?"

I don't like to talk about that part of my life. "Yeah, I was married once. She died."

Katia's smile falls. That sure put a damper on things. Maybe I should just tell the truth more often. "Oh, I'm sorry," she says. "What happened?"

"Cancer," I answer.

"That's awful. How long were you married?"

"A little more than three years."

"Kids?"

I'm not sure if I want to reveal this or not, but I do. "Yeah, one. I have a daughter going to college in Illinois."

"Oh, wow," Katia says. "Do you see her much?"

"Not often enough," I say truthfully.

"Hey, you like to eat?" she asks, sensing that she should change the subject.

I shrug. "I guess. Doesn't everyone?"

"I like to cook. You want to try one of Katia Loenstern's specials some night?" she asks.

I don't want to tell her that I like to cook, too. That would just give us something in common.

"Oh, I don't think so," I say. It pains me to have to tell her this.

She looks as if I'd just slapped her. "Really?" she asks.

"You'd be missing something, I tell you."

"I believe you. Thanks, really. But I just can't do that. I'm sorry."

"What's the matter? I said I don't bite."

"It's not that," I mutter. I try to put on the introverted, scared-of-women act to dissuade her.

"Don't you find me attractive?"

There's my opening. "No," I say.

I really thought that would do the trick, but instead she says, "Bullshit! You think I'm gorgeous. I can tell. Come on, what is it with you?"

I laugh and say, "Look, Katia, you're my instructor. I don't . . . I can't get involved, all right? Let's just be friends."

She shakes her head but keeps smiling. "Boy, I can't tell you how many times I've heard that one. Fine. Look, we all have pasts we want to hide. Don't worry about it. We'll be friends if that's what you want."

By now we're done with our coffees. I look at the time and say, "Well, I guess I'd better be going. I have some, uhm, sales reports to do this afternoon."

She sighs and says, "Okay, Sam. Will you be at the next class?"

"I should be. You never know, though, in my job."

We walk out of the diner together and she holds out her hand. I take it and give it a light squeeze.

"Okay, friend," she says. "I'll see you next time."

"Okay," I reply. And then we separate. She goes back to the studio and I begin the walk home, cursing at myself for being such a shit.

WHEN I get back to the house, I hear the phone ringing. I keep a regular unlisted home phone line. There's an extension in the kitchen, on the middle level, right when you walk into the house.

I pick up the receiver and I hear Sarah's sweet voice.

"Hi, Dad, it's me!"

"Sarah honey! I'm happy to hear from you," I say. I honestly get a warm, fuzzy feeling when I talk to her.

"Just wanted to let you know that Rivka and I are about to leave for the airport. We're *so* excited."

I tense up and say, "Whoa, hold on. The airport? Where are you going?"

"Jerusalem, Dad. Remember? We've been planning this for—"

"Sarah, we discussed this at length! I told you that you couldn't go."

"Dad! Come on, you didn't come right out and say I couldn't go. You didn't *want* me to go, but you didn't say I *couldn't* go."

"Well, you can't go. Israel's just too volatile right now. With the state of things in the world with respect to Americans, I'm just not comfortable with it."

Naturally, she sounds upset. "Oh, come on, Dad! I'm twenty years old! You can't stop me now! We're *on our way* to the airport as we speak! I have my tickets and everything!"

Aw, hell. What am I supposed to do about this?

"Sarah, I wish we'd talked more about this." I try to control my anger.

"Look, I'll call you when we get to Jerusalem. I'll try to figure out what the time difference is and not call you in the middle of the night. I gotta go."

I couldn't think of anything to say except, "Be careful. I love you." But she had already hung up. Damn it.

I guess I had forgotten all about her plans. Sarah wanted to go with her friend Rivka to Israel over spring break. I had told her I wasn't too crazy about her going to such a dangerous location but I guess I wasn't forceful enough. What can I do? Technically, she's an adult.

Sarah's a student at Northwestern University in Evanston, Illinois, just north of Chicago. She's a junior. I think. Sometimes I forget how long she's been in college. Rivka is her best friend and she happens to be from Israel. They're supposedly going to stay with Rivka's family in Jerusalem for a little less than a week.

I glance at the photo of Sarah that's stuck on the refrigerator with a magnet. She's the spitting image of her mother. Beautiful and smart. A class act all the way. The only thing she inherited from me was my stubbornness.

The memory of Regan giving birth flashes through my mind. It was a difficult labor and being on a U.S. military base in Germany didn't help. I was in the CIA at the time, working in Eastern Europe. Regan had a job as a cryptanalyst for the NSA. We met in Georgia, of all places. Not Georgia, USA, but the former Soviet state. We had a stormy affair and Regan got pregnant. The wedding was a small, quiet one on the base in Germany, and that's where Sarah was born.

I don't like to reflect on the three years Regan and I were together. It wasn't a happy time. I loved Regan and she loved me, but our professions interfered. It was a distant, difficult marriage. Regan eventually went back to the States and took Sarah with her. She reclaimed her maiden name, Burns, and had Sarah's legally changed. As for me, I dedicated myself entirely to the work, operating extensively in Germany, Afghanistan, and the Soviet satellites in the years leading up to the collapse of the USSR. Needless to say, I became estranged from Regan and Sarah.

I think Sarah was fifteen when Regan died. That was so goddamned hard. I hadn't spoken to Regan in years, and I tried my best to have a reconciliation with her when I learned that she had less than a year to live. Fucking ovarian cancer. It doesn't take a trained psychologist to figure out why I'm afraid of commitment now. Living with the guilt of not being there while Sarah was growing up and then facing the fact that the woman you love is dying will turn anyone off from relationships.

I became Sarah's legal guardian, and that's when I took the bureaucratic job with the CIA in the States, hoping I could settle into a suburban life and focus more on her upbringing. Unfortunately, I have enough trouble being comfortable around human beings in general, much less a teenage girl. It was an awkward, difficult time. I suppose, though, that it's turned out okay. After she graduated from high school, Sarah seemed to come around and appreciate me more. I've read that all teenagers go through the same thing. Once they leave the nest, they become your friend. Thank goodness that's what happened with us.

I wish I could see her more often.

I hear myself sigh as I force these thoughts out of my head. I walk downstairs to the office so I can check my *other* answering machine. My line to the NSA isn't a phone at all. It's really more of a pager embedded in a paperweight on my desk. If the pin light is on, that means I need to contact Lambert from a secure line outside the house. I don't ever call on my home line.

The pin light is on.

4

POLICE Constable Robert Perkins disliked his beat with a passion. Every night it was the same thing, except on Sundays when the theater was dark. Even days were bad because of matinees.

As the officer in charge of the area surrounding the National Theatre in London, PC Perkins felt that supervising traffic was below his station. Nevertheless, he did it without complaint. He didn't actually have to *direct* traffic—thank God for that—except in the case of an emergency, a royal event, or if some idiot did something to cause an accident. Perkins had walked this beat for the last twenty-two years and would probably be doing it for at least the next ten. Perkins could always put in for a transfer, but his superiors always frowned upon such requests. At age forty-three, he felt, he was becoming a bit long in the tooth for this type of work.

On weekday evenings traffic was even worse because of the business day rush hour. Waterloo Bridge loomed overhead, running from northwest to southeast across the

Thames to the South Bank. The mass of vehicles traversing that particular road never let up. At rush hour, before
the theater's evening performance, it was at its worst. The
"congestion charge" of £5 over and above the parking fee
didn't dissuade drivers from attempting to use the theater's small car park. Perkins wondered why more people
didn't just take the tube and walk. Certainly it was simpler
and less annoying.

Perkins usually stood at the intersection of Theatre
Avenue and Upper Ground because the only place
coaches could let off passengers was on Upper Ground
at the back of the theater. Thus, he was practically directly beneath Waterloo Bridge and had to deal with the
noise of the traffic above him. It gave him a daily
headache.

It was now 6:30 and the bulk of the evening traffic was
at its peak. Perkins stood at the crossroad and watched as
irritable coach drivers continued to stop, then move, stop,
then move. Civilian and taxi drivers moving along Theatre
Avenue had even worse tempers. They expected the world
to stop so that they could see the latest Shakespearean production.

Perkins had lived in London his entire life and had
never been inside the National Theatre except to investigate reports of theft, sick patrons, or the occasional bel-
ligerent guest. Not once had he sat in one of the three
theaters to watch something. He didn't really care to. He
wasn't into "high brow" entertainment. When he had told
his wife that, she'd replied that back in Shakespeare's day
the plays were considered entertainment for the lower and
middle classes. Perkins had nothing to say to that.

A blast of car horns on Theatre Avenue pulled his attention away from a density of taxis on Upper Ground. He
squinted in that direction and was aghast at what he saw

moving slowly along the street and eventually stopping on double red lines, halting traffic.

It was a large lorry pulling a flatbed covered with theater scenery. Three "actors" were performing on it for the benefit of pedestrians and cars trying to go around the lorry. Perkins had never seen anything like this in all his many years on the South Bank. For one thing, lorries weren't allowed on that particular road.

Perkins grabbed the radio from his belt and contacted his second-in-command, PC Blake, who was stationed on the other side of the theater.

"Yes, sir?"

"Blake, have you seen the lorry over here on Theatre Avenue?"

"What lorry?"

"There's a bloody lorry with actors on the back of it. They're doing some kind of show. It's causing all kinds of problems over here."

"I don't know nothin' about it, sir."

"Get on to the box office and ask them if this belongs to the theater."

"Will do."

Blake signed off and Perkins strode toward the lorry, preparing to give someone hell. He had to stop, though, and direct a number of cars around the lorry and then run back to the intersection to unclog a maze of taxis that formed in less than ten seconds. Perkins cursed and slapped the bonnet of one of the taxis, telling the driver to hurry around and lay off the horn.

Blake came back on the radio.

"Perkins here."

"Sir, the theater people don't know anything about it. They didn't provide this so-called entertainment."

"Right. That does it. Thank you, Blake."

Perkins replaced the radio and took a deep breath. He was angry now and he pitied the poor soul he was about to berate. He left the chaos at the intersection and walked with purpose to the lorry.

The actors were dressed in medieval attire and speaking lines that no one could hear due to the traffic on the bridge overhead. What was the bloody point? Perkins wondered.

The driver sat in the cab bobbing his upper body in a strange fashion. He appeared to be Middle Eastern—he had a dark complexion and black facial hair.

Perkins stepped up to the window and rapped loudly on it.

"Listen here! You've got to move! You're not supposed to be here!" Perkins shouted.

The driver didn't look at him. He continued to bob back and forth, muttering something to himself.

"Sir! Please lower your window! I'm speaking to you!"

Perkins rapped the window once more and then he understood what the driver was doing.

He was praying.

As soon as the realization hit him, Perkins's heart nearly stopped. He gasped and stepped back from the lorry, but it was too late.

The explosives were so powerful that they obliterated the lorry and its troupe of suicide "actors," eight vehicles on Theatre Avenue, and caused a section of Waterloo Bridge to collapse. Fourteen motorcars fell off the bridge, causing a massive, burning pileup. The side of the theater facing the blast was singed and several windows were broken. Sixty-two people were killed and nearly a hundred and fifty were injured.

Constable Perkins never had to supervise traffic at the National Theatre again.

* * *

EACH major broadcast network covered the disaster in the U.K., but it was BBC-2 that featured an exclusive interview with a Turkish terrorism expert that happened to be in London on business. A bright female reporter caught Namik Basaran as the fifty-two-year-old man rushed out of the Ritz Hotel to travel to Embankment and view the scene personally. Close beside him was his bodyguard, a broad-shouldered man wearing a turban.

"Mr. Basaran, can you tell us what your visit to London entails?" the reporter asked.

Basaran, a swarthy man with a noticeable skin condition, spoke to the camera. "I am the head of a not-for-profit charity organization in Turkey called Tirma. For the four years of our existence we have provided relief aid to victims of terrorist attacks all over the world. The United Kingdom is no exception. I hope to authorize the release of several thousand pounds to help the victims of this horrible tragedy."

"It is said that you're an expert on terrorism. Could you elaborate on this?"

Basaran shook his head. "No one is an 'expert' on terrorism. That is nonsense. Terrorism is fluid. It changes daily. Terrorism used to be hijacking an aircraft and forcing the pilot to take it to another location. This evolved into holding hostages aboard the craft to force governments to do something. Now we have hijackers willing to die on an airplane and kill every passenger along with them. Terrorists have become more desperate and bold."

A label identifying him appeared on the screen— "Namik Basaran, president and CEO, Akdabar Enterprises—Chairman, Tirma."

"Is it true that you're a victim of terrorism yourself?"

Basaran lightly touched the skin on his face. Had it been grafted? "That's a very painful subject for me and I'd rather not go into it here on television. Suffice it to say that I've experienced tragedy in my life and have dedicated the personal profits I make from my legitimate company, Akdabar Enterprises, to benefit Tirma. I have spent years studying the terrorist situation in the Middle East and other parts of the world and have made contacts that are beneficial for those of us who want to stamp out terrorism."

"Do you have any idea who was behind what happened on the South Bank this evening?"

Basaran's eyes flared as he said, "It's too early to say for certain, but I wouldn't be surprised if tomorrow the British government receives a message from the Shadows claiming responsibility."

"Sir, do you think the Shadows are the most dangerous terrorist network in the world? Some say that they have surpassed the prominence formerly held by such groups as al Qaeda and Hizballah."

"I'm afraid I have to agree that this is true. The Shadows are becoming more powerful every day. They are a force that the governments of the world will soon be reckoning with on a major scale. That's all, I must hurry. I want to see the site firsthand so I can make a report to our board of ambassadors back in Turkey. Thank you. Come along, Farid."

The bodyguard led Basaran out of the way of the camera, and they both got into the back of a limousine.

The reporter addressed the camera: "That was Namik Basaran, chairman of a victim-relief charity organization based in Turkey. If what Mr. Basaran says is correct, then the Shadows have struck again. To date this mysterious group of terrorists has claimed responsibility for several recent attacks in the Middle East, Asia, and Europe, the most recent one being the tragedy two weeks ago in Nice, France. This is Susan Harp for BBC-2."

5

I drive a 2002 Jeep Grand Cherokee when I'm at home in Maryland. It's one of the Overland models, a rugged 4×4 with a potent 265-horsepower V8. For the city, it's way too much car, but there are times when I like to take it over more rugged territory. I recently had an assignment for Third Echelon tracking down a suspected terrorist who was hiding out in Las Vegas. I drove my Cherokee cross-country and it was a blast. I happen to enjoy road trips. Anyway, I ended up taking the Jeep off-road several times during that mission. The car serves me well.

On the way down from Towson I listen to NPR and hear about a suicide bombing in London. It has just occurred on the South Bank and part of Waterloo Bridge was destroyed. They don't know how many people were killed or injured. It sounds pretty bad. I wonder if my meeting with Lambert has anything to do with this.

Lambert and I usually find a public place to meet. I avoid the government agency buildings in and around D.C. just in case someone's tailing me. Seeing me enter the NSA or the CIA buildings would certainly be a tip-off that I work for the Feds. Lambert and I vary the locations, but we usually meet in shopping malls. He knows I hate shopping malls, so I think he picks them on purpose just to annoy me. Lambert has a sick sense of humor.

Today I drive down to D.C. on I-95 and then swing west toward Silver Spring. I follow the directions to City Place Mall on Colesville Road, park the Jeep, and go inside. The Food Court is easy to find, and there's Lambert waiting for me at one of the tables. Today he's dressed in a short-sleeved knit golf shirt and khaki pants. He never wears his uniform when we meet in public. It looks like he's got himself a Big Mac Combo Meal and is actually enjoying it. I nod at him and approach one of the fast-food rackets to pick up something for myself. Since it's the middle of the afternoon and I'm not particularly hungry, I end up buying a slice of pizza from Sbarro's. How come every mall in America has the exact same combination of fast-food restaurants? It's one of the mysteries of the universe.

I may be a little older than Lambert, but I look younger. He reminds me of the actor Danny Glover. His curly hair has grayed completely, and the bags under his eyes show the strain of being in charge of a major intelligence department for the U.S. government. Don't get me wrong— he's a very energetic guy. He's ambitious and smart, and I'm not sure if he ever sleeps. He drinks more coffee than he sucks air. Lambert's the kind of guy who's always busy and never relaxes. He has a funny habit of rubbing the top of his crew-cut head when he's nervous.

Colonel Lambert has been in the Intel business since he was a young man. I know he had a lot of responsibility during the Gulf War. Today he's very well connected in

Washington, although I get the impression that he's mini-
mally trusted. He's never been acknowledged publicly, but
I believe he prefers it that way.

Third Echelon is an organization no one is supposed to
know about. The NSA—the National Security Agency—
is the nation's cryptologic establishment. It coordinates,
directs, and performs highly specialized activities to protect U.S. information systems and produce foreign intelligence reports. Since it's on the edge of communications
and data processing, the NSA is naturally a very high-tech
operation. For decades the NSA engaged in what I call
"passive" collection of moving data by intercepting communications en route. The First Echelon was a worldwide
network of international intelligence agencies and inter-
ceptors that seized communications signals and routed
them back to the NSA for analysis. It was a network vital
to the United States' efforts during the Cold War. As the
Soviet Union disintegrated and communications evolved,
high technology became the name of the game. The NSA
created Second Echelon, which focused entirely on this
new breed of communications technology. Unfortunately,
the immense volume of information combined with the
accelerated pace of developing technology and encryption
overwhelmed Second Echelon. NSA experienced its first
system-wide crash. As communications became more digital and sophisticated encryption more expansive, passive
collection was simply no longer efficient. So the NSA
launched a top-secret initiative—Third Echelon—to return to more, shall we say, "classical" methods of espionage powered by the latest technology for the *aggressive*
collection of stored data. In other words, it was back to the
nitty-gritty world of human spies out there in the field,
risking their lives for the sake of taking a photograph or

recording a conversation or copying a computer hard drive. Third Echelon agents are called Splinter Cells, and I was the very first one. We physically infiltrate dangerous and sensitive enemy locations to gather the required intelligence by whatever means necessary. Our prime directive, in a nutshell, is to do our jobs while remaining invisible to the public eye. We're authorized to work outside the boundaries of international treaties, but the U.S. will neither acknowledge nor support our operations.

Thus, Third Echelon, a sub-agency of the NSA, consists of an elite team of strategists, hackers, and field operatives. We respond to crises of information warfare—a war that is hidden from the media and the ordinary man on the street. You're not going to see our battles on CNN. At least I hope not. If you do, then we've failed.

"How's it going, Sam?" Lambert asks, chewing a bite of burger.

"Can't complain, Colonel," I reply, sitting at one of the plastic tables across from him. He once told me to call him "Irv," but I just can't bring myself to do that. "Colonel" is fine with me. It always strikes me as incongruous, us meeting like this. Here we are, two innocuous middle-aged men meeting in a shopping mall for fast food—yet we're about to discuss things that might affect the security of the United States.

Lambert gets right to the point. "Sam, another Splinter Cell has been assassinated," he says, looking me in the eyes.

I wait for him to continue.

"Rick Benton. Stationed in Iraq, but it happened in Brussels."

"I've heard of him. Never met him," I say.

"No, of course not. We keep you guys apart for a reason."

"What happened? Do we know?" I ask.

Lambert shakes his head. "Details are still coming in. The Belgian police are all over it, so we have to get the information through ordinary diplomatic channels, and you know how slow that can be. But we're getting cooperation from the Belgian Military Intelligence and Security Service. One of their guys was killed with Benton."

"What *do* we know?"

"Benton was in the process of obtaining some sensitive information from his contact in Brussels, an intelligence officer named Dirk Verbaken. Unknown assassins murdered both men in Benton's hotel room during the lunch hour. Apparently Benton and Verbaken got together for a face-to-face, but someone else knew about it. They were both shot, and there's every reason to believe that it's the same MO as what happened in Macau to Dan Lee. Same ballistics—caliber and so forth."

"You think it's the Shop?"

"It has to be. I can't think of another enemy organization that has an inkling that we exist. The Shop has been on notice for over a year now, and they know the NSA is on to them. Whether or not they're completely aware of Third Echelon and what we do is anyone's guess. Mine is that they *are* aware of us. How else would they be able to target two Splinter Cells in a three-month period?"

I shrug and venture, "They've tapped into our personnel records? Maybe they have talented hackers, too."

"Our firewall is impenetrable," Lambert replies. "Carly's too good at that stuff. We'd know if we were being hacked."

"There was the security breach that occurred nine months ago."

Lambert nods. "I've thought of that. It's a possibility. A

remote one, but yeah, you're right. Carly and I discussed this and there's about a one-in-three-hundred chance that someone got in. Improbable but not impossible."

"So what were Benton and this Belgian guy meeting about? What was his name?"

"Verbaken. The last report I received from Benton indicated he was investigating a possible connection between the Shop and 'something in Belgium.' He told me he was going to Brussels to meet with an intelligence contact there and that he would report in as soon as he was done. For months he was in the process of tracking a major Shop arms supply line coming into Iraq from the north. The customers are the various insurgents and terrorist factions that have been hounding our allies, the new Iraqi government, and *us* ever since the president declared that the war in Iraq was over. I know Benton was getting close to finding out some truths about those guys." Lambert took a long slurp of soda. "I'm afraid Benton turned out to be careless. It cost him his life."

"Is Belgium giving us any info on their guy? What was *he* working on?"

"Well, we have a clue. Benton's OPSAT was recovered from the hotel room. It was smashed to hell, but upon examination of the device our people were able to extract a minimum number of files that hadn't been transmitted to us. One was a shot of a page from a file belonging to Verbaken. When Belgian Intelligence saw the photo, they confirmed that it was from a missing file that detailed the activities of Gerard Bull."

"Gerard Bull?" I'm surprised. I haven't heard that name in many years. Gerard Bull was a Canadian arms designer and dealer who was active in the sixties, seventies, and eighties. He worked for our government for a while until there was a falling out. He served some prison time for illegal arms dealing. After he got out of prison, he worked extensively out of Europe. During the eighties he had close ties with Saddam Hussein and spent a lot of time designing and building high-tech arms for Iraq. His most famous "creation" was the design for what he called a "supergun." He called it the "Babylon." It was supposed to be a giant cannon-like weapon that could fire a payload an incredibly long distance. Alternatively, with the aid of boosters, a payload could be launched into space without the need of rockets. Bull never finished the project, but he did build a small prototype called the "Baby Babylon." It was dismantled and destroyed during the Gulf War. Bull was assassinated in 1990—in Brussels, to be exact. It is widely believed that the Mossad was responsible for the killing.

"So what's that all about?" I ask.

"I don't know," Lambert replies. "Belgian intelligence confirmed that Verbaken had recently added material to the file because he believed that someone previously associated with Bull was continuing the physicist's work for terrorists in the Middle East. Unfortunately, Verbaken hadn't completed his investigation and had not filed any detailed reports. He died without leaving anyone a clue as to where his notes are. They were probably *in* the file. And it's gone."

"Except for the one page recovered from the OPSAT."

"Right."

"Did the killers take the file?"

"We assume so. I wonder if they were after the file to begin with, or were the targets either Verbaken or Benton and the file was just gravy?"

"Or after both guys *and* the file," I suggest.

"There's that possibility, too."

We're quiet for a moment as we let these thoughts sink

in. I finish my pizza and ask, "You heard the news about London?"

Lambert nods grimly. "That's another thing I wanted to talk with you about. As you can imagine, we're all very concerned about it."

"The news report was very vague. What happened?"

"I was in my car when it happened," Lambert says. "I got on to the Pentagon immediately, and what they could gather in the few minutes after it occurred was that some suicide bombers were masquerading as actors or something. It happened by the National Theatre. A big truck packed with explosives blew up. Part of Waterloo Bridge crumbled. It's a big mess."

"Anyone claiming responsibility?"

"Not yet," Lambert answers. "But the modus operandi suggests the Shadows, don't you think?"

The Shadows. They're a bunch of shady characters who've grabbed some headlines lately. A relatively new barrel of terrorists, the Shadows operate all over the world but are believed to be headquartered somewhere in the Middle East. (Where else?) I can't remember who coined the name, but it wasn't them. I think it was a newspaper from the region—maybe Turkey—that referred to them as the Shadows and it stuck. From then on messages from the group were signed "the Shadows." I think they were flattered.

Third Echelon's been trying its best to collect data on the Shadows. Because they're so new it's been pretty difficult. No one knows if they represent a particular country. They're a lot like al Qaeda and other nomadic, independent terrorist factions. They've probably got a sugar daddy somewhere who provides all the cash. What we do know is that they've claimed responsibility for a rash of bombings over the last year. There was a really bad one in Nice, France, just a couple of weeks ago. Same kind of thing—a truck pulls up in some public place and blows up. Goddamned bastards. It's a shitty, evil thing to do.

"It's too early, isn't it?" I ask. "For them to issue a claim of responsibility, I mean?"

"Yeah. It'll be tomorrow. But I'll give you ten to one it's them."

I nod. "You're probably right."

"The interesting thing about all this is that there's a connection."

"How so?"

"That sheet of paper from the Gerard Bull file—the one from the copier?"

"Yeah?"

"It also mentions the Shadows."

"Really."

"The implication in the wording is that they're the Shop's biggest customers right now and possibly the group behind whatever it was that Benton was chasing in Belgium."

I sit back in my chair. "If we could establish a connection between the two groups—and identify the major players in each—"

Lambert smiles. "You catch on quick."

"So you want me to go to Belgium?"

"No. I want you to go to Iraq."

Iraq. Shit.

Lambert continues. "I want you to pick up Benton's trail there. Find out what he was investigating. He was sure suspicious about something, and damn it, he died before he could tell us what it was. You'll be drop-shipped to Baghdad." Lambert reaches into a briefcase and pulls out a manila envelope. He slides it across the table to me. "Everything you need to know is in there. Be ready to leave by army transport tonight at twenty-two hundred hours from Dulles. That should give you enough time to get home, make your preparations, and be back at the airport by twenty-one hundred."

Yeah, just barely enough time.

I nod and tap my fingers on the envelope without opening it. That can wait until I get back to Towson.

"Okay," I say. I have nothing else on the calendar.

6

I never pack much when I'm going OCONUS on assignment. An important component of my uniform is a slim custom-made Osprey backpack that fulfills a zillion functions. I can fit two or three changes of clothing inside, plus an assortment of Third Echelon equipment that I can pull out at a moment's notice. I have a medical kit that contains painkillers, bandages, antiseptic, and atropine injections to combat exposure to a chemical attack. I have a limited supply of flares—both chemical and emergency—for various uses. Chemical flares glow in the dark when you crack the inner containers. They're useful for attracting and distracting enemies. Emergency flares are standard road flares that emit heat, which can distract sensors like the ones found on automated turrets. I also keep a few frag grenades handy. These 14-ounce M67 babies consist of 2.5-inch steel spheres surrounding 6.5 ounces of high explosive. When these things go off, you don't want to be close, believe me. The high-velocity shrapnel will rip you to shreds. In addition to the grenades I usually carry at least one wall mine. This is a motion-sensitive explosive device that can be attached to almost any surface. I'm able to improvise in the field, too—I've found that I'm pretty good at deactivating enemy mines and adding them to my inventory if I need more.

Other tools of the trade include a standard set of lock picks, wrenches, and probes for bypassing basic cylinder locks. For more difficult enclosures, such as safes, I use what we call disposable picks that can be adjusted to different strengths, depending on what it is you want to open. They contain microexplosive charges that deliver a quick impact to any standard lock cylinder, shattering the pins. The downside of these things is that they're sometimes a little noisy. I've also got a nifty little camera jammer that emits microwave pulses. This is useful for disrupting the characteristic signals used in the microcircuitry of surveillance cameras. The only problem with the jammer is that it operates off a capacitor that you have to recharge. Then there's the optic cable—kind of like those things doctors use to stick up your ass to look around with when you're a lucky colonoscopy patient. It's very flexible and I can slip it under doors and through holes to see what's on the other side. There's even a night-vision enhancement.

My standard issue weapon is a Five-seveN tactical handgun with a single-action trigger. The twenty-round magazine comes equipped with a silencer and flash suppressor. I've already told you a little bit about the gun, but I don't think I mentioned that it has a T.A.K. integrated inside it. The Tactical Audio Kit is a laser-operated microphone that enables me to read the vibration off certain surfaces, mainly glass windows. The laser mic provides a zoomed camera-like field that can be aimed at different objects. It's great for listening to conversations, but I have to be careful to make sure I use it only when I'm concealed. The damn thing lights up red when it's on.

My uniform, which I've already described, folds up neatly and fits in a special pouch in the Osprey. My goggles are a lifesaver. They have two modes of operation—night vision and thermal vision. Night vision, of course, allows me to pick up illumination at the lower end of the infrared spectrum. This is great for exploring in the dark—the only drag is that the image is slightly grainy, so fine details are difficult to see. Thermal vision is an essential tool in darkness as well, for it captures the upper level of the infrared spectrum, which is emitted as heat rather than reflected light. This allows me to discern warm bodies through visual obstacles such as smoke and gas. One cool thing it does is that if I happen to examine a computer keyboard or keypad immediately after someone has touched it, the keys that were pressed will have a faint heat signature still on them. No well-equipped spy should be without thermal vision. A special fluorescent mode allows me to see fingerprints, stains, and dust disturbance that is normally invisible to the naked eye. This is useful when I'm searching for secret compartments.

My favorite weapon and tool has to be the standard issue SC-20K, a modular assault weapon system. This is something I can't carry with me when I travel. It usually needs to be drop-shipped by the NSA—along with my toy-filled Osprey—and left someplace where I can pick them up. Sometimes that can be a tricky maneuver in a country where we have no embassy. The SC-20K looks like a stocky rifle, but it's much more than that. The Bull Pup configuration makes it light and compact without sacrificing firepower (it uses 5.56×45mm ss109, 30 rounds, and it can be fired in semiautomatic or full automatic modes). There's a flash/sound suppressor combined with a multipurpose launcher that makes it an ideal appliance in the field, and for long-distance shots I can use the scope. The launcher is beneath the main barrel and it utilizes a number of different devices. I can shoot off a ring airfoil projectile, which incapacitates an enemy rather than kills him. A good head shot will knock a guy out, or if I hit someone in the torso, it'll stun him. I can launch sticky cameras that attach themselves to surfaces I can't climb to. These miniature cameras have full pan and zoom functionality plus night and thermal vision modes. The images are fed directly to my OPSAT. An adaptation of the sticky camera is the diversion camera. This honey has had its zoom motor as well as its vision enhancement apparatus replaced with a noisemaker and a CS gas canister. I can trigger it with my OPSAT from a distance, attracting enemies with sound and then dispensing the gas to stop them in their tracks. Similar to the sticky cameras are the sticky shockers, high-voltage discharge devices coated in adhesive resin. They stick to enemies and give them an incapacitating shock. Smoke grenades come in useful as well. These are standard CS gas canisters that stop groups of enemies cold. I like to treat them like bowling balls and aim for strikes. I have additional smoke grenades without CS that just produce black smoke to cover my tracks.

Finally, I need to activate my subdermal implants. These are transmitter/receivers that Third Echelon put in my neck next to my vocal cords and in my inner ear. When the devices are activated, I can receive voice messages from Lambert via satellite that only I can hear. It works best outdoors, naturally, but in most buildings it works pretty well. If I'm underground, it's not worth crap. By the same token, the PTT—Push To Talk—transmitter translates data for use with a voice synthesizer located at

Third Echelon. All I have to do is press the area of my neck near my Adam's apple and talk, or whisper, and what I say is sent to the synthesizer. Therefore, I can communicate with Third Echelon from just about anywhere. Pretty cool. The only drawback is that the signals can be picked up by the enemy pretty easily, so Lambert and I have an understanding that we communicate with text messages via the OPSAT first and use the implants only for urgent contact.

Once I'm packed, I make arrangements for my bills to be paid automatically for as long as I'm away. I confirm that I have plenty of cash in various accounts I can access just about anywhere in the world. I also make a phone call to the Krav Maga Studio and leave a message on Katia's answering machine, explaining that I was called away once again. She'll probably think I'm some kind of a nut. Alas.

I'll leave the Grand Cherokee at home. Lambert arranged for a car to pick me up and take me to Dulles. I wouldn't be comfortable with the idea of leaving my beloved Jeep in a long-term airport parking lot for what could very well be months.

There isn't much left to do when the house phone rings.

"Dad?" It's the sweet voice of my not-so-little-anymore girl.

"Hey, Sarah, I'm glad you called!" I say. I'm very happy to hear from her so I do my best to control my feelings about her going abroad against my wishes. Our last conversation wasn't a pleasant one. "Are you in Israel?"

"Uh-huh. It's the middle of the night, but we can't sleep. Rivka and I are still on Chicago time."

"How was the flight over?"

"Long, so I was glad that Rivka was with me. That made it more interesting. Hey, Dad?"

"Yes?"

"I'm sorry about the misunderstanding. You know, about me going."

Misunderstanding? In my mind there was no misunderstanding. She disobeyed my wishes but it was too late now.

"I'm sorry, too, honey."

"Dad, we had the most beautiful sunset tonight. It was all orange and red, and from Rivka's rooftop it looked like something out of a movie. It's beautiful here."

"And her parents are there with you?"

"Uh-huh. Her mom and dad are real nice."

"That's great to hear. Listen, honey, I have to go out of the country tonight, too. It's for work."

"Again? Didn't you just get back?"

I sigh. "Yeah. But you know how it is."

There was a bit of the old frustration in her voice. "No, I don't know how it is. You're so secretive about what you do. Where are you going this time?"

"I'm . . . I'm going to the Middle East, too. But don't worry, I won't be anywhere near you."

I hear Sarah talk to someone in the background and I distinctly hear a male laugh.

"Sarah, who's that with you?" I ask.

"Huh? Oh, that's Rivka."

"I thought I heard a boy."

"Oh, that's Noel, Rivka's boyfriend. He and Eli came over since we couldn't sleep. They're helping us party. You remember me telling you about Eli?"

"Is he that music student you were dating at college?" I ask.

"Yeah, that's him. He's back home in Israel this semester. So is Noel. He used to date Rivka. That's how Eli and I met, remember?"

I seem to recall hearing something about it last year.

During Sarah's sophomore year she dated a foreign student from Israel. Rivka, a foreign student herself, knew a whole group of them.

"What's Eli's last name, hon?" I ask.

"Horowitz. Eli Horowitz. He says he wants to meet you someday." I hear a male laugh again in the background and Sarah giggles.

"Well, I'd like to meet him, too," I say. I try not to sound too much like a father. "Why isn't Eli at school this year?"

"Oh, his student visa expired and he didn't renew it," Sarah answers. "Same with Noel. There was some kind of stupid technicality with them."

I don't know why, but I suddenly hear alarm bells in my head. Perhaps it's because of all the circumspection that foreign students have been receiving since 9/11. Immigration has cracked down on student visas since then and is ferreting out undesirables.

"Sarah, how much older is he than you?" I ask.

"Dad, please. He's just a couple of years older. Um, three." She sounds annoyed.

"Do his parents live there in Jerusalem?"

"Dad, what is this? What's with the third degree?"

"Honey, it's not a third degree," I say, trying not to sound exasperated. "I just want to know who you're hanging out with in a foreign country, that's all. And Israel can be a dangerous place sometimes. You can't be too careful. I'm your father, after all."

"But I'm also an adult, Dad."

"You're not drinking age yet," I counter.

"Oh, gee, like I have seven more months to wait," she says sarcastically.

I almost point out that that is nearly a year, but I let it go. I don't want the call to turn into one of our teenager vs. parent battles. Sarah and I went through some real knockdown drag-outs when she was in high school.

"All I'm saying is that you should find out a little more about him and his family before you get more involved, that's all," I say. I know it sounds lame.

"Dad, please. We dated for three months last year, but I guess you don't remember that. I know him pretty well already."

"All right, all right, I'll stop being a dad. Do you have plenty of money?"

"Sure, Dad. Thanks."

"And you remember the phone number in case you need to reach me?"

"I've got it memorized," she answers. This is a special toll-free number that she can call from anywhere in the world whenever I'm on assignment. It actually goes to Third Echelon and is then transmitted as a text message to my OPSAT, wherever I happen to be. No one but Sarah and I know the number. I instructed her long ago on how to use it, but only if it's an emergency situation. Anything trivial can wait until my return to Maryland.

"So, when do you fly back to Chicago?" I ask.

"Next Saturday. Just when I'm about to get over the jet lag I have to turn around and go back," she says.

"Yeah, that's the way it usually is."

"Look, Dad, I gotta go now. It's great to talk to you."

"Sarah, honey, you be careful, okay?"

"I will. You, too, with whatever it is you do." There's that touch of sarcasm again. She doesn't like that she knows nothing about my work and has said so on several occasions.

"Okay. Have fun. I love you."

"Love you, too."

She hangs up.

I begin to wonder if my uneasiness about her boyfriend is simply the normal reaction a father might have to his twenty-year-old daughter becoming intimate with an older boy, or is it something else? I probably shouldn't worry. Eli Horowitz lives with his parents. They're probably wealthy, too, in order to afford to send him to America to study. I wonder what really happened with his student visa? I might have to make an inquiry about it.

There's not a lot I can do about it now, I decide. I need to focus on the assignment at hand and study the documents that Lambert gave me this afternoon. They will reveal who my contact in Iraq will be and where I can pick up transportation, my SC-20K, the Osprey, and other equipment I may need. I imagine it'll be through the army. Someone at the top of the food chain there will have been briefed.

As I finish preparing for the trip, I glance at the photo of my daughter on the bedroom nightstand. I feel a sudden urge to hug her and give her a kiss. Instead, I lightly touch my lips to my index finger and then touch the portrait.

That'll have to do for now.

7

MESOPOTAMIA. That's what Iraq once was. The name "Iraq" didn't emerge until sometime in the seventh century. Mesopotamia was the location of Babylon and its legendary hanging gardens, regarded as the seventh wonder of the ancient world. The mythical Tower of Babel once stood in the land, and the area around Qurnah might have been the site of the biblical Garden of Eden. In the middle of the first millennium, Islam swarmed over the region and Mesopotamia became the cultural center of the Arabic universe. Many believe that writing began in the region. The tales of the thousand and one nights originated in Iraq. Magnificent mosques and palaces dominated the cities, built by powerful rulers who insisted on displaying the country's riches in tangible forms. Arabian Nights, magic carpets, sultans of swing . . .

It all sounds quite exotic and beautiful, doesn't it? It's too bad that our image of Iraq today isn't what it used to be. Now we think of Iraq as a very dangerous, unstable country—war torn, shadowy, and unfriendly. I'm not going to speculate on whether we were right or wrong to invade Iraq in 2003. There's no question that Saddam Hussein was bad news. His regime was cruel and merciless. But are the Iraqi people better off now? Who the fuck knows?

Today it's difficult to believe that the Middle East, and in particular Iraq, was once the "cradle of civilization." At least, that's what the historians claim. It's my business to know a lot about the Middle East, and I've extensively studied Iraq and the other countries in the region. That doesn't mean I fully understand any of them. The Middle East is truly a very different world from our existence in the United States, and the sad thing is that many Americans and the U.S. government refuse to acknowledge that the Middle East will never be like the West. But it's not my job to preach politics. I keep abreast of politics, but I try not to get too involved in them. I just do my job.

So many catastrophic events resculpted the world in the twentieth century. Prior to World War I, Iraq was part of the Ottoman Empire governed from Istanbul. The British mandate controlled the region after the war, and in 1932 the country was formally admitted to the League of Nations as an independent state—the first one in the Middle East. But the monarchy that had been installed by the British was overthrown in 1958 by nationalist Free Officers. In 1963 the Baathists took power, were overthrown, and succeeded in gaining control again in 1968. Until we toppled the Baath government in 2003, that's the way things stood in Iraq. During those thirty-five years, Iraq engaged in a war with Iran, a war with Kuwait, a war with the United Nations forces led by the USA, and a war with its own people in the northern, Kurd-populated region.

Ah, the twentieth century. Such a happy time.

These were the thoughts that swam through my head as

the U.S. Army transport touched down at the Third Army base outside of Baghdad. The plane stopped once in Germany. My ability to sleep anywhere at any time helped make the trip flash by in an instant. I was awake long enough to get off the aircraft in Germany, stretch my legs, and have a bite to eat. I slept through the second leg and woke up when the plane landed.

In between naps I thoroughly briefed myself on the current situation in Iraq. Even though an Iraqi government is in place, the U.S. still maintains a strong presence. The locals simply don't have it together to adequately police the country. The United Nations is committed to helping the country get on its feet again, but guess who's bearing the brunt of the work? The good ol' US of A, of course. And no one over here appreciates it. We deliver them from the evils of Hussein, and then they proceed to stab us in the back. Go figure.

Terrorist attacks continue to plague the country. You never know when a suicide bomber is going to drive his truck into yours. Every government officer and politician is a target because they're seen as puppets of the corrupt Satan—America, that is. These terrorists are anywhere and everywhere. Iraq is a big country. There are tons of hiding places. Look how long it took to find Hussein. He was caught hiding in a hole in the ground. There are a few million holes in the ground in Iraq.

The attacks are blamed on the usual nebulous "insurgents" and anti-American rebels. The name al Qaeda is still bandied about as being one of the primary instigators of unrest, along with other smaller terrorist factions that seem to pop up every day. Lately, though, it's the Shadows that provoke the most fear. Like al Qaeda, they don't mind patting themselves on the back in public after a particu-

larly nasty attack. They're more publicity-minded than al
Qaeda ever was. They send audiotapes, videotapes, letters, faxes, and e-mails to the various news organizations . . . signing them "the Shadows." Of course, many of
these missives could be pranks and copycat attempts, but
our people take each and every one seriously. It's what we
must do.

Although the army base is on the outskirts of Baghdad,
I notice the presence of many construction cranes in the
distance, no doubt rebuilding the once great city. The
2003 war inflicted a great deal of damage. The 1991 Gulf
War had also destroyed a significant portion of Baghdad,
including schools, bridges, and hospitals. These were rebuilt over the next decade, only to be leveled once again.
Baghdad has probably been demolished and rebuilt so
many times throughout history that it's a wonder that the
city still exists. Nevertheless, it's a very modern metropo-
lis. There are portions of Baghdad that resemble the
downtown areas of any major city in the West. On the
other hand, Islamic architecture abounds in many areas,
with pedestrian labyrinths of tight alleyways and court-
yards. The mosques are spectacular, covered in intricate
patterns of colored stones. Some neighborhoods of traditional housing still remain. Elaborate overhanging
balconies—*shenashil*—that are really upper rooms distin-
guish narrow streets of traditional quarters. Handsomely
decorated doorways front onto the street. One can get lost
wandering through the maze-like paths of the older sections that are full of character and charm. I had been to
Baghdad previously, before the war, and remember being
struck then by the beauty of the place, hidden behind a fa-
cade of pain, hardship, and despair. Today, I'm sure, it's
no different.

I debark and present my special NSA papers identifying me as an Interpol police detective from Switzerland. I use my own name, but this cover story will go much further in Iraq than if I went around saying I'm an espionage agent with the NSA. As far as my business in Iraq is concerned, I am researching a report that Interpol will publish on the current state of terrorism in the Middle East. Once I'm cleared to enter the base, a sergeant leads me to an office in the bustling command center. The sergeant never says a word, but he eyes me curiously. I must look like one strange civilian to him, especially since I have NSA clearance. The sergeant leaves me in the hands of my contact, Lieutenant Colonel Dan Petlow, who greets me in a businesslike fashion. When we're alone in his office, he tells me that he's the only army officer in Iraq who's aware of my mission. It turns out that he knows Colonel Lambert and has been in on the doings of Third Echelon for a long time.

"I was Rick Benton's contact as well," Petlow says before I can ask.

Petlow is about my age. I ask him how long he's been in the country, and he replies that he's lost track of the time.

"Not really, I'm just being facetious," he says. "I've been here sixteen months now. This country tends to sour you."

He offers me a soft drink and I take it. We sit under an electric fan because the AC in the building is being repaired. It feels like Phoenix, Arizona, outside, and it's an oven in the office.

"Tell me about Benton," I begin.

"He seemed capable but a bit reckless," Petlow says. "I met with him face-to-face only twice. Didn't know him well at all. He knew his stuff, though. He was an expert on all things Middle East."

"What do you know about his recent investigation?"

"The arms dealing? Not much. Benton kept that stuff close to his chest. He kept saying he was working on uncovering a Shop pipeline coming from the north into Iraq. He said the arms have been pouring into Mosul. That means they're coming from Iran and then through Rawanduz to get to Mosul, or they're coming from Turkey through the town of Amadiyah. Both of those villages are in KDP-controlled territory."

Mosul is perhaps the biggest city in northern Iraq. It's just out of the region controlled by the officially sanctioned Kurdistan Regional Government and the site of a lot of unrest, mainly between different Kurdish factions. Rawanduz is a village between Mosul and the Iranian border. Likewise, Amadiyah is a village north of Mosul, near the Turkish border. Two Kurdish political parties influence everything that happens in northern Iraq. In 1946 a recognized Kurdish hero named Mulla Mustafa Barzani formed the oldest one, the Kurdistan Democratic Party— the KDP—which has cultural ties to Iran. The second party, the Patriotic Union of Kurdistan—the PUK— formed in 1976 as a rival to the KDP. There are other, smaller Kurdish parties, but the KDP and PUK are the big daddies. In theory they share governmental responsibilities of Kurdish Iraq, but the KDP seems to have more power. In recent years the two parties have grudgingly cooperated with each other on many issues such as in the education and health sectors. But don't expect one to invite the other to a dinner party.

"What do you think?" I ask Petlow.

"I doubt the Turkish route theory. It doesn't make a lot

of sense. For one thing, Turkey is supposedly one of our allies and they're just as concerned about illegal arms traffic as we are. Another thing is that the route would be more difficult. Benton always thought that the arms originated in one of the former Soviet satellites. Maybe Azerbaijan. In order to get to Iraq from there, they'd have to go through Armenia and then Turkey. It's a straighter shoot out of Azerbaijan through Iran and into Iraq."

"So you're saying that I should look into the Rawanduz connection first?" I ask.

Petlow shrugs. "It's just an opinion. Doesn't mean I'm right."

I mull this over and say, "Southeast Turkey is a Kurdish region, too. There could be some cooperation going on between the tribes. There's also a lot of terrorist activity in that part of Turkey."

"That's true, too. Look, I'll be honest with you, Fisher. You don't have a lot to go on. What are you going to do when you get up there? Knock on doors? Benton didn't leave you anything to give you some direction, did he?"

"No, I'll just have to play it by ear at first. I figure I have to start in Mosul. I imagine I'll begin by investigating the sites in the city where illegal arms have been discovered. The goal is to find a lead pointing me in the right direction."

"Well, good luck." Petlow stands and picks up a duffel bag. "This came in the official pouch from Washington," he says, handing it to me. "It's for you."

The only weapon I carried on the plane is my genuine Marine Corps combat knife. It's got a 7-inch carbon steel blade with a blood groove and a 5-inch leather handle. I remove it from its sheath and cut the rope binding the end of the duffel bag. My SC-20K and Osprey are inside, along with boxes of various types of ammunition.

"I can use this stuff," I mutter.

Petlow then opens his desk and hands me a set of keys. "There's an unmarked Toyota Land Cruiser in the compound outside. It's yours to do with what you will. We don't need it back. We've checked it out and it runs fine. Believe it or not, imported vehicles do very well in Iraq. I know a car dealer in Baghdad who's gotten rich since the war began."

"How's security on the roads? What kinds of checkpoints can I expect?"

"You can expect checkpoints everywhere and some of them will delay you considerably. But if you dress appropriately, I don't think you'll have any trouble with the locals. You have such a swarthy complexion that you look like you might be Arabic. Do you speak Arabic?"

"Yeah." In fact, I speak seven languages. It's English I'm not so great at. I take the keys. "Thanks."

"Have you eaten? Would you like—"

Before Petlow can finish his invitation, a huge crack of thunder rocks the building. We look at each other and both immediately know that it wasn't thunder.

"Damn," Petlow mutters. "That was a big one." He shoots toward the door and runs outside. I follow him and join the throng of soldiers rushing from the building.

The air is dark and full of smoke. Sirens blare as emergency personnel appear on the scene. Men are shouting orders all over the place, and for a few minutes it's a mass of confusion. Eventually, though, the smoke begins to clear and I can see flames over by the fortified fence that separates the base from the outside world. A section of the fence is completely gone and in its place is a hulk of black, burning metal.

I stand out of the way and watch the professionals deal with it. These soldiers are obviously used to this kind of thing happening all the time. Fifteen minutes later Colonel Petlow sees me and takes me aside.

"It was a laundry van," he says. "Suicide driver, of course. The eyewitnesses say he drove straight for the checkpoint gate at full speed. One of the sentries fired at him to try and stop the thing, but it was too late. Damn explosives took out two of our men and a big chunk of fence. What a waste. What the hell do they think they're accomplishing? This is the third one in two weeks."

I commiserate and say that at least no one else was hurt.

"You know, these guys are getting their explosives from terrorist supply lines," Petlow continues. "There's no doubt about it. They couldn't have stockpiled it for all this time. Go plug up that pipeline, Fisher. I'm here if you need anything, so don't hesitate to call. You've got my number?"

I give him a bleak smile. We shake hands and then he rushes back toward the mess of burning debris.

8

SARAH Burns was having a wonderful time in Jerusalem. On the third night of her stay, she and Rivka decided to break the double-date routine and go off separately with their beaus. Rivka and Noel went to the movies. Sarah and Eli opted for a romantic stroll through the Old City and dinner in the New City.

Sarah had been brought up secularly and had no allegiance to any particular faith. She was one of those naïve but well-meaning people that was constantly bewildered by the fact that different races and religions found it difficult to get along. It was this purity of heart that made her so attractive, and she was well aware of it. Sarah often exploited this side of her personality in a charming, all-American girl-next-door persona. Academically she was very bright and accustomed to being an overachiever, but this didn't mean she was particularly worldly. Her mother, and later her father, had raised her in a protective environment that sheltered her from the liabilities of the street.

She was, therefore, unintentionally gullible—a trait she never realized might someday get her into trouble.

As she walked arm in arm with Eli, the young man with whom she was enamored, Sarah had no reason to worry about terrorists, suicide bombers, Arab-Jewish conflicts, or the peace process. The only thing on her mind that evening was whether or not she and Eli would eventually end up in a bedroom.

She had met Eli at the Northwestern University library during her sophomore year. Rivka Cohen belonged to a campus social club of Israeli students. She had arranged to study with a boy she was interested in, a fellow named Noel Brooks. Rivka asked Sarah to come along because Noel might bring a friend. Sarah needed to study for an exam so she thought, why not? She and Rivka found themselves at a table in the library and after a while Noel showed up with a companion. They sat across the table from the girls and introductions were made. His name was Eli Horowitz. Sarah thought he was the most beautiful man she'd ever seen. He had dark, curly hair, brown eyes, a closely cut beard and mustache, and was tall and muscular. He would have resembled Michelangelo's *David* if the statue had sported facial hair. Sarah attempted to continue studying, but she found the young man's presence quite distracting.

Eli, like Noel, was a graduate student from Israel. He was studying music and wanted to be a conductor. He didn't specialize in any particular instrument but claimed to be able to play several "not very well."

After the study session, the girls said goodbye to the boys and they went their separate ways. That night, Eli called to ask her out.

They dated for three months. Eli and Noel had an

apartment off-campus and Sarah found herself often staying there. As a sophomore, she still lived in a dorm, but the rules were lax enough that she could sign out to "stay with a friend." It got to where she rarely slept at the dorm.

Then, suddenly, both Eli and Noel were gone. Rivka and Sarah tried in vain to find out what had happened. At first they were hurt badly because they thought the boys had abandoned them without saying goodbye. Two letters arrived a month later, one for Rivka and one for Sarah. The boys explained that Immigration had deported them. Their student visas had been invalid—expired months earlier—and due to the heightened security rules regarding foreign students, they had no recourse.

Sarah kept in touch with Eli by e-mail once he was reestablished in Israel. He didn't reply often, which concerned her, but she figured he was busy looking for work or whatever. When he did write, the e-mails were full of love and adoration, many times loaded with sexual suggestions and invitations for her to come and visit. This encouraged Sarah to carry a torch for the young man.

And now, ten months later, here she was walking with him through the historic Old City of Jerusalem. Eli gave her a running commentary as they strolled through the narrow streets.

"You see, it's divided into four quarters. This is the Christian Quarter, the one we're in now. Over that way is the Muslim Quarter, and over there is the Armenian Quarter. The Jewish Quarter is straight across, to the east."

"You sound like a tour guide," Sarah said, laughing.

"I worked as a tour guide when I was a teenager," Eli said. "I'd take fat Americans all over the city in a company car. Sometimes I'd drive really fast and scare the hell out of them."

She slapped his arm and said, "You're awful."

They approached a somber church that appeared to have been built in a patchwork-quilt fashion. It was made up of several architectural styles but was impressive by its sheer antiquity.

"This is the Church of the Holy Sepulchre," Eli said. "It's built on the site where the Catholics think Jesus was crucified."

"Really?"

"Yeah. The Orthodox and Coptic churches believe it, too."

"You mean not everyone thinks it's here?"

"Nope. There's a place in East Jerusalem where most Protestants think it happened. You want to go inside?"

"I don't think so. I'd rather keep walking."

"Okay."

The couple moved south and east one block to the Lutheran Church of the Redeemer. Eli took her up the tower so they could see the excellent view of the Old City. As they gazed upon the marvelous vista, Sarah said, "You haven't told me where you live. Do you and Noel share a place?"

"No, I live alone now," Eli answered. "I have an apartment in East Jerusalem."

"Oh, yeah? You going to show it to me?" She squeezed his waist flirtatiously.

He smiled. "Maybe. You know East Jerusalem is the Palestinian part of the city."

"So?"

"I'm just saying."

After descending the tower they walked to David Street and headed west. When they reached the Jaffa Gate, Eli said, "This is the traditional doorway between the Old City and the New City." He pointed to an old building.

"That's the Crusader Citadel. That's where they think King Herod hung out."

"There's so much history here," Sarah said, wide-eyed.

"You hungry?"

"Starving!"

"Let's go eat. I know a very famous place in the New City."

They walked up the Jaffa Road past expensive gift shops and eateries until they came to the Village Green Restaurant.

"I've heard of this place," Sarah observed.

"Some people think it's the best restaurant in Jerusalem," Eli said. They entered, secured a table, and looked at the menu.

"It's kosher vegetarian," Eli explained. "No meat for you carnivores."

Sarah kicked him lightly under the table. "Hey, I like my hamburgers. But I like veggies, too. What's good?"

"I like their pizza."

She ended up ordering a meatless lasagna dish, vegetable soup, and a salad. Eli asked for a mushroom pizza and a bottle of kosher red wine.

As she watched him eat, she was reminded of her father's probing questions. She liked Eli a lot, but it was true she didn't know a lot about his background.

"Tell me about your parents," she said.

He shrugged, chewing on a piece of food. "What's to tell?"

"They live here?"

"Um, no. At one time they did."

"Where are they now?"

"My mother is in Lebanon. My father was Jewish and my mother is Muslim. They didn't stay together."

"I didn't know that," Sarah said. "Why haven't you told me that?"

"I didn't think it mattered."

"How old were you when . . . they divorced?"

He laughed inwardly. "They were never married. It was a bit of a scandal, I think. Not many Muslims and Jews have children together. My mother raised me until I was seven. Then . . . well, I went to live with relatives in Lebanon. I came back here when I was eighteen."

"Where's your father?"

"He's dead."

"Oh, I'm sorry."

He shrugged again. "It happened when I was young. It was a terrorist bombing. He was in the wrong place at the wrong time."

"Gee, Eli."

"Your mother is dead, too, isn't she?" he asked.

"Yeah. She died of cancer when I was fifteen."

"And your father . . . is he still an 'international salesman'?"

She looked at him sideways. "You say that like you're skeptical."

He laughed. "It's just that you don't seem to know much about what he does for a living. You never have."

"That's true, I guess."

"You see him much?"

"No, not really. He lives in Baltimore, or rather a suburb of Baltimore."

"That's near Washington, D.C., you know," he said.

"What do you mean?"

"He's probably in the CIA." Eli said it facetiously.

"Actually he did work for the CIA a long time ago. Not anymore, though. He was in the CIA when he met my mother."

"No shit?"

"That's right."

"What was he, like a spy or something?"

"I really don't know. Some kind of diplomat's aid."

Eli laughed. "Yep. Spy."

She laughed with him. "I guess, maybe. Anyway, I don't know *what* he does now."

"I see."

"So, Eli, are you going to stay in Israel or are you coming back to the States to get your degree?"

He took a sip of wine and said, "I'm thinking of going to Juilliard. I have an audition in the summer. I just have to get a visa."

"Really? Juilliard?"

"Uh-huh."

"So you won't come back to Chicago?"

"I don't think so, Sarah. But, listen, why don't you come live with me in New York after you graduate? You've got one more year, right?"

The question took Sarah by surprise. "You want me to come *live* with you?"

"Sure. Why not? You like me, don't you?"

"Well, yeah, but that's . . . that's like we'd be married or something."

"No it's not, silly. We'd just be living together."

She was flustered. "I'll have to get back to you on that one, Eli."

"There's plenty of time, I think," he said. He reached across the table, placed his hand over hers, and lightly squeezed it. Sarah was taken aback by his show of affection. She had no idea that he cared enough for her to ask her something like that.

What would a future with Eli Horowitz be like? she wondered. As an English major she could probably get a job teaching somewhere in New York. She'd have to get a certificate from that state, of course. Or maybe she'd just stay at home and be a writer. That's what she really wanted to do. Wouldn't it be an idyllic existence? She a best-selling author and Eli a famous orchestra conductor?

Sarah turned over her hand so that she could squeeze his in return.

It just might work, she thought.

9

I set out in the Toyota Land Cruiser and head north from Baghdad. The Iraqi security forces stop me at two different roadblocks on the outskirts of the city. They're very thorough. At the first one they ask to see my identity papers and passport. They ask me if I'm armed even though the papers indicate that I'm cleared with the Iraqi government to carry firearms. I comply by revealing the Five-seveN, but the SC-20K remains in the duffel bag. After a few minutes of suspicious looks and some frowns, they let me drive on. The second roadblock is much the same. They ask what I plan to do in Mosul and how long I'll be there. I tell them what I think will appease them and they let me go.

The highway is a modern one—newly repaved after the beating it took during the war and subsequent months of unrest. The city was brutal with stop-and-go congestion on every major street, but here there isn't much traffic. The open road feels good. I occasionally see military vehicles, even U.S. ones. Dilapidated pickup trucks and wagons carrying produce and other goods are fairly common.

The intensely bright sun beats down on the car, and I'm grateful that I remembered to bring an ordinary pair of sunglasses. The landscape is flat and barren. As I said before, it reminds me a little of southern Arizona. It's a rugged, cruel country and I wouldn't want to be stuck in the middle of the desert with no transportation. Thank goodness someone invented the air conditioner.

"Sam, you there?" Lambert sounds like what I imagine the Voice of Conscience to be. It's tinny and small and is lodged deep within my right ear.

I take one hand off the steering wheel and press the spot on my neck to activate the transmitter. "Yeah, I'm here, Colonel."

"How did everything go with Petlow?"

"Fine. He's got his hands full, though. This is still a very rough place."

"I know. Listen, I take it you're headed up to Mosul?"

"I'm on the road now. I'll be in Samarra in less than an hour."

"Forget Mosul. You need to go to Arbil," Lambert says. "That's why I'm contacting you via the implant instead of with text. We've just received word that the Kurdish police there have captured a brand-new shipment of weapons. Nasty stuff, too. Lots of AK-47s, but a nice little pile of Stingers, too. They've made an arrest—the truck driver that was bringing them in. He's not talking. The shipment is sitting in police headquarters in the town center. Since this is a fresh lead, I suggest you check it out before they move it. If you can determine where the arms came from, then you can follow the trail back to the source. Remember, that's Kurdish territory. You have no authority there, so you'll have to get in and out without the police knowing."

"Right," I say. "What's the best route from where I am?"

"Our intelligence suggests that you continue on to Mosul and then go east from there to Arbil. The main highway from Baghdad to Arbil runs parallel to yours, and the connecting roads aren't safe."

"Roger that. Anything else?"

"That's it for now. Good luck, Sam."

"Roger that. Out." I grip the wheel and keep driving. I eventually pass through Samarra and head toward Tikrit, the birthplace of Saddam Hussein. When I finally get through the roadblocks there, repeating the routine I perfected outside of Baghdad, I see nothing special about Tikrit. I'm happy to say there are no road markers proclaiming that "Saddam Hussein Was Born Here."

Mosul is Iraq's second-largest city. It's just on the edge of what is considered Iraqi Kurdistan. From what I understand, we get the word *muslin*, the famous cotton fabric, from Mosul. Apparently that's where it was first made. The ancient city of Nineveh is located outside of Mosul. I've heard there are a lot of archaeological ruins in the spot worth seeing if you're in a tourist frame of mind, but I'm afraid I have business elsewhere.

Another roadblock, another song and dance with my identity papers, and I'm now driving east to Arbil. This is officially Kurd country, for Arbil is considered the Kurdish capital in Iraq. Both of the two main Kurdish political parties, the KDP and the PUK, have their headquarters in Arbil. Considered to be one of the world's oldest cities, Arbil dates back past the Romans and Alexander the Great's time to Neanderthal Man, whose relics have been discovered there. The modern portion sits atop a mound that's been formed by successive building over centuries.

The scenery in Iraqi Kurdistan contrasts sharply with the rest of the country. Here there are high mountains and colorful, fertile valleys. The mountain ranges grow more impressive the farther north you go and are commonly referred to as "the Alps of the Middle East." Throughout history the mountains acted as a natural barrier for a society that has been eager to preserve its culture. Ethnically, the Kurds have no relationship with Arabs. They were allies of the U.S. during the Iraq War, in theory at least. I wonder if I'll be able to trust them.

The sun is setting as I approach Arbil. Lights up ahead indicate I need to slow down—another roadblock. Four men surround the Toyota when I stop. They're dressed in Iraqi police uniforms, but somehow I get the feeling that something's not right. Two men carry rifles and the third has a handgun.

As soon as I lower my window, the man with a handgun points it in my face. "We're going for a ride, friend," he says in Arabic. These guys aren't Kurds.

"I have my papers if you want to see them," I say in his language.

"Shut up!" he commands again. He waits until his three companions get in the backseat of the car. The guy with the handgun goes around the car and gets in on the passenger side. He keeps it trained at my head.

The man without a gun sitting in the backseat says, "Now drive that way," pointing to a dark dirt road leading off the highway. There's nothing I can do but obey. I put the Toyota in drive and follow their directions. The road moves off into the thicket. Were it not for the headlights, I wouldn't be able to see a thing.

"Where are we going?" I ask in Arabic.

"You'll see," the backseat driver says. "Just shut up and drive."

Three minutes later we're approximately a mile from the main highway. The man in back tells me to stop the car, leave the headlights on, and get out.

I have no choice but to comply. I open the door and step out, followed by all four men. It's now very dark outside, but the car's headlights illuminate the area well enough to see. The unarmed man, obviously the leader, roughly turns me around and pushes me against the car. "Get your hands up, on top of your head!" he orders.

I do so, but I'm getting pissed off. I'm not about to let these guys manhandle me. The asshole starts to frisk me. I'm thankful I left the Five-seveN in the glove compartment, but I need to think of a way to keep them out of the car.

"I'm with Interpol," I say. "I have clearance with your government."

"Shut up!"

The guy with the pistol grins at me. I see now that he's missing three teeth and is the ugliest son of a bitch I've seen since I got to Iraq. "Where did you get the nice car, my friend?" he asks.

The one frisking me, apparently looking for money, demands, "Where's your wallet?"

"I don't carry one," I say truthfully.

He grabs my shoulder and pulls me away from the car. All four of them are now facing me. The two with rifles hold their weapons across their chests, not aiming them yet. The guns appear to be Hakims. No-Tooth, though, has a Smith & Wesson 38 Special revolver. Probably a black-market item.

"I think we'll take your car, then," the leader says. The other three laugh. "We need it to move some boxes." They laugh some more. "There we were, sitting and waiting for some friends to bring us a truck to help us move our things, but I think your big car will do fine. May we borrow it?" More laughs.

"Where are you from, my friend?" No-Tooth asks. He twirls his revolver around his finger as if he were in a John Wayne Western. "We don't see many Westerners who speak Arabic."

"I'm Swiss," I say. "I'm a police officer with Interpol. I suggest you let me be on my way."

"Oh, you *suggest* that we let you be on your way?" the leader mocks me as he takes a step closer. "Listen, I suggest that you get down on your knees and pray because you're about to kiss the earth goodbye."

Come on, I think. Move just another step closer.

"You want me to get on my knees?" I ask.

"That's what I said!"

I look at the ground and point. "Right here?"

That does the trick. He takes another step and starts to say, "Yes, right th—"

Before he finishes I kick him fast and hard in the crotch. I don't stop there, though. I move in like lightning, using an advanced Krav Maga technique to grab hold of his upper body and pull him toward me as the toothless guy fires his gun. The leader takes the round in the back, and then I shove his body at No-Tooth with such force that they both fall to the ground.

Before the guys with rifles can react, I grab the barrel of one of the guns with my left hand, place my right hand beneath the butt, and use a levering jerk to yank it out of the surprised man's hands. Before the second rifleman can level his gun and fire it, I swing the butt of my new rifle around and clobber him in the face. He screams, drops his weapon, and falls to his knees, clutching his head. The first rifleman, now weaponless, growls, ready to rush at me. I slam the rifle butt into his nose and then use my right foot to kick him in the chest. Stunned, he stumbles away from me but doesn't go down. I then toss the rifle in the air, giving it a slight twirl so that it swings around like a baton. I catch it with the butt against me and the barrel pointing the way it's supposed to. I squeeze the trigger and the guy takes the round at point-blank range. He falls in his tracks.

I swing the Hakim around to No-Tooth, but he's no longer on the ground by the dead leader. I see him running into the dark thicket. I consider raising the rifle and taking him out, but I decide to let him go lick his wounds. I really can't imagine where he'll go in this rough terrain at night. The leader and one rifleman are dead. That leaves the guy whose face I smashed in. He's still on his knees, moaning. I think I broke his cheekbone.

"You," I say. "Stop whining and talk to me."

The man looks at me, wide-eyed. He can't believe I overpowered four men. The right side of his face is already swelling, giving him a lopsided appearance.

"Who are you?" I ask. "You're not the police."

The man babbles something in Arabic, and I raise the rifle butt, indicating I might strike him again.

He tells me his name and the names of the other three men. All generic Arabic names that seem to be interchangeable in the Middle East.

"Where did you get the police uniforms?"

He tells me that the police hired them to act as militia. That story doesn't ring true to me.

"Where are you from?" I ask.

Again, the babbling. This time I play rough. I ram the rifle butt into his shoulder. He cries out and falls back. I stand over him and ask him again where he's from.

"Iran," he tells me. He and his three companions are from Iran.

"What are you doing in Iraq?"

The man rolls over and clutches the dirt. I sense what he's about to do and shut my eyes just as he throws a fistful of dirt in my face. He jumps to his feet, but I'm ready for him. He grabs for the rifle and I jerk it up and forward. Even with my eyes closed, I manage to ram the side of the Hakim into his chin. I open my eyes and thrust the rifle butt into the man's chest. He falls to the ground, unconscious. It's possible I broke his sternum and maybe stopped his heart.

Shit. There are three dead men here. I have no choice but to abandon them. I don't like leaving bodies in my wake, but it can't be helped. I'm not going to waste time trying to hide the corpses, seeing that we're so far from the highway. If and when they're found, it will just have to be chalked up to the fact that Iraq is a very rough place.

I toss the Hakim to the ground and get in the car. I drive back to the highway and on into the city, wondering what became of No-Tooth.

10

I drive into Arbil shortly after midnight. The streets are deserted and the town is deadly quiet. There isn't much in the way of street lighting so the place is very dark and foreboding. Carly at Third Echelon had transmitted a town map to my OPSAT, so I find the police station with no problem.

I park the Toyota a block away, strip my outer clothes to reveal my uniform, don the headset, grab my Five-sevcN, put on the Osprey, and I'm ready to go. I get out of the car and creep along the street, keeping to the shadows. No one is around, but in my business you can't be too careful.

The Arbil Police Headquarters is small. It's a one-level building with a parking lot in back. I find it odd that there are no patrol cars there. The windows are covered with a thick screen mesh, so it's impossible to see inside. However, I detect illumination behind the windows in front. Either someone left an office light on or someone is inside. I go around to the back and quietly try the steel door. Locked, of course. It's a basic cylinder lock, so I use my picks. It takes me seventeen seconds to get it open. Not bad.

I look through the door and see a dark corridor. I position the goggles and switch on the night-vision mode. I scan the upper edges of the walls to make sure there are no cameras, and then I slip inside and shut the door behind me. With my back to one wall I slink to a door in the middle of the corridor and listen. Silence. I carefully open the door and look in the room. It's an ordinary office—desk, filing cabinets, a couple of chairs. I move on and come to a T. To the left is a door marked Secure Area in script I recognize to be Kurdistan. I'm not too familiar with the language. Arabic I can get by with, but Kurdistan—forget it. I recognize some words, but that's about it. If I have to speak with a Kurd while I'm here it might be difficult, although many Kurds speak Arabic as well.

The light I saw earlier is coming from the right. I inch along the wall and peer around the corner into a brightly lit space. It's the front outer office. There's a wall with a glass window that opens out to the reception area. On this side of the wall there's a man reclining in a chair, his feet on the desk. He is snoring loudly. I switch off the night vision and raise my goggles to get a better look.

The man is wearing a police uniform, but it looks as if it's two sizes too small. Something's not right.

I move into the room and stand behind the man. He's burly and has a Saddam Hussein-style mustache. I gently put my left hand over his mouth and pinch his nose. The policeman wakes, startled beyond belief. As soon as he leans forward, I grasp him in a "sleeper hold," which closes off the carotid arteries until he's unconscious. He falls forward and slides off the chair onto the floor. I figure he'll be out for about ten minutes if I'm lucky.

I take a cursory look around the desk and find nothing of interest except for a key ring in the drawer. I take it and go back to the corridor. Sure enough, one of the keys works in the Secure Area door, which opens to another corridor. I listen for signs of occupation and check again for cameras. They only keep one guy on duty? Very strange. I suppose there's not much crime in Arbil in the middle of the night.

I come to a locked door and try the key ring again. It opens on the third try. I'm conscious of my sharp intake of breath when I turn on the lights. It's some kind of store-room and it's full of crates. One is open and sits on the floor three feet away from me. A pile of Hakim rifles over-flows from the crate. I stoop to examine the weapons and see that they are clean and ready for use. I move to another crate, the lid of which has been previously pried open and replaced. I lift the lid and see more assault rifles—AK 47s. Another crate contains Soviet Makarov PMs, 9mm handguns that date back to the 1950s. They're also in ex-cellent condition. Yet another crate is full of SVD Dragunovs, gas-operated sniper rifles.

There are sixteen crates in all, most of them still sealed. This must be the captured cache that Lambert told me about. What do the Arbil police plan to do with it? Aren't they going to turn it over to the authorities, whoever they may be?

I have to figure out where the damn things came from. The first crate is unmarked, but the second one has an ink stamp on the side. In Arabic—Farsi, really—it reads Tabriz Container Company. Tabriz? That's in Iran! I move to the next crate and it has the same marking. In fact, nine of the sixteen crates bear the Tabriz stamp.

Either the weapons came through Iran or the supplier is simply using crates that were manufactured there. At any rate, it's a lead.

Against the far wall of the room is a stack of four large, flat cases. They resemble electric guitar cases only they're much wider. I unsnap the clasps and open the top one.

Stingers. Four cases of Stingers, two in each case. Un-fucking-believable. These are American made. How the hell did they get them? Off to the side of the cases are two shoulder-launchers for the Stingers. These babies are terribly effective against low-level aircraft, such as helicopters, and a single man can fire one like a bazooka.

I make notes of the inventory on my OPSAT, take a few photographs, and leave the room. I move farther down the hall to a large steel door with bars in a window. The jail perhaps? I turn to the key ring again and unlock the door. It squeaks with rust and I wince. Hopefully no one is back there. I look inside and see a row of six barred cells. A small desk is to my left, but it is unmanned. There's nothing here except a hammer lying on it. Upon closer examination of the tool, I discern a substance that appears to be dried blood and perhaps fleshy material and hair on the hammerhead. I turn to leave, but something in the first cell catches my eye. At first I think it's a bundle of blankets, but I see now that there might be a figure lying on the cot. I turn on the lights and step closer to the cell. It is indeed a body, completely covered by a blanket. Is he dead?

I move to the next cell and there's another guy, covered by a blanket. The third, fourth, and fifth cells contain the same. Number six is empty. I look on the ring and try the keys until I find one that opens cell number one. I pull the blanket back, and sure enough, there's a guy with a bullet hole in his head. From what I can tell, he was shot in the back of the skull and the round exited through the front of his face. He is unrecognizable, of course. I pull the blanket back farther and see that the man is wearing only his underwear.

The man in the second cell received the same treatment, although it looks as if he was tortured before being killed. There are burn marks, probably from a cigarette, on his upper body. The third guy's right hand is mangled, as if someone had pounded it a few times with a hammer. *The* hammer. The fourth man, like the first, was just shot.

I back out of the jail area and close the door behind me. I lock it again only because whoever had done this is sure to return. My friend in the outer lobby will be waking soon, and he probably knows a lot about what's going on here. Perhaps he's one of the killers

I go back to the front of the building and see that the guard is still unconscious. He's breathing steadily, so I'm sure he'll recover with just a bad headache to remember me by. I make my way to the first corridor and head for the back door but decide to check out the office I saw upon entering. I open the door, step inside, and use my night vision to avoid turning on lights.

I have good reason to believe that this is the office of the chief of police. There are a couple of citations on the wall and a photo of the chief shaking hands with a man I figure is one of the Kurdish politicos. I look closely at the photo and I could swear that one of the dead guys in the jail cell is the chief. I'm not positive because the victims' faces were bloody messes. Even so, if I had to bet on it, I'd say that the guy in the photo is the man in the second cell, the one who had been tortured before being executed.

On the desk are several manila folders full of mug shots. I open the top folder and am surprised to see none other than No-Tooth. In fact, the top four photographs in the pile are the same four men who tried to steal my car and leave me for dead outside of Arbil. Notes on the back of each photo are written in Kurdistan script, but I can make out the words *terrorist*, *wanted*, and *Iran*. On the back of No-Tooth's photo is another word I recognize—*Shadows* with a big question mark beside it.

It's all very clear to me. Those four bandits I encountered outside the city were here earlier. They killed the four *real* policemen and placed the corpses in the cells after stripping off and donning the uniforms. The bandits had wanted my Land Cruiser. To move the crates of weapons? One of them had said they were waiting for a truck to "move some boxes." Are those guys the Shop's customers? The Shop is selling arms to the Shadows? I have to say I'm not surprised. If the Shadows are the terrorist group *du jour*, then it makes sense that the Shop, the biggest illegal arms dealer in the world, would want them as customers.

I hear a car door slam outside. Shit. As keys rattle in the back door, I flatten against the wall of the office and hope whoever it is doesn't come in here.

Two voices. One man is laughing and speaking rapidly—in Arabic. I catch the words "police," "taking care of," and "move the boxes." The men walk past the office and continue to the outer lobby. I hear exclamations of surprise and concern when they find my friend on the floor. There's a groan and a slap and another groan. The guard is coming around. One of the men orders the other one to check on the weapons, and I hear him ask for the keys. More talk, the sound of moving things on the desk, and an angry shout. The keys are gone, of course. They're in my pocket.

The angry guy sounds familiar. I figure it's probably in my best interest to get a look at him. I reach into the Osprey and pull out a handy tool I call the "corner periscope." It's really a lot like a dentist's tool—it's a thin piece of metal with a small round mirror at the end. The metal is bendable so I can adapt it to just about any kind of space. It's best for looking around corners when you don't want to be noticed.

I quietly creep out of the office and snake down the hall with my back to the wall. When I reach the corner by the front office, I stick the mirror out and position it so I can see.

The guard is sitting in the chair, rubbing the back of his head. The angry guy is sitting on the desk in front of him, his back to me. The other man is behind the chair and looks concerned. He doesn't look familiar. Both of the new men are wearing police uniforms. I want the angry guy to turn around so I can see his face.

"What are you going to tell Ahmed?" the second man asks. I can now follow the conversation pretty well.

"I'll worry about that later," answers the angry guy. "It's more about what Ahmed will tell Tarighian!" He grabs the guard by the chin. "You sure you didn't see who did this to you?" The guard shakes his head. "Allah help me. Tarighian will be most displeased. We'd better find a way to break down that door. If our stuff is gone . . ."

Tarighian? Who the hell is Tarighian?

The angry guy turns slightly and I see his face. It's my old buddy No-Tooth, the one that got away. I knew I'd heard his voice before.

I could take them out if I wanted, but that's not my directive. I move away, down the hall and toward the back door. There's a garbage can beside the door, so I quietly lay the key ring inside. No need to make it easy for them. I'm sure the proper authorities will have the means to break down the doors if they have to.

I slip outside and run to the shadows on the opposite end of the parking lot. I crouch and then move quickly to the street, satisfied I'm not being followed. I run in the darkness to the Toyota, get inside, and crouch low in the seat just in case the goons come out and start to look around.

Using my OPSAT, I send a message to Colonel Petlow in Baghdad. I explain that the Arbil policemen were murdered by Shadows terrorists who are attempting to remove a shipment of illegal arms from the station. I blind-copy the report to Lambert in Washington and wait.

Approximately thirty-five minutes later I hear sirens. I'm surprised by the rapid response. I was afraid the terrorists would get away with the goods by the time the Iraqis or the U.S. Army arrived. I see three police vehicles pull up in front of the station, followed by a U.S. Army jeep with four soldiers inside. I'd like to give them a hand, but I need to stay innocuous. So I sit back with an intention to watch and enjoy the fireworks.

But to my horror the terrorists suddenly appear from behind the building, firing AK-47s at the policemen. Three Iraqi police fall to the ground and the others jump behind cover. I recognize No-Tooth as the terrorist ringleader. He throws something into the midst of the vehicles, and a few seconds later it explodes with a powerful blast. The grenade destroys the U.S. Army jeep and most likely kills or seriously wounds the four American soldiers. I now seriously consider joining the fight, but before I can make a move a van pulls around from the back of the building. The terrorists jump inside and the van speeds away with a screech.

I curse at myself for not doing something sooner—but what could I have done? I'm not supposed to interact with the local law enforcement without authorization. Could I have made a difference? I honestly don't know. Next time, though, I think I'll go with my instincts and buck the directives.

Approaching sirens wail some distance away, and a few seconds later I see more police cars and an ambulance arrive at the scene. There's nothing I can do now; I have to let the Iraqis handle it.

Disgruntled, I start the Toyota and drive away.

11

ANDREI Zdrok was in a foul mood.

His driver let him off in front of the Swiss-Russian International Mercantile Bank, pausing long enough to receive instructions regarding when to return to pick up his employer. The Mercedes sped away and Zdrok strode toward the heavy glass doors. Just before entering the building, though, he looked at his Rolex and saw that he had fifteen minutes before the meeting. He decided that a bagel and coffee might go a long way toward improving his frame of mind.

He made a detour and crossed the avenue to the bakery. Even Andrei Zdrok agreed with the food critics that Zabat's was the best bakery in Zurich. That it happened to be in the financial district was a plus for its proprietors. They sold hundreds of bagels, muffins, rolls, and pastries daily to the bankers and accountants who worked in the area. By coincidence, there was also a bagel shop across the street from the other Swiss-Russian bank branch located in Baku, Azerbaijan. Zdrok often frequented that establishment as well, although it wasn't as good.

Zdrok went inside Zabat's, bought an onion bagel with cream cheese, a coffee—black—and paid for it with a five-franc bill. He told the server to keep the change. He did this often and had a reputation in the bakery of being the "generous man in the Brioni suit."

Zdrok returned to the bank, entered the lobby, and nodded to the security guard standing just inside the door. A banking customer was already at the teller window; two more were in the private safe-deposit rooms. As one of the many private financial institutions in Zurich offering numbered bank accounts, the Swiss-Russian, as Zdrok referred to it for short, dealt only with wealthy international clients. In a city where money was the lifeblood, the Swiss-Russian was well on its way to becoming a major player in worldwide finance. The beauty of it was that the bank was small and not very well known. The authorities paid little attention to it. Zdrok made sure that all of its legitimate business was aboveboard and clean so that trouble never came knocking. He didn't want too much circumspection into what really went on behind the scenes of the Swiss-Russian International Mercantile Bank.

Zdrok unlocked the gate that led to the "employees only" area, glanced back into the lobby to make sure nothing was amiss, then entered the conference room, where his three associates were waiting. Not surprisingly, they had also purchased bagels or muffins with coffee prior to attending the meeting.

Anton Antipov was fifty-two years old. A former colonel with the KGB, he had formed a partnership with Andrei Zdrok shortly after the fall of the Soviet Union. He was tall, imposing, and had a reputation for being a sadist.

Zdrok had never witnessed anything supporting this rumor, but he had heard plenty of stories. Antipov had been in charge of one of the gulags outside of Moscow during the eighties, and he had connections throughout the underworld and black markets in Russia and Eastern Europe. As Zdrok's right-hand man, Anton Antipov merely had to invoke his name in some circles to elicit respect—or fear.

Oskar Herzog was fifty-three years old and hailed from the former German Democratic Republic. At the time of his country's reunification, Herzog was one of the most dreaded prosecutors in East Berlin. He put away for life or sentenced to death hundreds of alleged political criminals. Associates called him "The Hatchet" behind his back until one day when he heard the nickname. Instead of becoming angry, he embraced the moniker and encouraged others to perpetuate it. He figured it might help instill apprehension in his enemies.

General Stefan Prokofiev was fifty-five years old and claimed to be related to the famous Russian composer that bore his surname. As a high-ranking officer in the Russian army, Prokofiev spent most of his time in Moscow. He made the trip to Zurich only when Zdrok called a meeting, which wasn't very often. Prokofiev had been one of the top military advisers in charge of weapons development while his country was still under Soviet rule. In 1990 he was promoted to general and became the liaison between the military and the physicists who designed and created Russia's modern armaments. Prokofiev had a reputation of being a communist hard-liner, although he had no qualms at all about making the equivalent of forty million U.S. dollars a year in Zdrok's organization.

Andrei Zdrok, the undisputed leader of the quartet, was fifty-seven years old, had the looks of a former matinee idol in his distinguished retirement years, dressed as if he were the richest man in the world, and had an IQ of 174. Originally from Georgia, Zdrok grew up in a family that ran banks for the Soviet Union. He took over the business when he was in his twenties and quickly learned how to make money for his personal use while serving the tenets of the Communist party. By the time the USSR fell, Andrei Zdrok was one of the ten wealthiest men in Russia. He immigrated to Switzerland, set up the Swiss-Russian, brought in as partners the three other men in the room, and proceeded to double his fortune every year. Zdrok had an insatiable appetite for money, and he always managed to find ways to make it—no matter how many lives might eventually be lost as a result of his business.

These four men were the brains behind the Shop.

In Zurich business meetings always began on time. Zdrok noted that he still had two minutes. He sat at the table, took the bagel out of the bag, and placed it in front of him. The other men watched without saying a word. They had already finished their breakfasts.

Zdrok took a bite, savored the flavors that bombarded his taste buds, and then washed it down with a sip of hot coffee.

At ten o'clock sharp he said, "Good morning."

The others mumbled a greeting in return.

"Gentlemen," Zdrok said, "our first order of business is the shipment that was lost in Iraq. What the hell happened?" He looked at Antipov and raised his eyebrows.

Antipov cleared his throat and said, "The Iraqi police stopped the transport and confiscated everything. Stingers and all. It was extremely lucky on their part, most unfortunate on ours."

"Where did it happen?"

"The town of Arbil. It was on the way to Mosul, where our customer would have then distributed the goods as usual."

"Have we heard from the customer?" Zdrok asked.

Herzog answered, "Yes, and he is very upset. He's asking for a refund."

Zdrok rolled his eyes. "Is he mad? He knew the terms. The shipment is under our protection up to a point, but once it's in the customer's territory and in *his* hands, then it's his responsibility."

"I told him that," Herzog said. "He isn't happy."

Zdrok looked at General Prokofiev and asked, "What do you plan to do about this?"

Prokofiev shrugged. "An offer for a replacement shipment has been made. We can get the arms together in a few days. Because he and his organization have been good customers, I said he could pay upon receipt. He'll have to pay twice, but at least he'll get the goods."

"Did he take the offer?"

"Yes."

Zdrok looked at Herzog. "Make sure you follow up about the payment as soon as the shipment is in his hands."

Herzog nodded and made a note in a pad he had in front of him. "The customer did say that he's going to attempt to retrieve the shipment. His people know where the police are keeping it."

Zdrok said, "Well, that's their business. If they want to try it, they're certainly welcome to do so. Next item. Operation Sweep."

Antipov cleared his throat again and said, "The information on the man known as Rick Benton proved to be reliable, as you are aware. The intelligence we received may prove fruitful in unmasking more American agents. We have several names. Now all we have to do is match each name with the correct person. It shouldn't take too long. We have operatives working on this as we speak."

Zdrok nodded in approval. "That is good news. The Americans have been hovering much too closely to our organization. We must continue to weed out and eliminate their agents. The one that hit us in Macau damaged our Far East operations a great deal. It will take months, maybe years, to reestablish our business in that region. I especially want *that* man."

"Vlad and Yuri are on it," Antipov said. "We'll get him and the others, but keep in mind that it's not easy. These agents are called 'Splinter Cells' because they work alone and undercover. Their own government pretends they don't exist. We've taken out two of them so far. We're nearing confirmation on the identity of another one in Israel, and we're getting close to one in America."

Zdrok cracked his knuckles and nodded. "Vlad and Yuri. They're careful, right? They leave no trace?"

"None. They are as professional as they come. They were my most trusted executioners in the KGB," Antipov replied.

"What did they learn in Belgium?"

"Not only did they eliminate Benton but also a Belgian intelligence officer that Benton was working with. These men knew far too much about what we've been distributing to our number-one customer. Hopefully the material we took from Benton's hotel room will be one-of-a-kind documents. I've taken the precaution to destroy all of it. This should slow down our enemies. In addition, much of our new information about Third Echelon came from Benton's personal computer, which we have also destroyed."

Zdrok waved his hand slightly. "Fine. I leave you in charge of it. Proceed as you see fit. But I want results by the end of the week. If they discover who we are or where we are, it's not going to be pretty. The sooner we get rid of these American bloodhounds, the better off we'll be."

With that, Zdrok took another bite of his bagel and the meeting was over.

12

THE lovemaking was as good as it had been in Illinois. As they lay entwined in the narrow twin bed in Eli's small studio apartment, Sarah was convinced more than ever that he was "the one."

She knew she had better get up and phone Rivka. She was supposed to have been back by ten o'clock at the latest. Now it was nearly noon. They had slept in, waking only to make love. How many times had they done it since coming back to his place the night before? Four times? Five? Sarah smiled inwardly and sighed.

"You okay?" Eli asked.

"I sure am," she said, snuggling closer to him.

"I heard you sigh."

"It was a sigh of contentment."

"Oh, I see." He kissed her. "I am glad you're content."

"How about you? Are you content?"

"You better believe it."

She yawned and squeezed his lean torso. "I could stay here forever."

"Me, too," he said. "But I'm getting hungry. How about you?"

"Who needs food when you can have sex?" she said as she placed her hand on his crotch.

"Hey, hey, what are you, a junkie?" He laughed but didn't bother to move her hand.

"With you, yes!"

Eli sat up. "Okay, then I think it's time you go cold turkey for a little while. I'm really hungry. I'm not kidding."

Sarah loved his Israeli accent. There was something about a foreign accent that turned her on. "Shall I make you breakfast?" she asked.

"No, no, I'll make *you* breakfast. Or lunch, I think. My God, look at the time."

"Oh, boy, Rivka's gonna be pissed at me. I can't imagine what her parents will think."

Eli waved her comment away and said, "Don't worry. Rivka spent the night with Noel. I bet they slept late, too."

"Still, it's scandalous behavior, don't you think?"

"You're a big girl. You're an adult, right?"

"I'm twenty. I can't drink in America yet."

"Yeah, but you're *legally* an adult. That's what counts." He slipped out of bed and walked across the room to the bathroom. She enjoyed watching his backside.

"Anyone ever tell you that you've got a cute tush?" she called out as he closed the door. He didn't answer. Sarah sighed again and finally swung her legs out from under the covers and sat upright. Naked, she went to the kitchen area and looked in the cabinet to see what was there. Typical bachelor apartment, she thought. Nothing but junk food and sugary cereal.

"Eli, do you have coffee?" she called, but the shower started and he couldn't hear her.

She opened another cupboard and found some instant

coffee. "Yuck," she said. She shrugged and took it, found a pot to boil water, and tried the tap. The water was brownish. Sarah made a face, turned off the tap, and put the coffee back in the cupboard. She looked around her and realized that Eli's apartment was decidedly a dump. Last night, in the dark, she hadn't noticed. She did remember that the neighborhood where he lived appeared to be a poor one, almost a ghetto. The room smelled moldy. She hadn't noticed the odor earlier because she had been tipsy on wine. Now as she examined the apartment she felt a little repelled.

"Hey, Eli, can I take a shower, too?" she called.

"Sure, come on in!"

She smiled and opened the bathroom door. The little cubicle was steamy from the hot water. At least he *had* hot water, she thought.

First things first. She put the toilet seat *down*, sat, and urinated. Without thinking she flushed the toilet, eliciting a yelp from Eli.

"Sorry!" she said as she opened the shower stall and joined him.

They took turns lathering each other's bodies, pausing every now and then to kiss. He became aroused again and she grasped him firmly with a slippery hand.

"Oh, please, no more," he said. "I'm raw!"

She giggled and said, "I don't think your penis agrees with you."

"My penis *never* agrees with me," he said, closing his eyes.

"That's typical for guys, isn't it?" she whispered as she continued playing with him.

Afterward they stepped out of the stall and used the same towel to dry off. "You don't have another towel?" she asked.

"Sorry. I'm poor and destitute."

That prompted her to ask a question she'd been considering for a while. "Eli, do you have a job?"

"A job? Sure, I have a job." He looked in the mirror, took a razor, and started to shave without lather.

"What is it?"

"I work for a delivery service. I'm off this week so I can see you."

"What kind of delivery service?"

"You know, I deliver packages and stuff."

She pictured the car he drove and shuddered. It was a relic from the early nineties. When she first got in the passenger seat, she imagined that she was in a cartoon car that went *putt putt pfft pop* as it creaked along the road.

"You don't do anything with your music?"

"No, that's hard to do."

Come to think of it, she thought, she had never heard him play an instrument. In fact, there was no evidence at all in his apartment that he was interested in music. No sheet music, no CDs of classical music, no busts of Beethoven—nothing.

He glanced at her off the mirror. "What?"

"Nothing," she said. "When will you know about Juilliard?"

He shrugged. "Those things take time." He nicked himself with the razor. "Look what you made me do."

"How did I make you do that?"

"By asking me difficult questions."

"You should use shaving cream."

"I've always done it this way. Go on, you're making me nervous!" He pushed her out of the bathroom and shut the door.

Sarah sighed once more, walked over to her pile of clothes that she had dropped on a chair, and dressed.

* * *

ELI ended up making the instant coffee himself. They sat at the excuse for a breakfast table as Sarah called Rivka on her cell phone. Her friend was slightly upset with her for not calling earlier. Rivka's parents were not too happy, either. Sarah apologized and said she'd be there in an hour.

"Why don't you just come stay here for the rest of your visit?" Eli suggested.

"Oh, I don't think that'd be a good idea," Sarah replied.

"Why not? Don't you like me?" He winked at her.

She punched him and said, "Of course I do! But, you know, I'm staying with Rivka's parents and all. How would it look?"

He shrugged. "It would look like we're together."

She shook her head. "I wouldn't feel right. Sorry." She took his hand.

"It's okay. Your daddy might not approve, either."

That struck her as an odd thing to say. "I don't think my father would even know. He doesn't keep tabs on me like that. We live in different cities, remember?"

"Oh, right. Your father is the CIA spy."

"He is not."

"What's his name again?"

"Sam Fisher."

"Why not 'Sam Burns.'"

"My mother changed our last names legally after the divorce."

"Right. Sam Fisher. Sam Fisher—Government Agent."

She punched him again. "Stop it. He is not."

Eli kept at it. He hummed the "James Bond Theme" and pointed his finger like a gun. Sarah laughed. "Cut it out," she said.

"Okay. But I still think he's a government agent and not some kind of salesman."

"Why do you say that? Why do you even care?"

"I don't know. I guess I just want to know what my future father-in-law is like."

Sarah blinked. "Your what?"

"You heard me."

"Eli."

He grasped her hand and said, "I know, it's too soon to talk that way. But listen, if you do decide to come live with me in New York, it might happen. I care for you, Sarah. Really."

She looked down. "I know. Me, too."

"Tell me about your mother. What was her name?"

"Regan."

"She worked for the government, too?"

"Yes, I told you that. She was in the NSA."

"National Security Advisory?"

"Agency."

"National Security Agency—whatever."

"She was stationed in Georgia. You know, the former Soviet satellite."

"Uh-huh."

"That's where she met my father. At the time he *was* in the CIA."

"Once a spy, always a spy, that's what I always say." She gave him a look. "Sorry. Go on."

"Anyway, they had this torrid love affair and eventually got married. In Germany. That's where I was born, on a military base there."

"Army brat."

She nodded. "I guess so."

"But they didn't stay together?"

"No. It lasted three years. I really don't remember

much about my father living with us at the time. I was three when he left. My mom always said that the breakup was mutual—in fact it was her idea for him to go away—but I can't help thinking that he abandoned me. I guess any kid whose father leaves would think that."

"So what happened?"

"Mom took me back to the States. She continued to work in Washington and raised me by herself. I didn't really get to know my dad until I was a teenager. I'd see him every now and then, and he was like this *stranger* who'd come see us, claiming to be my father. He'd bring me presents and stuff, but it all seemed very detached. Then there was a period of time I didn't see him at all. Several years. It was between the time I was nine years old and . . . fifteen, I guess."

"Where was he?"

"I don't know. Mom never said. Maybe she told him to stay away, I really don't know. Anyway, it was after mom was diagnosed with ovarian cancer. That's when he showed up again. He came to see her in the hospital and even tried for a reconciliation, but it wasn't to be. After she died, he became my guardian."

"And then you lived with him?"

"Yep. And it was weird. I was in high school and suddenly I lived with a man who was supposed to be my father. It was rough going at first, but I guess it turned out all right. We became friends, especially after I graduated and went to college." She shrugged and smiled. "Now I think he's a great guy."

"Even though he's so *mysterious*." Eli exaggerated the word with a whisper.

"Oh stop."

"Hey, I'm going to run downstairs and get a couple of sandwiches. How does that sound?"

"Okay."

"Stay here and I'll be back in a few minutes. You want *meat*, right?"

She laughed. "Whatever. I don't care."

"Coming right up."

He got up from the table and left the apartment, leaving Sarah shaking her head and wondering how she got involved with such an interesting man.

Downstairs, Eli stood outside the deli below his apartment, pulled out his cell phone, and made a quick call.

"Everything checks out with Sam Fisher," he said. "He was with the CIA in the nineteen-eighties and he married a woman named Regan Burns. She died of cancer and they had one daughter. He lives in Baltimore, Maryland, and supposedly works as a 'salesman.'"

Eli listened to the voice on the other end and then said, "Right. Definitely. It's just as you suspected. It's him— he's the one."

_13_

I have to enter Iran illegally. Iraq wasn't a problem because of the U.S. presence there. Iran, however, is a different story. Of course, an ordinary tourist or official
governmental representative could simply apply for a visa
and enter the country. Despite the prevalent notion in
America that Iran is a hostile and dangerous place, it is actually a relatively warm and friendly place. I have been to
Iran on numerous occasions, mostly to Tehran, and I've
always found the people to be helpful and welcoming.
Things have relaxed in the country since the heyday of the
Islamic Revolution. There was a time when the _komite_, the
religious police, were comparable to the Gestapo. Not
anymore— today they are hardly visible on the streets.
Nevertheless, you have to watch yourself. You must abide
by the laws, especially the religious ones, stay away from
rallies and demonstrations, and avoid talking about politics.

But since I'm on a Third Echelon assignment, I can't

very well get a visa and enter the country by the normal channels. Even my Interpol cover won't fly in Iran, and I certainly wouldn't get anywhere telling the Immigration authorities that I'm with the NSA. So, even more than in Iraq, I have to be invisible.

The worst part about it is that I have to abandon the Toyota Land Cruiser in Iraq and make my way across the border on foot. Once I'm in Iran, I have to find transportation to Tabriz. Walking isn't an option.

I drive east before dawn, through Rawanduz, until I'm a mile away from the border checkpoint. I pull off the highway at the first dirt road I see, drive a ways, and stop. I make sure I have all my belongings, and then I leave the keys in the car. Some lucky son of a bitch is going to find himself a free SUV! I get out and walk across the rugged terrain, avoiding the highway, until I see the checkpoint in the distance. I'm on a hill overlooking the highway. I count three armed guards stopping vehicles traveling in both directions. On the other side of the border is another checkpoint run by the Iranians. The sun hasn't risen yet, but I have only an hour or so before daylight destroys my chances of getting across today.

I strip down to my uniform, stuff my outer clothes in the Osprey, and make my way down the hill. I dart from one large bush or tree or boulder to another, pausing at each step to make sure I haven't been seen. It's unlikely. My uniform is dark and there are no lights on the hill. The guards' attention is focused on the vehicles entering and leaving the country.

In fifteen minutes I'm at ground level, lying on the slope of a ditch, my head barely peeking over the top so I can see the checkpoint. They don't expect anyone on foot to try and cross over. If I stay down and move laterally east, I should make it. I wait until a car approaches the checkpoint and one of the guards talks to the driver.

Employing a crablike maneuver on all fours, I traverse the ditch. I'm parallel with the checkpoint when one of the agents steps out to smoke a cigarette. He walks to the side of the building that faces me and gazes at the night sky. I can't take a chance of him seeing me, so I lie perfectly still.

Shit, he's starting to walk toward the ditch. He's lost in thought, tugging on the cigarette, probably wondering what he'll have for breakfast when he gets off his shift. However, I'm close enough that he could possibly spot me if I move.

Then one of his associates calls for him. The guard acknowledges the summons, takes one last drag on the cigarette, and then tosses the butt toward me. It lands a foot away from my face and it's still burning. Luckily he doesn't bother to look where the butt fell—he's forgotten all about it as he walks back to the building.

I take the opportunity to pick up the butt and rub it out in the dirt.

Once again I apply the crab walk to move farther east. Now I have two checkpoints to watch. At this time in the early morning there is very little traffic. I'm fortunate that there were one or two cars going through to mask my transit thus far. Now, though, there's nothing. The road is deadly quiet. The Iraqi border guards retreat into their checkpoint building, but there's a lone Iranian outside of his. He's standing there, looking west, as if a parade of cars is on the way and he's preparing himself to inspect them. What's he doing?

The guy calls out to the Iraqi checkpoint. He waits a few seconds, then calls again. Someone's name. In a moment the cigarette-smoking Iraqi I saw earlier comes out of his building. He shouts back to the Iranian. I don't understand what the Iranian says, it's in Farsi, a language I can't speak. I have an easier time *reading* Farsi than speaking it, because written Farsi is very similar to Arabic. The Iraqi nods and the two men walk toward each other. Shit, what's going on? They meet halfway between the two checkpoints, and I realize I have nothing to worry about. The Iraqi pulls out his cigarette pack and offers one to the Iranian. They share a joke, I think, for they talk and laugh, and after five minutes they separate and stroll back to their respective positions.

All clear. I literally crawl into Iran.

I continue to walk in the darkness, remaining off the highway. The sky is beginning to turn deep orange and red. The sun will be up within minutes. I have to find a place to stay put through the day, and I think I see a good possibility about a mile ahead, where the highway crosses a bridge.

Ten minutes later I'm at the bridge just as the sun peeks over the hills directly in front of me. The bridge spreads across a ravine that appears to be a good two hundred feet deep. This is very hilly country—these foothills eventually become the volcanic Sabalan and Talesh mountain ranges.

Bridges are among my most frequented hotels. The accommodations are not always of the four- or five-star variety, but they usually offer me what I need the most— privacy.

I make my way down the hill to the edge of the highway, then inch down the steep slope next to the bridge. I grab the steel supports and climb up and around to the inside. It's an easy ascent to the underside of the highway, where a hollow section—a ledge—runs the complete length of the bridge. It's about four feet wide, with head-space of a couple of feet. It's perfect for me to lie in, as long as I don't roll over in my sleep and fall off. It's never happened before.

Before retiring for the day, I send a text message to Lambert via my OPSAT, telling him I'm in Iran and on my way to Tabriz. I then eat a very satisfying pack of rations. It's not a gourmet meal by any means, but it reduces the hunger pangs and lulls me into the disposition to get some shut-eye.

And that's where I sleep most of the daylight hours—underneath a bridge, the highway into Iran directly over my prone body.

MY OPSAT wakes me at nine o'clock that night, after the sun has set. The constant rumbling of vehicles passing over the bridge hasn't kept me awake—on the contrary, there's something akin to white noise about it. I slept like a log.

I carefully slip out from my crawl space under the bridge, grasp the support, and climb down to the ground. I move away from the road and into the brush, where my presence will go unnoticed. I sit behind a tree and check my OPSAT. Lambert has left a message—

CONTACT REZA HAMADAN IN TABRIZ BAZAAR
"TABRIZ CARPET COMPANY" HE IS ON CIA PAYROLL
AND EXPECTS YOU

Okay. Now the trick is finding a ride to Tabriz. Hitch-hiking isn't an option, so I start the long walk to the next

town, which is Mahabad—about thirty miles away. I estimate I can make it in seven or eight hours. The drawback
is the up-and-down terrain, which contributes to the wear
and tear on my legs and feet. I silently thank Katia Loenstern for all the leg exercises she had us do in Krav Maga
class. It's tough going and I have to stop and rest several
times, which makes me realize it's going to take a lot
longer than I initially thought. What the hell, I've had to
rough it many times in my career, though, and this is a relatively tame sojourn compared to some.

Along the way I pass through a couple of seemingly
deserted whistle-stop villages. While Iran is a very modern country, the rural parts still contain vestiges of the
past. You'll see shepherds dressed in the same type of
clothing that was worn hundreds of years ago. Not everyone drives cars. If I happen to get hurt or ill, I'm on my
own. There aren't going to be any emergency clinics on
the road. This thought flits through my mind when I hear
wolves howling in the deep woods to my left.

It's nearly morning when I finally reach Mahabad. Not
a large town, but bigger than a village, it's a rural community that is just beginning to rouse from slumber. I hear the
musical intonations of Islamic morning prayers drifting
through the air—something I have to admit I find very
soothing. Besides the dominant Persian population of
Iran, the region where I'm headed is full of Kurds and
Azerbaijanis. Persians are direct descendents of the
Aryans that first inhabited the land about four thousand
years ago, and they make up over half the total population
in the country. Nearly everyone in Iran is a Shiite Muslim,
the Islamic branch that dictates the cultural, religious, and
political direction of the country. Sunni Muslims make up
a small ten percent or so. It's interesting to note that in the

rest of the world, almost all Muslims are of the Sunni variety—but in Iran, and most of Iraq, the majority is Shiite.

I wander into town, now dressed in casual clothing with my uniform underneath. It's not as hot here in the mountain region, so I'm fairly comfortable. Most Persians are light-skinned and can pass for a Westerner if they have to. I blend right in, even with my darker complexion. I probably look as if I've just come off the bus from Tehran. No one looks twice at me. As long as I don't have to talk I'll be fine.

Most of the men are wearing the traditional *jeballa*, a full-length robe, and many wear turbans. In the bigger cities you'll see men wear Western clothing—suits, casual trousers, and shirts. The women, however, are almost always covered in the *hejab*, the modest dress. This is usually represented by the *chador*, a tentlike cloak that is draped loosely over the head, legs, and arms. Nothing that suggests the shape of the body can be worn. All bits of skin except for the hands, feet, and face above the neckline and below the hairline must be covered. In the cities women can get away with wearing a full-length skirt or even trousers worn beneath a long dark coat known as a *roupush*. The hair is covered by a simple headscarf. Here, though, everything's more traditional, more old-fashioned.

I find what I'm looking for at the edge of town. It's a sort of minor truck stop for commercial vehicles traveling to the north. I walk around to the back of the place where I can't be seen and sit down to wait for my ride. Thirty minutes later it arrives.

It's a ten-wheeler truck—perfect for my needs—with the words "Tabriz Moving Company" painted in Farsi on the side. I wait until the right moment, when the driver is inside the station using the washroom, then I run to the back of the rig, crouch, and crawl beneath the hot flatbed. I turn my belt all the way around so that the buckle is on my back and pull out the hook. I then lodge my body up above the axles, facedown, and position myself so I can hold on to and rest my legs on parts of the chassis with the hook securing me in place. It's not the most comfortable way to ride a hundred miles, but I've done it many times, and it really isn't so bad as long as you keep your wits about you, don't fall asleep, and never let go.

Five minutes pass and the driver gets back in the cab. The engine fires up and we're off. For the next three hours I have a lovely view of a speeding blur of highway, four feet below my face.

TABRIZ is the largest city in northern Iran and is occupied primarily by Azerbaijanis. It seems to be an unsightly spread of high-rise apartment buildings, but the areas in the old town center are more representative of traditional Iran. After slipping out from under the truck, I make my way to the bazaar, just south of the Mehran River. It's the oldest and largest bazaar in all of Iran and is typical of the maze-like medinas of most Middle Eastern countries. I arrive midday, just as business is bustling. The teahouses are full, lined with men smoking water pipes or having lively conversations over Persian tea. The hawkers are out in force, soliciting every person that walks by to come into a particular shop and buy something. The atmosphere is much more relaxed and pleasant than it was in Iraq—understandably so.

I wander around like a tourist until I find the Tabriz Carpet Company, an unusually large shop that specializes not only in Persian carpets but also in silk and spices. A woman greets me when I enter and nods enthusiastically when I ask for Reza Hamadan. She goes through drapes to a back room while I examine the intricate work of the carpets on display. I'm always amazed by the craftsmanship that goes into these things. Carpets are not made just to cover your floor—in this part of the world a carpet is a symbol of wealth or an integral part of a religious or cultural festival. From what I can see here, Reza Hamadan is a master carpet maker.

He comes out of the shop, dressed in a loose-fitting white shirt with baggy sleeves, dark trousers, and sandals. He appears to be in his fifties, clean-shaven except for a small, Chaplin-esque mustache. His deep blue eyes sparkle and exhibit warmth.

"I am Reza Hamadan," he says, extending his hand.

I shake it. "Sam Fisher."

"I have been expecting you, Mr. Fisher. Welcome to Tabriz," he says. His English is very good.

"Thank you."

"Come with me to a more comfortable place. My wife will mind the store." He calls to the woman I saw earlier. She enters the shop, smiles, nods her head at me, and allows us to go through the drapes and into the back room. Hamadan leads me to what appears to be his office. The walls and floor are covered in magnificent carpets, a mahogany desk that looks English sits in a corner, and large pillows occupy the middle of the room.

"Please sit. Would you like some tea?" he asks.

"I would love some."

"Please," he says again, gesturing to the pillows. I sit cross-legged and then find it's better to lounge sideways. It feels really good to be off my feet. Hamadan leaves the room and returns a few moments later with a tray. "Normally my wife would serve us, but she has a customer."

It's what I expect—*chay*, the unofficial national drink. It's a strong tea, served hot and black in a small glass cup. I'm not a huge fan of the stuff, but at the moment it tastes like heaven. The highway dust of the trip from Mahabad has infiltrated my throat, and the tea works wonders in clearing the air passages.

"How was your journey, Mr. Fisher?" Hamadan asks.

"As pleasant as it could be," I say tactfully.

"I'm glad to hear it. Now that you are here, I am authorized to lend you a car. It's my son-in-law's and he is away on business for an extended period of time. Feel free to use it as long as you need it. You can take it anywhere except into Iraq."

"That's quite kind, thank you."

"I suppose you have questions for me?"

"I do, but before we get to business, I'd like to ask you something personal."

"By all means."

"How did you get to be a CIA mole?"

Hamadan grins, revealing a wide set of sparkling white teeth. "I spent my early twenties in the United States, during the 1970s, before the fall of the Shah. I went to a small college in West Texas, where other Iranian students attended. The school had an exchange program with Iran at the time. I studied political science and English. During that period, men from your government came to talk to us. It was quite blatant—they wanted to recruit young men to help the U.S. spy on Iran. The money was good. I was young and didn't know better, so I accepted. I've been earning extra income from the CIA ever since. I have no complaints."

"Fascinating," I said. "It's a small world, isn't it?"

"It grows smaller daily. Now then, to the business at

hand." He sets down his teacup and looks me in the eyes. "Mr. Fisher, I have many connections in the underworld and in law enforcement in this country and surrounding areas. Before your government contacted me and said to expect you here, I had heard your name mentioned in . . . other places."

"Oh?"

"Mr. Fisher, there is a price on your head. You are a marked man."

14

"**WELL,** that's nothing new," I say.

Hamadan looks at me as if he's sizing me up. "I detect that you are either a very brave man, Mr. Fisher, or a very foolish one."

"Call me Sam, please."

"Very well, but you must call me Reza."

"All right, Reza. What exactly do you mean?"

"You appear not to take what I say seriously."

"Of course I do. I take all death threats seriously."

"Forgive me, then. Perhaps I mistook your self-confidence for indifference."

"Reza, I've been in this business for a long time. It takes a lot to shake me up. Now, why don't you tell me what it is you know?"

He nods and smiles. "I like you already, Sam. You have . . . what's the word? Aplomb." He takes a sip of tea and continues. "I assume you knew Mr. Benton?"

"Not personally. Rick Benton worked for the same organization as I."

"I had dealings with Mr. Benton. I was one of his informers. I liked him as well. I find it difficult to believe he was killed. He was also a man with great self-confidence."

"Go on."

"You must know that Mr. Benton was trying to track down the Shop. He wanted to know where they were based, who was in charge, how they worked. For the last two years this had become his obsession. I helped him the best I could. I found out things for him, guided him in certain directions. I believe he may have shown his hand too soon, though. The Shop became aware of him. Mr. Benton told me as such right after your man in the Far East was killed. Mr. Lee?"

"Yes. Dan Lee. In Macau."

"Right. After that happened, Mr. Benton told me that he thought the Shop had a list of names. Names of possible agents with the National Security Agency. He was afraid the Shop had begun a campaign to eliminate everyone on the list."

I consider this. "I don't question Rick's suspicions, but I think you both give the Shop too much credit. If the Shop really does have a list of names, then I can't imagine how they got it."

"That is exactly what Mr. Benton said. Very mysterious."

"I tell you, Reza, I'm not going to worry about it," I say. I mean it, too. I have more important things to think about. I spend a great deal of energy watching my back when I'm on an assignment. It's routine. "Now, what can you tell me about Rick's investigations?"

"Mr. Benton was working on tracing an arms supply line coming into Iraq. He believed the arms come from Azerbaijan, but he wasn't completely sure. I tend to agree with him. If this is true, then there are two routes the arms could take—one through Iran, and one through Armenia and Turkey. I'll tell you what I think. I don't believe they're coming through Iran, although maybe the Shop wants to give us that impression. There are arms that do come into Iran, but they do not *originate* in my country. I know for a fact that our government is working very hard to keep illegal arms out of Iran. They do not want to be perceived as a contributor to international terrorism, despite how the world arena has portrayed us. Our government is particularly concerned about radical terrorist groups that may have Iranian connections."

"Like the Shadows, for instance?"

Hamadan smiles again. "You are very perceptive, Sam."

"They are quickly becoming a priority for us," I explain.

"Yes, well, as they should. There have been some suspicions in the media and in our government that the Shadows are based in Iran. I hope it's not true. I don't believe it."

"Reza, whatever enlightenment you can provide would be appreciated."

"I don't know much, either. Only that the group is taking credit for a lot of attacks lately. Are we even sure that the Shadows really exist? Could they be al Qaeda or another one of the established groups merely trying to confuse us?"

"No, I don't think so. Their methods are slightly different. Results are the same, though. I actually think I met some Shadows in Arbil the other day."

"Really?"

"Yes. That reminds me. What do you know about the Tabriz Container Company?"

Hamadan wrinkles his brow. "Why?"

"There was a shipment of arms confiscated in Arbil. The stuff was in crates made by the Tabriz Container Company."

Hamadan shrugs. "It's a large company here that makes boxes, crates, containers. . . . Their warehouse is located outside the city."

"I'm going to check them out."

"It can't hurt, but I can't imagine that this company is involved in anything illegal. They sell their products to all kinds of clients. The Shop might be buying the containers through a middleman or a front."

"Could be. Here's another question for you. Have you ever heard of anyone named Tarighian?"

"Tarighian?" Hamadan looks surprised. "*Nasir* Tarighian?"

"I don't know his first name."

"If you're talking about Nasir Tarighian, you're talking about an Iranian war hero. He was a hero during the Iran-Iraq War."

"Tell me about him."

"He was very wealthy, owned several businesses, and was very active politically. He got into a little trouble in the early 1980s by speaking out against the Islamic Revolution. When the war started he underwent a tragedy—his home was destroyed and he lost some relatives, killed by Iraqi bombs. After that incident he swore revenge against Iraq. He formed an anti-Iraqi militia—a terrorist group, really. They made frequent raids across the border. They were merciless—they killed innocent civilians and destroyed a lot of property. Tarighian became something of a cult hero here in Iran, but the government didn't approve of his actions. They were going to step in and stop him, but before they could, the Iraqi army ambushed Tarighian and his little band of soldiers. Tarighian was killed and the militia was wiped out."

"Tarighian's dead?"

"That's the general consensus. He hasn't been heard from since. No bodies were recovered from the battle, I might add."

"Hmm. I heard a member of the Shadows mention that name in Arbil."

"I shall make inquiries," Hamadan says. "However, the one name I have heard associated with the Shadows' leadership is a man named Ahmed Mohammed. Have you heard of him?"

"Yes, I heard his name in Arbil as well and I remember his name coming up in reports," I answer. "I'm sure he's on the FBI wanted terrorist list."

"Mohammed is an Iranian, a known terrorist who is wanted by our government for a number of crimes. My sources tell me that he is a major player in the Shadows. He may not be the supreme boss, but he most likely plans operations and has them carried out."

"Well then, I'll be sure to watch out for him."

Hamadan stands and goes to his desk. He opens a drawer and removes an accordion folder. He brings it back to me. "This is Mr. Benton's. He sometimes stayed in a room we have above our shop. In fact, he was here just before he went to Belgium. He left that material here and I found it in the room. Perhaps the material will be useful. You are also welcome to stay here in the room if you wish, Sam."

"Thanks." I open the file and find several papers and some photos. I remove the first photo and have a look. There are two men in the picture. One of them looks vaguely familiar to me. He's obviously Middle Eastern, is in his fifties, and appears to have a skin condition. The other guy I don't know.

"Ah, yes, that's something else," Hamadan says. "Mr. Benton had made contact with that man." He points to the guy who looks familiar. "His name is Namik Basaran. He's a Turk. Mr. Benton believed that Mr. Basaran has inside information about the Shadows."

"Namik Basaran. I think I've heard of him."

"You might have seen him on television. He's an entrepreneur who owns a huge conglomerate in Van, Turkey. It's called Akdabar Enterprises. Do you know it?"

"No."

"They deal mostly with construction, oil production, and steel. Besides that, Basaran runs a charity organization called Tirma, the mission of which is to provide relief for terrorist victims around the world. He founded Tirma with his own money. Namik Basaran is a publicity hound, so he always goes on the news to speak out against terrorism whenever there is an attack. He has been known to help the Turkish police in their search for terrorists, and he seems to have connections in all the surrounding countries."

This charity organization rings a bell. Perhaps I have heard of this guy. "Have you met him?" I ask.

"Never, but we have done business together. I sold him some carpets to decorate his offices. I hope to meet him someday. He's a very generous man, but I must say I believe he's more interested in getting his face on TV than in anything else. But at least he puts his money where his mouth is."

"Who's the other man in the photograph?" He appears to be Eastern European, not Arabic or Persian. Another guy in his late fifties or maybe early sixties.

"I don't know. Neither did Mr. Benton."

"Where did Rick get the photo?"

"I don't know."

I return the photo to the folder and nod. "Well. It looks like I have some homework. If you don't mind, I'm going to take you up on your offer for that room, get some rest, and then check out the container warehouse tonight."

"Very good. I will show you to the room."

I follow Hamadan out of the office and up a flight of stairs. It's a small but very homey bedroom with a futon and dozens of pillows. There's an attached bathroom as well. As far as I'm concerned, it's pure luxury. I thank Hamadan and tell him I'll see him at dinner. Then I settle down to relax. Before I go to sleep I check the OPSAT for messages. There's one from Lambert that says, simply, "Talk to me."

I press the implanted transmitter in my throat. "Colonel? Are you there?"

After a moment I hear Lambert's voice in my ear. "Sam? Where are you?"

"In Tabriz. At Reza Hamadan's place."

"Good, you made it. Listen, I have some nasty news. Another one of our Splinter Cells was murdered yesterday. Marcus Blaine."

Blaine. Again, I didn't know him personally, but I know who he was. He was Third Echelon's man stationed in Israel.

"How did it happen?" I ask.

"We don't know yet. Details are very sketchy, but the preliminary report indicates that it may be the same killer or killers who got to Rick Benton and Dan Lee."

That's when I begin to take what Hamadan said about the Shop having a list of names a bit more seriously.

15

ANDREI Zdrok sat in his office in the Swiss-Russian International Mercantile Bank, gazing out the window at the streets of Zurich's financial district. This had been his home for several years and he loved it. Zurich was a very expensive place to reside, but he had the means to take advantage of everything the city had to offer. His chateau on the shore of Lake Zurich was his pride and joy, and the only time he ever left the home was to come into the bank. When he wasn't working, he indulged himself in expensive hobbies. Zdrok owned six automobiles that were considered collector's items, including a 1933 Rolls-Royce that Paul von Hindenberg once owned. His most prized possession, however, was the Swan 46 yacht that he had recently purchased. He liked to sail it leisurely along the length of the lake and sometimes slept on it. Zdrok considered it a small slice of heaven on earth.

The Shop had done well. The enterprise had begun modestly, operating at the beginning out of Georgia. He

and Antipov had made the first arms sale, and then they recruited Prokofiev and Herzog to join the team. The Shop
grew in size and influence, supplying arms of all kinds to
whoever was able to pay for them. Zdrok had no political
aspirations or loyalties. The almighty dollar was his only
motivation.

The business really blossomed during the Bosnian conflict. Zdrok moved the base of operations to Baku, Azerbaijan, for security reasons and opened the first
Swiss-Russian bank in Zurich. A second branch was built
in Baku two years later. By using the front of the two
banks, Zdrok was able to assemble a discreet machine that
handled marketing, acquisition, delivery, and profit laun-
dering. Finding the right employees to do the grunt work
had been time-consuming—he had to be sure that his men
would remain loyal. He paid them well, which went a long
way toward insuring their devotion. At any rate, the common soldiers of the organization didn't know a lot about
the operation. Thankfully, to date no one with any real
knowledge of the Shop had ever been caught by the law.

Andrei Zdrok felt justified in enjoying his life in Zurich.

The biggest problem they now faced was rebuilding the
Far East pipelines. The business had been hurt badly but
not irreparably. The Shop had intelligence of its own, and
Zdrok was certain that the Americans' National Security
Agency was responsible for the damage. Operation
Sweep, the initiative he created to hunt down and eliminate Western spies, was already in place and active when
the events in Macau occurred. Now the operation had become a priority.

Zdrok thought about the Far East situation and how it
could be repaired in a timely and efficient manner. It was

possible to bring in another partner, the leader of a Chinese Triad called the Lucky Dragons with whom the Shop had done a lot of business. His name was Jon Ming and he was quite possibly the most powerful gangster in China. He resided in Hong Kong, his Triad's home for decades. Even when the handover occurred and other Triad clans moved out of the former British colony, Ming and the Lucky Dragons stayed. He had a special relationship with the Chinese government. He had the ability to pull strings and keep lawmakers in his pocket. Yes, Ming might be the answer to the Shop's problems, but Zdrok wasn't sure how the other partners would feel about bringing the man aboard.

There was also an American he knew in the Far East who might be able to help. Zdrok's partners would most certainly be opposed to working with *him*, but Zdrok thought it might be advantageous. After all, the man was known to and trusted by the U.S. intelligence agencies. Zdrok decided to put that thought on hold and wrestle with it later. There was time.

The phone rang. He picked it up and said, "Zdrok." He listened to the short message from the caller and replied, "Thank you." He hung up the phone, swiveled his chair to face the computer, and logged on.

His technical director had assured him that sensitive Shop files used a complex encryption that could never be hacked into. Even if auditors came to the bank and insisted on confiscating the hard drive, they would never be able to access the information. Therefore, Zdrok kept all of the Shop's records, plans, and operations on his office computer.

He brought up the file marked Sweep, short for Operation Sweep, the campaign to eliminate those who wished to harm the Shop. They were the enemy, these intelligence agents from foreign powers who insisted on disrupting Zdrok's business of making money. Didn't he have a right to pursue the vocation of his choice? Who were they to tell him that he couldn't sell his goods? Makers and sellers of guns do not kill people. What his clients did with the products was not his concern.

A list of names, some in black font and some in red, appeared on the screen. Zdrok highlighted the first name that was still black—Marcus Blaine—and changed the color to red. Like the two other red names, Dan Lee and Rick Benton, Blaine was now considered "Deleted."

Two more entries remained in black. Zdrok clicked on the first one, the man whose name they believed to be Sam Fisher. Zdrok quickly reread the details that had been gathered on Fisher—that he was supposedly a CIA agent in the 1980s and was married to an NSA agent named Regan, that he worked out of the Washington/Baltimore area, and that he was the oldest Third Echelon Splinter Cell. Most significantly, he may or may not have a daughter in her late teens or early twenties. No one knew what Fisher looked like, but the information they possessed was good enough to track down a possible suspect. The Shop's man in Israel had done well.

Zdrok picked up the phone and dialed a number. When the call was answered, Zdrok said, "All right, I'm convinced. It's time to act with regard to Fisher. Find out where he is. Don't use force yet—that will be a last resort. Psychological pressure will probably work. After all, she's young."

16

AFTER a good night's sleep on a real futon mattress, I wake refreshed and spend more time going through the material in Rick Benton's file. There really isn't a lot there. He must have kept most of his records on a personal computer, which I understand was never recovered, or in his home, which was thoroughly scoured by NSA personnel. Nevertheless, there are a few items worth deciphering.

The first of these is a page of doodles. Benton had written several words on the page and had drawn arrows between the names, apparently attempting to connect them or show their relationships. The words are: *Shop, Shadows, Tarighian, A. Mohammed, Zdrok,* and *Mertens.* The first two labels I know, of course, and the third one has become a name I want to investigate. "A. Mohammed" I just learned about from Hamadan. The other two are mysteries to me. The Shop seems to be the dominant name on this makeshift chart. An arrow points from the Shop to the Shadows. Another arrow goes from the Shadows to A.

Mohammed, but a dotted arrow points to Tarighian. There's also a big, underlined question mark next to the name. Mertens also has a question mark beside it, and a two-way arrow connects it to the Shadows. The only free-floating word is Zdrok, and there's a circle around it.

I have no clue what it all means, so I type a text message on the OPSAT, photograph the chart with the built-in camera, and transmit the files to Lambert. Maybe he and his team can make sense of it. Why didn't Benton communicate all this stuff to Washington as soon as he got it? Lambert is right—Benton *was* reckless. Maybe he got too cocky for his own good, which sometimes happens in this business.

I also copy the photograph of Namik Basaran and send it to Washington with instructions to identify the other man in the picture.

Whatever Benton discovered about the Shop and the Shadows, it was enough to get him killed. I feel as if I'm stepping into a pool of murk that has remnants of his blood in it. I just hope I can solve the puzzle before the same forces that caught up with him happen to cross my path.

AFTER nightfall I drive Reza's two-door Pazhan, a jeep-like vehicle made in Iran, out of Tabriz toward the container company's warehouse. It's located just west of the city limits in a nonresidential, industrial zone. The Pazhan is a funky old thing, probably twelve years old. The Iran government doesn't allow many foreign-made cars into the country. You'll find Japanese brands but certainly no American ones. Iranian automobiles are notorious for being bad for the environment, but they have a substantial monopoly on the market.

The Tabriz Container Company's warehouse is a large building that appears to be thirty or forty years old. There isn't much in the way of lighting around the building at this time of night, probably because there isn't a lot to steal.

I park the Pazhan a quarter of a mile away, off the main road. Wearing my uniform and headset, I walk to the building, traverse the empty parking lot, and stand for a moment with my back to the wall, near the employees' entrance. There's a lone bright bulb over the door. I load the SC-20K with a ring airfoil projectile and aim at the light. Got it—the front of the warehouse is plunged in darkness. I hope the sound of the bulb breaking doesn't attract any security guards.

I stand in front of the door and peer through the square window in the center. There are a few lights on, but it's difficult to discern the geography of the place from here. I use the lock picks to open the door and slip inside.

It's an empty reception office. A door with keycard access leads to the rest of the warehouse. I drop the goggles over my eyes and activate the thermal-vision mode. I'm in luck—someone very recently went through the door. The keys most often punched show traces of residual heat as long as not much time has elapsed. The trick is to press them in the correct order. Logically the key that's the faintest would be the first one and the brightest key would be the last. Distinguishing the differences of luminescence on the three keys in-between is the hard part.

On this particular pad only four keys show heat. That means there are only four numbers in the code or one of five numbers is used twice. I'll need a little help with this one, so I aim my OPSAT screen at the keypad and snap a shot. I then use the controls on the OPSAT to play with the contrasts in the image. This gives me a digital readout of the amount of luminescence it's picking up. The 2 key is the brightest, so it's either pressed twice or it's the last of four numbers. The 4 is the next brightest, followed by 8 and 3.

I try 3, 8, 4, and 2. Nothing happens.

I try 2, 3, 8, 4, and 2. Nothing happens.

I press 3, 2, 8, 4, and 2. Nothing happens.

I punch 3, 8, 2, 4, and 2. Green light. The door unlocks. I'm lucky the system doesn't set off an alarm after three unsuccessful tries, which many do.

I'm in the warehouse. The only illumination is up here at the front. There's a desk by the door, presumably used by a foreman or some such employee. A book lies open, facedown, on the desk. I know I'm not alone here because of the heat signatures on the keypad.

The rest of the place is full of, well, containers. Boxes, crates, barrels, cans, stacks of flat cardboard that will eventually be folded into boxes, and even plastic kitchen containers along the lines of Tupperware. Amazing.

I move in and start down an aisle of crates. They're all marked with the same Tabriz Container Company stamp I saw in Arbil. I tap on one of the crates and hear a hollow echo—it's empty. Just in case, though, I reach into the Osprey and pull out a metal detection wand. It's like the thing they use at airports to wave around your armpits and between your legs if you happen to beep when you walk through the metal detector.

As I continue down the aisle, I wave the detector across every other crate. They're all turning up empty until I cross an aisle to go to another section. This time, the wand buzzes over some crates, and a little too loudly for my comfort. I use my combat knife to pry off the top slat and peer inside. Engine parts—big deal.

"Salaam?"

I freeze. There's my missing individual who leaves heat signatures on keypads. The voice comes from the other side of the warehouse. Shit. He must have heard the detector buzz.

"Salaam?"

It's closer. He's coming this way. I quickly move back the way I came, treading lightly, hoping he's not sure exactly where the sound came from. I keep moving until I reach a darker aisle. I quickly negotiate the shelving here, climb on top of a crate, and pull myself to the top shelf. They'd need forklifts to place and remove objects from this height. I lie facedown and wait.

Sure enough, I see the lone elderly night watchman walk slowly into my aisle. He's not sure what he heard or if he heard anything at all. Nevertheless the poor guy looks scared. This tells me there's nothing in this warehouse that's of any interest. If there were illegal arms here, the Shop wouldn't guard them with a lone sixty-year-old grandfather.

He eventually gives up and returns to the desk at the front of the warehouse. I can see him clearly from where I'm lying. He sits, opens the book, and begins to read. Every now and then he looks up and scans the aisles in his view, then goes back to reading. Damn. How long am I going to have to stay here?

I really don't want to do it, but I have no choice. I'm not going to spend the rest of the night in this goddamned warehouse. I slowly pull the SC-20K off my shoulder and reach for another ring airfoil projectile. I load the rifle and aim for the old guy's head. At this range it shouldn't do much damage. It'll knock him out for a while and he'll have a nasty headache when he wakes up, but that'll be it.

I aim at the back of his head and squeeze the trigger. Perfect shot. The watchman slumps forward and looks as if he's fallen asleep while reading.

I climb down from my lofty position and head toward the back of the warehouse. Everything looks innocent enough and I'm about to call it a night and leave when I notice the office. It's in the back corner—an enclosed room with windows and a door. It's unlocked, too.

Using the night-vision mode so I don't have to turn on the office lights, I riffle through the papers on the desk. Most of it means nothing to me. However, I do come across a blank "shipping manifest" form that is written in both Farsi and English. Where there's one, there must be more. I turn to the filing cabinets and pull them open one by one. I eventually find a drawer that's full of shipping manifest forms—and these are filled out. I scan the dates and find the folder for last month's shipments. Again, I don't understand a lot of it, but I do recognize certain city and country names.

The Tabriz Container Company apparently ships its products all over the Middle East. I see that they have customers in Iraq, Turkey, Lebanon, Syria, Jordan, Egypt, Afghanistan, Saudi Arabia, Kuwait, and even Israel. There are clients in Russia, Azerbaijan, Armenia, Georgia, the Czech Republic, and Poland.

So those containers I saw in Arbil could have come from anywhere. This has turned out to be a false lead.

Then I see something that's interesting. I find some Shipping Manifests to Akdabar Enterprises in Van, Turkey. This is the company that Reza told me about. The one owned by that humanitarian guy, Basaran. There are also manifests to his charity organization, Tirma. A coincidence?

I put everything back the way I found it and leave the office. When I get back to the front of the warehouse, I see that my friend the night watchman is still counting sheep.

I approach him silently and determine that he's breathing steadily. He'll be all right. I go out the front door, walk back to the Pazhan, and drive into town.

At daybreak I'll head towards Turkey. I think it's time I meet this Namik Basaran fellow and see what he's really all about. I'll send a report to Lambert, say goodbye to Reza, and chalk up my visit to Iran as educational but ultimately a dead end.

17

SARAH had been drunk on two previous occasions, and neither of them had been pleasant. The first time was when she was in high school. She and some girlfriends had been at a party in which the boys had gotten hold of a keg of beer. It was an unchaperoned event, and just about everyone had too much to drink. Some parents found out about it and there was hell to pay at school the next day. Sarah's father had been disappointed but didn't punish her too severely. He just made sure that adults would be around the next time his daughter went to a party.

The second time was about a month after she had left home to go to college in Evanston. She was with a boy she had just begun dating, and one night he procured a bottle of Jack Daniel's. He mixed it with Coke and she drank three glasses. It made her violently sick, much to the boy's chagrin.

Who was it that said the "third time's the charm"? This thought went through Sarah's head as she sipped the glass of red wine. Rivka had already announced that she planned to drink enough to get "tipsy," and the boys proclaimed they were going to drink much more than that. Sarah decided that she, too, would drink enough to feel a buzz. She just didn't want to feel sick.

They were in a bar in the New City. It was a place Noel had been to several times, and he was sure the girls wouldn't be asked for IDs. They weren't. Noel and Eli started by buying two bottles of wine, and then the quartet sat in a booth in the back of the smoky dive, unseen by the few patrons that were too lost in their own drinks to pay much attention to the laughing, happy young people.

At first Sarah thought the bar looked dumpy and was depressing. Eli assured her they would liven up the place. Sure enough, after one bottle was empty, the boys and girls were having a grand time in the little back room. Eli and Noel could be very funny, especially when they told off-color jokes, and Sarah and Rivka were thoroughly entertained by them. It didn't hurt that in-between laughs the boys planted kisses on their dates.

"Hey, I've got an idea," Eli said. He looked at Noel. "What do you think, Noel? Irish Car Bombs?"

Noel's eyes widened and he grinned. "Yeah!"

"Huh? What's that?" Sarah asked.

"Irish Car Bomb! You'll love it," Noel said.

"Irish Car Bomb?" Rivka asked, giggling. "What are you talking about?"

"It's a drink, silly," Eli said. "I'll be right back." He got up and left the room, heading toward the bar.

"You didn't know this was an Irish pub, did you?" Noel asked the girls.

"This is an Irish pub? In Jerusalem?" Sarah asked.

"It doesn't look like an Irish pub," Rivka said.

A few minutes later Eli returned with a tray carrying four pint glasses of what appeared to be beer and four shot glasses of an odd, creamy brown liquid.

Eli sat down and pointed to a pint glass. "This is a half-pint of Guinness." He then pointed to a shot glass. "This is Irish whiskey mixed with Bailey's Irish Cream." He then proceeded to take the shot glasses and drop them—glass and liquid—*into* the pint glasses. The whiskey and Irish cream mixed with the Guiness. Once that was done, he put a completed "Car Bomb" in front of each person at the table, took the one in front of him, and chugged the entire contents without breathing. When he was done, he slammed the empty pint glass on the table—the empty shot glass rattled inside of it—and burped loudly.

"Wow," Sarah said.

"Drink up, before the cream curdles!" Noel commanded. He took one of the glasses and chugged the mixture faster than Eli had.

"Come on, ladies," Eli said. "Your turn."

Rivka took one of the glasses and asked, "I'm supposed to drink it all at once?"

"Chug it," Noel said. "That's what you're supposed to do."

"You can't sip it," Eli added.

"Okay, here goes." She turned up the glass and started drinking. The shot glass slid down and hit her nose. She almost laughed but kept going. The boys chanted, "Go, go, go, go . . . !" When she got it all down, Rivka slammed the glass on the table as she had seen the guys do it.

"Wow, that was great!" she said.

"Your turn, Sarah!" Eli said.

"I don't know," Sarah said, eyeing the drink warily. "I've never chugged anything like that. I'll probably choke."

"No, you won't. Just gulp gulp gulp. Don't stop to breathe. Do it fast."

She took hold of the drink and smelled it.

"Don't smell it, drink it!" Noel ordered, playfully poking her arm.

"It's good, Sarah," Rivka said, smiling. "Really."

Sarah shrugged and put the glass to her lips. Then she started to drink. And drink.

"Go, go, go, go, go!"

When she was done, she slammed the glass on the table.

"Yeah!" the others cried.

Sarah felt proud of herself. She wiped her mouth and said, "Yum!" Eli beamed at her and then leaned over to kiss her. It was a mushy open-mouthed one.

"Whoa, Sarah!" Rivka cried. She laughed. Noel laughed. Eli and Sarah broke apart and laughed as well.

That was when Sarah realized the room was spinning more than it was five minutes earlier. She felt light-headed and woozy.

"I'm getting drunk," she said, but it didn't sound like those particular words to her. She laughed again. Rivka burst out laughing, too, and reached for her friend. The two girls leaned on each other, laughing so hard that tears fell from their eyes. Eli sat with his arms folded across his chest, watching them and keeping an eye on his watch.

It should take about ten minutes, he thought.

He poured another glass of wine for the girls but left his and Noel's glasses empty.

"Tell us about your uncle Martin, Noel," Eli suggested.

Noel raised his eyebrows and said, "Oh. Okay. That's a good story." The girls smiled and looked at him, ready for more hilarity. "I have this uncle, his name is Uncle Martin, and he used to live in the basement of a tenement building. His hobby, if you can believe this, was collecting mice feces. I kid you not. You know what he did with the feces?"

"What, Noel?" Eli asked.

The girls were beginning to lose it. Their mouths hung open and their eyes drooped, but they hung on to every word Noel was saying.

"He liked to use the feces to make art. He would mix the stuff with water and use a paintbrush to paint. And you know what he would paint?"

"What would he paint, Noel?" Eli asked.

"Mice!"

He continued the nonsensical story for several minutes. Sarah tried to concentrate on it, but the words kept fading in and out. It was as if she were in a waking dream.

The words droned on. Eventually she couldn't understand them anymore. She had to close her eyes, just for a minute.

Noel stopped talking.

Rivka was out. Her head was on Sarah's shoulder. Sarah's eyelids fluttered and finally fell. She began to slide over in the booth, but Eli caught her and held her up.

"Wow, that was fast," Noel said.

"Always is," Eli agreed.

"I'm glad you gave them the correct glasses."

"Come on. Let's get them out of here." He pulled Sarah out of the booth and let her lean on him.

"What's going on?" she slurred.

"Sarah, I'm taking you home. You're drunk," Eli said.

"I am?"

Noel helped Rivka up. She whimpered a little. "Rivka, come with me. We have to go home now," he said. Rivka started to cry a little.

"My stomach hurts," she mumbled.

"Let's go," Noel said.

Eli left money on the bar as they helped the girls out. He winked at the bartender and said, "I guess those Car Bombs were a little too strong."

When the night air hit Sarah's face, she became aware that she was outside. "What's going on?" she asked again, but her voice sounded far away.

"I'm taking you back to my place." She thought it was Eli's voice. The nice man was helping her walk, though. She shouldn't have drunk so much. She knew that drinking didn't agree with her. Now she felt awful. She just wanted to climb into bed.

The last thing she remembered before passing out was a car door slamming as she fell into the passenger seat.

ELI drove his beat-up 1995 Chevrolet Cavalier out of the New City and headed north, toward Atarot Airport. Sarah was snoring lightly in the seat beside him. Before he had left the street where the bar was located, he watched Noel get Rivka into his car and drive away.

Eli was happy that he didn't have to do what Noel had to do.

The Rohypnol worked amazingly well. He had broken up the two white tablets, one in each shot glass, and waited until the powder dissolved before bringing the Irish Car Bombs back to the table. Sarah and Rivka never knew what hit them. Car bombs, indeed.

It was approaching midnight when he turned off the main highway and took a little-used route toward an industrial area of the city. Eli could hear planes overhead, flying in low for a landing at the small airport. When he had first gone to the warehouse to prepare it for Sarah's arrival, he wasn't happy about its location. He would have

preferred it to be farther out of Jerusalem and not so close
to the airport. But orders were orders. Apparently Yuri and
Vlad's people already owned the building. Eli supposed it
didn't really matter. As long as he was paid what was coming to him.

It was at the end of a curving road full of derelict ware-
houses and condemned office buildings. Vlad had said it
was "where Jesus lost his sandals." This wasn't far from
the truth. Aside from the proximity to the airport, the
warehouse seemed to be in the middle of nowhere. The
building was dark and would have appeared deserted were
it not for the two sports cars parked in front. The Ferrari
and the Jaguar were a little too conspicuous for Eli's comfort level, but what was he going to tell those guys? Get a
couple of ugly old cars like his?

He pulled the Chevy next to the Jaguar and shut off the
motor. He looked at his sleeping passenger and softly
said, "Sorry, Sarah."

Eli got out of the car and went to the front door of the
building. He knocked and waited until the little window
slid opened. Dark eyes peered out.

"You going to help me or not?" Eli asked.

The door unlocked and opened and the two Russians
came out.

"She okay?" the one called Yuri asked.

"Yeah. She's out cold, though," Eli said.

"Let's get her inside, then," the one called Vlad said.

They walked to the car and opened the passenger door.
When he saw Sarah, Vlad remarked, "Hey, she's a beauty!
This is going to be a more interesting assignment than I
thought."

"Shut up, you horny bastard," Yuri said. "Help me."

The two men pulled her out of the car and carried her
to the building.

"Don't drop her," Eli said. "Be careful."

"Don't worry, kid," Yuri said. "She's worth gold."

Eli followed them inside and shut the door behind him. The warehouse was clear in the middle, but the sides were full of old and broken kitchen and bathroom appliances. A loft, supported by two concrete columns, jutted out halfway over the ground floor, serving as half of a second floor. It, too, was covered in junk. The men carried Sarah across the floor of the dusty warehouse, through a door on the west wall, and into a moldy-smelling corridor lined with three offices. They went into the third office, which was empty except for a cot, a small table, and a chair. The cot was made up with blankets and a pillow. Adjoining the room was a bathroom containing a toilet, a sink, and a shower stall.

There were no windows, of course.

Yuri and Vlad placed the unconscious girl on the cot, covered her with a blanket, and left the room. Vlad locked the door and motioned for Eli to follow him into one of the other rooms.

"You did good," he said. "I have your money."

The middle room was both an office and a bedroom, as it contained another cot along with a desk and phone. Yuri stood in the doorway and watched as Vlad opened a drawer and removed a large white envelope. He tossed it to Eli, who opened it and glanced inside.

"It's all there," Vlad said. "But you can count it if it will make you feel better."

Eli wanted to do just that, but he thought it would make him look weak. He didn't want to appear weak in front of these guys.

"I'm sure it's fine," he said. "How did . . . how did the other thing go?"

"What other thing?"

"That guy Blaine?"

"Oh, Blaine," Yuri said. "That went . . . very well."

Eli nodded. "Well, I guess your people are pretty happy, then. I think everything I found out from her"—he gestured with his head toward the next room—"will be accurate. Her father is the one you're looking for."

Vlad spoke again. "Like I said, you did good. Now, we've made you a nice cozy place to sleep in the loft in there. Sorry, but there are no more vacancies back here. Yuri sleeps in the next room, I have this one, and our guest has the other one."

"I know," Eli said. "I'll be all right."

"How about the girl's friend?" Yuri asked.

Eli shrugged. "I don't know. I haven't talked to Noel. He got her in the car and drove away. I assume everything is fine. By the way, don't you think you should move your cars?"

"We were going to do that," Yuri replied. "We'll put 'em in the back and cover them with a tarp. You should do the same."

The three men left the warehouse, moved their vehicles, and met back in the little office.

"Good," Yuri said. "Let's get some sleep, boys." He held out his hand to Eli. Eli shook it, and then he grasped Vlad's hand. He nodded and left the room, following the corridor back to the warehouse. He ascended the wooden stairs leading to the loft and found the sleeping bag in the back corner.

As he undressed and climbed into the bedroll, Eli wondered if he was going to hell.

18

SOUTHEASTERN Turkey is beautiful, but it's a bitch to travel through. It's extremely rugged terrain. I'm afraid that Reza's Pazhan doesn't have the *oomph* to continuously travel up and down the mountain roads. The car slows down considerably on an uphill incline. While northeastern Iran is also mountainous, it doesn't compare to this part of Turkey. The Caucasus range is vast and the roads are not as well kept. I'm lucky that it isn't winter, for then it would *really* be difficult. It can be bitterly cold and snowy between December and April, and I'm pushing it by being here at the very end of March. On the higher slopes there's still a lot of snow and ice, and I've taken to adjusting the temperature controls on my uniform to keep me warm.

Another thing that distinguishes the region from the rest of the country is that eastern Turkey is more "Asian" than "European." As it was once upper Mesopotamia, the land and people still retain remnants of that long-lost culture, thereby giving the region a much more exotic feeling than the rest of Turkey. By the same token, people here are more conservative, more suspicious, and less warm toward strangers than in the Westernized European half of the country. It's also dominated by the Kurds, perhaps a fifth of the total population.

During the past decade the region was plagued by terrorism instigated by the Kurdistan Workers Party, the PKK, considered to be one of the more dangerous terrorist groups in the world today. They recently changed their name to KADEK (Kurdistan Freedom and Democracy Congress) and yet again to KONGRA-GEL (the People's Congress of Kurdistan) in attempts to diminish the perception that they support terrorism. The jury's still out on whether or not this is true. At any rate, Turkish police and antiterrorism forces are plentiful in the southeast, and I'm prepared to be stopped at checkpoints without warning.

Reza supplied me with the necessary identity papers and visa. I'm back to being a Swiss detective for Interpol. Getting across the border isn't a problem, although I'm asked a lot of questions. I'm pretty good at bluffing my way out of interrogations from your everyday variety policemen. They let me drive on after issuing a strict warning to stay off the roads at night, to not talk to Kurds who ask me to carry items for them, and to report any suspicious activity.

I drive to Van, a midsize town on the eastern shore of Lake Van, the largest body of water in Turkey, excluding Istanbul's Sea of Marmara. Mount Ararat is nearby, a spectacular sight but also the location of a Turkish military facility that is off-limits to civilians. I can't be caught dead anywhere around there.

With help from Third Echelon's navigation capabilities, I find Akdabar Enterprises on the very edge of town, overlooking the vast lake. It strikes me as an odd place for a construction and steel conglomerate site. Why Van? Perhaps its main clientele consists of Kurds in the region. Who knows? I realize now that the place gets its name from Akdabar Island, one of the more important islands on the lake. One of Van's few tourist attractions is the tenth-century Church of the Holy Cross located on Akdabar.

I park the Pazhan on a hill overlooking the expansive complex so I can get a bird's-eye view of the place. Using a pair of Third Echelon's binoculars, I see that a tall wire fence surrounds the property. In the very center is an open courtyard with two flagpoles at opposite ends. A Turkish flag is on one while the Akdabar logo sails on the other. A large refinery sporting two tall smokestacks appears to be the dominant landmark; it's probably where the steelworks are located. There are a couple of big oil drums near the edge of the water, along with smaller constructions that are probably workers' quarters and offices. From what I can see there are several armed guards patrolling the grounds—along the fence perimeter and around the buildings. The oil drums, certainly a target for terrorists, have a particularly strong security presence. Other guards ride around in three-wheelers, golf cartlike vehicles that I suppose are faster than walking.

The most impressive thing is that the plant has its own airstrip and hangar. I see a cargo plane with Akdabar's logo painted on the side readying for takeoff. Basaran must do very well for himself indeed.

Reza was able to provide me with a letter of introduction to see Basaran. Although the two men have never met, their business connections should be enough to get me in. I'm counting on the letter and my Interpol credentials to get me in the front door. I want to meet Basaran personally in order to get a sense of the guy. If he knew Benton, then perhaps he'll be forthcoming with information.

I dress in civilian clothes, put on a tie, leave the Osprey in the car, and drive down to the visitors' parking area. I present my papers and letter to the guard at the front gate and ask to see Basaran.

"Do you have an appointment?" he asks in heavily accented English.

"No, I'm afraid not," I say. "I'm sorry, but I had no time to arrange it. I just entered the country. If Mr. Basaran is busy I can come back later . . . ?"

"Wait here." The guard went into the checkpoint booth and made a call. I could see him reading from Reza's letter, nodding his head, and glancing at me. Finally he came back and said, "If you don't mind waiting a little while, Mr. Basaran will see you when he gets out of a meeting." He gave me a map of the complex, pointed to the group of small buildings by the lake, and told me to drive there and park in the accompanying lot. He gave me a visitor's pass and admonished me not to drive anywhere else on the property.

Over by the lake the view is spectacular. It's a clear day and the water stretches out to the horizon, much like Lake Michigan does at the edge of Chicago. The buildings here are modern constructions and apparently house the administrative offices, an employees' facility that includes lockers, dressing rooms, a gym, a cafeteria, and vending, and the Tirma charity organization headquarters. By the way, Carly back at Third Echelon pointed out that the word *tirma* means "silk" in Farsi. My question is, why Farsi? Why not Turkish?

The waiting room in the main administrative building is modern and comfortable. It contains pretty much the kind of furniture you'd expect in a reception area—and I note the surveillance camera in the corner keeping a record of who goes in and out. A pretty Turkish reception-ist sits behind the glass window and glances at me every now and then. It's refreshing to be in a predominantly Muslim country where the rules are relaxed enough that women can reveal their hair and the skin on the arms and legs.

I wait approximately twenty minutes and another lovely Turkish—or maybe Kurdish—woman fetches me and leads me to a door to the right of the receptionist that requires keypad code access. Part of my training with Third Echelon was to try to memorize codes by watching someone press the keys. Depending on how fast the per-son was, I eventually achieved an eighty-eight-percentile success rating. I stand beside the woman and fake a cough just as she begins the sequence—this creates the illusion that I'm not watching. Her fingers quickly zip over the pad, but I'm able to catch it—8, 6, 0, 2, 5.

The door opens and she leads me through a hallway adorned with Middle Eastern artwork. As we walk I quickly enter the code sequence into my OPSAT so I won't forget it. We turn a corner and I notice another sur-veillance camera on the ceiling, and then we enter the head man's spacious, and very Western, office. In fact, there's a Picasso hanging on the wall. In one corner of the room stands a table displaying a scale model of a fancy modern building.

Namik Basaran greets me at the door, grins broadly, and holds out his hand as I'm ushered into the room. A very large guy, wearing a suit and a turban, stands to the side and eyes me closely.

"Mr. Fisher, welcome to Turkey," he says in good En-glish. I shake his hand and thank him. I notice that he's squeezing a rubber ball in his other hand. He chuckles and says, "It's for tendonitis. It's also a nervous habit!" He walks over to his desk and drops the ball into a drawer. He turns to the big guy and says, "You may leave us, Farid, thank you."

The big guy nods, glares at me once more, and leaves the room.

"My bodyguard," Basaran explains. "And driver. And assistant. A man in my position can't be too careful. Poor Farid, I took him into the organization from the street. He's an Iranian, a victim of Saddam Hussein's regime. Farid doesn't speak—his tongue was cut out while he was a prisoner in Abu Ghraib Prison during the Iran-Iraq war. Now, would you like something to drink? Tea? Coffee? Something stronger?"

I shrug and say that I'll have whatever he has.

"Well, personally at this time of day I prefer a small cup of *çay*. Is that suitable?"

I groan inwardly but smile and reply, "That would be fine."

Çay is Turkish tea that comes from the Black Sea area and is usually served with tremendous amounts of sugar. It's a bit on the strong side, but I can grin and bear it when I have to. Basaran walks to his wet bar, pours the tea into tiny tulip-shaped glasses, and brings them over. We sit on black leather chairs at a low table beneath the Picasso. A wall-sized window to our left overlooks the lake.

It's difficult to determine how old Basaran is, but I'd guess early fifties. He's medium-height, and, as in the photograph, there's a noticeable skin condition on his face and hands. I'm not sure what it is. It's not as bad as skin grafting, but it doesn't look as if it's due to some disease, either.

"Very impressive place you have here, Mr. Basaran," I say.

"Thank you. It's very gratifying to achieve the success one yearns for in one's youth and then still be alive to enjoy it."

"I'm particularly impressed with your airstrip. How do you use it?"

He shrugs. "We ship materials all over. Currently I'm in the process of building an elaborate indoor shopping mall in Northern Cyprus. That's a model of it over there on the table. Beautiful, isn't it? We ship materials daily to the island. As you can guess, I'm a firm supporter of Turkey's right to claim Cyprus. I'm helping the cause by building up the north, giving the people more modern facilities and attractions. This mall will be the largest shopping center of its type in the Middle East." He shakes his head and sips his tea. "The ongoing struggle with the Greek Cypriots there is tragic. Why can't they just accept us and be done with it? But that's a whole other conversation. Now. Tell me what brings you to Van, Mr. Fisher. I read your letter of introduction from Mr. Hamadan, and I see that you work for Interpol. How can I assist you?"

I give him my spiel on how I'm compiling an extensive report on terrorists in the region. Interpol will publish the report and send it to law enforcement agencies all over the world, but most important, it will help in combating terrorism here in the Middle East. "Mr. Hamadan suggested that I speak to you, as I hear you're an expert on terrorism here in Eastern Turkey," I say. A little flattery usually goes a long way.

"You give me too much credit," Basaran says, but he smiles and enjoys the compliment. "I wouldn't call myself an expert. That's ridiculous. But I do know some things.

I've followed the various groups in this area for many years and even met some of the leaders. That is not to say that I'm friendly with any of them. As a Turkish entrepreneur—and a successful one—they probably hate me as much as they hate anyone else in Turkey who favors a Westernized lifestyle. I could probably talk for hours about terrorism, Mr. Fisher, so unless you have specific questions, we might need to postpone our meeting for another time. I am very busy today."

I decide to drop another name. "I see. Rick Benton also said you'd be very helpful."

I notice a flicker in his eyes. "You know Mr. Benton?" he asks.

"Only by his work," I say. "I never met the late Mr. Benton."

Basaran's mouth drops slightly. "The *late* Mr. Benton? Is he . . . ?"

"Yes," I reply. "He was murdered in Brussels just last week."

"That *is* tragic. I'm sorry to hear it. Do they know who did it?"

"No, it's a mystery."

Basaran takes a sip of tea. "I met him one time. He asked me questions about some of the terrorist groups operating in this part of the country, just as you have asked. I assure you, I am compelled to speak out against terrorism whenever I have a public forum. It is important to me and to my family."

I'd like to find out more about his family but decide that now's not the best time.

"You do know about my charity organization, Tirma?" he asks.

"Yes, that's one reason why I wanted to meet you."

"Tirma is a personal project for me. I've pledged much of my income to help fight terrorism, and Tirma allows me to make a difference—if only a small one."

"It's not-for-profit, I take it?"

"Certainly. With an all-volunteer staff, I might add. If you'd care to quit Interpol and work for us for free, we would be more than happy to have you!" He laughed boisterously.

I laugh, too, but quickly swing the conversation back to the topic at hand. "Well, since you're pressed for time, I do have a couple of specific questions."

"Fire away."

"What do you know about the Shop and what do you know about the Shadows?"

Basaran nodded, as if he was expecting the question. "Mr. Benton asked me the same thing. Those two groups are becoming the hot topics on everyone's list. As far as the Shadows are concerned, our friend Tarighian has certainly taken the word *mystique* to a new level."

"Tarighian?" I feign ignorance.

"Nasir Tarighian," Basaran says. "He's the money behind the Shadows. Didn't you know?"

"I thought Nasir Tarighian died in the 1980s."

"That's what he wants everyone to believe. But he's alive and well, and financing and directing the Shadows' operations with a firm hand. I'm afraid that no one knows where he is, though. Or much about his personal life, either. He's a very mysterious man, just like his organization. It is said that Tarighian lives like a nomad, much like Osama Bin-Laden. He and his band of merry terrorists travel from one place to another so they can't be caught. I imagine they live in caves in the mountains somewhere."

"Any guesses as to what country they stay in the most?"

"I think it's Armenia, Georgia, or Azerbaijan. It's safer for them there. If they were in Turkey, they'd probably be caught. If they were in Iran, they'd probably be caught. If they were in Iraq, they'd most *certainly* be caught. But I really don't know. Perhaps they move from country to country periodically."

"Do you know an Ahmed Mohammed?" I ask.

"Yes, indeed. He's the more visible leader of the Shadows. Perhaps *leader* is not the right word. He receives instructions and money from Tarighian and then sees that things get done. He's very much a wanted terrorist, and I'm *sure* he is always on the run. He is a snake, that man."

"No idea where he is?"

"None. Anywhere and everywhere. Like Tarighian."

There's a knock at the door.

"Excuse me a moment," Basaran says. "Come in!"

A thin man with unkempt blond hair enters the room. He is a Caucasian and appears to be in his late forties or early fifties. "May I speak to you for a moment?" he asks Basaran. I can't place the accent, but it's European.

Basaran stands and says, "Professor, how many times a day must you interrupt me?" He winks at me and says, "The professor is a stickler for details. Please excuse me a moment. I'll be right back."

As soon as they are gone, I quickly stand, reach into my jacket pocket, and remove three miniature sticky bugs. They're a lot like the sticky cameras I use except that they're audio-only. I move to Basaran's desk and quickly stick one bug underneath, attaching it to one of the legs up high where it won't be noticed. I hurry over to the scale model and place another bug on the underside of the table. Finally I attach the third bug underneath the small table where we're currently sitting. I resume my place, pick up my teacup, and am mid-sip when Basaran returns.

"I'm sorry, please accept my apologies for the interruption," he says. "I'm afraid I must cut short our talk. Something has come up that requires my attention. However, if you are free for dinner tonight, I would be more than happy to meet you and we can continue our discussion."

I stand and say, "Why, I'd be delighted. Just tell me where and what time."

He gives me the address of a restaurant in the harbor area, and we arrange to meet at eight o'clock that evening. We shake hands and I'm escorted out of the building.

I drive out of the Akdabar complex and park on the hill where I was earlier, turn on my OPSAT, and tune in to the little bugs I left in Basaran's office. Reception is very good, but I know the farther away I am, the less quality I'll get. I recognize Basaran's voice. He's talking in English with another man. It doesn't sound like the professor fellow I saw briefly.

BASARAN: "And what is their answer?"

OTHER GUY: "The suppliers refuse to refund our money for the first shipment. The goods were confiscated in Iraq and were under our control at the time. The suppliers say it's not their responsibility."

BASARAN: "Damn them to hell. What happened to the shipment was not our fault and they know it. Bastards."

OTHER GUY: "Not only that, but the payment for the replacement is due in two days."

BASARAN: "It's highway robbery, that's what it is. Damn Zdrok! Fine, do what you have to do. Proceed with the payment. And tell Professor Mertens to expect me in his lab in twenty minutes."

Mertens? I recall the name scrawled on Rick Benton's chart. Was that the "professor" I saw in Basaran's office?

I hear the door open and close. There is silence for a moment, and then I hear Basaran mutter again, "Damn Zdrok." After that the door opens and shuts once more and the room is quiet.

Tarighian. Mertens. Zdrok. It's all trying to come together.

19

LIEUTENANT Colonel Petlow knew that the confiscated arms would be excellent bait for the Shadows.

After he had received Sam Fisher's report from Arbil, the U.S. Army took the initiative to secure the arms shipment that was held in the police headquarters and move it to an unspecified location. The Shadows had shown they were keen to get it back, so a plan was instigated to draw the terrorists out. The Iraqi police were also under pressure to find those responsible for murdering the members of their force, as well as make up for the botched arrest raid that occurred outside the Arbil police headquarters. The debacle was more an embarrassment for the Iraqi police than the U.S. Army. In fact, the Pentagon blamed the Iraqi government's lack of adequate police training for the deaths of the four American soldiers, who were officially along on the arrest raid only as observers. So in a unique instance of military and civilian police cooperation, the two organizations worked together to formulate a plan to draw in the escaped terrorists.

One of the more positive developments to come out of Iraq gaining its own government in the summer of 2004 was that informers were more willing to cooperate with Iraqi police, intelligence officers, and the military. These people, most often civilians but sometimes men who had served in various Iraqi militias, were interested in not only receiving monetary compensation for their efforts but also in developing a favorable relationship with those in power. Sometimes a reliable informer would be granted special status with employment or tangible means such as property. In a country like Iraq, which was still finding its way back to the level of economic existence it held before the war, many people jumped at the chance to get ahead.

Thus, informers were paid to spread the word around Arbil that the arms confiscated from the Shadows were being kept in a cave that was in control of a Kurdish army platoon. Furthermore, the Kurds were reportedly green and undisciplined.

In reality the arms were nowhere near the cave. The U.S. Army positioned two platoons at the site with orders that if the Shadows didn't try to retake the arms within two weeks, then the soldiers would be reassigned. Petlow figured it was worth the time and expense to deploy the troops in this way.

It was a dependable informant named Ali Bazan who came through with the goods. He had at one time been a top lieutenant to the militant Shiite cleric who waged a guerilla war against the U.S. in the spring of 2004. Now working for the young Iraqi government and police force, Bazan made contact with the alleged terrorists who were itching to find and take back the arms taken from them. Bazan duped them into believing he was on their side and was helping them achieve their goal. They foolishly

shared with him their plans to attack the Kurdish platoon
at the cave on a given morning.

Sure enough, in the early hours of the same day that
Sam Fisher drove to Turkey from Iran, a group of twenty
militants laid siege to the cave. They were armed with
AK-47s and handguns of various makes and models. The
U.S. platoons were armed with standard issue M16A2s,
M4A1s, M203 grenade launchers, M67 fragmentation
grenades, and M84 stun grenades. There was no contest.

The terrorists struck first with six men storming the
cave opening, guns blazing. As they engaged the men inside, the Shadows quickly realized they weren't fighting
Kurds. The American firepower overwhelmed the attackers and the six men were killed. This brought forward the
remainder of the terrorists, who found themselves surprised by the sudden appearance of the U.S. army at their
right and left flanks. The Americans had hidden in
dugouts covered by trapdoors camouflaged with dirt,
rocks, and vegetation.

The gun battle lasted twenty-two minutes. Thirteen of
the terrorists were dead and the rest were captured. The
U.S. lost two men. The seven prisoners were brought to a
temporary base outside of Arbil and lined up outside of
Petlow's quarters.

Sam Fisher had made copies of the relevant file photos
he found in Arbil and forwarded them to Petlow. The lieutenant colonel, along with a representative from the Iraqi
police force, had a chance to take a look at the dead militants first but didn't recognize any of them as being the
men that Fisher had seen that night. Petlow then confronted the seven prisoners, one by one. They were a
mangy bunch, men who had lived in the brush and
avoided the law for months at a time.

None of them looked familiar. As he briefly interrogated each man with the Iraqi policeman serving as interpreter, Petlow had a sinking feeling they had failed to catch the men they were looking for. But as he spoke to the fourth man in line, something sparked his memory.

"Open your mouth," Petlow ordered the prisoner. When the man did so, Petlow saw he was missing some teeth. He was the man Fisher called "No-Tooth." The man responsible for the deaths of the four U.S. soldiers.

Petlow gave the order for the Iraqi policeman to interpret. "They're all under arrest, of course, but this one is to be charged with the murder of the Arbil police officers and our soldiers. We'll start serious interrogation this afternoon. In the meantime, tell this guy that he's in some serious shit."

SARAH had slept for nearly sixteen hours. When she awoke she was understandably confused and disoriented. She had no idea where she was. She sat up too quickly, bringing on a wave of nausea. A hot flash immediately surged through her body and she broke out into a sweat. Sarah knew she was about to be sick and started to panic. Out of the corner of her eye she saw the door to the bathroom and bolted for it. She made it to the toilet just in time.

When she was done, Sarah sat on the dirty floor beside the toilet for a few moments before attempting to stand.

Where the hell was she? What *was* this place? And more important, where was Eli? And Rivka?

She stood slowly, using the toilet seat as leverage. A stained, cracked mirror over the sink reflected a pale, frightened girl of twenty. She looked terrible.

A washcloth and towel sat on the edge of the sink. She turned on the cold water and let it run. At least it wasn't brown, like in Eli's apartment, so she splashed her face and let the water run down her neck. It felt good. She realized she was terribly thirsty, but she didn't want to drink the tap water.

She carefully went back into the other room and saw nothing in there but the cot she had slept on and her purse on the floor next to it. She went to the door and turned the knob, only to find it locked.

"Hello?" she called. "Eli?" It was eerily quiet on the other side of the door. "Rivka? Somebody?" She felt the panic build again as she knocked loudly.

When she heard footsteps on the other side, Sarah backed away, ready to let Eli have it.

The man who unlocked the door and peeked inside was not Eli. He had a cold, cruel look about him, and he grinned lecherously at her

"Good morning, Princess," he said. "You slept a long time. How are you feeling?"

"Who are you?" she demanded. "Where am I?" She was suddenly so frightened and confused that she felt light-headed again. She staggered and her knees buckled. The man rushed into the room to catch her and help her to the cot.

"Whoa, miss, sit down. There, there."

She reclined on the pillow and then asked again, more softly, "Who are you?"

"My name is Vlad. I think you need some more sleep."

"Where am I?"

"Just sleep," he said and turned to walk out.

"Wait!"

But he was out the door and she heard it lock.

What the *hell* was going on? Who was he? Where were her friends?

She heard an airplane overhead. Was she near an airport? Come to think of it, she had dreamed of airplanes, or so she thought. She remembered an unpleasant state of consciousness that she wasn't sure was real or part of her sleep. She thought she might have been carried someplace by men who gripped her ankles and wrists too tightly. Even now, as she touched her arms, they felt bruised. She also recalled a feverish tossing and turning, which may or may not have occurred there on the cot, and hearing the occasional roar of overhead planes.

Surely Eli would show up soon and explain what was going on. Right now she felt too dazed and confused to care very much. Perhaps she should try to sleep more. If this was what a hangover felt like, she never wanted to take another drink.

She admonished herself that she hadn't been the most model twenty-year-old girl while on her trip to Israel. She had had sex several times, had drunk alcohol, had stayed at a boy's house overnight . . . what would her father think?

Her father! She could call *him*! There was that special number she could dial on her cell phone and send a message to him. She didn't know where he was, but he was sure to get it. Sarah reached for her purse on the floor and frantically looked inside it for her phone.

It wasn't there, of course. Nor was her address book. Damn, she thought. What now?

A key rattled in the lock again. This time the door opened to reveal Eli.

"Eli! My God, what the . . . where are we?"

He closed the door behind him, set a bottle of water on the floor, and stood in front of her. The expression on his face disturbed her.

"What's wrong? Eli? What is this place?"

"Sarah, as long as you cooperate they won't hurt you," he said.

She wasn't sure that she'd heard him correctly. "What? Where am I? Where's Rivka?"

"Shut up," he spat. "Listen to me. You're a hostage. You're all alone. You can't escape, so don't try. Don't try to scream for help, because no one will hear you. We're miles and miles from anyone."

She couldn't believe what she was hearing. "What? Eli?"

"I'm sorry, Sarah. That's just the way it is."

"Are you . . . who was that guy who came in? He said his name was Vlad."

"You're not listening to me, Sarah," Eli said. "You are a fucking *hostage!*"

She gasped. He really meant it. This wasn't a joke. The look on his face was something she had never seen before. This wasn't the Eli she knew. This wasn't the funny, tender Eli who had once made love to her. This was someone who scared her.

"What's going on, Eli? Why are you doing this?" she asked.

"We want to know where your father is."

The enormity of what he said nearly made her faint. She took a deep breath and said, "So that's what this is about. My father." She shook her head and turned from him.

"Tell us where he is and you'll be all right. If you won't, then . . . I can't be responsible for what Vlad and Yuri will do to you."

"Vlad and Yuri? What about what *you've* already done to me, Eli! Fuck you, Eli!"

Eli stood there unfazed. There was a knock on the door and Eli said, "Come in."

It was Noel.

"Noel!" Sarah said. "What the hell is going on? Where's Rivka?"

Noel looked at Eli, who shook his head.

"Noel? *Where's* Rivka?" Sarah asked again.

Noel shrugged at her. He looked at Eli again and then walked out of the room.

My God! she thought. Something *bad* had happened to her friend. She knew it. She felt it in her gut.

Eli turned to follow Noel and said to her, "Your father is an American government Splinter Cell, and you're going to help us find him. We have your cell phone and your address book. After we finish examining these items, if we haven't found the means to contact him, then we will come back to you. If you know how to get in touch with him, then you had better tell us. I wouldn't want to see you . . . hurt."

She stared at the young man she thought would someday be her fiancé.

"Think about it," he said. "I'll be back in a while. There's some water for you. I'll bring you some food, too. But this isn't a hotel, Sarah, so don't expect room service whenever you want it."

He opened the door and left. The sound of the door slamming and locking reverberated in the small room.

Her private cell.

GENERAL Prokofiev couldn't make the meeting. He had business in Moscow and would be returning with an important piece of equipment for exclusive use by the Shop. As one of the top officers in the Russian military, Prokofiev had access and clearance to an unbelievable amount of material. If something was lost or diverted, the buck stopped with him—and he was certainly not going to tell his superiors about it. It was one method by which the Shop obtained much of their product.

Andrei Zdrok spent twenty minutes going over the

sales of the last month and outlining the Shop's profit margin. He also detailed the company's losses and what it meant for them.

"If we don't reestablish our position in the Far East within the next two months the Shop will lose six point three million dollars," he said. "Gentlemen, I do not want to give up my chateau on Lake Zurich. If we have to recruit another partner, then we will. Jon Ming has expressed interest on numerous occasions. What do you think of the notion of bringing on a Chinese partner?"

Herzog shrugged. "If we have to in order to save the company, then fine. But let's try to repair the Far East damage ourselves first."

Antipov said, "Never. I hate the Chinese."

Zdrok almost smiled at his associate's bigotry. "At least you're honest, Anton." He then moved on to another important topic and announced, "I'm happy to report that we have the identity of the next Splinter Cell on the list. His name is Sam Fisher. He lives in Baltimore, USA, and is not assigned to any particular territory. The NSA sends him out to do specialized missions—the *difficult* assignments. We believe he was responsible for Kim Wei Lo's death in Macau and for the damage done to our interests there. His identification has given us an opportunity to dispose of him. Someone close to him is now in our control, and hopefully she will lead us to Mr. Fisher . . . or lead him to us, more likely."

Antipov and Herzog nodded.

"Mr. Fisher will not be an ordinary enemy. He is probably the best trained and formidable opponent we have faced. The other Splinter Cells were mere children compared to Fisher."

"What would you like us to do?" Antipov asked.

"Nothing," Zdrok answered. "I have assigned our enforcers to the task."

More nods. Antipov and Herzog had no problem with that.

Zdrok turned to Antipov. "Anton, I want you to handle this situation with the Shadows. It's turned into a mess."

"How do you want me to handle it, Andrei?" the former KGB officer asked. "Do everything I can to patch things up, or do everything I can to insist on implementing our policies?"

Zdrok said, "Let me put it this way. If their management doesn't see eye to eye with us, then fuck them. We don't need them. I don't care who the hell they are. I have a feeling that they're treading down a road that will bring them serious consequences. This new project of theirs makes no sense to me. But then again, I'm not a fundamentalist Muslim."

Antipov asked, "Then I should . . . ?"

"Cut them off," Zdrok said. "If they give us any more trouble about money or refunds or credit or *shit*, just cut them off."

Antipov nodded, but it was clear that he wasn't sure if he agreed with the boss.

Zdrok ignored him. He knew that Antipov would do his job and perform it mercilessly. Zdrok took a breath and then had another idea.

"On second thought, we might look to Mr. Mohammed for a solution," he said.

"Ahmed Mohammed?" Antipov asked.

"Yes. He's the one who really does all the work for the Shadows, isn't he? Why not get word to Mohammed that should *leadership* in the Shadows suddenly become *questionable*, then the Shop will continue to support *him*."

"I think that's an excellent idea," Antipov said. Herzog nodded as well.

"Good. I'm off to Baku," Zdrok said. "I'll be in touch. If you need me, you know how to find me."

With that, he stood and left the room. Antipov and Herzog looked at each other, shrugged, and got up from the table.

The Shop had a unique four-man leadership. They each had specific jobs and duties. Each man commanded a legion of underlings. Each of the four partners had tremendous wealth and power.

But there was never any question as to who was in charge.

20

I go to my dinner appointment with Namik Basaran and arrive at the restaurant on time. It's a little place overlooking Lake Van in a tourist-oriented square and marina. There are a couple of chartered boat services, a travel agency, gift shops, two hotels, and several restaurants. It's not far from Akdabar Enterprises.

Basaran and his bodyguard are waiting for me inside the restaurant. The big man glares at me again but departs as soon as his employer gives him a nod. Basaran is wearing the same suit he was wearing when I saw him earlier. I've put on a different tie but have on the same sports jacket. My Osprey can fit only so much civilian clothing. I'm wearing my uniform underneath, not just for practical purposes but also because the night air is cool up in the mountains. A breeze wafts in from the lake and produces quite a chill.

The maître d' greets Basaran warmly, calling him by name. Basaran asks for a table by the window and then leads the way. I happen to enjoy Turkish food. Like the people in many European and Asian countries, the Turks make an event out of dinner, and it can sometimes last for hours. I get the feeling that tonight will not be one of those occasions, as Basaran is a busy man.

Basaran orders a dry red wine made in the region along with raki, an aniseed drink a lot like Greek ouzo or Arab arak—it burns wonderfully on the way down. We start with appetizers, or *mezeler*, consisting of finely chopped salad, roasted pureed eggplant, and pepper and turnip pickles. A lentil-and-mint soup enriched with an abundance of paprika follows. The main course is a lamb casserole, filled with cubed roasted meat, green beans, tomatoes, eggplant, zucchini, peppers, and a lot of garlic. A good adjective to describe Turkish meals is *hearty*.

Basaran begins the conversation by saying, "I just heard on the news that there was another terrorist bombing attributed to the Shadows."

"Oh?" I hadn't heard anything.

"In Iraq again. A motorcade carrying two members of the Iraqi government was targeted. They were both killed."

I shook my head. "That's precisely why the nations of the world have to get together on this."

He looks at me skeptically. "But Mr. Fisher, you are from Switzerland, right? Are not the Swiss notoriously neutral when it comes to the problems of the world?"

"That's a misconception, I'm afraid," I answer. "Just because we don't participate in wars doesn't mean we don't care."

"What do you think of the United States' policies in the Middle East?"

Yikes. I have to be careful here. I don't want him to suspect that I'm not really from Switzerland.

"I suppose I'd have to say that it's . . . disappointing," I reply. I don't like admitting it to myself—I actually believe that.

"Ha!" he says loudly. "Disappointing is an understatement. Look, I was no admirer of Saddam Hussein and I sympathized with Iran during the Iran-Iraq war, but what the United States did in Iraq was monstrous. How stable is that country going to be from now on? There will always be insurgents wanting to take it down again, simply for the purpose of showing the world that America made a big mistake. Sometimes a country's culture requires that the people be told what to do. Democracy doesn't work everywhere."

"I think America must have learned that lesson from Vietnam, don't you think?" I suggest.

"Bah. They learned nothing. Or if they did, they forgot it. Don't you agree that American policy in the Middle East has turned many of their former friends against them? The Arabs hate them. The Turks, well, I can say many of them hate America. Not all. But overall, Muslims have been given the impression that the U.S. is out to stamp out their religion."

"We both know that's not true," I say. My hackles are starting to rise.

"We do? Oh, I see, then it's really about *oil*! Am I right?"

I have to keep my thoughts close to my chest. "Oil is a very valuable commodity, not only in the U.S. but all over the world. Keeping a stable Middle East is important for everyone, not just Americans with their freeways and sports cars."

Basaran shrugged. "I suppose you're right. Still, I fear that Arab opinion of America has been so badly damaged that recovery may be impossible."

I tend to agree with that statement, but I think it's best to change the subject. "So, tell me, how did you get so interested in fighting terrorism? Or rather, providing relief for terrorist victims?"

"Everyone has a passion, don't they? Mine is helping victims of evil doers. I have seen first hand the tragedy that befalls families when their loved ones are killed by a suicide bomber or by a land mine or by a hijacked airplane that is flown into a building."

"Forgive me if I'm being too outspoken here, but I sense that terrorism has affected you personally."

Basaran's eyes cloud over for a second. I hit a nerve, I know I did. "Doesn't terrorism affect everyone personally?" he asks, avoiding the question.

"The thing is, terrorism is a means to an end that really doesn't accomplish what the terrorists hope to achieve," I answer.

"What do you mean?" he asks.

"Governments don't usually change their policies because of terrorism."

"That's not entirely true," he says. "Look what happened in Spain when the Madrid train was bombed. The people voted out the existing government. Make no mistake—terrorism makes its point in a number of ways. People today are more frightened of terrorism than of anything else. Look what's happening in Iraq. That can't go on forever. Pretty soon something will break and the terrorists will win there."

"Do you really believe that?" I ask.

Basaran suddenly slams his fist on the table, startling other diners around us and surprising me. "Iraq will fall again! I know it will. Iraq will fall and American interests in the region will be in jeopardy. You just wait and see!"

He quickly gains composure and says, "Forgive me. I get carried away sometimes."

The outburst seems to have come from nowhere. Does Namik Basaran have something against Iraq? It's obvious he's not fond of American foreign policy, but there's something else at work here. I decide to steer the conversation in yet another direction.

"Mr. Basaran, we were talking earlier about the Shadows, and we didn't get around to discussing the Shop. Can you tell me anything about them?"

Basaran appears embarrassed by his show of emotion. He sits for a few seconds and sips his raki as if he's considering what information he should reveal.

"The Shop," he begins, weighing his words, "are despicable. From what I can gather, they are interested only in making money. They do not care whom they harm in the process. They don't give a damn about political, religious, or sociological issues. They provide a service and they're very good at it. There have been many clandestine arms dealers in the world but none as nefarious and well organized as the Shop."

"Who are they? What's their chain of command?" I ask.

"No one knows. It's run like a mafia family, though. There's a boss and his trusted lieutenants, and then each lieutenant has an order of battle beneath him that spreads like a genealogical chart. They have their fingers everywhere, not just in the Middle East. I imagine they have a branch in Switzerland, my friend."

"I don't doubt it."

"As for the leadership? It is rumored that the Shop is led by a small group of wealthy bankers, former military officers, and corporate presidents from Russia and the former Soviet satellites."

"Russia. That's what I've always thought. Any idea of who the big boss is?"

Basaran looks around to make sure no one is listening. He leans forward and whispers. "I've heard a name. I don't know how accurate it is. Have you ever come across the name Zdrok?"

Interesting. It's the name Rick Benton had written on his chart. It's also the name of a man I heard Basaran curse earlier today.

"I may have heard that name before," I say. "Who is he?"

"Andrei Zdrok. He's from Georgia, I believe. Very wealthy financier. If he is not the head of the Shop, then he's very high in its bureaucracy."

"Have you ever met him?"

Basaran shakes his head. "Of course not. As I said, I don't know if he exists. It's just a name that has come up. It may mean nothing."

I doubt it. I sit back and reflect on this. Basaran has just lied to me. He wouldn't curse a man that didn't exist. I now know I can't trust Namik Basaran any more than I can trust the terrorist I called No-Tooth. I'm going to have to take a closer look at Akdabar Enterprises after the sun goes down.

We are served strong coffee—*kahve*—and baklava for dessert. Finally Basaran offers me a Turkish cigar, and we sit for a few minutes gazing out the window at the dark lake. Turkish tobacco is pungent and produces thick smoke. I make a show of smoking it but try not to inhale.

"I love it here," Basaran says. "The sunsets on the lake are particularly rewarding."

"Are you from here originally?" I ask.

"Actually I'm from a small village at the foot of Mount Ararat called Dogubayazit. Do you know it?"

"I'm afraid not."

"Drab little place. I was happy to leave when I was old enough."

"You've managed to build yourself a very successful life."

Basaran waves his cigar. "Luck. A little luck and making some smart investments. That's all. I'm not qualified to really *do* anything. I'm good at running my company. It helps to have vision, I suppose. It took vision to imagine the shopping mall in Northern Cyprus. That's a project that comes from the heart."

"When do you foresee the mall being finished?"

"It almost is! It's been under construction for three years. I expect to open the doors within weeks, but I hope to have a completion ceremony in the coming days."

"Congratulations."

"Thank you."

"And what does the Republic of Cyprus have to say about it?"

He waves his cigar again. "Those damned Greek Cypriots can go hang themselves. They'll be in a bother for a while and then settle down. That's the way things are in Cyprus. It heats up for a period, then cools down. It keeps everyone on his toes. What's important is that the opening of the shopping mall will show the world that the Turks are in Cyprus to stay."

I wonder if the south will be that easily conciliated. For a guy who spends a lot of money, time, and energy supposedly fighting terrorism, Basaran sure is opinionated about politics. Reza warned me as such.

When the waiter brings the bill, Basaran snatches it up and waves his cigar again. "Do not protest. This is my pleasure." He looks at his watch and says, "Alas, I must call an end to our very pleasant evening together. I do wish you luck with your Interpol report, Mr. Fisher. I hope to have a copy of it when it is published."

"Certainly. Thank you very much for the dinner."

"Not at all."

We stand after he leaves a stack of bills on the table. We say good night to the maître d' and step outside into the brisk night air. The big bodyguard appears from the shadows to stand beside his master. Basaran holds out his hand and I shake it. "Good night, Mr. Fisher. Pleasant journeys."

"Thank you. You, too."

I have to cross the surprisingly busy main street that cuts through the square. I wait as five cars rumble by and casually look back to the restaurant and see Basaran and the bodyguard still standing there, watching me. I give them a little wave and Basaran does the same. I turn back to the road and see the approaching headlights of a sixth car some distance away. I figure I can make it across the square before it gets here. As I step off the pavement, the car's wheels screech and the vehicle speeds toward me.

For the first time in my life I freeze. Even as it's happening I realize I'm unable to move and I don't know why. Normally I would have reacted by instinct and leaped to the side, but for some reason that I cannot fathom I don't know what to do. I'm a deer on the road, caught in the beams.

Something prompts me to look back at Basaran. He, too, seems to be frozen in place, his eyes glued to me. Why isn't he moving? Shouldn't he be shouting "Mr. Fisher, look out!" or something like that?

And that's what jars my senses. It's *his* reaction to what's happening that causes me to break out of my immobility. The headlights are a mere couple of car lengths away, propelling toward me at ninety miles an hour. I leap away, fall on my hands, and roll backward just as the car roars past. It's an old Citroën. I turn my head to watch them, and the car screeches to a halt, half a block down. I see the silhouettes of three men inside. Namik Basaran and the bodyguard are still behind me in front of the restaurant and haven't moved.

The Citroën's driver throws the car into reverse and begins rolling back at a high speed. A guy in the passenger seat thrusts his upper body out the window and leans over the hood—and he's holding an AK-47. I jump to my feet and run for cover, but there's nothing but the storefronts behind me. The shooter fires and the street becomes a crashing war zone. I slam forward and hit the ground as bullets rip over my head. The windows of the travel agency behind me shatter, and someone inside shouts. The Citroën squeals to a halt again, ready to move forward for another volley. I'm aware of other civilians, alerted by the noise, looking out of restaurants and shops.

When the gunfire begins again, the bystanders scream and run. I realize I have to lead the killers away from the pedestrians, so I do what might be considered a foolhardy thing and jump to my feet. I run into the middle of the road and stand behind the Citroën as it moves along the street. They seem to have lost sight of me. Should I run for my car? It's about fifty yards away in a small lot on the opposite side of the square. No, it's too risky. By the time I got there, they'd be on top of me. The Pazhan could never withstand a round of fire from an AK-47.

The shooter points and says something to the driver. They've spotted me. The Citroën performs a wild U-turn and accelerates in my direction. I run to the opposite side of the square, the side next to the water. A short brick wall separates the road from the marina and a small lot where seven or eight cars are parked. I sail over the wall just as the bullets begin to fly again. Chips from the stones in the wall scatter like shrapnel, so I hug the ground. I hear the car zoom past, shrick to a stop, and back up, swerving closer to the edge of the road.

This time my instincts don't fail me. I roll like a log toward the parked cars and then squirm between a Chevrolet pickup and a Volkswagen. The passenger sprays the side of the street, perforating the two vehicles with dozens of bullets. Windshields and headlights explode and tires are blown. I snake beneath the pickup as the rounds ricochet within inches of my body. The noise is deafening and must surely be attracting the local police. I *hope* it's attracting the local police!

I crawl on my belly out from under the front of the pickup, putting the truck between them and me. I keep low and rally toward the dock where dozens of small boats are moored. The guy stops shooting, but I hear the Citroën's door open and slam shut. Now they're on foot.

I run to the edge of the dock and weigh my options. I could jump into the water and swim. Or I could jump into one of the sailboats to my left or right, but by the time I untie one and push it off, they'd be in the boat with me. The last recourse would be to draw my Five-seveN from the holster I wear at the small of my back and fight back. That could cause problems with the local authorities, though, and my mission is too sensitive to get involved in foreign legal problems. I don't fancy spending the rest of my life in a Turkish prison.

The shooter appears at the other end of the dock. He raises the AK-47 and fires. The wood splinters in a million places at my feet as I turn and dive into the cold, murky water.

It's a shock. Thank heavens I'm wearing my uniform; otherwise I'd be freezing. It's dark as hell, but I don't risk using the LED on my OPSAT for illumination. They might be able to see me from the surface.

As I swim away from the shore, bullets chop through the water, producing that otherworldly slow-motion effect you get when you fire a gun into water. Even in the pitch black I can see the trails of the rounds cutting lines on all sides of me. One comes dangerously close to my ear, and I feel the heat emanating from it as it groans past. I quickly reverse direction and swim back toward the dock and hope they can't see me. I'm pretty good at holding my breath. That's another thing that Krav Maga classes teach you—stamina and resistance to pain. My lungs are strong—the last time I timed myself holding my breath, I clocked a little less than four minutes. It was Katia Loenstern that pushed me to achieve a score past three minutes. I'll have to remind myself to be nicer to her when I get back to Baltimore.

I make my way to the line of sailboats on one side of the dock. I feel the hull of the first one and swim on, past the second and third. I figure it's been at least two minutes since I submerged because my lungs are burning. When I can't take it anymore, I dare to surface between the boats so I can catch a breath. As I hold on to the side of one of the rocking crafts, I hear two men talking on the dock above me. They're down at the end, maybe thirty feet away. It sounds as if they're arguing. I can't understand the language, but I know it's not Turkish. Actually it sounds like Farsi, but I'm not positive.

The man with the gun suddenly lets loose with another barrage of gunfire into the water, and the other one shouts at him to stop. More arguing. Then I hear the men walk toward the shore, their boots clomping on the wood above me. I dunk my head and position myself directly beneath the sailboat and wait. More gunfire darts the water between the boats, but I'm safely out of the way.

Where the hell are the police in this town? This is one time when I wouldn't mind some interference.

Another minute passes and I feel the pressure in my chest. The gunfire stops and I need to suck some air, but I'm not moving yet. I wait at least another thirty seconds—when I know I can't take it anymore—before coming back up. When I do, I gasp for oxygen as quietly as possible and listen. I hear nothing. They're gone. Maybe they think I'm dead.

I wait another three minutes before pulling myself up and onto the dock. I walk back to the square and hear a police siren approaching from the distance. The Citroën is gone and the street is deserted. I run to the Pazhan and get in, even though I'm soaking wet. I start the car, back out, and head out of town before the cops arrive.

I do notice that Namik Basaran and his goon are no longer standing in front of the restaurant.

21

AFTER midnight I park the Pazhan on the hill overlooking Akdabar Enterprises and survey the scene. There are plenty of floodlights illuminating the compound, and I see a handful of security guards patrolling the premises. This isn't going to be easy.

First I tune in to the bugs I left in Basaran's office. The OPSAT's silence tells me that the room is empty. I quickly leave my civilian clothes in the car, take my SC-20K and sling it over my shoulder, adjust my headset and goggles, regulate the temperature control of my uniform, and I'm off.

Once I'm at the bottom of the hill near the wire fence, I crouch behind a large shrub to assess the situation. Two huts are directly across the fence from where I am—and this will be a good place from which to operate. I wait as a guard walks past, between the huts and the fence, heading toward the front gate. His beat must be this entire side of the compound—so I estimate his return trip to be a little less than ten minutes.

Armed with heavy-duty wire cutters, I clip the fence enough so I can bend the loose section out far enough for me to slip inside. I close this "trapdoor" behind me and carefully position the cut ends together so that unless someone carefully inspects them, the fence appears normal.

I quickly skirt to the space between the two huts and pause to map out my plan of attack. I want to hit the administrative building, especially Basaran's office. I'd also like to get inside the Tirma office and see what I might find in there. Finally, the big warehouse and steel mill must hold some secrets. It will be a busy night.

I decide to begin at the end of the complex near the lake—the Tirma building and Basaran's office—and then make my way back this way. The key is to stay in the shadows. My uniform is embedded with photosensors that detect and let me know how much light falls on me. When I switch on the OPSAT meter, I can see exactly how invisible I really am. At the moment I'm at thirty-two percent. It's very luminous throughout the compound, and my only screens are the broad shadows of buildings, cast by the floodlights. Walkways between buildings are so bright it's like daylight.

The corner periscope comes in handy here. I use it to look around the corner of the hut and determine that the walkway is clear. I scan the pole supporting a floodlight and don't spot any cameras. I go for it.

I run across the walkway and stop at the next building, my back to the wall. I then inch around to the next corner and repeat the process. I count six buildings between my goal and me. It goes smoothly until I reach the fifth building. The periscope shows two guards in the walkway, smoking and talking. I have to find a way to distract them, so I take the SC-20K off my shoulder and load it with a diversion camera. If I wanted to, I could set the camera to also trigger CS gas, but I don't wish to leave traces of my presence if I don't have to. The main thing is simply to get the guards out of the way.

I load the gun and aim at a building directly in line from where I am, some fifty yards away. I check to make sure the suppressor is fitted correctly, take a bead, and squeeze the trigger. The soft *pfft!* sound blends with the night breeze and is unheard by my two buddies. Through the scope I see that the sticky camera adhered to the upper part of the building's side—a little low—but it will have to do. I sling the rifle back over my shoulder and tap the OP-SAT to activate the diversion device. There are a variety of sounds in the menu that I can pick, from animal noises to a recording of "Alexander's Ragtime Band." I decide on a static white noise, one that's loud enough for them to hear. They'll think it's a malfunctioning loudspeaker and go over to investigate it. I hope.

Sure enough, the two guards look over at the sound. They mumble to each other and then walk in that direction. Hurrah. Now's my chance. I inch around the corner, and the light meter on my OPSAT goes up to the danger area. I'm in full sight. I run to the sixth building on my route, exposed for approximately eight seconds. By the time I'm there, the guards have reached the diversion camera and are probably wondering what the hell it is.

The path is clear for me to scoot across the road and small parking lot to the Tirma building. It's very different from the rest of the structures in the compound. The two-story Tirma building seems to have been designed after an American Colonial house, something you'd see in a middle-class New England neighborhood. It's made of wood, is painted white, and has two fat columns on opposite sides of the front door. Instead of a number to mark the building's location, the word *TIRMA* is displayed on the molding above the door. Very strange.

I slink around to the back of the building, where there is less chance of being spotted. Luckily there's no lighting back here. I can look out across the vast lake and see the town square marina about a mile along the shore. The wind coming off the lake is icy cold.

There's a back door, presumably used as an emergency exit, and a couple of windows on the ground floor. I try the windows first, but they're both locked. It'll have to be the door. Once again my lock picks are useful, and I'm able to open the simple bolt lock in six seconds.

I'm inside the building, in a room that's apparently used for putting stuff that doesn't fit anywhere else. There are stacks of folding chairs that I guess must be for big meetings. I see shelves full of office supplies and a bunch of boxes beneath them. There's a soft drink vending machine here, too.

This room leads to a hallway that shoots straight to the front door on the other side of the building. I listen carefully for any signs of occupation and hear nothing. I move on and see that the hallway connects to a large conference room, complete with a big-screen television and A/V equipment, and another room that appears to be a social parlor. They must hold fund-raising cocktail soirees in there. The largest room on the floor contains samples of the various goods that Tirma sends out for relief. I figure the complete stock is stored elsewhere on the campus, in one of the storage sheds or a warehouse. These include medical supplies, dried food, water bottles, grain, and articles of clothing. Besides a couple of modern bathrooms there's not much else on the ground floor, so I quietly ascend the staircase to the second. The place is furnished with thick carpet, even on the stairs. My movements are relatively silent except every now and then the wooden floor creaks beneath the carpet. That can't be helped.

Upstairs I find four offices. One is obviously for support staff—there are three desks, computers, filing cabinets, a copy machine—what you'd normally find in an office. The other three offices are probably for administrators of the charity organization. In one of them I find a lot of company literature printed in several different languages—pamphlets and brochures explaining Tirma's purpose and goals. I take a handful; some are printed in English, some in Farsi, some in Turkish, and some in Arabic. I place these in my Osprey and move on.

The other two rooms are executives' offices. I boot up the computers in each room and spend a little time at them. I don't need any security passwords, and I'm able to browse through the files easily. I'm unable to find anything suspicious, even when I search for the names *Tarighian, Mohammed, Mertens,* or *Zdrok.*

For all intents and purposes, it appears that Tirma is a legitimate charity organization.

I make my way out of the building and exit through the door I came in. The next stop is Basaran's office, inside the building that's a couple of doors down. This one's going to prove more difficult. It's very well lit and I'm sure the security is stronger. There may be people inside. I stay in the back and dart to the next structure—the employees' cafeteria—and then the next . . . until I'm looking at the main administrative building where I met Basaran earlier. There are no guards in the back, but I know that at least one is patrolling the front.

The back door has a keypad lock. I'm betting that the same code is used throughout the building, so I punch my

OPSAT to recall the sequence I noted earlier. I press the buttons 8, 6, 0, 2, 5 and the door unlocks. I know there are surveillance cameras all over the place, so I open the door just a sliver and use the corner periscope to peek inside. Sure enough, there's a camera trained at the door.

If I wanted to I could take it out with the Five-seveN pistol, but that would only call attention to the fact that someone had been in the building. I'd rather get around it another way. The camera appears to be a standard off-the-shelf model that continuously records, but only if there's sufficient lighting in the room. There has to be a switch just inside the door—I maneuver the periscope until I see it, then reach my hand in quickly and flick off the lights. I then enter the room and shut the door. With my night-vision goggles I can see fine, but the camera is recording nothing but darkness.

I move out of the room and look through an archway to the outer lobby, which is well lit. Glass windows face the front and I can see the guard standing with his back to me, looking toward the parking lot. He's bundled up, smoking a cigarette, and probably hating every minute of this assignment. I scan the ceiling, walls, and corners for more cameras and find one aimed directly at the front doors. I can easily scoot past this one because I'm already in the building. While the guard's not looking, I move across the outer lobby, through the double wooden doors and into the main receptionist's office. Thank goodness the lights are already off.

I go to the keypad, punch in the same code, and enter the hallway leading to Basaran's office. The lights are on here and I see no way to turn them off. I know there's an-other camera around the corner up ahead, so I use the periscope again to take a look. It's a motion-detection camera that pivots in a wide arc. Midway in the arc is

Basaran's office. There's no keypad for his door—they must figure that once you're past the reception desk, you're clear to roam wherever you want.

I have to distract that camera. I take the camera jammer out of the Osprey and turn it on. The thing vibrates a little, so I know it's working—I sure can't see the microwave pulses coming out of it—and it works best if you're moving at the same time. So I aim the jammer in front of me, turn the corner, and quickly move down the hall. I hear the camera lens zoom in and out as it attempts to focus on whatever it thinks it detects, but it's very confused. I open Basaran's door and slip inside just as the camera regains its functionality.

The overhead lights are off in the office, but mood lighting is on—behind the wet bar, on the desk, and here by the door. Curtains cover the big glass window overlooking the lake, and fortunately they're closed.

First, I examine the desk and its contents. The drawers hold nothing of interest—just a bunch of personal items, credit card bills, employee phone numbers, and other papers relating to the company. There's also that hand exerciser, the rubber ball I saw Basaran squeezing when I first met him. I boot up the computer and see that a password is required to gain access. Damn. If only I had Carly St. John's expertise now. I had informed Lambert I'd be coming here tonight, but Carly didn't have much notice to try to hack Akdabar's server. There's not much I can do.

I shut down the computer and then notice for the first time that there's a framed photograph sitting on the desk. It shows a veiled woman with two young girls, ranging maybe six to eight years old. Basaran's family? The thing is, they don't look Turkish. Most Turkish women, even very religious ones, don't wear veils as they do in, say,

Iraq or Iran. I quickly snap a copy of the picture and store it in my OPSAT, then move to the filing cabinets.

The lock picks open the cabinets easily, and I find more documents relating to Akdabar Enterprises—employee records, accounting books, and other boring stuff. One drawer, however, contains files marked Cyprus. I pull these out and thumb through them. I see records relating to the shopping mall that Basaran is building—expense reports, schedules, press releases, and company memos. The place is located near the city of Famagusta, a seaport that is perhaps Northern Cyprus' most strategic urban center after the capital, Lefkosia.

At the back of the drawer is a document portfolio with twine tied around it. I remove it, untie the twine, and look inside. It's full of copies of blueprints that have been reduced in size. They show portions of some kind of machine—there's a base that takes up a couple of prints, an engine shown from several sides, and what looks like a series of cylindrical pieces that fit together. I'll be damned if it isn't some kind of weapon.

The machine's designer is named "Albert Mertens," and this name is on every page. Surely he's the same Professor Mertens I met earlier in the day. I snap some photos of the plans for good measure.

I put everything back the way I found it and approach the door. The damned camera jammer uses so much power that it's basically just good for one go, and then it has to be recharged. I don't risk using it again, so how do I get out without the camera seeing me? I think for a moment and get an idea. I go back to Basaran's desk, open the drawer, and remove the rubber ball. I return to the door, open it a crack, and roll the ball down the hall in the opposite direction from where I need to go. The camera whirrs and follows the ball as I slip out and close the door behind me. It will just have to be a mystery as to how the ball got into the hall.

Moving back to the outer lobby is not a problem. When I look out the front, I see that the guard isn't there. I quickly scoot around to the corridor that leads to the back door. The lights are still off, so I'm okay. I carefully open the door, peer outside, and leave the building.

I guess it wasn't as difficult as I thought it'd be.

Now I need to zigzag back across the complex and take a look inside the steel mill/warehouse. I retrace my steps, bouncing from building to building and avoiding the glare of the floodlights, and finally make it to a shed across from the courtyard that's in the center of the compound. The lights are bright here and I see two guards standing lazily by the flagpoles. Not only that, but there are more surveillance cameras perched on the poles. The big building is on the other side. I could go the long way around the courtyard, building to building, but that increases the chances of my being seen.

As I ponder the problem, I hear the sound of a vehicle approaching. It apparently entered through the front gate and is now driving down the main road toward the courtyard. Concealed by shadow, I lie in the grass beside the shed and watch as the car stops so that the driver can speak to one of the guards.

It's the Citroën, the car that chased me earlier! Three men are inside, as before. Son of a bitch. Further proof that Basaran had something to do with the incident in the town square. No wonder he stood there doing nothing. Shit, is my cover blown? Does he know who I am? And the bigger question is—why? Basaran's supposed to be on *our* side, isn't he?

But I could be jumping to conclusions. These guys in

the Citroën could be acting independently of Basaran, for
all I know. Maybe Basaran has enemies within his own organization. It's possible.

Then something odd occurs. The two guards get into
the Citroën and drive away toward the airstrip on the far
side of the compound. The courtyard is empty. It still
doesn't solve the problem of getting to the other side
without the cameras seeing me. Do I dare shoot them out?

The answer comes to me as I look to my left and see a
shed housing the three-wheelers, those golf carts I saw the
guards driving earlier. I run to the shed and climb into a
cart. No key is needed because it runs on electric power.
There's a nice canopy over the driver's seat —so if I hunch
over and keep my head down, I'm fairly certain that the
cameras won't make me. On the surveillance video I'll
probably just look like another guard. I decide to risk it.

The thing starts up and I drive into the courtyard. I hear
the cameras move as they pick me up, but I don't worry
about it. I putter along at a slow speed as if I'm just another lazy guard doing his rounds. For authenticity I stop
once and pretend to rummage around in the floor of the
cart, then continue on.

I make it across, get out of the cart, and begin to explore the sides of the big building. The main employee entrances and loading doors are closed, locked, and directly
under floodlight beams. On the far side, though, there's a
garbage Dumpster sitting directly beneath an open window. I scramble up the Dumpster and peer into the place.

For the most part the space is dark. There are lights on
here and there, but it's a very big building. I crawl through
the window and drop to the floor on my hands and feet
like a cat. Lambert once told me that I'd make a pretty
good cat burglar if I were into that sort of thing. I let him
think I may have been at one time.

It's a typical steel mill. There's the huge furnace, belts, worktables, overhead trolleys, forklifts, and everything else that accompanies a legitimate construction plant. As I explore the place, I'm beginning to think I'm wasting my time here. There's nothing out of the ordinary. I'm about to give up and get the hell out when I turn a corner and see a lone guard sitting in a chair in front a heavy steel door on rollers. He's holding an AK-47 and is staring straight ahead, probably counting the minutes until his shift is over. I wonder what he's guarding.

This time I decide to act aggressively. I load the SC-20K with a ring airfoil projectile, aim for the guy's head, and fire. *Zap*—the guard falls over, unconscious. I rush over to him, pick up the round, and return it to my Osprey. He won't know what happened to him, but he'll have a fairly big knot on his head when he wakes up.

I unbolt the big door and slide it open. It's a storeroom containing dozens of crates and boxes. I step inside and— *bingo*. I recognize the crates as having the same stamp as before, from the Tabriz Container Company. With my reliable combat knife I pry off the crate lid. Guns. AK-47s. I pry open another crate—Hakims. Explosives. Bomb-making materials. Pistols. More rifles. Ammunition.

Just what the hell is Akdabar Enterprises doing with a shitload of weapons?

I continue to examine the containers, closing them as I go, and eventually find a shipping manifest still stuck on one of the crates. The originating location is an address in Baku, Azerbaijan. I note it in the OPSAT and decide I've seen enough. I snap a few shots of everything and leave the storeroom. I close the heavy sliding door and latch it. The guard is still in Dreamsville.

As I make my way to the window where I entered, I hear the rusty screech of a door opening. It's the front employee entrance. I rush to cross the floor, but it's no good—whoever it is will see me if I continue on this path. I hear a single set of footsteps clomping toward me at a slow pace, so I just have time to slip behind a column and stand perfectly still.

The man discovers the unconscious guard and grunts. It's a sound that's familiar to me, so I risk peeking around the column. The newcomer is none other than Farid, Basaran's big bodyguard. I have to get out of here quickly before the goon sounds the alarm. I look around for an escape route and find no other recourse but to climb onto the tall conveyor belt mechanism and grab hold of a pipe that runs the length of the room, forty or fifty feet off the ground. While Farid is bending over the guard and trying to revive him, I dart across the floor, step onto the base of the mechanism, use a set of cranks as leverage, and climb the thing like a monkey. The machine resembles a gigantic old-fashioned jukebox with the conveyor belt coming out of a "mouth." It's not easy to climb, especially toward the top, which is rounded. After two tries I manage to clutch a handhold on top of the machine and pull myself up. Sliding off would be a disaster, so I take a moment to catch my breath and concentrate.

I look down and see Farid standing by the guard, who is now sitting up and rubbing his head. No time to lose. I can easily reach the pipe, so I grab it and begin traversing it, hand over hand, my body dangling precariously high over the floor.

Bang! The gunshot comes from below. Shit, Farid has seen me. I continue to move along the pipe, but the guy's taking potshots at me with a pistol. He doesn't have a very good aim, praise the Lord. As I approach the end of the pipe near the far wall, where I can easily climb down to the floor, the gunshots stop. He's figured out he'll meet me there, and sure enough, he's standing below me when I reach my destination.

With my helmet and goggles on, I'm hoping he doesn't recognize me. Besides, I'm pretty high above him. I hear him grunt at me, motioning me to come down. He expects me to climb down and take my punishment like a man. So what do I do? I let go of the pipe and drop the forty or fifty feet directly on top of him.

We both crash to the hard floor and I feel a sharp pain in my shoulder as it hits the concrete. It's a good thing Farid is so big; otherwise I could have caused a lot more damage to myself. He made a nice cushion. I quickly scramble to my feet, ready to take on the brute—but I see he's sprawled faceup, not moving. His arm is bent unnaturally behind his back, obviously broken.

Fine. Saves me the trouble of killing him. Before the other guard can run over to see what's happened, I move quickly to the spot where I came in, climb some crates to reach the window, and squeeze through.

Outside, I get back in the three-wheeler and drive around the building and head through the courtyard toward the side of the complex where I originally entered. I don't see a soul. Eight minutes later I park the vehicle near the fence, skirt through the shadows until I find the incisions I made at the beginning of my adventure, pull open the trap, and squeeze through the hole.

Damn, my shoulder hurts. It could be a sprain, but I don't think it's a bad one. I've taken some pretty hard knocks in my time and this is nothing.

When I'm away from the complex and back in the Pazhan, I send Lambert a message:

URGENT—FIND OUT ALL YOU CAN ABOUT NAMIK BASARAN, ALBERT MERTENS, AND ANDREI ZDROK.

22

LIEUTENANT Colonel Petlow was tired. He had overseen the interrogation of the prisoners for nearly twenty-four hours. After the "Iraqi prisoner abuse" scandal that had rocked the world several months ago, the U.S. government was being overly cautious with regard to what could or could not be done during interrogation sessions. As a result, interrogations became matters of time. A lot of time.

The prisoner Petlow was most interested in, of course, was No-Tooth, whose real name was supposedly Ali Al-Sheyah. Petlow preferred to call him No-Tooth.

Although no one had realized it at first, No-Tooth had been wounded during his capture. He had taken a bullet in the side, but it hadn't damaged any vital organs. The round had entered and exited, leaving a bloody hole that wasn't noticed until No-Tooth had been booked and placed in a prisoner holding pen. Then the man fainted and was taken to a mobile army surgical unit to be stitched up. That's when the doctors saw that the prisoner was already feverish and hosting a bad case of pneumonia. Such were the hazards of living as a nomad in an unstable country.

Petlow thought that No-Tooth's condition might work to an advantage. The man was fairly drugged up and probably more comfortable than he had been in months. Armed with new directives from Central Command to find out the identities of specific individuals, Petlow decided to give No-Tooth a try before going to bed.

The surgical unit was housed in an air-conditioned portable building that had clean running water. Things had improved immensely since the days of Vietnam, when an army hospital was just as filled with deadly bacteria as the jungle itself. Depending on the seriousness of the wounds, an injured soldier or prisoner could find it pleasant staying in the hospital.

Petlow was aware of this when he entered with his interpreter. He filled out the necessary paperwork and asked the sergeant in charge to give them some privacy. After checking with the doctors, a folding screen was placed around No-Tooth's bed and Petlow and the interpreter took seats beside him.

"Mr. Al-Sheyab, do you recognize me?" Petlow asked. The interpreter translated the questions and answers as the two men spoke.

No-Tooth grinned and nodded. They didn't call him No-Tooth for nothing.

"I'd like to ask you some questions. Will you talk to me?"

No-Tooth grinned wider and shook his head.

"Why not?"

No-Tooth cursed in a language that Petlow didn't understand. It wasn't Arabic. Maybe Farsi? The interpreter left the prisoner's words to Petlow's imagination.

"But, Mr. Al-Sheyab, we've saved your life. You would

have died. You had pneumonia. You'd been shot. Aren't you comfortable now?"

No-Tooth shrugged.

"I suppose then, if you're feeling fine, that we can move you back to the prisoners' holding area," Petlow said.

No-Tooth's eyes widened and he shook his head.

"Why not? You seem to be doing better. I think I'll have the doctor release you so we can interrogate you properly."

"No," the prisoner said. "What is it you want? Please, I feel terrible and I am in a lot of pain. Don't move me."

Petlow almost smiled. "All right. I want you to look at some photographs. I'm going to ask you if you can pick out a certain person, would you do that?"

The prisoner stared at Petlow and almost snarled. But he didn't say no.

Petlow plowed ahead. He opened a folder containing several black-and-white photos of various Middle Eastern men. "Does the name Ahmed Mohammed mean anything to you?"

Again, No-Tooth grinned.

"I understand that Ahmed Mohammed is one of the leaders of your organization, is this correct?"

No-Tooth shrugged, but he did it coyly. Petlow took that as a yes.

"How about Nasir Tarighian?" Petlow asked. "Do you know Nasir Tarighian?"

This time No-Tooth's eyes widened and he stopped smiling. He shook his head.

"Is it true that Nasir Tarighian is the man who provides the money behind the Shadows?"

No-Tooth refused to respond.

"You *do* know him, don't you? Nasir Tarighian? Well, we *know* that Tarighian is the financial leader of your group, which calls itself the Shadows. I understand that you confessed to being a member of the Shadows when you were arrested."

No-Tooth spoke in a monotone. "I am proud to be a Shadow. We will liberate the Middle East from Western oppression and return it to its Islamic roots." He said it as if he was repeating a mantra.

"Mr. Al-Sheyab, I don't believe you are a Shadow," Petlow said.

No-Tooth's eyes became fierce. He didn't like being called a liar. "What do you mean?" he asked.

"I'm saying you don't know if Tarighian is your leader or not. You can't be a Shadow."

"I am a Shadow! I am proud to be a Shadow! We will liberate the Middle East from Western oppression and return it to its Islamic roots!"

Petlow showed the prisoner the first photo. "You can't say that this man is Nasir Tarighian, can you?"

No-Tooth scowled at the photo and said, "That's not him! You don't know what you're talking about."

Petlow switched to the next photo. "We think this is Tarighian. Do you?"

"No! You stupid Americans don't know a great man when you see one. That is Ahmed Mohammed." Petlow knew that. Mohammed's face had been well known to the authorities for some time.

Next picture. "Then I guess this can't be Tarighian, either."

"That's not him."

They went through seven photographs with negative results. On the eighth shot Petlow asked, "Well, we *know* this isn't him."

No-Tooth held up a hand. A visible change came over

the prisoner's facial expression, as if he had just looked upon his Lord and Savior.

"Nasir Tarighian," he whispered reverently.

Petlow nodded and marked the back of the photo.

"Thank you, Mr. Al-Sheyab. Get some rest now, all right?" Petlow said.

No-Tooth looked at Petlow with confusion. He knew he had somehow been tricked into revealing something and his foggy mind allowed it to happen. He cursed once again at Petlow and the interpreter as the two men got up and left. The prisoner shouted at them, "I am a Shadow! I am proud to be a Shadow! We will liberate the Middle East from Western oppression and return it to its Islamic roots!"

Petlow hurried out of the hospital and ran toward his quarters. He had to get this information to Washington as soon as possible.

SARAH'S stomach growled for the sixth time since she began clocking the noises. She didn't care, though. She was determined to see her hunger strike through. No matter how starved and weak she became, Sarah resolved not to eat the food they brought her. They *had* been consistent. One of them had brought her a separate meal for break-fast, lunch, and dinner, but until they let her go, she wasn't eating. To hell with them. If they considered her a valuable hostage, she wouldn't be worth much dead.

Most of the time it was one of those creepy Russians who came in. They said their names were Vlad and Yuri, which were probably fake—or else why would they tell her their names? Unless they really planned to kill her all along once they got what they wanted. This was the reasoning that motivated Sarah to go on a hunger strike.

She had been in the little room for two nights and was beginning her third day. Once she asked if she could go outside just to get some fresh air. They wouldn't let her. Now the room smelled of her sweat. The bathroom stank due to bad plumbing. She showered daily just to feel better, but the last half-day hadn't been easy. She was beginning to feel the effects of not eating. All she wanted to do was lie on the cot and sleep.

Sarah was dozing, daydreaming about an Asian barbecue restaurant in Evanston that she and Rivka liked to frequent, and her mouth started watering. Her stomach growled again and she willed herself not to think about it. It was hard. She missed her home. She wanted to leave Israel more than anything.

The sound of the key in the door startled her. It always did. The place was usually deathly quiet until that damned key rattled.

The door opened and she saw Vlad's cold face peek inside.

"Go away," she said.

"I brought your breakfast," he said. He came in with a tray. The dish was covered, so she couldn't see what it was. It smelled cooked, though, and that went a long way toward breaking down her defenses.

Vlad set the tray on the floor by the cot and then sat in the chair. "You'd better eat, Princess. We are becoming very tired of your behavior."

"Go to hell," she murmured.

Vlad chuckled. "You still have spirit, eh, Princess? Even after not eating for so many hours? What is it now, two days? That's nothing. Do you know how you'll feel in a week? Me and Yuri, we made a bet to see how long you will keep this up. He says you'll eat tomorrow. Me, I think you have more willpower and will last another two days.

What do you think? Is Yuri going to win, or am I going to win?"

"Take the tray and go. I'm not going to eat it," she said.

"You know, Princess, I think what you need is a little more encouragement," Vlad said. He scooted the chair closer to the cot. She looked at him with alarm and recoiled.

"Now, now," he said. "Don't be afraid of Vlad. I won't hurt you. I make you feel real good. I have a way with the ladies. They all say so." He reached out and stroked her hair.

"Get your fucking hands off me!" she spat as she jerked up and away from him.

This angered Vlad. "You little bitch!" he shouted. He grabbed hold of her shoulders and threw her back onto the cot. She struggled with him, but he moved his heavy body on top of her. She felt his scratchy, unshaven face against her cheek as he nuzzled her neck. Sarah attempted to fight him off, but she was no match for his weight and girth. When she felt his wet tongue on her ear, she lost control.

"No!" she screamed. "Help!"

Vlad covered her mouth with one thick hand. "Shut up!" he commanded. "It's time you learn to obey your masters!"

She felt his other hand grope between her legs, and she tried in vain to kick him away.

Oh, my God, she thought to herself. *This* is what it's going to be. It all comes down to *this*. She closed her eyes tightly and prepared herself for the ordeal that was surely coming.

"What the *fuck* are you doing?" It was an angry voice at the door.

Suddenly the horrible, heavy weight came off and she could breathe again. She was aware of a struggle in the room.

It was Eli. He had come in and pulled Vlad away. The older man stepped on the breakfast tray, causing it to spill its contents over the floor. Now the two of them were fighting. Vlad swung at Eli, but the young man was faster and more agile. He dodged the blow and sneaked in one of his own, hitting Vlad on the nose.

"You goddamned bastard!" Vlad said. He wiped his face and smeared blood over his upper lip. "I'm going to kill you!"

The door opened again and Yuri entered.

"Stop!" he shouted. "Stop it right now!" He pulled his Heckler & Koch pistol and pointed it at Vlad. "Move back, Vlad! Now!"

Eli and Vlad halted and lowered their fists. Both of them had traces of oatmeal on their clothes. The floor was a mess.

Vlad looked at his partner as if Yuri had betrayed him. "I was just going to have some fun. I'm going crazy here. This isn't what we usually do—guard hostages. You know that."

Yuri kept the gun pointed at him and said, "We do what we're told because we're well paid. Don't forget that." He looked at Eli. "And you, don't you ever attack him again. If he acts up, as he sometimes does, you come and get me."

Eli stood his ground, breathing heavily. "Keep him away from her," he said.

Yuri took the gun off Vlad and pointed it at Eli. The VP70 appeared huge in his hand. "You don't give me orders," he said. "Never."

"Fine," Eli said.

The two stared at each other for a moment and then Yuri said, "Stay and clean up this mess. Let's go, Vlad.

Out of here." Vlad grunted and left the room. Yuri kept his eyes trained on Eli and followed his associate out. The door slammed shut.

Eli turned to Sarah, moved to the cot, and sat down beside her. "I'm sorry for that," he said.

Sarah whirled around and slapped his face. "Get out of here and take that tray with you," she said.

Eli stood, rubbing his face. "I guess I deserved that. I have to clean this up."

"Leave it, I don't give a shit if my room's a pigsty. It was a pigsty before it was covered in breakfast," she said.

"Look, Sarah," Eli said. "You're just making this worse for yourself. I don't have to be nice to you, you know."

"Oh, *really*? You don't have to be *nice*? You didn't have to *kidnap* me, either!"

"Goddamn it, Sarah, all we want to know is how to reach your father. I know you have a way to get hold of him. If you don't tell us, you're going to suffer. I can't stop that. Vlad will have his way with you. I guarantee I won't be able to prevent it. And Yuri, if he gets started on you, it's all about pain. Those guys are experts, Sarah. So far they haven't been given the orders to hurt you, but if the orders come, they won't hesitate to do it. Now, tell me, is your father here in the Middle East?"

Sarah folded her arms in front of her, still shaken by what had just occurred. Eli's words frightened her, and she wasn't sure what to do.

"Sarah. Talk to me. Is he in the Middle East? We have reason to believe he might be in Turkey at this moment."

Sarah brought her knees up to her chin and buried her face. The tears came freely.

"I see," Eli said. "Stubborn to the end. Fine. Well, you just think about it some more, then. Oh, and by the way, I brought you something to read. Maybe it will help you make up your mind." He reached into his back pocket and pulled out a folded newspaper. He tossed it on the cot beside her, picked up the tray and dishes, left the spilled oatmeal on the floor, and went out of the room.

After she heard the door lock, Sarah looked at the newspaper and saw that it was in English—and a picture of Rivka was on the front page. Sarah picked up the paper and stared at the front-page headline, her heart racing in terror.

ISRAELI WOMAN FOUND DEAD IN EAST JERUSALEM

The story related how a twenty-year-old woman was found strangled to death, her body lying in a trash heap in an alley. Police suspected Palestinian militants for the slaying, but an investigation was under way.

At the bottom of the page was a photo of both Rivka and Sarah. Sarah recognized it as one that Rivka's parents had taken earlier in the week. The caption read:

MISSING AMERICAN WOMAN LAST SEEN WITH SLAIN ISRAELI

23

THE Caucasus Mountains. Would you believe that the Soviet elite thought of these small republics—Georgia, Armenia, and Azerbaijan—as a holiday paradise? They have everything: sunny beaches, snowy mountains, luxurious orchards, and some of the best wine in Eastern Europe. Or is it Asia? It's hard to say. The region seems to connect Asia with Europe, and it's a mixture of cultural elements from both continents. Now that the Soviet Union is no more and these countries are more or less independent, all we hear about are the ethnic conflicts that plague the area. But I've never had any problems here. In fact, I kind of like it.

I drive out of Turkey in the Pazhan, which is beginning to worry me. The engine's starting to make a *cough-cough* noise every now and then. I just hope it makes it to Baku. The mountain roads are tough on even the sturdiest of vehicles.

I travel north and enter Armenia just west of Yerevan. I have no trouble at the border. My Interpol credentials get me through, and it helps that these places are far less suspicious than the other countries I've visited on this assignment. I have to cross over the mountains, north of Lake Sevan, to access the straighter, more level road heading east into Azerbaijan. The distance in miles really isn't that much, but the up-and-down nature of the trip stretches the time frame. I just try to relax and enjoy the gorgeous scenery.

I reach my destination after nightfall. Baku, or Baki—depending on whom you talk to—is the largest city in the Caucasus. In America they say that Chicago is the "windy city," but it has nothing over Baku. Baku's name, in fact, comes from Persian words that mean "city of winds." Perched on the shore of the Caspian Sea, Baku is bombarded by strong gales on a frequent basis. Another distinctive aspect of Baku is that it's surrounded by gaseous and flammable oil fields. Since oil is the country's main commodity, most of Baku is an industrial city that works to refine the huge amounts of petroleum. What's amazing is there are areas of earth that literally flame up because gas is coming out of the ground. So Baku is sometimes called the "land of fire," as well. Back in the times of the Greeks, many of the myths grew out of this area because of its unusual natural characteristics.

It's not a very attractive city. I find it very polluted, especially on the outskirts, but I believe this is a legacy of former Soviet rule. The inner city and the harbor area have lately been built up to attract more tourists. It's trying to be downright cosmopolitan, albeit a little more conservative than, say, Istanbul.

If I wanted to I could stay at a four-star hotel, but that's not my style. I prefer budget places where no one pays much attention to the guests. I find such an establishment located on board a former Caspian Sea ferry that sits on a permanent mooring beside the Port Office in the area known as Boom Town. The place is a dump but the cabins have hot water and privacy. I don't plan to stay long.

After a welcome night's sleep I greet the morning refreshed and ready to work. I have a breakfast of bread and honey with yogurt at the teahouse near my so-called hotel, and then I walk through Boom Town to the address I found on the shipping manifest in the Akdabar storeroom. Those weapons were definitely shipped from Azerbaijan, and whatever business occupies the address had something to do with it.

It turns out to be a bank just off Fountain Square, the center for people watching in Baku. The fountains happen to be working today, so the café terraces are busy and lively. Since I'm wearing my civilian sports jacket and trousers, I blend in easily. No one notices the casually dressed businessman enter the Swiss-Russian International Mercantile Bank except the security guard at the front door. He's standing outside as if he were actually a hotel concierge waiting to hail a taxi for a guest. I notice there's a retinal scanner by the door—which will make my entry during off-hours all the more difficult. I'll have to think about that one.

As I open the door, the guard nods at me and asks me something in Azeri. I simply smile, point to the information desk, and go inside. It's a fairly small bank lobby with two teller windows and two executive desks on the floor. A barred gate leads to an area behind a wall, which I presume are back offices, the vault, and maybe safe-deposit boxes. I go to the table that holds bank literature, pick up a pamphlet, and pretend to study it as I case the place. There are two surveillance cameras up in the corners and appear to cover the entire lobby. I glance through the teller windows—only one is occupied—and see a pretty Azeri woman in her thirties counting manat, the official currency. There's not much room back there, so I figure all the good stuff in the bank is through the barred gate.

While I'm studying the place, a man enters from the street, stands and speaks quietly to the guard, and then walks over to the teller window. I recognize him as the man with Namik Basaran in the photo that was in Rick Benton's folder. He's dressed impeccably in an expensive suit and has the demeanor of a king. I make him out to be perhaps the bank manager.

He speaks to the teller for a moment and then moves to the barred gate. He unlocks it with his own set of keys, enters, closes and locks the gate behind him, and disappears. He didn't look at me once.

It's funny how all the little pieces start falling into place. Whoever this guy is, he's obviously pretty chummy with Basaran. In the photo they look like old pals who have enjoyed a longtime business relationship. Of course, the guy could simply be Basaran's banker. Much remains to be seen.

I take a couple of pamphlets and leave the lobby. As I walk by the guard I don't look at him—instead I study one of the pamphlets as if I'm trying to make up my mind whether or not to use the bank's services. He says something that probably translates to "Have a nice day, sir," and I grunt affirmatively without looking up.

I walk south to what is referred to as the Old Town. It's a little maze of alleys that probably should be more impressive than it is. There are some interesting medieval monuments scattered about, but it's mostly made up of nineteenth-century oil-boom structures and Soviet-era tenement buildings. I find a harbor *restoran* that specializes in barbecue and have a seat outside. The waiter brings me Azeri's standard fare—barbecued chicken and *shashlyk*, which is marinated lamb kebab. I find the "fast food" in this town better than the restaurant menus.

When I'm done I walk along the harbor and contact Lambert via my implant.

"Colonel, are you awake?" I ask. "Colonel?"

He answers after twenty seconds or so. "Sam?"

"It's me, Colonel. Did I wake you?"

"Um, yeah, but that's all right. We haven't spoken in a while. Are you in a secure place?"

"I'm walking along Baku harbor. There's no one around. I thought I'd check to see if you have news, because I have some."

"I do," Lambert says. "But you go first."

"You know the address I found attached to the arms at Akdabar Enterprises?"

"Yes?"

"It's a bank. The Swiss-Russian International Mercantile Bank. Right off of Fountain Square in Baku."

I hear Lambert chuckling. "What's so funny?" I ask.

"It's such a coincidence. We've been hard at work gathering information about those men you asked for. Just a second, let me get to my portable transmitter. . . ." I wait a few seconds. He probably has to get out of bed and go into his office. After a moment I hear him again in the depths of my ear. "I'm uploading a photo. Take a look."

In a flash my OPSAT displays a picture of the guy I just saw in the bank. The same guy in the photo with Namik Basaran. "Got it," I say.

"That's Andrei Zdrok."

"No shit."

"That's him."

"Son of a bitch. You won't believe this, but he's here. I

just saw him in the bank. He walked in like he owned the joint and went into the back offices."

"Well, he does own the joint," Lambert says. "Unfortunately there's not a lot on him we could dig up, but what we've found is interesting. He's a Russian banker—he's actually from Georgia—and he's the *president* of the Swiss-Russian International Mercantile Bank. He resides in Zurich, Switzerland, where the main branch of the bank is located. The only other branch is there in Baku."

"Okay."

"Our intelligence reports suggest that Zdrok has ties to organized crime, but nothing has ever been proven. He's never been accused of anything or had any problems with the law. He's on a watch list, though. The Russian government suspects he might be a major player in the black market."

"Colonel, I have reason to believe he may be one of the top dogs in the Shop," I say. "Rick Benton thought so, I think. You saw the chart I sent you?"

"I've made that same connection, Sam. I label the guy Russian mafia."

"I'm going to have a look inside the bank tonight. No telling what I might find."

"In the meantime we'll see what else we can dig up."

"And don't forget there's his connection with Namik Basaran. They obviously know each other and Basaran lied to me about it. Basaran's dirty, Colonel. I don't care what kind of charity he runs, the guy's a phony."

"So far he's clean, Sam," Lambert says. "The Turkish government insists he's the equivalent of a saint."

"What about his background? Do we know anything about him? He's got skeletons in his closet, I just know he does. I saw a photo in his office of a woman and two girls—I'd bet they're his family, but where are they now?"

"We're still digging. I'm afraid there isn't much on the guy before the nineties."

"Well, that's enough to make me suspicious. A man in his forties just doesn't magically materialize in a country without some sort of history. Find it, Colonel."

"We're doing our best. Oh, here's one report I'm looking at now . . . hmm, it's a memo from a Turkish intelligence officer that's apparently been disputed by his superiors, but he claims that Basaran isn't really Turkish."

"I'd like to talk to this officer. Who is he?"

"Well, unfortunately, he's dead. Doesn't say how or when he died . . . just says he's deceased."

"Shit."

"Now, there's the other fellow you wanted to know about. . . ."

"Mertens?"

"Albert Mertens. Dr. Albert Mertens was one of Gerard Bull's right-hand men during the years when Bull was an arms designer and dealer. Mertens was one of the top physicists on the fabled 'Babylon Gun.' Remember that?"

"Sure. When we were talking about Gerard Bull in Washington, I happened to recall it. It's the supergun that could fire a payload at a target a thousand kilometers away. Saddam Hussein commissioned Bull to make one so he could attack a neighboring country without more expensive cruise missiles. Wasn't it able to fire not just conventional explosives but also biological or chemical warheads, or even nuclear bombs?"

"You're right, Sam. Luckily the thing was never finished."

"Okay, so what's this Professor Mertens doing working for Basaran?"

"I don't know, but it's got us concerned. You see, Mertens served seven years in a Belgian prison for illegal arms dealing. According to the data we received, Mertens was transferred during the seventh year to a mental institution and was committed. The guy's a raving lunatic. Then, five years ago, he disappeared from the clinic. Either he escaped on his own or someone broke him out. We don't know. The Belgian police have been looking for the guy ever since."

"So what's Basaran up to?" I ask. "Has he got Mertens building him a supergun? And if so, why? Basaran's supposed to be on *our* side, but it's looking more and more like he isn't."

"Let's just keep moving forward, Sam. You're doing a great job."

"Any luck on Nasir Tarighian?"

"Not yet. The research team does have a lead on obtaining a photograph of the man. As soon as it's available, you'll be the first to get it."

"Fine. I'll send you a report tonight after I've had a look inside that bank."

"Just be extra careful, Sam," Lambert says. "If this Zdrok guy is really part of the Shop, he'll have your intestines for dinner if you're caught."

"Don't worry, I intend to stay off the menu."

24

IT'S a little after midnight when I make my way through the streets, sticking to the shadows and pausing every now and then to make sure no one is following me. Not only is it important to make sure you're not seen as you move forward, you need to have eyes in the back of your head as well.

There are a few late-nighters in Fountain Square. I can't imagine why, because it's cold as hell with the wind coming off the Caspian. I avoid the place altogether and take backstreets to reach the bank. As expected, there's a lone security guard standing outside under a light, bundled up and rubbing his arms to keep warm. I see his breath wafting from his nose and mouth. Unfortunately that's also a hazard for me when it's cold outside. There's not a lot I can do to mask my breathing except stay in the shadows and avoid light.

I have to move quickly for this to work—he mustn't see me coming. I choose a dark spot along the street and then dart across so I'm on the same side as the guard. I crouch and draw my Five-seveN. I'm approximately thirty feet from the guy, but he can't see me. Like a cat, I run lightly and noiselessly right up to him and halt with the barrel of my pistol at his temple.

It takes him a few seconds to realize what has just happened. He doesn't move his head but tries to look at me with his eyes. With my free hand I take the Glock from his holster and toss it away. The guard asks me something, probably, "What is it you want?" or something like that. I don't answer. Instead, I turn him around to face the retinal scanner. I point to it and he gets the idea. At first he shakes his head, but I tap him with the barrel again. The guard slowly leans forward and looks into the scanner.

I hear the door unlock.

While he's still in this position, I club him hard on the pressure point at the base of his skull. He drops like a sack of Azeri beets. I get a good grip under his arms and drag him into the shadows. For good measure I kick his Glock into the sewer drain.

I lower my goggles, turn on the night vision, and open the bank door. In two seconds flat I crouch and shoot out the overhead lights with the Five-seveN—*one, two*. I shut the door and now it's dark in the lobby. The surveillance cameras can't see me.

Bypassing the teller windows, I go straight to the barred gate and use the lock picks to open it. Beyond that is a small room to the left that holds a minimal amount of safe-deposit boxes. Across from that is an office, presumably Zdrok's. Down the corridor is the vault. I go into Zdrok's office.

His computer is on, but the monitor is off. I switch it on and examine the hard drive. His e-mail address is easy to pick up, so I note it in my OPSAT. Armed with this infor-

mation, Carly St. John can hack into his server and retrieve everything he's sent and received that hasn't been
deleted. The rest of the files are Excel and Word documents that appear to be legitimate bank business. I do find
a folder that's encrypted, and I try all the basic hacker
tricks to get inside. No luck. I'm also unable to copy the
file into my OPSAT. Whatever's in there, Zdrok made sure
he's the only one that can access it. I end up making a
copy of the folder's properties so I can send it to Carly.

A quick search of the desk and filing cabinets reveals
nothing of interest. I'm beginning to feel as if I've struck
out. Perhaps Zdrok keeps all the good stuff in Zurich. I sit
in his chair for a moment and look around the room.
Sometimes this helps inspire me to try something I hadn't
thought of. I notice that the interior designer placed polished mahogany panels on the walls, arranged in a geo-
metric, artistic pattern. The panels jut out slightly, creating
an embossed effect. I stand and cross the room for a closer
look. On a whim I switch the mode on my goggles to fluorescent. In this mode I see that the panels' top edges are
very dusty.

I move to the other wall and examine the panels there.
The dust on one panel reveals evidence of disturbance, as
if someone had gripped the panel and inadvertently wiped
the top edge clean in some spots. I carefully grip the panel
and pull. What do you know—the thing snaps out and pivots on a hinge, revealing a small safe. I dig into my thigh
pocket to retrieve a disposable pick and adjust the amount
of force I'd like the microexplosive to have. To open a safe
it has to be on full strength. That can make a bit of noise,
not to mention a mess.

Screw it, they're gonna know I was here anyway.

I arm the pick and position it next to the knob. When

I'm confident it's in the right place, I take a step back, brace myself, and push the firing pin on the side of the pick.

The blast feels like the equivalent of three Black Cat firecrackers, the kind I used to ignite on the Fourth of July when I was a kid. The damage it does, however, is much worse—there's now a hole in the front of the safe. I can easily reach through it, turn the tumblers, and open the door. I'm always amazed by the fact that every time I use one of these things, nothing within the safe gets damaged.

Inside is a stack of papers, facedown. Some are clipped or stapled together, others loose or in manila folders. Upon examining them I see they're records of money transfers to what appears to be a numbered Swiss bank account—which means it's private and secure. The amounts of the transfers are in the millions of dollars. I also note they're from a variety of organizations and individuals, but the locations are not indicated. In some cases there's simply a number—a transfer from one numbered account to another. Trying to trace these accounts back to whom they belong isn't going to be easy, if it can be done at all. Nevertheless, I snap pictures of several pages to see what Third Echelon can do.

The last document—that is, the record most recently placed in the safe—does denote the name of the customer. The money came from Tirma in the amount of eight million dollars. The transfer is dated tomorrow and the memo notation reads "Replacement." Damn. What's an alleged charity organization doing spending eight million dollars? They just bought a shitload of stuff. More proof that Namik Basaran isn't what he seems.

Many of the records reference another Azerbaijan address in regard to the payee. I don't recognize it, but I think it's in the suburban outskirts of Baku. I make note of the location, snap a shot of the document, replace everything neatly in the safe—even though the front is blown away—and stand in the middle of the room. I open the Osprey and take out two sticky cameras. I climb onto the desk so I can reach the air vent above it, pry off the grating, and attach the camera so it aims out and down at the desk. The second camera I place in the bookshelf and set it to the far left, on top of a large book. It isn't noticeable unless you pull out the book or stand right in front of the shelf and look closely. Finally I wedge an audio bug on the underside of Zdrok's desk.

Now I'm ready to leave, but as I step out of the office into the hallway, the blasted alarm goes off. I nearly jump out of my skin—it's about as loud and abrasive as an alarm can be. I edge to the end of the hall, near the barred gate, and hear shouting outside. Just my luck—someone must have discovered the unconscious guard I left outside, or he came floating back to reality earlier than I expected.

Well, I can't go out the way I came in, can I? The front door bursts open just as I turn and head back through the corridor to look for an emergency exit. I don't wait to see who comes in. I toss a smoke grenade behind me and run. It explodes, filling the entrance to the corridor with thick smoke. Men shout at me from the lobby, even though I'm certain they haven't seen me yet.

I do find an emergency exit in the back of the building, near the washrooms. There are warning notices all over it, which means another alarm will go off if I open the door. Too late to worry about that now.

I push the bar on the door, shove it open, and am greeted by another siren that resounds through the building. I leap into the alley, alight in a crouch, and look up to see two policemen standing fifty feet away, guns in hand. One yells at me, levels his pistol, and *fires*! What happened to "Don't move *or* I'll shoot"? The hell with it, he misses anyway. I bounce to my feet and run toward the other end of the alley—but I quickly see this wasn't a wise move, because there's a sixteen-foot wall there. A goddamned dead end.

I've never been one to be stopped by something as insignificant as a wall. First, though, I have to get rid of the pests firing bullets at me. The cops are either drunk or blind because they're lousy shots. I draw the Five-seveN, drop to my knee, twist my torso, take aim, and discharge two rounds for each man. It's as if they're both punched in the chest by an invisible sledgehammer. I figure they're probably wearing bulletproof vests, but the force of getting hit, even in a vest, is enough to knock you down.

This gives me time to pull out the cigar holder from the pocket on my left calf. I call it a cigar holder because it's a long cylindrical tube—but it has many uses. I then reach into the Osprey, find the length of rope I keep there for emergencies just like this one, and attach the end of the rope to the cigar holder. I push the button on the holder and four steel prongs snap out, creating a portable grappling hook.

I swing the hook twice and throw it over the wall. The hook catches on the bricks, and I give the rope a good tug or two to make sure it'll take my weight. Then it's just a matter of climbing up the wall, retrieving the hook, and jumping down to the other side.

Now I'm on a street around the corner from the bank. The sirens are still blaring, so I can't stay and watch the excitement. I run across the street to the nearest building and flatten myself against a side bathed in shadow. I need a moment to get my bearings. From here I can see the front of the bank. Three police cars have pulled up, lights blazing. The original guard is sitting up against the wall, rubbing the back of his head. I don't know how many cops are in there looking for me but as soon as they figure out I've left two of their buddies in the alley, they're going to be hunting for me like angry bees.

Before I can slip away into the darkness, a policeman appears at the end of my street and sees me. He shouts and draws his weapon. I immediately turn and run in the opposite direction. I hear gunshots and now there're more of them aware of my presence. I turn the corner and suddenly I'm at Fountain Square where a small handful of people—college age kids, really—are still huddling together, laden with heavy overcoats, smoking cigarettes and drinking vodka. It takes a real hardcore crowd to remain outside after midnight in this kind of wind chill. I have no time to stop and chat—I dart across the square just as two policemen appear behind me in pursuit. Another gunshot proves to me that the cops in Baku don't care much about innocent bystanders. The group of young people scream and disperse in all directions, which is a good thing for me. Suddenly there are several moving targets in the square, and I'm hoping this will confuse my hunters.

As they fire more wild shots at me, I make it across the square and skirt into a dark alley. The grappling hook I fashioned is still coiled around my shoulder. If I can get a minute to use it again, I'll take to the rooftops. But first I have to take care of Mutt and Jeff behind me.

I find a nook in the wall that's deep enough to cover me in shadow. I stop running, slip into the cranny, and wait until I hear the two cops enter the alley. They slow down, suddenly realizing I'm not in sight. The men speak to each other in low voices—one of them seems to be adamant that I came this way, the other is not so sure. With their weapons in hand they walk slowly toward me. The element of surprise is key here, so I hold myself back until just the right moment. When I see both of their backs, I step out of the nook and move between them. I grab their shirt collars, one in each hand, and slam the two men together. A pistol discharges and the owner drops it. The two cops are shaken but have the tenacity to turn and face me. Using the Krav Maga technique of moving forward in offense and positioning myself on the opponent's dead side, I prevent the armed cop from shooting me. The "dead side" of an opponent is his "outside." If you face an enemy who has his left foot forward, you must move forward and to your right. Moving in this direction places you in a position where the opponent's hands or feet can't readily strike you since you're at his side. This also allows you to clobber the guy because he's on your "inside." And that's just what I do. A quick jab to his arm causes him to drop his weapon. I swing to the right, raising my leg for a kick, and slam my boot into his chest. He goes down. The other cop is too shocked to budge. I move in, punch him hard in the stomach, and then pound him on the back of the head when he bends over in agony.

The alley's quiet after that.

I take the rope and grappling hook off my shoulder, swing it like a lasso, and throw it onto the roof of the building closest to me. I hear shouts and running footsteps in the square, so I have no time to lose. Getting up the wall is easy, and once I'm at the top I have a bird's-eye view of the Old Town. Below me, three more policemen enter the alley and rouse their stunned colleagues. I move to the other side of the roof so I can see Fountain Square and the bank beyond it. The number of patrol cars has increased and there's a lot of activity around the building.

Using the rooftop route, I head northeast toward the harbor, one shadow at a time.

_25_

THIRD Echelon's headquarters is nowhere near the National Security Agency, which is housed on Savage Road in Fort Meade, Maryland. The NSA is halfway between Baltimore and Washington, D.C., but Third Echelon resides in a small, nondescript building in the nation's capital, not far from the White House. The reason for this separation is because technically Third Echelon doesn't exist. Most NSA employees will have never heard of Third Echelon. As one of the most classified, top-secret organizations in the government, only those on a "need to know" basis are aware of the faction.

Third Echelon's mission is to activate individual operatives—the Splinter Cells—in targeted locations to assess and access information vital to the security of the United States. Third Echelon is not the CIA or the FBI. While men such as Sam Fisher have a license to kill in the line of duty, it is never an objective. Thus it is important that Third Echelon's support team in Washington provide the most accurate and up-to-date information to the Splinter

Cells. It could mean the difference between successful missions with or without bloodshed.

Colonel Irving Lambert and his team had pulled an all-nighter reviewing NSA satellite photographs of the Middle East and evaluating various reports pertaining to Fisher's assignment. After Lambert studied the revelations concerning Namik Basaran and the possibility that he may not be what he seemed, he directed the team to have a close look at Akdabar Enterprises' construction site in Northern Cyprus.

Carl Bruford, Third Echelon's director of research analysis, sat with Lambert at the light table examining the photos with a magnifier. Bruford, a thirty-one-year-old man from Illinois, was considered an expert on reading between the lines of intelligence reports and deciphering cryptic messages.

"I'll be damned if I can see anything weird," Bruford said. "The site looks like what Basaran says it is—a shopping mall. It's finished, too, from the looks of it. I don't think it's open to the public yet. There are still a lot of construction vehicles going in and out of the site, but the parking lot is empty."

Lambert rubbed the top of his head and frowned. "I don't like it," he said. "Keep looking. But I'll send this info to Sam anyway."

"Right. Oh, Chief, I had a thought that, I don't know, you might want to consider."

"What's that, Carl?"

"Doesn't Fisher have a daughter?"

"Yes, he does. She's a college student in Illinois."

"Northwestern, right?"

"Yes. Why?"

"I don't know. Just a feeling, but shouldn't we check up on her? I mean, since Fisher's out of the country and all.

And, you know, since three of our Splinter Cells are dead."

Lambert made a face and rubbed his head again. "You think we're losing Splinter Cells due to a hit list?"

"I do, Colonel."

"And you think Sam's probably on it?"

"Don't you?"

Lambert looked away and Bruford thought he could see the wheels turning in the man's head. The colonel turned back to Bruford and said, "Yeah, go ahead. Be discreet, though. We don't want to alarm her."

"Will do."

The colonel went into the next room, where Carly St. John was busy working on hacking into Basaran's server. Probably Third Echelon's Most Valuable Player, St. John was a computer programmer extraordinaire, a woman who had the ability to dismantle the most complex code and put it back together the way she wanted. At twenty-eight St. John was the youngest member of the team yet one of the most senior—she held the position of technical director. And while she didn't consider herself attractive, men who met her fell in love at first sight. She was petite—five feet, one inch tall—and had a brunette bob-cut and sparkling blue eyes. She had heard the description "pixie" far too many times.

"How's it coming?" Lambert asked her.

"Well, I'm getting closer," she replied. "It's pretty tough encryption, but I think I have a handle on it. I've got Basaran's bank account hacked, now I just have to work on the Swiss account."

"Sam says that Basaran is supposed to transfer the money tomorrow. I'd really like to sabotage that wire transfer."

"I know, Chief," St. John said. "Give me the rest of the day, okay?"

Lambert squeezed her shoulder and left her alone. He went back into the Operations Room and saw Bruford hanging up the phone.

"No answer at Sarah Burns's apartment in Evanston, Chief," Bruford announced.

"I thought she lived in a dorm."

"That was last year. She's a junior now and lives in her own apartment."

Lambert rolled his eyes. "Sheesh, time flies. Keep trying, but you might contact our man in Chicago to have a look-see. He probably has nothing to do."

Bruford chuckled and picked up the phone again. "Right."

Lambert went into his private office, a small space that allowed him to get away from the hustle and bustle for a few minutes at a time. He sat in his swivel chair, scanned his e-mail inbox, and took a sip of the now-cold coffee. He made a face, thought about going to get a fresh cup, but decided he'd rather shut his eyes for a bit. He was dead tired. All-nighters were for college kids.

But as soon as he closed his eyes the fax machine began to beep. He glanced at the cover page and saw that it was from Lieutenant Colonel Petlow in Baghdad. Lambert figured that perhaps he should go ahead and get a fresh cup of hot coffee—by the time he returned, the fax would be finished. Four minutes later he was back in the office, java in hand, ready to examine Petlow's fax.

TO: Colonel Irving Lambert
FROM: Lieutenant Colonel Dan Petlow
RE: Nasir Tarighian

Dear Colonel—

Pursuant to your instructions I have had my intelligence people work on the Tarighian business 24/7, and we now have something to report.

Nasir Tarighian was/is a wealthy Iranian citizen who was politically active during the Iraq-Iran War. In 1983 his home in Tehran was bombed and destroyed, killing his wife and two daughters. He formed a radical anti-Iraq terrorist outfit that made frequent sojourns across the border to Iraq, where he and his men performed vicious raids against innocent Iraqi civilians. In Iran and in parts of Iraq, Tarighian's band of terrorists was already beginning to be known as the Shadows. The Iranian government disapproved of Tarighian's methods and exiled him, but he left behind a populace that considered him a war hero, a sort of avenger for the Iranian people. In November 1984, Iraqi soldiers ambushed the Shadows—in Iraq. The force was wiped out and Tarighian was believed to have been burned to death in a massive explosion. No remains were found. But the Shadows live on to this day. In the last five to ten years they have regrouped and became better managed and financed. Terrorist Ahmed Mohammed has been linked to the group and may be directing their operations in the field. Four years ago the rumor mill perpetuated the story that Nasir Tarighian was alive and well and still leading the Shadows from outside of Iran. Since no one had really seen him, Tarighian remained a mythical figure—part righteous warrior, part ghost.

However, one of our prisoners here is apparently a top lieutenant in the Shadows and knows Mohammed personally. We believe he knew Tarighian in the 1980s. After lengthy interrogation he identified a photo of a

man we believe is Nasir Tarighian. I attach that photo
for your use.

Dan

Lambert turned to the photo. His heart rate increased
as he realized that his and Sam Fisher's instincts were correct.

The man in the picture was Namik Basaran. There was
no question about it. Here, though, he was dressed in an
Arabic robe and a turban. The shot was taken outdoors
circa 1984.

Lambert opened his file and studied the more recent
photo of Basaran with Andrei Zdrok. Yes, it was the same
man. Basaran had apparently undergone some skin grafting and plastic surgery, which was what made his face
look as if he had a dermatological condition.

Now it was clear. Nasir Tarighian had reinvented himself
as Namik Basaran, obtained Turkish citizenship, and used
his already-amassed wealth to establish Akdabar Enterprises in Turkey. No wonder Basaran had no history prior to
the 1990s! By using the front of Akdabar, and especially
the "charity" organization Tirma, Basaran/Tarighian had
been funding and giving strategic direction to the Shadows
for years. He may not be personally *running* the Shadows,
but he was certainly providing them with what mattered—
money.

Lambert suddenly felt wide-awake.

26

OF the two major ports in the Turkish Republic of Northern Cyprus, Kyrenia and Famagusta, the latter has the most colorful history. Located on the east coast of the island, it is a walled city that has been utilized throughout the ages—by a number of landlords—as a convenient strategic base from which to control the Mediterranean Sea. Today the harbor is used mainly for shipping and trade, whereas Kyrenia is more of a passenger terminal. The TRNC government had questioned why Namik Basaran would want to build a shopping mall just outside of Famagusta. Wouldn't Kyrenia make more sense? Kyrenia had more people and more traffic. Basaran stuck to his guns, saying that Famagusta was the most historically important city in Northern Cyprus. After all, it was the location of Othello's Castle, the inspiration for Shakespeare's famous play. Famagusta needed building up, he claimed. It demanded a refurbishing. Once a proud seaport, Famagusta had declined in respectability and Basaran aimed to change that.

The TRNC, unwilling to challenge such a valued supporter of the republic, allowed him to go ahead and strike ground.

Now, three years later, Famagusta Center was finished and Basaran was ready to begin leasing space to vendors. After a few finishing touches were added, Famagusta Center would be unveiled to the world.

Of course, Namik Basaran, aka Nasir Tarighian, had no intention of ever using the site as a shopping mall. Its proximity to Famagusta and the east coast was chosen simply for strategic reasons. He felt no compunction to help the Turks in their fledgling republic. It had all been a decade-long ruse just to arrive at this moment.

Tarighian and his chief weapons designer, Albert Mertens, walked around and inspected the massive structure that occupied a space large enough for a sports stadium. Topped by a reflective dome, the building might have been mistaken for some kind of planetarium or observatory if it weren't for the TRNC and Turkish flags hoisted on flagpoles and recognizable Western logos such as the McDonald's arches and the Virgin Megastore script mightily displayed on neon billboards.

"Isn't it beautiful, Professor?" Tarighian sighed. "The architect did a nice job with the building, don't you think?"

"Yes, indeed," Mertens said, but he wasn't smiling.

"And you're sure the Phoenix will be ready in two days?"

"Barring any unforeseen problems, yes."

"It's a shame that it will never open for business. We might have made a little money selling Big Macs."

Mertens didn't laugh.

"What's the matter, Professor?" Tarighian asked. "You seem a little unhappy lately."

"I've told you before, I don't agree with your proposed . . . plan," he said.

Tarighian stopped walking and threw up his hands. "Do we have to go through this again?"

Mertens turned and pointed his finger at his boss. "You know we have one shot and one shot only. Why waste it on Iraq? Don't you want to make the strongest statement you can possibly make?"

"Professor, enough!" The force in Tarighian's voice silenced the physicist. "I've made up my mind, so don't mention it again. Let's go inside. They're waiting for us."

Mertens nodded resignedly.

"Professor, you're a brilliant physicist," Tarighian said. "I couldn't have done this without you. But do me a favor and stick to what you know best and leave the strategic and military decisions to me."

"Fine."

Tarighian slapped Mertens on the back and said, "Good. Come on."

THE five men gathered in the bowels of the shopping mall were Nasir Tarighian's closest aides and lieutenants. Each of them was responsible for a faction of the Shadows' operations. Ahmed Mohammed, an Iranian, was responsible for the Political Committee, whish issued *fatwas*, or edicts purporting to be based on Islamic law, including orders for deadly attacks. He was also the unrecognized number two in the organization, the man responsible for making sure operations in the field were carried out properly. Nadir Omar, a Saudi, led the Military Committee that proposed targets, supported operations, and ran training camps. Hani Yousef, an Iranian, ran the Finance Committee, which provided fundraising and financial support in league with Tarighian. Ali Babarah, a Moroccan, headed the Information Committee, which was responsible for propaganda and recruitment. Finally, Ziad Adhari, an Iranian, led the Purchasing Committee, the machine that procured weapons, explosives, and equipment. These five men rarely met face-to-face for security reasons.

Tarighian and Albert Mertens joined them in the small conference room on the ground level. Farid, his broken arm in a cast and sling, stood by the door. Tarighian took the chair at the head of the table, as expected. Mertens sat next to his second-in-command, German physicist Heinrich Eisler. Mertens was happy to have an ally in Eisler, who was ten years his junior. Despite the disparity in backgrounds and age, the two men shared similar ideologies. They were also once roommates in a mental institution in Brussels. Eisler had a habit of whittling on small pieces of wood with a Swamp Monster combat knife, which was made of 420 stainless steel, a full 1-1/2 inches wide and 1/8 inch thick. Mertens knew that aside from the fact that Eisler was a brilliant physicist, he was very handy with the bladed weapon. When they lived in the institution, Eisler wasn't allowed to keep a knife. Ever since they had been "released," Eisler was never seen without it.

Tarighian, the man the world knew as Namik Basaran, stood and addressed the room. "Gentlemen, thank you for coming to Cyprus for this meeting. We praise Allah for delivering you safely and for the secure return to your posts. I thought it important that you be here in person as I outline my plans for what has been the realization of a dream. It's a dream I've had for twenty years. Now it will finally come to fruition."

He paused to make sure he had everyone's attention.

"The Phoenix is complete. It is ready, thanks to the genius of Professor Mertens." Tarighian held out his hand toward the physicist. The other men in the room turned to him and nodded, but there was no applause. These men were too serious for that kind of self-congratulatory nonsense. Mertens remained stone-faced.

"You've been wondering, I know," Tarighian continued, "what I want to do with the Phoenix. Today I shall tell you." He looked at every man in the eyes and announced, "It is time for Iraq to pay for what they did to Iran during the 1980s."

The committee heads shifted in their seats. Three of them leaned forward, their interest sparked.

"I am going to destroy Baghdad," Tarighian said softly. "And the destruction will be such that the city will be unrecognizable. Iran's revenge on Iraq will be swift and complete."

Nadir Omar cleared his throat. "Sir, with all due respect . . . ?"

"Yes, Nadir?" Tarighian faced his lieutenant.

"What will this accomplish for us?"

"Don't you see?" Tarighian held out his arms. "The resulting disorder in Iraq, and in the Middle East as a whole, will set the entire region against the West—in particular, against America, for not 'protecting' Iraq from terrorism. Iraq's government is made up of puppets, we all know that. The entire *world* knows that. America continues to monitor the country and influence the decisions made by the Iraqi leadership. This must end, once and for all. With such a disaster occurring in Iraq under America's watch, the entire Muslim world will react. America will be driven out of Iraq and perhaps even the rest of the Middle East. And then . . . with that opening, Iran will take America's place."

Two committee heads eyed each other.

"And Iran's government knows this?" asked Ahmed Mohammed.

"Not yet, but once the deed is done, then I will reveal myself to the world. Can you see the headlines in Tehran? 'Nasir Tarighian is still alive!' My followers in Iran will most assuredly back me. They will pressure the government to do what Iran has wanted to do but hasn't dared to do for nearly two decades. Iran will invade and conquer Iraq because Iraq is weak and under Western management! The West has tried to make Iraq a democracy in the image of a Western country, but it won't and will never work. Muslims should be the caretakers of the Muslim world. My loyal armies in Iran and neighboring countries are waiting for this showdown, and the Shadows will lead them into Iraq. And we will be victorious!"

Mertens nudged Eisler under the table.

Ahmed Mohammed cleared his throat and said, "Sir, if I may be so bold as to venture an opinion?"

"Yes, Ahmed?" Tarighian acknowledged.

"I do not believe the men who have claimed to be serving Islam in the Shadows will agree to destroying a city in what is essentially a Muslim country. I herewith express my disapproval for the whole thing."

Tarighian folded his arms in front of him. There was a tense moment as he glanced at Farid, who appeared ready to do something about the insurgent. Finally Tarighian merely smiled and said, "I appreciate your candor, Ahmed. Your objection is noted. Now I would like to meet with Ahmed and Nadir to discuss the next steps. The rest of you please stay and enjoy my hospitality. I'm sure Professor Mertens will be happy to show you the completed Phoenix." With that, Farid opened the conference room door with his one good hand and made a gesture indicating that the meeting was over.

Tarighian didn't notice that Mertens and Ahmed Mohammed exchanged a look that only they understood.

* * *

THREE hours later Nasir Tarighian shut himself in his private office and stared into the mirror on the wall. He normally hated mirrors, but ever since he had resolved to proceed with the project to bring Iraq to her knees, he wanted a daily reminder of why he was doing it.

He had never forgotten that fateful day when the bombs fell in Tehran. The air-raid sirens were loud and always frightened his daughters. On that morning school had been called off and the children were at home with their mother. Tarighian was busy at a political rally protesting the war and the current government's strict religious rules. When the bombing began he left and went straight home, running the six miles to be with his family. He imagined the face of his wife and how happy she would be to see him as he walked through the front door of their lovely, two-story home. He had worked hard to give his family such a house. Nasir Tarighian had been one of the fortunate Iranians who had shared in the former Shah's wealth by advising him on a number of policies. Needless to say, Tarighian was not a fan of the Islamic Revolution and Iran's newfound religious fervor. Nevertheless he was a loyal Iranian and he hated the Iraqis for what was happening to his country.

As he ran, Tarighian remembered the night before, when he embraced his wife and children and told them not to worry. Allah would protect them. The bombs would not strike their house. They would be safe.

But he was wrong.

The bomb hit the house just before he made it home. He recollected a wave of intense heat and a deafening noise that would haunt his dreams for the rest of his life. He recalled flames and smoke, flying debris, and screams.

He remembered finding the charred bodies of his family in the rubble.

Tarighian looked in the mirror at his own scarred face and prayed to Allah. He admitted to his god that he knew he had not been a good Muslim. He didn't pray five times a day. He had never made the pilgrimage to Mecca. He had to forgo the more orthodox rituals of Islam in order to perpetuate the pretension of being a Turk. He had lived a lie for twenty years, and he promised to prostrate himself, confess his many sins to Allah, and reap his punishment—after he obtained his revenge.

He had seen the faces of his most trusted men in the meeting today. They thought he was crazy. They thought he was embarking on a disastrous journey. He smelled the insurgency within his ranks. But didn't this happen to all leaders at some point in their tenures?

It didn't help that an intruder had infiltrated Akdabar Enterprises in Van. Farid said it was only one man, but no one saw his face. It was unclear where in the complex other than the steel mill the intruder had been. The surveillance cameras picked up nothing out of the ordinary, although there was the odd appearance of Tarighian's exercise rubber ball in the hallway outside his office. Was that supposed to be the intruder's idea of a joke? Could he have been the American that had posed as a Swiss Interpol policeman? Surely the man calling himself Sam Fisher was dead. The men had assured him the American never came out of Lake Van.

Enough of that, Tarighian told himself. Think of the matters at hand. Should he do something about the negativity within his organization? What could he do at this point other than continue on the course he was on? No, he shouldn't worry about his own men. They would continue to obey him, he knew that. They would remain loyal. He had instilled devotion in them. After all, he was the source of the Shadows' funding; he was their lifeblood. He was Nasir Tarighian and they viewed him as a prophet. It was he who would lead the Islamic nation out of the depths of misery and to a superior position in the world arena.

This was his destiny.

MERTENS and Eisler finished leading the tour around the facility and watched as the committee heads immediately got on cell phones to their lieutenants back at their respective bases. Mertens pulled Eisler to the side and said, "I told you. He's quite mad."

"I didn't believe it until now," Eisler said. "What are we going to do?"

Mertens shook his head. "I don't begrudge Tarighian his desire to seek revenge on Iraq. But it's a personal vendetta. He wants to avenge the deaths of his wife and children. It has nothing to do with Iran. He's delusional to think that Iran is going to back him on this. He was exiled from his country a long time ago. What makes him think he'll gather support now? Just because he's a cult hero, a mythological warrior? He's insane."

"Do you have a plan?"

Mertens put his hand on Eisler's shoulder and said, "Yes. I do. And so does Ahmed Mohammed."

27

ARMED with Third Echelon's revelations about Namik Basaran, I head out of Baku in the Pazhan to the address I found in Zdrok's safe. The built-in GPS in the OPSAT leads me to a heavy industrial area south of the city on the Abseron Peninsula, probably the most polluted part of Azerbaijan due to the predominance of petrochemical plants and oil refineries. The land itself is semidesert, the earth is scorched by oil, and derelict derricks stand like forgotten sentinels amidst a panorama of desolation. The images invoke a bizarre postapocalyptic hell on earth.

The sun is setting as I reach my destination. I'm surprised to see that the building is a *diaper* factory and warehouse. Who are they kidding? I've heard of deadly weapons of mass destruction, but this is ridiculous.

I wait until it's completely dark, but the night sky tends to glow from the fires of the surrounding refineries. There's not much I can do about it, so I hope for the best and leave the Pazhan dressed in my uniform. I make my way around to the back of the building, where I find a loading dock with a long ramp inclining toward it, a large folding steel door, and an employees' entrance. A vast, flat field stretches three hundred feet or more behind the building and I'm perplexed as to why nothing is built there. No time to wonder about that now.

The lock picks work easily on the employee door and there are no burglar alarms. Too simple. I utilize the corner periscope to peek through the door before opening it wider. This part of the building is a warehouse, of course, full of boxes and crates with the diaper company logo on them. Work lights illuminate the place much too brightly for my taste. I scan the ceiling and corners and see in the mirror a lone surveillance camera trained at the door. Damn. There's no way I can get inside without it seeing me, even if I blast it with the Five-seveN. I have to figure out something else.

I move to the side of the building and get lucky. Two hinged slat windows are ajar approximately fifteen feet above the ground. I look around for something to stand on and remember seeing an empty oil drum by the loading dock. I go back to retrieve it and roll the thing until it's in position. I climb onto the top, pull myself through the window, and jump to the floor inside.

I'm still in the warehouse portion of the building. I see several sealed barrels near the loading door—presumably full of gasoline for the truck that sits in a bay next to the dock. I've never seen so many boxes of diapers in my life, if indeed that's what they are. There's also a large open space on the floor, probably where more diapers sat until they were shipped, but it's huge—maybe a hundred by a hundred feet.

Before moving, though, I look for more cameras and find none. The only one in the warehouse is aimed at the

employee's entrance. Good. I dart to the nearest crate and
pry it open with my knife. Inside I find . . . diapers. I move
to the next crate and repeat the process. More diapers.

I take a look at the truck, a twenty-four footer—that
can hold a lot of diapers. The lock picks open the padlock
in the back, and I find the vehicle completely empty.

A folding vertical steel door separates the warehouse
portion of the building with the diaper-making half. I figure they raise the door and use forklifts to bring boxes of
diapers from one side to the other. I take a peek into the
factory area and see the heavy machinery that's employed
to make the diapers. Before I check out that space, I want
to see the rest of the building.

I go to the front of the warehouse, locate a door to the
rest of the building, and open it carefully. The hallway beyond is dark and empty. I flip on the night-vision goggles
and go through. As expected, there are a couple of offices,
an employee room with vending machines, a broom
closet, and an electrical room. I take a look at the latter and
study the circuit panel. I find switches for the warehouse
and front-area spaces, but that leaves a series of additional
switches that have no labels. What are these circuits for?

I make my way back to the warehouse and stand in the
square open space, trying to figure out what I'm missing.
There's got to be something here and it can't just be diapers. Directly in front of me is the huge vertical folding
door that opens when the loading dock ramp is in use. It
suddenly hits me that the boxes and crates are stacked
evenly and in straight lines on three sides around me. It's
almost as if there was an imaginary square drawn on the
floor and the rules state that no crates or boxes can be
stacked within the square. Could it be that they leave this
space free for a reason?

Using the fluorescent mode on the goggles, I look at the floor and finally notice an honest-to-God faint outline of a square. Then I see a pair of tire-tread tracks leading from the door to the edge of the outline.

Could it be . . . ?

I jump up and land with force. The echo below me indicates that the floor is hollow. I'll be damned—it's a trapdoor. There's a whole other level beneath the warehouse. So that's what the extra circuit breakers are for.

Without moving in front of the surveillance camera, I go into the small foreman's office near the employees' entrance. I examine the desk and walls, and sure enough, there's a locked compartment on one wall that appears to be a telephone access box. I quickly try the lock picks but it's a more complicated obstacle and might take too long with the conventional tools. I pull out a disposable pick, set the charge, and blast a hole in the box. Now it opens and there's a thick heavy switch inside. I throw caution to the wind and flip it up.

The big empty space in the warehouse begins to lower, like an elevator.

I leave the little office and approach the opening in the floor. There are lights on below and I hear movement. I whip the SC-20K off my shoulder, check that it's loaded with bullets, and wait.

As soon as the platform is completely lowered to the bottom level, two men dressed in *jeballas* and turbans walk onto it. They're carrying AK-47s around their shoulders but are at ease. Apparently they believe whoever's up here is a friend.

One of them calls to me in Arabic and then realizes I'm not who he thinks I am. The other man shouts something in alarm, and both of them swing the guns into their arms. I let off two rounds, hitting them both squarely in the chests. The guards drop the weapons and fall to the platform, their blood spreading across the robes.

I listen carefully for more signs of occupancy. The silence tells me it's safe. It's a good forty feet to the bottom, so I use the rope and grappling hook/cigar holder to fashion a vertical passage down. I slither to the lower level.

The place smells like fuel—aircraft fuel.

I notice that the perimeter of the moving platform is lined with built-in lights, flush on top. Off to the side are sets of wheel chocks, the things they use at airports to block wheels to keep aircraft from rolling. There's a fuel tank with an extra-long hose attached—just the kind that's used to fill up an airplane. A fire extinguisher sits nearby.

I'm in a fully functional but empty hangar. The flat field behind the building serves as a runway. The plane rolls up the ramp, onto the loading dock, and into the warehouse, where it is lowered to the underground hangar. I'll bet the platform turns so they can point the plane in the proper direction for its next liftoff.

Leave it to the Shop to keep a secret airplane hangar underneath a diaper warehouse. But where's the airplane?

Without warning I hear a gunshot and feel the heat of a bullet whiz past my face. I drop to the platform instinctively and roll toward one of the corpses. The maneuver sends a bolt of pain through my injured shoulder, but I grit my teeth and ignore it. The shot came from the portion of the lower level directly beneath the factory area. Using the dead man as cover, I glance over the body and see more crates and boxes—many of them stamped with the familiar Tabriz Container Company logo. Then I spot movement behind one of the crates. How many guys are there?

More shots. They hit the dead Arab, but I'm concerned the rounds might go through him and strike me. I take the risk of swinging the SC-20K off my shoulder, which puts me in the line of fire for a couple of seconds, and then I drop facedown. I lower the goggles and aim the rifle in the direction of the sniper, but one of his bullets strikes the platform directly in front of my face. Shards of concrete perforate my cheeks and mouth and it burns like hell. Thank *heaven* for the goggles, which are made of a highly concentrated Plexiglass that's nearly impossible to shatter. The shards would have blinded me for sure.

I take a moment to wipe my face on my right sleeve. There's a lot of blood, but I imagine that the wounds are small. Hopefully they'll be like shaving nicks—bleed a while, and then coagulate. I overlook the pain and concentrate on finding my prey. Then I see him. It's another Arab and he's the only one back there. He must have seen his buddies get killed and then decided to hide until I came down. I take aim and squeeze the trigger. I miss—he's covered well, but I watch him move to cover behind a crate.

I've got him now. My bullet will go right through the crate, depending on what's inside it.

I fire and—*holy shit!*—there's a massive explosion on his side of the floor! I don't know what I hit, but it sure was nasty. The space fills with thick black smoke—something I didn't want to happen because I'm not finished down here.

I jump up, grab the fire extinguisher I saw earlier, and run to the fire, which luckily is contained within a small space. I aim the extinguisher and let her rip.

It takes about a minute to put out the fire. As the smoke clears I see the charred remains of the sniper. The guy's in a few pieces and it's not pretty. The crate he was crouching behind is obliterated, but I was successful in keeping the rest of the cache safe from harm.

The draft from the platform opening in the ceiling sucks out the smoke pretty quickly, so I move to the other boxes and crates. I know what I'm going to find in there, but I open a crate just so I can say "I told you so" to myself.

Guns. Explosives. Military gear. Stingers. Uniforms. Surveillance stuff. Damn, it's a Terrorist Kmart. I've just found one of the Shop's main storehouses. When orders come in through the Swiss-Russian International Mercantile Bank, product is shipped from here. Maybe they use the airplane to deliver goods. Perhaps it's out calling on customers at this moment.

I snap a few pictures of the place with the OPSAT and wonder what I should do. I could leave it to the military to bomb the shit out of the place, or I could take peremptory action and do something myself. Glancing over at the first two dead Arab guards, I get an idea. I go back to the cache of goods and look in the boxes where I found the uniforms. There are flaksuits, camouflage wear, and traditional Arabic dress such as *jeballas* and turbans. I take a *jeballa*, but I'll be damned if I know how to wrap a turban. Instead, I go over to one of my dead friends and steal his headgear. I try it on without unraveling it and find that it's a perfect fit.

I take a frag grenade from my Osprey, set it to manual mode—which allows me to ignite it from a distance by pressing a button on the OPSAT—and I place it underneath the hangar's fuel tank. For good measure I place another grenade on the control panel that operates the platform. Before I climb the rope back to the upper level, I shove the dead guards off and onto the floor. I ascend the rope, replace it in my backpack, and go back to the foreman's office. I flip the switch to raise the platform and wait until it's in place.

I exit the building the way I came in. I make a careful countersurveillance sweep of the area and determine I'm alone. I run back to the Pazhan and change—I put on the *jeballa*, fix the turban so it looks correct, and then saunter back to the building.

This time I use the picks to open the employee entrance and walk inside, in full view of the surveillance camera. It will record an ordinary Arab walking into the warehouse. I take one of the Tirma pamphlets I stole from Basaran's place in Turkey—excuse me, I mean *Tarighian's* place— and drop it on the floor where I'm standing. I then proceed to set and plant frag grenades all over the place. I pay special attention to the gasoline drums. As I go around the building, I drop Tirma pamphlets.

Finally, when I'm done, I leave the building and drop the remainder of the Tirma literature on the loading dock, the ramp, and on the runway field. Investigators will surely find whatever Tirma pieces are not obliterated in the coming fireworks.

Back at the Pazhan, I get rid of the *jeballa* and turban, sit in the car, and activate the OPSAT trigger. The diaper factory goes up in a massive fireball that turns the night sky into an orange-and-yellow backdrop. I'm sure the thunderclap is heard for miles.

I drive away from the disaster area and can't help smiling. I'd love to be there when Andrei Zdrok gets the news that his terrorist department store has been blown to kingdom come. And with the "evidence" I left behind, hopefully he'll think the Shadows are responsible. Beautiful.

As I approach the city limits of Baku, I receive a message on the OPSAT from Carly St. John. I laugh out loud when I read it, for it serves my little plan that much more.

HI SAM. JUST LETTING YOU KNOW THAT I'VE SUC-CEEDED IN DIVERTING TARIGHIAN'S MONEY TRANSFER TO A TEMPORARY HIDDEN ACCOUNT IN OUR OFFSHORE BANK. THAT'S ONE PAYMENT THE SHOP WON'T GET.

—CARLY

28

THE Russian military lagged behind the United States in stealth technology and only recently began to aggressively pursue an updated, modern approach to air defense development. The cause was advanced considerably by the recovery and sale of a shot-down U.S. Air Force F-117A stealth fighter during the 1999 war against Serbia. Serbs reportedly sold the remains of the American aircraft directly to the Russians. Since then, Russian fighter maker Sukhoi began to use the S-37 Berkut, or "Golden Eagle," as a test bed for developing technologies for the next generation of military aircraft. The S-37 eventually evolved into the modern Su-47.

Western intelligence speculates that the new Su-47 is a stealth fighter. To date the truth is not known to the U.S. or Great Britain, but Russian military insiders are well aware of the state of affairs. The stealth fighter does exist, if only in a prototype stage, and it is destined to compete with the F-117A.

An impressively designed aircraft, the Su-47 has

swept-forward wings and a shape not unlike the Su-27 series. This configuration provides many benefits in aerodynamics at subsonic speeds and at high angles of attack. The foremounted canards are somewhat triangular and placed unconventionally far from the cockpit and close to the wings. The rear tailplanes are small but sleek and of unusual design. A strange hump behind the canopy encloses computer systems. There are two ordinary-looking D-30F6 engines and an IR targeting tracking blister mounted just in front of the canopy. With a wingspan of nearly seventeen meters and an overall length of twenty-two and a half meters, the Su-47 is the perfect size aircraft for stealth missions.

It was General Stefan Prokofiev who made one of the prototypes available to the Shop. He was in charge of the development team that was the liaison between Sukhoi and the Russian military. As a handful of prototypes emerged from the factory, Prokofiev made sure that one of them "disappeared" during a test flight. In reality it was stolen and diverted to one of the Shop's secret hangars located in southern Russia.

The only consolation Andrei Zdrok could attribute to the disaster that befell the diaper factory in Azerbaijan was the fact that their Su-47 was currently safely at rest in a different hangar in southern Russia. To replace the aircraft would have been extremely difficult, if not impossible, and it was a loss that Zdrok did not want to incur. Losing the twenty-three million dollars' worth of arms, equipment—and the Baku facility itself—was bad enough.

He was furious.

Too many strange things had happened in the past couple of days, and he was convinced it was not a coincidence. First, an intruder broke into the bank and blasted a hole in his safe. Nothing was taken—although Zdrok was certain that the documents were most likely photographed—and a great deal of damage had been done.

And now the warehouse/factory had been destroyed. By whom? Initial reports by his own investigators indicated that the Shadows might have had something to do with it. The site was littered with Tirma literature. Was that an accident or had it been done on purpose as a protest against the Shop's refusing to refund the money for the Shadows' lost arms shipment?

A knock on the door rustled Zdrok from his mind racing.

"Come in," he said.

It was Antipov. The man entered the room, stepped over the rubble that still lay on the floor, and shut the door. "The two policemen are fine," he said. "Their vests stopped the bullets. The night sentry insists that the man who made him use the retinal scanner was definitely American." He handed a CD to Zdrok and said, "This is from the camera at the warehouse. What was left of it, anyway. I think you'll find it interesting."

Zdrok took the disk and put it in his computer. They watched the clips together.

A man dressed in a *jeballa* and turban entered the back entrance. . . . He set grenades . . . he dropped leaflets . . . and then he left.

"Who is he?" Zdrok asked. "*He*'s not American."

"Who knows? He's obviously an Arab militant. He deliberately left that Tirma stuff. It's a message, Andrei. Tarighian is sending us a message."

"What does he want, a goddamned war?" Zdrok fumed. He took out the disk and gave it back to Antipov. "I'm going to call the bastard."

He picked up the phone, consulted the directory in his computer, and dialed the number in Cyprus.

"Yes." It was Tarighian, otherwise known as Basaran.

"It is I," Zdrok said.

"Are you on a secure line?"

"Of course."

"How are you, Andrei?" Tarighian sighed. He sounded tired and stressed.

"I could be better."

"Why, what's wrong?"

"What's *wrong*? You don't know?"

"Know what?"

"Our facility south of Baku was destroyed last night. By one of your men."

"What?"

"We have him on tape. He left Tirma shit all over the place so we'd know it was you."

"I don't believe this! What the hell are you talking about? You're accusing *me*?" Tarighian sounded way too offended. Zdrok smelled a rat. The man was an actor—after all, he'd been acting a part for the last twenty years.

"Only a handful of people know about that place," Zdrok said. "And I trust every one of them with my life. Except you."

"What are you saying? That I was somehow responsible for this?"

"My friend, if you think you can get away with this, you are sorely mistaken."

"Andrei, it sounds to me as if we're being set up. It was not me, I swear it."

"Oh? Is this the American agent you told me about, then? Is he the one who maybe infiltrated our bank in Baku?"

"Your bank in Baku? I know nothing about that!"

"We think an American broke into the bank the other night."

"Well, no, I don't think it was the man who was here. My men said they killed him. He drowned in Lake Van. Although I must tell you that our facility in Van was breached the other night. My bodyguard was hurt. A lone operative was seen in the steel mill, but he escaped."

Zdrok was aghast. "Tarighian, if this man was a CIA or NSA agent and he obtained some of our secrets from you, I can't tell you how much you and your organization will suffer."

"For the love of Allah, Andrei, we're on *your* side!"

"We're not on anyone's side but our own. You know that. I don't care about your bloody *jihad*. What you're planning to do with the materials we sold you over the last three years is foolish. I wouldn't be surprised if your own men turn against you. All I care about is the business. And speaking of that, why haven't we received payment for the replacement of goods that was sent to you? That was supposed to be in the account this morning, if you recall."

"What?" Now Tarighian really sounded concerned. "That money was transferred. I gave the order personally."

"It's not here."

"That's peculiar. I'll have to—"

"It's more than just *peculiar*, Tarighian. I suggest that you drop everything and look into the matter right *now*."

"Andrei, we're trying to finish our project. You know I have grand plans for what we've been building."

"Yes, I know. And I can imagine you're currently having cash-flow problems, too. But I don't care. Prove to me that you didn't do this terrible thing to me and pay me what you owe me."

Zdrok hung up without giving Tarighian a chance to respond. He looked at Antipov and said, "So he thinks the American is dead? The girl in Israel hasn't talked yet, so I suppose it's time we convince her to do so. If he's really dead, we'll soon know for certain." He picked up the phone again and made a call to Jerusalem.

"DAMN Zdrok," Tarighian said to Mertens as he hung up the phone.

They were in Tarighian's private office inside the Cyprus shopping mall complex.

"What is it now?" Mertens asked.

"They're screwing us," Tarighian replied. He dialed another number and waited. "Hello, Hani?"

Tarighian's head of finance was on the other line. "Yes?"

"Was that payment transferred to the Shop?"

"Yesterday, sir."

"You're sure?"

"Of course I'm sure. I did it personally."

"They say it wasn't received."

"Impossible."

"Look into it, will you? I have enough problems right now."

"Yes, sir."

Tarighian hung up and glared at Mertens. "I suppose you want to tell me again how crazy this scheme is."

Mertens shrugged. "As a matter of fact . . ."

"All right, Professor. If Baghdad isn't a suitable target, then what is? Are you going to say Israel again?"

"Of course! I cannot believe you are blind to this. Tel Aviv or Jerusalem should be the target because Israel is the key objective in the Middle East. Destroy Jerusalem and the region really *will* be in chaos. And it will avenge the assassination of Gerard Bull."

"So *that's* what this is about? Your former boss?"

"He was much more than a boss. He was my mentor. He was like a father to me."

"There is no proof that Israel was responsible for Bull's murder."

"There is every indication that the Mossad was responsible. I was there. I was working with Gerard when it happened. I swore to avenge his life then and I intend to do it."

"Not with my money you don't," Tarighian said. "Just because you were Gerard Bull's right-hand man doesn't give you the privilege to question my motives. Professor, you have done a wonderful job with the Phoenix, but in Allah's name I will not tolerate insubordination. Now that the Phoenix is complete, you are *expendable*. Don't forget that."

Tarighian's cold brown eyes stared holes through Mertens, and the Belgian physicist saw—not for the first time—why so many men respected and feared the man. Tarighian possessed that rare quality known as charisma. Great men throughout the ages used charisma to influence others, whether it was for good or for evil, and Tarighian was no different. He had seduced Mertens long ago, convincing the Belgian to devote his life to designing and building a weapon for the Shadows. The pay was an additional incentive, of course, along with protection from the Belgian authorities who had been looking for him ever since his escape from the mental institution.

For Mertens, though, he was not in it only for the money. By working on Tarighian's project, Mertens had fulfilled his goal of continuing the dreams of Gerard Bull, the man who taught Mertens everything he knew. Mertens was not a Muslim, nor did he care about the Shadows' objectives to drive the West out of the Middle East and take over Iraq. He had no loyalty to Jews, Muslims, or Christians. His devotion was to Bull and the man's genius. Mertens owed it to Bull to fulfill the man's prophecy.

"Very well," Mertens said. "I apologize. But you should know that many of your own men are unhappy with what you plan to do. They do not agree with your decision to attack a city in a Muslim country."

"Are you talking about Ahmed Mohammed by any chance?" Tarighian growled. "I will deal with him in due time. Ahmed has been my friend and ally for over twenty years. If he is disgruntled, he'll get over it. Now get back to work. I don't want to hear another word about it. I expect the Phoenix to be fully operational tomorrow and we'll begin tests in the afternoon. Is that clear?"

Mertens bowed his head slightly. "Absolutely." He stood and left the room.

He walked down the dark, empty corridor to his own office, where Heinrich Eisler was waiting for him, whittling on a piece of wood.

"Well?" Eisler asked.

"I've had enough of Nasir Tarighian and the Shadows," Mertens said. "It's time to take matters into our hands. I'm placing a call to Mohammed."

_29_

SARAH wiped the tears from her cheeks, rose slowly from the cot, and walked weakly into the bathroom. The dirty mirror reflected a frightened mess of a girl. Her eyes were bloodshot, her hair was stringy, and the makeup was long gone. Sarah hadn't showered in a couple of days— what was the point? The hunger pangs no longer bothered her, but she felt extremely feeble. Now it was just a question of how much longer she'd be able to perform other normal functions.

Over the years she had been aware of other kidnappings in the Middle East. The stories were always on CNN or in the newspaper. Americans were abducted while performing their jobs or while serving in the military. Sometimes the hostages were rescued . . . more often not.

What would the bastards eventually do to her? So far they hadn't mistreated her physically, although the creep named Vlad had come close. She hated Eli now, but in many ways he'd been her protector. There was no telling what the two Russians would do if Eli wasn't around.

Several times she had been tempted to tell them how to contact her father. Sarah was loath to involve him, but she also suspected that he could get her out of this situation. If Eli was right and her father really was a government spy of some kind, he would have the resources to rescue her. Perhaps he could bring the army in and blow her asshole kidnappers to hell.

On the other hand, the kidnappers wanted him for a reason, and Sarah didn't think it was a good one. She could see the hate in their eyes and hear the venom in their voices when they spoke of him. Sarah was certain they wanted to kill her father, and she understood full well that she was the bait to lure him into their clutches. She was resolved not to let that happen.

How many days had it been? She had lost count. She now realized she should have done what she'd seen prisoners in movies do—scratch on the wall with something and make a mark for every passing day. She knew she'd been there less than a week but more than four days. If she hadn't been kidnapped, she'd be home now. She would have said goodbye to Rivka and her family and—

Oh, Rivka.

What happened to her friend haunted Sarah and tore at her heart. It was all her fault. If she hadn't been Rivka's friend, the girl would still be alive. During one of Eli's frequent visits to her room, Sarah asked him what had happened to her. How did she die? Eli refused to tell her. He said he didn't really know—only that she was dead. Sarah asked him if Noel was responsible and Eli simply shrugged. How could he be so cold? How could *both* of them do what they have done? She and Rivka had given the boys their bodies, their love, their devotion. She and Eli had spoken of living together in New York and maybe getting married someday. Had Rivka and Noel done the same? Had he convinced her to trust him and look forward to a future with him?

Bastards.

Sarah finished her business in the bathroom and lumbered back to the cot and lay down. She then heard a familiar knock on the door. Eli again. The key turned in the lock and the door opened. She didn't look at him but felt his presence as he stood over her.

"You want anything to eat yet?" he asked.

She didn't answer.

"Come on, Sarah. You better eat something. You're . . . you're going to need your strength."

Sarah refused to acknowledge him.

"Look, Sarah, we've had new orders come through. Vlad and Yuri—they've been given the go-ahead to be more, um, aggressive. This is your last chance. You have to tell us what we want to know. Where is your father? How do we get a message to him?"

Her silence finally got to him. Eli grabbed her by the hair and pulled her head up. She shrieked and he shouted, "Goddamn it, Sarah! Talk to me! I can't be responsible for what they're going to do!"

The tears welled in her eyes, so she closed them. That way she wouldn't have to look at him.

He let go of her and she burrowed herself into the blankets and pillow, sobbing.

"Sarah," he said, a little softer. "Vlad and Yuri . . . they're going to come in here and make you talk. I promise you, they will make you. So please. Tell us what we want to know."

She mumbled something.

"What?" he asked.

She lifted her head and said evenly, "Go to hell."

Eli sighed, moved toward the door, and said, "I'm sorry, Sarah." And then he left.

Now Sarah was really frightened. What were those two men going to do to her? Please God, don't let it be rape. Anything but that.

She felt movement in the room and heard the door slam shut. Sarah looked up and saw them—Vlad and Yuri—standing near the cot. Vlad had a coil of rope. Yuri carried a tool kit.

"Hello, Princess," Vlad said. "Are you ready to have some fun with us?"

Adrenaline pumped through Sarah's body as she leaped from the cot and ran toward the bathroom. Vlad caught her around the waist and swung her back to the cot. She fell on it hard, collapsing it.

Vlad uncoiled the rope.

CARLY St. John finally had a good night's sleep after spending two days straight on hacking Tarighian's and Zdrok's bank accounts. Now she had a new assignment and it was just as urgent. Lambert had given her digital files of phone conversations that Sam Fisher had recorded in Turkey, and he wanted a splice job. This meant she had to take pieces of the conversation, cut them up, and put them back together so the speakers were saying something very different from the original.

The subjects were Nasir Tarighian, aka Namik Basaran, and an unknown subordinate. They spoke in Farsi, not Turkish. After Third Echelon's crack interpreter translated the dialogue into English, Carly heard the original conversation like this—

MAN: "But surely the Shop can see that it wasn't us?"

TARIGHIAN: "No, the Shop can't see, Zdrok is blind to everything but his own little world."

MAN: "Let me get this straight. The diaper factory was attacked by someone—"

TARIGHIAN: "An Arab."

MAN: "—and he blew up the building."

TARIGHIAN: "And left Tirma material all over the place."

MAN: "So obviously someone wants to create a rift between you and the Shop."

TARIGHIAN: "The rift was already there. They just made it wider."

MAN: "So I suggest you tell him that you're convinced it was an outside job. Someone is setting you up."

TARIGHIAN: "I told him that, but he didn't listen. Now he doesn't take my calls. Damn it, doesn't he know who I am?"

MAN: "Has Hani found out what happened to the money transfer?"

TARIGHIAN: "*No*. We sent the money. According to Hani's records the transfer made it safely into Zdrok's Swiss bank account. However, Zdrok claims he never got it."

MAN: "You did give the order for the transfer, didn't you?"

TARIGHIAN: "Of course!"

MAN: "Then why would he lie?"

TARIGHIAN: "He's angry that the first shipment of arms was confiscated in Iraq. The Iraqi police arrested the men red-handed. Ahmed and his men tried to mount an operation to retrieve it, but that failed. We had to bite the bullet and pay for a completely new shipment. So far Zdrok says he hasn't been paid."

MAN: "He delivered it without us paying up front, right?"

TARIGHIAN: "Yes. His one Good Samaritan act. Now he wants his damned money yesterday."

MAN: "So he probably thinks you're trying to put him out of business."

TARIGHIAN: "Yes, that's probably what he thinks."

MAN: "Surely the Azeri police will catch someone for the crime."

TARIGHIAN: "Not likely, you fool. The media's already blaming the Shadows for it. Ali put out a statement denying responsibility but you know how far that goes."

MAN: "So what now?"

TARIGHIAN: "The man better apologize for his behavior and exonerate us of this crime. And he should not charge us for the new shipment. The man's a billionaire, he can write it off."

Carly heard the sound of a knock.

TARIGHIAN: "Come in."

ANOTHER MAN: "You're wanted in the control room."

TARIGHIAN: "I'll be right there."

And that was the end of it. A second file contained the following short exchange between Tarighian and the same man.

TARIGHIAN: "The Filipinos behave as if they're in the West. They are a godless bunch."

MAN: "The Shadows' influence on them will change things."

TARIGHIAN: "The authorities can't deny that Islam is growing in the Far East. Our cells in the Philippines and Indonesia will soon make strikes but not until—" (garbled).

MAN: (garbled) "—and the United States will then relent."

TARIGHIAN: "All they care about is money. I've hit them where it hurts and I'll continue to do so. Come on, let's worry about the Far East after the Phoenix project is completed."

And that file was over.

Her intercom beeped. She pressed the Talk button and said, "Yeah?"

"What do you think?" It was Lambert.

"It doesn't seem too difficult," she answered. "I've got plenty to work with."

"It has to sound convincing. I can tell Sam we need more material if you can't put something together that will—"

"Don't worry, Chief, I can do it. Is that pizza here yet?"

Lambert laughed. "For such a small person you sure eat a lot."

"My brain cells need feeding—they soak up all the nutrition."

"The delivery should be here in another five minutes or so."

"Let me know, I'm starving."

Carly released the intercom and went back to her computer. Sometimes the work was like this and she never went home. Here she was with a bedroll in her office. There were periods of time when she felt as if she were back in the dormitory at Harvard. She could remember all-nighters when she'd catch a nap for an hour or two and then hit the books again. During finals she never left her room.

Her mother always complained that she wasn't married and didn't date. If her mother only knew that Carly was busy saving the country and didn't have the time or the will to see anyone, perhaps the woman would leave her alone. Of course, knowing her mom, she'd probably say that "settling down and raising a family" was more important. No, thanks. Carly was content to live a celibate lifestyle and drown herself in work. If human desire ever raised its ugly head, she wasn't beyond picking up some hunk for a one-night stand. Commitment, for her, was a four-letter word.

When the pizza arrived, she took a plate-full of slices back to her office. She never sat with the other employees in the break room. She was aware of her reputation as aloof, but she didn't care. Lambert knew better, and that's all that counted.

Carly began the work by cutting all the lines of speech into individual phrases. If a word or phrase needed repeating, she copied it and created a new file. It wasn't long before she had all the puzzle pieces needed to create the picture.

Four hours later she called Lambert into her office. He came in, sat, and rubbed the top of his head.

"Listen to this," she said. She manipulated the mouse and clicked something on her computer.

TARIGHIAN: "Zdrok is blind to everything but his own little world. He's angry that the first shipment of arms was confiscated in Iraq. The Iraqi police arrested the men who had it. Ahmed and his men tried to mount an operation to retrieve it, but that failed. We had to bite the bullet and pay for a completely new shipment. So far, Zdrok says he hasn't been paid."

MAN: "So he probably thinks you're trying to put him out of business."

TARIGHIAN: "Yes, that's probably what he thinks."

MAN: "You did give the order for the transfer, didn't you?"

TARIGHIAN: "Not likely, you fool."

MAN: "The Shadows' influence on them will change things."

TARIGHIAN: "The Shop behave as if they're in the West. They are a godless bunch. All they care about is money. I've hit them where it hurts and I'll continue to do so."

MAN: "Let me get this straight. The diaper factory was attacked—"

TARIGHIAN: "The rift was already there. We just made it wider."

MAN: "An Arab—"

TARIGHIAN: "I sent him—" (garbled) "—and left Tirma material all over the place."

The recording stopped. Carly looked at Lambert and raised her eyebrows. "Well?"

Lambert smiled. "I think it'll work. Send the file to Sam."

30

I receive Carly's file of the doctored conversation between Tarighian and one of his henchmen and it's great. Carly also sends me a second file with the English translation. The folks at Third Echelon really know their stuff. It must have been extremely difficult reconstructing a conversation without speaking the language, but then Carly St. John is brilliant. I have to admit I find her attractive. She's a tiny little thing and smart as a whip. I've never made any moves toward her, though. For all my skittish tendencies toward women, you'd think that seeing someone in the same agency would be all right. At least she'd understand my line of work, and I wouldn't be putting her at risk simply by knowing me.

I'll have to think about that one.

For now, though, I need to send Andrei Zdrok my little present. I'm surprised to find a bagel shop in Baku right across the street from his bank and decide that's as good a place as any from which to keep a surveillance going. I position myself at a corner table, have some breakfast, and read the newspaper, poised where I can look through the window at the street. The proprietors don't seem to mind that I'm loitering as long as I keep filling the coffee cup. Finally, at a little after ten o'clock, I see him get out of a Mercedes in front of the bank. He's dressed as sharply as always. When the Mercedes drives off, though, Zdrok doesn't enter the building. Instead he turns, looks in my direction, and crosses the street toward the bagel shop. Shit. It's quite possible Zdrok knows what I look like. Tarighian's cameras had surely captured my mug when I first visited his office. The guy could have sent my picture to Zdrok.

I stand and walk toward the washroom. Zdrok enters the shop just as I go through the door. I enter the stall and wait a few minutes until I'm fairly certain that he's made his purchase and left. I move to the door and open it slightly.

Damn, he's heading this way! There's nothing I can do about it so I turn to the sink and start washing my hands. The door swings open and Zdrok walks in. I see that he has a sticky pastry in one hand and he's wolfing it down. He stands beside me, obviously waiting for me to finish with the sink so he can wash the goo off his hands.

I don't look him in the eyes, but I nod, smile, and move away from the sink. I grab a couple of paper towels as he rubs his hands in the running water. I feel him looking at me in the mirror—in fact, he's *staring* at me. I have to get out of here, fast. I finish drying my hands and walk toward the washroom door.

"Do I know you?" he asks in Russian.

I stop. My Russian isn't perfect, but I can get by. "Excuse me?" I say.

"Were you in my bank the other day?" he asks.

What does he mean? "I beg your pardon?"

"Didn't I see you in the bank? The one across the street. You were there the other day, at the information table."

Whew. So that's what this is about. "Um, yes, I was."

Zdrok smiled. "I'm Andrei Zdrok, the bank manager. If there's anything I can help you with, please let me know."

I nod and say, "Thank you," and then leave as if I'm embarrassed. I walk straight through the bagel shop and out the front door. I turn left and stride purposefully away from the bank and hope that Zdrok doesn't follow me. It's unlikely, but I don't want to take any chances.

I stop at a newsstand and pretend to browse the magazines, keeping an eye on the bagel shop. After a moment I see Zdrok exit and cross the street to the bank. He doesn't look my way. He's probably forgotten all about the encounter. I'm counting on it, anyway.

Once he's inside the building I move back down the street and enter an old-fashioned phone booth. These relics are pretty much a thing of the past in America, but you'll still find them in Europe.

I cradle the phone between my head and shoulder and activate the OPSAT. I'm able to send an e-mail anywhere in the world with the thing as long as I have an unhindered signal to the satellite. It works best when I'm outdoors, but it'll do all right in some buildings. For this, though, I don't take any chances. I want Zdrok to get *this* e-mail.

His address is stored in the OPSAT so it's a simple procedure to send Carly's file. For a message, I type in Russian, "I thought you'd find the attached conversation interesting." I sign it "A Friend" and send it.

I leave the phone booth and walk the two blocks back to where I parked the Pazhan. I get inside, put on my headset, and listen to the bug in Zdrok's office. At first there's nothing but static. After a few minutes, though, I hear someone walk into the room and the subsequent creak of the chair as he sits in it.

He picks up the phone and makes a call. "Ivan, find out where General Prokofiev is. I want to talk to him," he says. It's Zdrok, all right. He hangs up the phone and I hear him typing something on his computer keyboard. Good. Maybe he's checking his e-mail. There're a few minutes of silence and then I hear Carly's file, broadcast loud and clear on the computer's speakers.

TARIGHIAN: "Zdrok is blind to everything but his own little world. He's angry that the first shipment of arms was confiscated in Iraq. The Iraqi police arrested the men who had it. Ahmed and his men tried to mount an operation to retrieve it, but that failed. We had to bite the bullet and pay for a completely new shipment. So far, Zdrok says he hasn't been paid."

MAN: "So he probably thinks you're trying to put him out of business."

TARIGHIAN: "Yes, that's probably what he thinks."

MAN: "You did give the order for the transfer, didn't you?"

TARIGHIAN: "Not likely, you fool."

MAN: "The Shadows' influence on them will change things."

TARIGHIAN: "The Shop behave as if they're in the West. They are a godless bunch. All they care about is money. I've hit them where it hurts and I'll continue to do so."

MAN: "Let me get this straight. The diaper factory was attacked—"

TARIGHIAN: "The rift was already there. We just made it wider."

MAN: "An Arab—"

TARIGHIAN: "I sent him—" (garbled) "—and left Tirma material all over the place."

I wish I could see Zdrok's face. He's probably sitting there with his mouth wide open. Silence fills the room again. He's not moving. I hope he's in shock. After a minute goes by he plays the file again. When it's done, there's more silence. He plays it a third time and then picks up the phone.

"Ivan, have you found General Prokofiev yet? Well, hurry!" He hangs up. I hear him type some more. Maybe he's forwarding the file to all his buddies in Russia or wherever they hang out.

After a minute the phone rings. He answers it with a "Yes?" I switch on the OPSAT's record mode and listen.

"General, where the hell are you?" he asks. "I see. Where's the plane? Yes, *our* plane, what did you think I—? Yes. I see. Listen, this is what I want you to do. I want to order an air strike on Akdabar Enterprises in Van, Turkey. Yes, I know what I'm doing. I have proof that the Shadows are double-crossing us. They never sent that money and have no intention to do so. And I know now they are responsible for what happened at the hangar in Baku. Yes. I just sent you an e-mail, did you get it? Well, check it, damn it! I'll wait."

There are a few moments of silence, but I can hear Zdrok breathing heavily. The guy's blood pressure has probably shot up.

"I'm still here," he says. "You have it? Listen to the file. I'll wait."

More breathing. A cough.

"Well? You see? No, no, I just want to—General, this is not negotiable. These are my orders. Send the plane to Turkey and bomb the shit out of that facility. I want it done today. Right. Keep me informed. Thank you, General."

He hangs up the phone and I hear him stand and walk out of the room.

I stop recording and play back the file. His voice comes through clearly. He said all the right things and it's beautiful. Apparently Tarighian's people are going to see some fireworks later today. Too bad the big man won't be there. I know he's down in Cyprus now. Carly got hold of his e-mail address easily enough, so I prepare the file and type the same message in Russian—"I thought you'd find the attached conversation interesting." I sign it "A Friend" once again and send it to Tarighian.

As I drive away from Fountain Square and head toward my floating hotel, I hear Lambert's tinny voice in my ear.

"Sam? Are you there?"

I press the implant in my throat and speak to him. "I'm here, colonel."

"You're finished in Azerbaijan, Sam," he says. "All the evidence you've managed to capture in pictures is enough for us to move against the Shop. We're going after the Swiss-Russian banks there in Baku and in Zurich. We're also making arrangements to move in on Nasir Tarighian. Good job."

I tell Lambert about Zdrok's conversation I just recorded. "He's going to do some damage to Tarighian's operation in Turkey and it's gonna happen soon," I say. "You might want to alert the Turkish air force. If they're on the lookout for a small plane capable of dropping bombs, they can kill two birds with one stone. Let the Shop do their thing on Tarighian's place and then knock their plane out of the sky."

"Good idea, will do. Now listen, Sam. I want you to go to Cyprus. We need to know exactly what Tarighian is up to. All we know is that he's built a shopping mall in the north, but he's got to be hiding something."

"I agree."

"Go to the American Embassy on Azadliq Avenue there in Baku. Find our man George Tootelian and he'll set you up with transport out of the country. We're going to fly you to Tel Aviv, where you'll catch a ride to Cyprus. Tootelian's expecting you. I'll talk to you again once you're in Tel Aviv. Have a good trip."

"Thanks, Colonel."

He signs off as I arrive at my hotel. I'll need to check out and head for the embassy, but I'm hungry and want a bite to eat first. Knowing the efficiency of our embassies abroad, they'll have me on a plane before I'm able to fill my belly.

My OPSAT beeps and I check it for an incoming message. It's coded so I know it's—Christ, it's from Sarah! It's the first time she's ever used the private number to reach me.

But as the words appear on the screen, my heart skips a beat. I feel a growing dread that threatens to erupt into full-blown panic. I want to tear off the OPSAT and throw it into the Caspian Sea. I want to scream at the heavens for allowing this to happen.

The message reads:

WE HAVE YOUR DAUGHTER. YOU HAVE 72 HOURS TO COME TO JERUSALEM FROM WHEREVER YOU ARE.

The message goes on, ordering me to phone a specific number when I arrive and ends with the parting shot:

NO TRICKS IF YOU WANT TO SEE HER ALIVE AGAIN.

31

FOR the Shop, one of the advantages of keeping a top Russian general in a major administrative position was his ability to procure and modify military equipment. When the Su-47 prototype stealth plane was presented to Andrei Zdrok, the aircraft was still in the stage in which design alterations could be made. The plane was originally conceived to carry air-to-air missiles, such as the R-73 (AA-11 "Archer") or the R-77 (AA-12 "Adder"). However, Zdrok thought that air-to-surface missiles would be more useful for the Shop's purposes, and he asked General Prokofiev to adapt the Su-47 to fire tactical ASMs.

The Soviets lagged behind in developing air-to-surface missiles. The first one introduced, in the late 1960s, was the Kh-66 Grom, a solid-fuel, radio-guided missile with a general appearance similar to that of the U.S. Bullpup-A. This was followed in the 1980s by the Kh-25 series, modular weapons that allowed field fit of different guidance heads, including radio and laser-seeker systems. The Kh-25 gave way to the bigger Kh-29, another solid-fuel ASM.

Designed by Molniya Design Bureau, it has a NATO designation of AS-14 "Kedge." The Kh-29 was built to be
carried by small and medium tactical aircraft such as the
MiG-27, Su-17, Su-24, and MiG-29 and was specifically
designed for use against hardened targets. It has a reinforced nose section and the warhead takes up almost half
the weight of the missile. Today it comes in three styles—
a laser-seeker Kh-29L, the TV-guided Kh-29T, or the fire-
and-forget thermal imaging guidance Kh-29D. All three
versions have been heavily exported and can be encountered almost anywhere in the world.

It seemed to General Prokofiev that the Shop's stealth
plane could be most easily adapted to carry the Kh-29L,
with its semi-active laser homing head 24N1. Weighing
approximately 657 kilograms, the missile has a minimum
range of 1,000 meters and a maximum of 8,000. With a
speed of 3,000 meters per minute, the thing is fast and
deadly.

The Shop kept three hidden hangars for the Su-47—
one in Baku, which was now destroyed, one south of
Moscow in the tiny village of Volovo, and one south of
Kiev in a small hamlet called Obukhov. The stealth fighter
was in the hangar at the latter location when the orders
came through to attack Akdabar Enterprises. The Shop's
ace pilot, Dimitri Mazur, lived and breathed with the
plane. He had apartments near each of the three locations
so that wherever the plane had to go, he was there to take
it. He then baby-sat the aircraft until the next assignment.

Three hours after Zdrok gave the order to attack the
Shadows, Mazur eased the Su-47 off the runway and rose
to an altitude of 10,000 feet, where he would stay until he
was a good distance from Kiev. Within ten minutes the
plane ascended to 30,000 feet and turned in the direction
of southeast Turkey. While in flight Mazur kept in contact

with the Obukhov control center, but for all intents and purposes he was on his own. Mazur worked from a set flight plan that he prepared before takeoff, and he served as his own navigator. The rules were that if he got into trouble, he was to destroy the plane by activating a self-destruct mechanism. Prokofiev had installed explosives within the plane for this purpose because he couldn't afford having the Su-47 discovered by the Russian government. Pilot Mazur was well aware of his obligations should events transpire that might force him to eject. What he didn't know was that Prokofiev had fixed the system so that the pilot wouldn't be able to eject—he would meet the same fate as the plane itself. This was done to protect the integrity of the Shop and keep its directors in the clear. Should the government recover fragments of the plane, it would be chalked up to one of the many mysterious bureaucratic snafus that occurred when the Soviet Union fell apart.

Fortunately, the Su-47 had thus far performed beautifully. Most of its missions had been to transport small loads of weapons. Only once had it been used aggressively, and that was to obliterate the home and storehouse of an arms-dealing competitor who had refused to cooperate with the Shop.

Mazur thought it unwise to fly the plane during daylight hours, but who was he to question orders? Regardless, he looked forward to flexing the plane's muscles. He enjoyed the feel of the recoil when the missiles launched and found pleasure in the reverberation of the impact. But what he really wanted to do some time was to fire a nuke. He could fly the plane in above the target, let loose with the ASM, and speed away unseen. The Shop had yet to acquire a nuke, but the Kh-29s were plentiful and potent. The Su-47 normally carried fourteen air-to-air missiles, but since it was modified, the plane's armament capacity was ten ASMs. This was enough to destroy a small village.

As the plane crossed the border into Turkish airspace, Mazur contacted Obukhov control and informed them he would be in sight of the target area within the half-hour. The Turkish air force patrolled the eastern portion of the country with vigor since it was in close proximity to Iraq and often had dealings with the PKK. A stealth plane wasn't completely invisible by any means, so Mazur had to be extremely vigilant and avoid the flight patterns of other aircraft. The goal of stealth technology is to make an airplane imperceptible to radar. There are two different ways to create invisibility—the airplane can be shaped so that any radar signals it reflects are bounced away from the radar equipment, and the airplane can be covered in materials that absorb radar signals. Most conventional aircraft have a rounded shape. This shape makes them aerodynamic, but it also creates a very efficient radar reflector. The round shape means that no matter where the radar signal hits the plane, some of the signal gets reflected back. A stealth aircraft, on the other hand, is made up of completely flat surfaces and very sharp edges. When a radar signal hits a stealth plane, the signal reflects away at an angle. In addition, surfaces on a stealth aircraft can be treated so they absorb radar energy as well. The overall result is that a stealth aircraft can have the radar signature of a small bird rather than an airplane. The only exception is when the plane banks; there will often be a moment when one of the panels of the plane will perfectly reflect a burst of radar energy back to the antenna.

Mazur descended to 20,000 feet and finally to 10,000 upon approaching Van. He guided the plane to the lake and descended another 5,000 feet. Now he could be seen from the ground no matter what he did, but he would quickly unleash the payload and be out of there before anyone had time to react.

The Su-47 flew low over Akdabar Enterprises, and Mazur discerned the large steelworks building with its smokestacks, the airfield, and the numerous smaller buildings that appeared the size of bugs. Mazur set his sights on the big building first and fired two Kh-29s, one after the other. The recoil in the cockpit felt heavenly. The missiles hit their target—how could they miss?—and the plane pulled up as the explosions engulfed the space beneath it.

Mazur banked and came around for another pass. This time he aimed for the administrative buildings by the shore. The computer centered on the target and Mazur released the weapon. It was a direct hit, turning Tarighian's office structure into a mass of flames and rubble. The Tirma building was next on the list. He had strict instructions to be sure and hit the white colonial-style building. Mazur flew the plane over the lake, banked, and approached the target from behind the edifice. The fourth missile launched and hit the Tirma headquarters dead in the middle.

Mazur could see dozens of people running on the ground and congregating in the center courtyard. He didn't know if they were soldiers or civilians, and he didn't care. He shot missile number five directly into the courtyard, reducing Akdabar's payroll by at least forty percent.

The sixth missile went into a section of the big steelworks building that was still untouched by fire. Now the entire structure was demolished, collapsing in a fiery heap of blackened metal. Mazur fired his seventh missile into a row of smaller sheds, causing a fire to spread over the grassy open areas of the compound. Missile eight blew up the front gate and security checkpoint, where several guards attempted to shoot the plane out of the sky with pathetic handguns.

Mazur figured he was done. He still had two more missiles, but the compound was covered in black smoke. He couldn't see more targets if he tried. Mazur contacted the base and declared his mission accomplished.

Before he could turn and head north, the passive radar beeped a warning—something was in the air with him. According to the screen, four aircraft were approaching the site from the west.

What the hell?

Mazur banked over the lake again, turning so he could see what he was up against.

F-16C fighters from the Turkish Air Force—the Taktik Hava Kuweti Komutabligi—were zooming directly toward him. The 2nd TAF HQ in Diyarbakir had received word that an enemy aircraft with hostile intentions would be in Turkish airspace near Van. Unfortunately, the air force base at Mount Ararat housed only helicopters, so the fighters had to come from the next nearest base. By the time the orders were received and the fighters made ready, they were minutes too late—but not too late to stop the enemy from escaping.

Mazur gasped and pulled up, anxious to get away from them. He soared high and shot north over the lake, but the fighters stayed on his tail. The pilot hadn't prepared for a situation like this. He felt fear for the first time in his life.

Two warning alarms went off at once. The fighters had launched two AIM-9X Sidewinders.

Evasive action! Evasive action! Mazur struggled to keep calm and remember what he was supposed to do in an emergency, but the alarms were too loud. He couldn't concentrate. Panic overtook him as he forced the plane into a dive, hoping he could outmaneuver the missiles and lure them into the lake. The Su-47 dipped dangerously low, maybe 1,000 feet from the surface, before Mazur pulled up and leveled out. The Sidewinders attempted to correct their trajectories but failed. They hit the lake like meteors, exploding on contact. Two massive geyser-like splashes filled the sky, but ultimately produced no harm on the fighters' enemy.

Mazur ascended once again. Now it was simply a matter of outrunning the fighters. Before he could throttle the engines and shoot forward, the warning alarms sounded again. This time two more AIM-9Xs sliced through the air on a collision course with the plane. Mazur swerved and managed to dodge the first missile, but in doing so, he flew right in line with the second.

Unfortunately for Mazur, the Su-47 was a work-in-progress prototype and the heat exhaust suppression had not yet been perfected. A stealth plane with such a capability could have fooled a heat-seeking missile. The new AIM-9X, however, expanded the capabilities of older AIM-9 models by developing a new seeker imaging infrared focal plane array, a high performance airframe, and a new signal processor for the seeker/sensor. The Su-47 was a goner.

The impact jolted Mazur hard and he heard the explosion deep within his inner ears. He felt the aircraft drop in altitude dramatically, and the sky outside his windscreen was a blur. Warning alarms shrieked and lights flashed all around him, telling him that the plane was a goner.

Eject! Must eject! Mazur blindly grappled for the controls, unlocked the release switch, and pushed the eject button.

Nothing happened.

He struggled with the mechanism, cursing and crying. Was it a malfunction? Surely it couldn't be . . . sabotage?

Mazur didn't realize another Sidewinder was launched at the aircraft as it dived recklessly toward Lake Van. In one gigantic powerhouse of impact, the Su-47 and its pilot became a hundred thousand burning particles that flittered slowly down to the water.

TARIGHIAN had been away from his office for the last three hours, overseeing the installation of some replacement parts in the Phoenix. Albert Mertens had tested the targeting system that morning and found the weapon's accuracy was off by 6 degrees. That was unacceptable. Mertens swore he could correct the problem in six hours. When Tarighian entered his private office where he could fret and curse alone, he meant to try and relax. It had been a stressful week. He had a bad feeling about Mertens and didn't look forward to making good on the threat he had made. Tarighian had decided that the best thing would be to eliminate Mertens after the Phoenix had performed its function.

He sat at his desk and looked at his computer screen. An icon indicated that he had a dozen unread e-mails since yesterday. He checked the in-box and saw that the messages were mostly from his various committee heads. Not many other people knew his e-mail address.

One e-mail stood out, however. It was from "A Friend." Tarighian opened it, expecting a piece of spam advertising how to get a bigger penis or the latest deal in obtaining prescription drugs. What he saw instead took his mind off his worries about the Phoenix. A conversation he would find "interesting"? What could that possible be? He opened the attached file and listened to the recording. He immediately recognized the voice as belonging to Andrei Zdrok.

"General, where the hell are you? I see. Where's the plane? Yes, *our* plane, what did you think I—? Yes. I see. Listen, this is what I want you to do. I want to order an air strike on Akdabar Enterprises in Van, Turkey. Yes, I know what I'm doing. I have proof that the Shadows are double-crossing us. They never sent that money and have no intention to do so. And I know now they are responsible for what happened at the hangar in Baku. Yes. I just sent you an e-mail, did you get it? Well, check it, damn it! I'll wait."

There was a pause, after which the voice continued. "I'm still here. You have it? Listen to the file. I'll wait." Another pause and a cough. Then—"Well? You see? No, no, I just want to—General, this is not negotiable. These are my orders. Send the plane to Turkey and bomb the shit out of that facility. I want it done today. Right. Keep me informed. Thank you, General."

Tarighian felt as if his blood was boiling. Just to be certain that he wasn't dreaming, he played the file again.

As if on cue, the phone rang. He heard his voice shake when he spoke and he couldn't help it.

"Hello."

"It's me." Nadir Omar, his Military Committee head.

"Nadir, I'm so glad you called. I just had the strangest—"

"Are you sitting down?" Omar normally never interrupted Tarighian.

"Yes."

"Akdabar Enterprises has been destroyed."

Omar's words were worse than the recorded conversation. Tarighian felt the blood rush from his head.

"Are you there?" Omar asked.

Tarighian cleared his throat. "Yes."

"Did you hear what I said?"

"Yes. I . . . I know. I just heard about it."

"We don't know who did it. Or why. But the Turkish Air Force—"

"It was the Shop, Nadir. I have proof."

"What?"

"The Shop. They did it."

"No. I don't believe it."

Tarighian created a new e-mail, addressed it to Omar, attached the conversation file, and clicked Send. "I just sent you an e-mail. Listen to the attachment. Then forward it to the rest of the committees. I . . . I'm hanging up now. I need a few minutes to myself."

"What are we going to do?"

"Talk to me later." Tarighian hung up the phone and sat in his chair, stunned.

Twenty years of his life . . . up in smoke. The lives of his employees—how many were lost? It was too early to tell. Millions upon millions of dollars' worth of equipment and goods—gone in an instant.

Tarighian clenched his fists and cursed.

The *Shop* had done it. Zdrok had made good on his threats. The filthy Russian had started a war with his most influential customer. The Shadows would make him pay. For the sake of Allah and the future of Islam, the Shop would pay for this.

Tarighian was perfectly willing to use the Phoenix to exact revenge. The problem was that he had no idea where to aim. The Shop had many bases. He knew about the one in Baku, of course, and he knew that Zdrok owned a bank in Zurich. But how could he possibly damage the Shop with such a big weapon? It would be like hitting a tiny ant with a ten-ton weight. He had to think of something else.

Get hold of yourself! Think rationally!

Tarighian knew he had a job to do. He had to stay focused. Stay the course. Complete the goal that was originally set and then go after the Shop. No matter how traitorous the Shop had been, the true enemy was still the West. The Puppet Iraq and its overseer, the United States, must fall. The Shop could wait. They were peanuts. He wasn't about to waste the Phoenix on the Shop.

There was one problem, though. The Turkish authorities would wonder why Akdabar Enterprises had been destroyed. They would investigate possible motives for such an attack and look more closely into Namik Basaran's background. His true identity could be uncovered. The intelligence forces of the entire world would then focus on Basaran, aka Tarighian, and eventually trace him to Northern Cyprus.

For the sake of Allah, they had to hurry! The United Nations could come sweeping down on them within hours.

He picked up the intercom and punched in the code for Mertens. When the physicist answered, Tarighian said, "The Phoenix will rise in twelve hours. Sooner if possible. That's an order. Make it happen or you will face a firing squad."

_32_

LIEUTENANT Colonel Irving Lambert wiped the sweat from his brow as he hurried from the Operations Room to the conference room where his team was assembled. Like the others in Third Echelon's Washington, D.C., office, he had been up all night. None of them had received much sleep the past couple of days. Sometimes it got to be like that.

For an hour he had been on the phone with the secretary of defense, who had coordinated the attack on the stealth plane with Turkey. The fact that the fighters had been minutes too late to stop the destruction of Akdabar Enterprises was a political wrinkle that would be smoothed over as soon as the truth about Namik Basaran was confirmed. At any rate, the Turkish government was understandably skeptical about the NSA's claims. Furthermore, Turkey wanted to involve the United Nations in any further actions against Basaran if indeed he was really the terrorist supporter Nasir Tarighian. That was going to take time.

But Lambert was convinced that Tarighian was in possession of some kind of large weapon in Cyprus. He didn't know what it was, but the presence of Albert Mertens, the physicist who had been Gerard Bull's right-hand man, indicated that it was a weapon of mass destruction.

Third Echelon had to act alone for now.

He looked at his watch as he entered the conference room. Since it was early morning in Washington, it would be late afternoon for Fisher. He'd be arriving at the Dhekelia garrison in the Republic of Cyprus—the southern portion—about now. Lambert knew he shouldn't let personal feelings interfere with the job at hand, but he couldn't help worrying about his best Splinter Cell. As the team in Washington was able to monitor all incoming and outgoing communications on Fisher's OPSAT, they were aware of Sarah Burns's situation as soon as Sam was. Lambert considered pulling Sam out. He had spoken to Fisher and assured him they would work around the clock to try and locate Sarah, but Sam had a job to do. Fisher was beside himself, insisting that he needed to be in Israel to find her, but Lambert was forced to order him to stick with the mission. Tarighian would be a desperate man at this point and was liable to do anything with whatever weapon he had in his hands. Fisher reluctantly obeyed, but it might have been at the cost of the friendly relationship with his boss.

"Morning, Chief," Carl Bruford said.

"Morning, everyone," Lambert replied. Along with Bruford, the team included Carly St. John, Research Analyst Mike Chan, and Chip Driggers, who had the catchall title of logistics coordinator. Mike Chan was roughly the same age as Bruford and specialized in cryptography.

Driggers was in his forties, an army buddy of Lambert's who had been recruited for his painstakingly compulsive eye for detail.

Lambert sat and looked at Bruford. "What have you got?"

Bruford cleared his throat and said, "Our man in Chicago went to Sarah Burns's apartment in Evanston. It's on Foster Street, not far from the university. He got the super to let him in. The first thing he did was to take a look at her computer. He found several e-mails to and from a boy named Eli Horowitz, who lives in Jerusalem. From what we gather, this guy's a former boyfriend or maybe he still is one. That's not certain. At any rate, they made plans to meet up in Jerusalem. We know she went to Israel with her friend Rivka Cohen, whose parents haven't seen Sarah since . . . well, last Thursday."

Lambert and the rest of the team were fully aware of what had happened to Sarah's friend.

"Go on," Lambert said.

"Okay, we started looking into this Eli Horowitz. He's twenty-three years old and is an Israeli citizen. He was a student at Northwestern University last year, and we assume that's how he met Sarah. He was enrolled as a music major, but his grades sucked. Immigration came after him in late spring last year because his student visa had expired . . . and get this—he's on a terrorist watch list with the Department of Homeland Security."

"Shit," Lambert said.

"Anyway, with those two strikes—expired visa and his name on a list—he was immediately deported."

"Known associates?" Lambert asked.

"A Noel Brooks was at Northwestern the same year and the two were roommates. Brooks is also Israeli and was deported at the same time as Horowitz. He wasn't on the terrorist watch list, but his visa had expired. Other than him, we have no other information on known associates."

"Is there any mention in the e-mails of where this guy lives?"

"No. Only that he lives in Jerusalem and that he was going to show Sarah the sights when she got there. I think she's pretty intimate with the guy. Some of those e-mails were . . . suggestive."

Lambert sighed. "Okay, it's a start. Get onto tracing Horowitz's movements after his deportation. We have to find out where he lives *today* and get the Israeli National Police to bring him in for questioning. Or should we ask the Security Police to be involved?"

"I'll find out."

"Get on it. It's tedious, I know, but it's the only lead we've got." Lambert looked at Chip Driggers and asked, "Have you heard from Fisher?"

"Not since he left Tel Aviv. I expect him in Cyprus any minute," Driggers said. "I've arranged with the British military there to supply him with diving equipment and anything else he might need. Shouldn't be a problem."

"And what about our friends in Zurich and Baku?"

"We've alerted the Azerbaijan and Swiss authorities as well as Interpol and our own FBI. The local law enforcement agencies are preparing raids as we speak. We should know something by lunchtime. I'm afraid, though, that the Turkish air strike on the Shop's stealth plane most likely tipped them off that the jig was up. They could be long gone by now."

"Yeah, I know, it was a risk," Lambert said. "I hope the Azeris and Swiss understand the gravity of the situation and realize who these people are."

"I believe they do, Colonel."

Lambert nodded and then looked at Carly. "And what have you got for me?" he asked.

She shrugged. "I'm just trying to find out everything I can about that shopping mall in Cyprus. I'm mapping routes to the place from Famagusta, pinpointing the best spot for Sam to go ashore, that kind of thing. I want to have everything he'll need ready to go in an hour or two."

"Good. Well, we have work to do, people. Let's get it done."

"Sir?"

"Yes, Carly?"

"What about the fallout with the Turks? Hasn't our government been able to convince them that Namik Basaran is really Nasir Tarighian?"

"No. That's why we can't go to the police in northern Cyprus to help us. If they knew we were planning to possibly muck up their new shopping mall, they'd probably fight on Basaran's side even if they know the truth about him. I'm afraid the secretary of defense—and the president—have ruled out letting the Turks in on what we want to do. They're not happy about what happened to Akdabar Enterprises in Van. In hindsight I guess it wasn't a good move on our part."

"Hell, we got the Shop's stealth plane," Bruford said. "That counts for something."

"True, but now they see Tarighian—or rather, Basaran—as a victim. One of their respected businessmen and philanthropists was irrationally attacked by a Russian terrorist organization. That's how they see it."

"I'll try to put together a convincing presentation you can give to them," Carly said.

"That might help, Carly. Thanks."

With that, the meeting adjourned. Lambert went back to his office, eyed the large electronic map on the wall,

and focused on the current trouble spots lit in red—
outside of Famagusta in Cyprus, Jerusalem, Baku, and
Zurich.

He hoped he could diminish the priority of these four
places by the end of the day.

ANDREI Zdrok hadn't worked so hard in years.

He carried the box of file folders out of the bank, loaded
them in the back of the Mercedes, and went back inside. He
and his driver, Erik, had been at it for the past two hours.
Zdrok didn't dare tell the bank staff what was happening.
When the authorities arrived, they would have to deal with
it on their own. If he could clear out his office of any incriminating evidence, then the bank employees shouldn't
have any problems other than perhaps a night in an interrogation room. And if they were detained, well, tough luck.

Zdrok looked at his Rolex and saw that it was getting
late. When Erik passed him with another box, he said,
"Hurry. We have to leave." Erik nodded and said, "There's
only one more box."

"I'll get it," Zdrok replied. He went through the lobby
and was suddenly confronted by Gustav Gomelsky, the
bank's assistant manager and the man who really ran
everything.

"Andrei," he said, "I demand to know what's going on.
Why are you doing this?"

"Gustav, I don't have time to explain it to you. You'll
find out soon enough." Zdrok attempted to push past him,
but Gomelsky grabbed him by the arm.

"Are we in some kind of trouble?"

Zdrok stopped and stared at the man. Softly but with
menace, he whispered, "Get your hand off of me."

Gomelsky swallowed and released his boss. He had always been a little afraid of Andrei Zdrok because he knew so little about the man. "Sorry, sir, I was just—"

"I'm leaving this office and relocating," Zdrok said. "That's all you need to know for now. I'll be in touch." Fat chance, Zdrok thought to himself.

"What about the police investigation?" Gomelsky asked.

"What do you mean?"

"The break-in! The other night. Your safe was blown, remember?"

"Oh, that." Zdrok had practically forgotten about it.

"The inspector will want to know where you went. The case is still under investigation, you know."

"Tell him I'm away on business."

"Don't you think he'll be suspicious that you cleaned out your office? Andrei, you're putting us in a very awkward position."

Zdrok lost his temper, grabbed the man by his jacket, and got into his face. "*Shut. The. Fuck. Up!*" He released Gomelsky and shoved him away. "Deal with it and leave me alone," he said.

Zdrok went on past the teller windows into the back and to the remains of his office. It was a shambles. He and Erik had torn out the computer, the files, emptied the desk and the blown-out safe, and the phone. Antipov was doing the same thing in the Zurich branch and Zdrok wished he could be there to oversee it. Antipov was thorough, but Zdrok liked to make sure nothing was missed. If he could clone himself, he would do it.

How long would it be before the authorities arrived? Zdrok was certain that it would be no later than tomorrow.

Those goddamned terrorists. The so-called Shadows, Nasir Tarighian and his band of religious fanatics. Why did *they* have to be the Shop's best customers? They had compromised the Shop's cover, and now Zdrok was faced with having to reorganize under a different, unknown camouflage in another country.

And what was the cost? Zdrok had no idea what it was, but he knew it was going to be in the billions. The loss of the stealth plane was a huge blow, but having to relinquish the two banks was a disaster. The very worst part was leaving his chateau on Lake Zurich. He'd never make it back to his home to retrieve his personal belongings. Zdrok had to abandon the place and everything in it. A fucking eight-million-dollar write-off and there was nothing he could do about it. Christ, the *automobiles*! He had forgotten all about them. His beloved collection! And his precious yacht! At least he was fairly certain he had left nothing incriminating in the chateau. It was simply the home of an eccentric banker who had expensive tastes.

Zdrok clenched his fists and shook them at the ceiling.

Someone would pay for all this. Andrei Zdrok swore, then and there, that once he had reestablished the Shop in a new location and regrouped, he would exact revenge on the parties that set this catastrophe in motion—namely the United States of America.

33

I'M not happy.

My daughter is in jeopardy and needs me. I'm up against a mad religious fanatic who finances terrorism and is intent on causing some kind of mass destruction. I'm on a British military base on an island in the Mediterranean, and I have to perform a job I don't particularly feel like doing. I'll be the first to admit I'm distracted. For me the first priority is to go find Sarah. For my country the first priority is to stop the mad religious fanatic. The only thing I can hope for is that I finish the country's assignment in record time so I can tackle the personal one as soon as possible.

Cyprus. It's a beautiful place, but it's rife with tension. Back in 1963 some British officer drew a green line across the island's map when violence broke out between the Greek and Turkish Cypriots. The United Nations tried to keep the peace along what has since been referred to as—surprise—the "Green Line." Then, in 1974, the Greek government attempted a coup, and the Turks responded by invading and occupying the area north of the Green Line. Today, the United Nations recognizes only the Greek Cypriot side, the Republic of Cyprus. The so-called Turkish Republic of Northern Cyprus is not recognized by any nation other than Turkey. It's a situation that has provoked a great deal of mistrust and conflict ever since.

Britain maintains important military bases in the southern portion of the island. In fact, the British Sovereign Base Areas cover about three percent of the island's land. The Royal Air Force occupies the Western Sovereign Base Area in the Episkopi Garrison and the Akrotiri airfield. I'm over on the eastern side, in the Dhekelia Garrison. Because Cyprus was once a British crown colony, these areas remained under the UK's jurisdiction when the Treaty of Establishment created the independent Republic of Cyprus in 1960.

The army presence at Dhekelia consists of sixty-two Cyprus Support Squadron Royal Engineers and sixteen Flight Army Air Corps (equipped with Gazelle helicopters). There are also a variety of supporting arms such as the Royal Logistics Corps, Royal Army Medical Corps, Royal Electrical and Mechanical Engineers, Royal Military Police and others located in both Sovereign Base Areas. Dhekelia, also known as a "cantonment," is home to a total British population of just over 2,000 people.

It seems to me to be a fairly cushy assignment for the Brit soldiers. Dhekelia is on the northern shore of the wide sweeping Larnaca Bay and is situated some 15km northeast of the important coastal town of Larnaca and 20km west of Ayia Napa, the premier tourist resort for the club music scene in the Eastern Mediterranean. Dhekelia Cantonment has an abundance of sporting and recreational facilities, with the emphasis, naturally, on water sports. When I arrived by military transport, I could see some die-hard skiers in the bay getting in some last-minute thrills before sunset.

Captain Peter Martin, a proper British soldier in his thirties, escorts me to the mess, where I am fed a fine meal of roast chicken, mashed potatoes, and asparagus. A good Western meal would hit the spot and I'm starving. Captain Martin sits and briefs me on his orders and how he plans to proceed in helping me.

"I'm to take you out in a boat after nightfall," he says. "We'll sail around Cape Pyle and Cape Gkreko and then turn north up the coast. After three miles or so I'll stop and let you out. You'll swim another half-mile or so underwater to the Famagusta harbor, where you'll go ashore and make your way to the shopping mall site. Once you're out of the boat, we have no knowledge of your being anywhere near Cyprus. You'll have to make your way back across the border by sea. I'll give you my mobile number. When you're ashore I'll come and collect you. If I don't hear from you, then I'll have to assume that you've either found another way off the island or that you're dead. Is that clear?"

"Clear and very blunt," I answer.

"We'll fit you with some SCUBA gear. We can't give you the best stuff; we need that for our own men. It will be spare equipment, fairly old, but I assure you that it's in good working condition. If you're able to bring it back, we would appreciate it. If not, don't worry about it."

"Thank you for that," I say, swallowing my last bite of chicken. "As long as the tanks are full."

"I guarantee that you'll have the same quality air that we do," the captain says, smiling.

"What do you know about the shopping mall? Surely you've done some recon on the site?" I ask.

"We have indeed and I can honestly tell you that it looks completely legit. They've been working on it for three years, and not once have we seen anything remotely suspicious."

I have nothing to say to that. I find it difficult to believe that Tarighian is really building a shopping mall for Turkish Cypriots when he devotes the rest of his energy financing the Shadows' directives to kill and maim as many non-Muslims as they can.

After dinner Captain Martin takes me to the army's diving club, which overlooks gorgeous Larnaca Bay. I ask the captain if Cyprus is good for tourism, and he tells me that it's a fabulous vacation spot. When the Greek and Turkish Cypriots behave themselves, Cyprus is a fantastic island paradise.

"Actually the Turkish side of the island is even prettier," he says. "Mostly Turks and people from other Muslim countries visit the north. Everyone else comes to the south."

Captain Martin gives me a single tank, an MK2Plus regulator, a Glide 500 buoyancy compensator device, a Smart-Pro wrist computer, Twin Speed adjustable fins, a standard weight belt, and a frameless face mask. Everything fits nicely over my uniform, which will keep me warm enough, but I'll have to fasten the Osprey on my chest. Martin also gives me a small Diver Propulsion Device—a portable hand-held mechanism that propels a diver by dragging him through the water. This saves the diver's strength. I'm ready to go, but first I need to check in with Lambert.

I try my implant first. "Colonel, are you there?"

"I'm here, Sam. I take it you're in Cyprus?"

"Roger that. Everything's proceeding according to plan. They're treating me well."

"Glad to hear it."

"What have you found out about Sarah, Colonel?"

"Sam, we're doing everything we can to find her. Listen to me, now. You've got to let us handle this. There's still a good forty-eight hours or more before they expect you to be in Jerusalem. We have a lead on a suspect, and we're following up on that."

This is good news. "Who is it?"

"Sam, it's a bit premature—"

"Goddamn it, Colonel, this is my *daughter* we're talking about." Needless to say, I'm a little pissed off. "If you want me to keep my mind off her and on this job here, then you'd better tell me everything you know."

"Right, Sam. I'm sorry. There's this boyfriend. Do you know about him?"

I have to think to remember his name. "A boy from Israel, isn't he?"

"Yes. Name of Eli Horowitz."

"That's him. Yeah, I remember Sarah mentioning him. What about him? Is *he* the suspect?"

"She made plans to meet up with him in Jerusalem. We checked him out, and we learned that he was deported from the U.S. last year for an expired student visa. And for being on a terrorist watch list."

"Oh, shit," I say. I don't care who hears me.

"We're trying to find him as we speak. We've got people in Jerusalem hunting him down right now."

"What about Sarah's friend? The one she went with to Israel . . . what's her name? Rivka."

I hear Lambert sigh. When he does this, I know I'm not going to like what he has to say. "Sam, Rivka Cohen's dead. She was found in an alley in East Jerusalem, strangled to death."

"Oh, for God's sake, Colonel!" I'm losing my mind here. I want to pick up something and smash it to pieces. "I can't be here, Colonel. I've got to go to Israel *now*."

"Sam, you don't have the resources that we do. Believe me, we're in a better position to find Sarah than you are."

"It's *me* they want, Colonel. My daughter is just the bait."

"That's exactly why I can't let you go yet. Please, Sam. You have a job to do there, and we need you to do it. I know this sounds horrible, but you've got to forget about her for now."

I suck in a breath and say, "All right, Colonel. I'll do your little errand tonight, but come tomorrow morning I'm going to Israel—no matter where I am or what I'm doing. I'm picking up and leaving this fucking island, and I'm going to find my daughter. Do I make myself clear?"

I can't believe I just spoke to my commanding officer that way. But then again, I don't hold a military rank. Colonel Lambert is really just my *supervisor* and I'm his employee. It's not the same thing.

"I understand, Sam," Lambert says. "I don't blame you."

That calms me down a bit. "Thanks, Colonel. Sorry. I, er, got a little carried away."

"Don't worry about it. Just do what you have to do tonight and let us know what you find out."

We sign off and I look out the window at the bay. The sunset casts a bloodred spill over the choppy surface, and I wonder if that means anything.

At ten o'clock, well after dark, we board what's called a Rigid Raider—a fast patrol craft with a fiberglass reinforced plastic hull and a single 140-horsepower outboard motor. It's normally used to patrol harbors and inland waterways. The thing holds about eight or nine guys, and the captain tells me there's an even larger version of the Rigid Raider that holds up to twenty men. On this particular voyage a pilot and a private join the captain and me. From what I can tell, they know nothing about my mission. I imagine they're just following the captain's orders.

The pilot keeps the speed down so as not to attract too much attention. It's not uncommon to see these patrol boats at all times of the day or night, but I figure they think it's best that we keep a low profile. The boat moves along past Cape Pyle and then around the easternmost tip, Cape Gkreko. The water seems choppier here, and the captain tells me that there are strong currents on this side of the island. He wants to get me as close as possible to the Green Line because it's going to be a strenuous swim.

I can see the lights of Famagusta from here. The captain tells me to get ready and he helps me with the BCD and tank. The pilot turns off all the lights on the boat and cuts the engine down to a quiet putter.

"This is your stop," the captain says. He holds out his hand and I shake it.

"Thanks for everything," I say.

"Thank me when I pick you up in the morning." He doesn't say *if* he picks me up in the morning.

I put on the fins, lower the face mask, secure the SC-20K on my back, and I'm good to go. I climb over the side while holding on to the ladder, insert the regulator into my mouth, hold on to the DPD, and dive backward into the cold, dark water.

34

THE captain was right about the strong currents, but the DPD prevents the swim from becoming a struggle. I forge ahead, allowing the device to pull me along at a speed of roughly a knot per hour. I figure I can climb out of the water near the docks and use the moored boats as cover. I seriously doubt there will be much activity there at this time of night.

The DPD's headlight casts a ghostly glow on the floor, and I can see masses of brightly colored coral shelves and an abundance of fish. Not being much of a fisherman, I can't identify them, but I know none of them are dangerous. Apparently there are no sharks in the Mediterranean, but barracuda have been known to take bites out of swimmers. Moray eels are also nasty creatures that are a must to avoid. At any rate, what I see here would fit nicely inside a restaurant aquarium.

The computer tells me I swam a distance of three-quarters of a mile when I finally see the wooden posts supporting the Famagusta docks. The water is dirtier here as a result of pollution from the dozens of moored boats. I surface with just my face above the water so I can evaluate the situation.

There are boats of all sizes—catamarans, motorboats, sailboats, several small yachts—and a brightly lit boardwalk. I see a lone night watchman in a shed on the boardwalk. The Turkish Republic of Northern Cyprus flag flies on a tall flagpole that's next to the shed.

This is easy. I swim to the dock and follow the edge to the shore. When I'm able to touch bottom I crawl up, remove my fins, and climb out of the water into the shadows. I avoid the boardwalk altogether and make my way up a concrete slope to level land. This is where I'm most vulnerable to being seen, so I quickly skirt into a grove of trees that abuts the docks. I get lucky and find a water drainage pipe built into the ground where I can store my SCUBA gear. The sky is clear and I don't expect rain, so the stuff should be safe nestled inside the pipe. I strip off the tank, BCD, and other gear and leave it. I retrieve my headset and goggles from my Osprey and I'm ready.

It's a three-mile hike to Famagusta Center. Since I'm keeping to the shadows and avoiding streetlights, it takes me nearly an hour to get there. Now it's nearly three in the morning and I have two, maybe three hours before dawn.

The property is in a clearing outside of Famagusta, just off the main highway. At the moment a wire fence surrounds the grounds. Signs written in Turkish and English read: Keep Out—Construction Hard Hat Area. Other signs proclaim—Famagusta Center, Opening Soon! Vendor Space For Rent! The place is well lit with floodlights, trucks carrying debris periodically leave a loading dock area at the back of the complex, and men in hard hats go in and out of various entrances. That's a clue right there that something's afoot—construction employees normally don't work in the middle of the night. These guys appear to be working feverishly to meet some kind of deadline. Lambert's probably right—Tarighian means to use his weapon as soon as possible.

I'm unable to see an area of the fence that's not covered by the bright lights. I'm beginning to wonder how the hell I'm going to get inside when providence intervenes. A pair of headlights appears on the road near where I'm crouched, and they're headed my way. When it's close enough I see that it's a professional electrical company's van, and there's a lone driver inside. The van passes me, not traveling very fast, so I jump up and toss a rock at it. As the van slows I run behind it and slap the back doors a couple of times, loud enough for the driver to hear me. He slows even more and stops. When he lowers the window, I'm there with the Five-seveN pointing at his nose.

"You're going my way," I say. "Can I have a lift?"

He doesn't understand the words, but he gets the meaning. I keep the gun trained on him, walk around the front of the vehicle, and get in the passenger side. I tell him to drive on as I crouch on the floorboard, my pistol stuck against his potbelly. He's obviously frightened and I tell him to calm down. He nods and proceeds.

We get to the gate, where he stops the van and lowers the window. The guard there asks him something in Turkish and the driver replies, reaching for a clipboard on the passenger seat. He shows the guard the front page on the clipboard, and we're cleared to go through. I take the opportunity to rise and peer through the windshield. I see a parking area where several vendor and construction vehicles are stationed, so I point him over there. As soon as he parks the van and shuts it off, I get in the seat beside him, motion him closer, then conk him on the back of the head.

"Sorry," I say, but he doesn't hear me. I lay him on the

floorboard, look to see if anyone is watching, take the keys, and then get out of the van.

There seem to be several public entrances to the building made up of glass doors that are most likely locked at this time. The workers and guards are using the loading dock I saw earlier. This appears to be for a major department store, the biggest vendor in the complex. I want to avoid the heavy traffic areas and find another way in, so I opt for a set of glass doors. I scan the lightpoles for security cameras and see none—but that doesn't mean there aren't any. I'm afraid I have to be a little reckless at this point. I'm running out of time and I want to get in and get out as quickly as possible. So what do I do? I walk out into the light, head for one of the public entrances, and use my lock picks to get inside.

No one sees me that I know of.

I'm inside the building. The lights are off here in a main corridor that passes through the shopping center. Empty storefronts line the sides of the hallway, and I find it odd that none of them are named yet. For a mall that's set to "open" soon, from what I can see there are no real stores inside.

I move toward the central core of the mall, a wide open space that connects three wings and a passage to the un-named, big department store. Overhead is the huge domed ceiling, and there seems to be a line on the underside dividing it into halves. A few lights are on here, so I hug the walls and try to use natural cover to mask my movements. Then I hear the sound of a motorized vehicle in one of the other dark wings, so I crouch and wait for it to come into view. It turns out to be one of those three-wheeled golf carts like the ones they used at Akdabar Enterprises in Turkey. Two guys dressed in security guard uniforms are inside.

The cart rolls past me, headed for the department store wing. It's now or never, so I make my move. I run and chase the back of the cart, jump onto the back end, and surprise the two guards. Before they can react and say, "Hey!" I slam their heads together. One guy goes out, but the other one must have a hard head. He leaps out of his seat at me, pushing me flat onto the back of the vehicle. It continues to move forward but swerves for a wall. The guard hits me hard in the face, producing a star-filled slate in front of my eyes, but I bring up my knee in a classic Krav Maga below-the-belt crotch crunch. This causes my opponent to freeze with shock and pain.

At that moment the cart crashes into the wall. It's a good thing it wasn't traveling at a very high speed, or it might have attracted some attention. Instead it makes a dull *thud*, and my happy nemesis flies off me and smashes into the steering wheel. I rise and punch him hard in the jaw and he's out, like his friend.

Neither guard is armed, but I relieve one of them of a security keycard. I imagine it will come in handy at some point.

I creep into the dark department store, which is— surprise, surprise—empty. But on one wall there's a double door that looks like a big elevator. Of course, now I see what this place is. It's not a department store at all but some kind of staging area. Supplies and stuff are brought in through the loading dock and taken to this double door—which I assume is the main entrance to whatever it is that Tarighian's hiding. I start to move toward it, but I hear footsteps in the darkness near the loading dock area. I wait until I see two guards walk out of the shadows and to the double door. One of them inserts a keycard, the doors open, and they go in.

When the doors close, I run across the floor and use the stolen keycard to open them.

I nearly gasp aloud when I see what's on the other side. There's a long ramp sloping to a brightly lit underground level that's full of workers. I leap to the side, out of the doorway, and roll to a position behind a stack of crates. I *think* no one saw me. They're all too busy, like worker bees preparing the nest for the honey harvest. From here, though, I have a better chance to look around and comprehend what I see.

Quite literally, it takes my breath away.

It's a goddamned missile silo. Or something like that. The level I'm on is really a circular, perimeter "balcony" that looks down onto the lower level, much like a rotunda. In the middle of the bottom floor sits a gigantic cannon-like apparatus made of alloy and steel. The base appears to be about a hundred feet square and looks as if it weighs a few tons. Surrounding the base is a massive mechanism of hydraulics that raises and lowers the weapon. The cannon-barrel is about 100 meters long, several meters thick, and sits perpendicular to the ground floor, pointing straight up. The thing probably raises from a deep well in the ground so that it extends the full length into the air.

My God! I suddenly realize what it is! I *recognize* it! I remember seeing pictures of the original designs, back when Gerard Bull attempted to develop one of these things for Iraq in the 1980s.

It's a Babylon supergun, complete and ready for use. The shopping mall is nothing but the enclosure for the weapon. When they want to fire it, I imagine the supergun is raised to the ground level, where it sits in that central, empty space beneath the domed ceiling. The two halves of the dome separate, like an observatory, and the barrel extends into the sky as far as it will go.

Incredible! No, it's fucking *fantastic*! I have to admit I'm impressed. The thing is absolutely beautiful. It's the sleekest, most awesome weapon I've ever seen in my life.

Now I realize what those blueprints were that I saw in Tarighian's office in Turkey. Albert Mertens, Gerard Bull's right-hand man, designed this thing. And it's a jaw-dropping masterpiece.

From what I remember of Bull's original Babylon supergun and what it's able to do, this version looks very similar. I'm guessing here, but I'd say that's a 1000mm gun that utilizes tons of propellant to fire a humongous projectile over a range of up to 1,000 kilometers.

I immediately snap some pictures of it with my OPSAT and then type a text message to Lambert. I tell him what I've found and that I'm going to try and sabotage the thing. At any rate, he needs to get the United Nations, or NATO, or whoever the hell he can persuade to help out, over here as soon as possible and bomb the *shit* out of the place before Tarighian has a chance to use it. From the looks of all the activity, it's pretty damned close.

Sheesh. Sabotage the thing. How am I going to do that? The only weapons I've got with me are the frag grenades and my SC-20K. That'll be like flicking paper clips at an armored tank.

Maybe the best thing is to set the grenades to go off in a bit, perhaps cause a diversion, and give me time to get the hell out of here. I can only hope Lambert will come through with the big guns. I reach into the Osprey and pull out a grenade, set it to go off in forty-five minutes, and place it out of sight but very near the double doors.

I begin to move slowly around the perimeter of the upper balcony. Whenever I find a good spot, I place another frag grenade and set it to go off simultaneously with the first one. I continue to do this all the way around the balcony, which thankfully is devoid of workers. They're all down below, hurrying like mad to finish whatever they're doing.

When I'm on the opposite side of the balcony from the double doors, I see the bright windows of the control room. It's a bunker built into the floor that's probably made to withstand the supergun's huge recoil. Several men are inside the control room, and I recognize one of them—Namik Basaran, aka Nasir Tarighian, looking out a window at his baby.

I make my way around, placing three more frag grenades, and now I'm ready to disappear. Sarah Burns, darling, here I come. I head for the double doors and prepare to use the keycard to open them—but I hear my OP-SAT beep quietly. A message is coming through from Lambert. It reads—

U.N. FORCES ON THEIR WAY. GET OUT NOW!

You don't have to tell me twice, Colonel. I raise the keycard, ready to slip it through the slot, when suddenly the doors open. Four armed guards are standing there, and I'm caught with my thumb up my ass.

One of them sees me—and my strange alien uniform—and shouts. Before they can react, I bolt through them, shoving the two inner guys apart. They fall into the outer guys, knocking them to the floor. I run like a madman as I hear more shouting behind me. A gun fires and a bullet whistles past my head. I begin countermaneuvers of zigzagging and bouncing off the walls like a pinball to make myself less of a target.

Then the alarm sounds. As they say, all hell breaks loose.

I run into one of the wings containing nonexistent stores and head for the exit, the one I came in. When I'm about forty feet from the doors I see two guards on the other side of the glass. I pause long enough to swing the SC-20K off my shoulder, unlock the safety, and blast away, shattering the glass and killing the men. I barge forward like a bull, ready to smash through the remaining shards of glass, but a volley of gunfire behind me forces me to hit the floor. I roll to the wall and try my best to squeeze as close as I can to it, but the bullets are frighteningly near. The rifle's still in my hands, so I let loose a barrage of rounds at my pursuers while lying on my back. I hit two of them, but the others jump for cover. This gives me the seconds I need to jump up and run through the broken glass doors. A shard cuts into my uniform at the shoulder, ripping the outer layer and opening a water tube. I fall to the ground outside the complex, roll, and leap to my feet without breaking the momentum of my progress.

The parking lot is clear. I'm almost free.

I run to the electrical van, pull open the door, and find that my buddy is no longer on the floorboard. What the hell, forget him. I put the key in the ignition and start it up, ready to throw it into reverse and tear out of the parking lot.

The cold metal of a gun barrel presses against the back of my neck.

I look in the rearview mirror and see my old friend the electrician behind me. He says something in Turkish and he doesn't look too happy. I guess I must have hurt his head earlier and it's payback time. I slowly raise my hands and he relieves me of my SC-20K. He then opens the panel door and tosses my gun to the ground just as a dozen of Tarighian's armed guards surround the van.

35

"**MR**. Fisher," Tarighian says as they march me into the control room. "Is spying on my facility a part of your Interpol report?"

"As a matter of fact, it is," I reply. I know it sounds lame, but I can't think of anything else to say.

I scan the room to see what my opposition consists of. Besides Tarighian and the three guards holding me, I see Farid the bodyguard and Albert Mertens busy at a desk with another man. The odds would be pretty fair if I didn't have my hands tied behind my back. They've also taken my Osprey, my headset and goggles, my weapons, and emptied all my pockets.

If looks could kill, Farid's expression says it all. He's obviously put two and two together and figured out I'm the one who broke his arm. I give him a smile and a wink.

Tarighian looks at me with those cold, brown eyes. "You should have stayed in Lake Van, Mr. Fisher. That's where I thought you ended up."

"Sorry to disappoint you."

"You know, when I turn you over to my men, they will murder you and videotape it at the same time. They'll upload the tape on an Islamic Web site and the whole world—and all of America—will see you beheaded. You *are* American, are you not? You're not Swiss, like you said."

I don't answer.

"I assure you that if I had the time I could make you talk. But I'm in a bit of a hurry. I fear I'll have to expedite your sentence and make sure you're no longer a threat to me before I begin this morning's operation."

"And what might that be?" I ask. I hope to appeal to his ego. "That's an impressive-looking machine out there. What's it do?"

Tarighian's eyes flickered and he moved to the window. "It is lovely, isn't it? I call it the Babylon Phoenix. The Babylon because it's a reimagining of Gerard Bull's supergun that was designed for Iraq in the 1980s, and the Phoenix because it has been reborn from the ashes of its ancestor."

Hearing the mention of his creation, Mertens looks up and smiles at me.

"This is your doing, I gather?" I ask him.

The Belgian ignores me, but Tarighian answers for him. "Yes, Professor Mertens did an excellent job. To my specifications, of course."

"What's your game, Tarighian? What are you going to do?"

Upon hearing his real name, the man smiles at me. "You know who I am. I was afraid of that. Who do you work for, Fisher? The CIA? The FBI?"

"The NSA, not that it matters."

He shrugs. "No, it doesn't matter. You will be dead within the hour." He gestures toward the supergun and says, "The Babylon Phoenix utilizes nine tons of special supergun propellant that can fire a 600 kilogram projectile over a range of approximately 1,000 kilometers."

"That's what Bull's supergun was supposed to be able to do."

"Yes. Alternatively, I could launch a 200-kilogram object into orbit with the assistance of a 2,000-kilogram rocket. The barrel, when fully extended, is 156 meters long with a one-meter bore. The launch tube is 30 centimeters thick at the breech, tapering to 6.5 centimeters at the exit. Like the V-3, the gun is built in segments. Twenty-six six-meter-long sections make up the barrel, totaling 1,510 tons. Added to this are four 220-ton recoil cylinders and the 165-ton breech. The reinforcement around the breech is fifty feet of solid concrete, steel, and rock. From our base here in Cyprus, we can hit any target in the Middle East we wish."

"But it's crazy," I say. "You shoot the thing once and you'll have the entire world on top of you in no time."

"You're right," he answers.

"You only want to fire it once?"

"Yes. Once is all I need."

"And what, may I ask, is your target?"

"I'm afraid you will go to your death not knowing that," Tarighian says.

"Then can you tell me what kind of payload you're firing?"

Tarighian scratches his chin and says, "Why not? I'm using a 600-kilogram MOAB, or as you call it, a Massive Ordnance Airburst Bomb. I think you know what this can accomplish?"

I knew what he was talking about. It's similar to our CBU-72 Fuel-Air Explosive. It's an incendiary, advanced cluster bomb carrying ethylene gas that explodes in the air, creating a fireball and explosive wave that spreads quickly over a much greater area than traditional explosives. The aftereffects of the explosion are very similar to those of small nuclear bombs but without the radiation. It's a nasty, deadly device. Talk about a weapon of mass destruction—this is certainly it.

"You're evil," I mutter. Tarighian's eyes flare and he approaches me. He turns his head slightly, as if he's preparing to strike me, but instead he spits a glob of phlegm at me. It hits me in the face and dribbles down my cheek.

"That's what I think of America," he says. He moves away and addresses Mertens. "Begin the calibration. It's time."

Mertens nods and picks up a phone. After a moment he says, "Begin calibration. Raise the Phoenix."

Six seconds later the control room shakes and a loud hum reverberates throughout the complex. Through the windows I see the ceiling part and slide away, revealing the dome two levels above. The supergun and its heavy platform begin to rise on a hydraulic lift toward the ground floor above us.

Tarighian, satisfied that everything is working properly, turns to me and addresses the guards. "He's seen enough. Take him to the incinerator room and kill him."

Farid grunts and makes a face at Tarighian. "I'm sorry, Farid," he says. "I need you with me. Perhaps you'd like to hurt him a little right here?"

The brute smiles like an ogre. Even though his good arm is in a cast, I'm sure his other one can pack a wallop as well. The guards hold me steady as Farid faces me. He raises his free arm, makes a fist, pulls it back, and puts his entire weight into a punch that nearly knocks my head off.

For a moment I hear a ringing in my ears and see nothing but bright lights. A tremendous spear of pain shoots through my now-broken nose into the back of my brain. Before I have time to recover even slightly, Farid hits me hard in the stomach. The guards let me fall to my knees as I gasp for breath. Blood pours from my nose onto the floor.

I hear Tarighian say, "That's enough. Take him away and get rid of him. Be sure you videotape it. Make it gruesome. You know what to do."

The men roughly pull me out of the control room.

36

THERE was a seven-hour time difference between Cyprus and Washington, D.C. At precisely the moment that Sam Fisher infiltrated the shopping mall complex, Colonel Irving Lambert finished a phone call with the secretary of defense and waited impatiently at his desk for news from his Splinter Cell. He knew that Fisher had arrived safely in Cyprus, had received diving equipment from the Brits, and was on his way to Tarighian's "shopping mall" outside of Famagusta.

In anticipation of Fisher's report, Lambert had already been in discussions with not only the secretary, but also the top military brain trust at the Pentagon, the president of the United States, and the secretary of state. In turn, these people were in touch with their counterparts in the Middle East. Should a strike in Cyprus become necessary, Lambert wanted an immediate response. As of the current time, all the appropriate players were ready and willing—except for Turkey. Even in the face of proof, the Turkish authorities refused to believe that Namik Basaran was really Nasir Tarighian, mastermind and patron of one of the world's most dangerous terrorist organizations. The prosperity he had brought to southeastern Turkey was unquestionable. He had created jobs for hundreds of unemployed. He had contributed food and money to just causes. He had created a great deal of goodwill between Turkey and her neighbors. How could this man be the evil being that the United States claimed?

Lambert's intercom buzzed. "Yes?" he said, pushing the button.

"We've got some news on Horowitz," Bruford said.

"I'm on my way."

Lambert rose, grabbed his coffee cup, and rushed to the Operations Room where Bruford and other team members were working. Carly St. John had her hands on a printout that she was studying closely.

"What have you got?" Lambert asked, taking a seat at the table.

"Eli Horowitz isn't an Israeli," Bruford said. "He's from Azerbaijan. He entered Israel when he was sixteen on the pretext that he was a Jewish refugee from Russia. The Mossad has just confirmed that Horowitz—which is his real name by the way—has used a number of aliases throughout his life. When he was living in Azerbaijan, he was arrested on conspiracy charges with a group of terrorists associated with the Kurds there. Because of his age and some political connections, he was set free. On a later occasion he was arrested in Georgia in possession of a cache of illegal weapons. He was about to stand trial when he miraculously escaped from jail. It was a daring operation that involved several participants. Georgian authorities believed the jailbreak to be the work of a powerful Russian mafia."

"The Shop?"

"Very likely. That terrorist watch list he was on, when it was tardily discovered by U.S. Immigration, identified Horowitz as a mule for the Shop."

Lambert slapped the table. "Okay, so we've definitely established he's a bad guy. How the hell do we find him?"

Carly spoke up. "The Mossad has been very cooperative. They found his apartment in East Jerusalem and ransacked it. The boy left the place as if he was planning to return. All of his clothes and belongings were there—including a computer."

Lambert raised his eyebrows, and Carly wiggled hers in reply.

"And we might have something," she said. "This is a printout showing the contents of the hard drive. Although there isn't anything that directly connects him to the Shop, we've retrieved some recent e-mails that indicate he was planning something before Sarah Burns came to Israel. Most of the mail prior to two weeks ago was deleted, but the Mossad is delivering a subpoena to Horowitz's ISP as soon as they can. What we do have are some of the last communications between him and Sarah, much of which we already uncovered on Sarah's computer in Illinois, but also some e-mails between Horowitz and someone named Yuri. We've traced this Yuri's e-mail address, and the server is at the Russian-Israeli Bank in Jerusalem."

"The Russian-Israeli Bank? Is that legit?" Lambert asked.

"It is. It's a private and fairly young institution. The bank opened two years ago, and the board of directors consists of nothing but Russians."

"Interesting."

Then Carly smiled, pausing for dramatic effect. "And

here's the clincher. The bank is a subsidiary of the Swiss-Russian International Mercantile Bank."

Lambert raised his fists above his head. "Praise the Lord! We need the Israel Security Forces to get in there and tear the place apart. Now."

Bruford replied, "It's already in the works. The bank manager and its employees are going to have a rude surprise when they arrive at work in the morning—which should be happening any minute over there."

"Great work, people," Lambert said. "Now if we'd just hear something from Fisher, my ulcer might settle down."

Chip Driggers spoke up. "Colonel, there's a transmission coming through!"

Lambert rose and went over to Driggers's terminal. "Is it Sam?"

"Looks like it. He's sending some JPG files."

When the image appeared on the monitor, both men's jaws dropped.

"Holy shit, what the hell is that thing?" Driggers asked.

Lambert rubbed his eyes and looked again. "It's a god-damned Babylon supergun. We should have known. We should have *known*!"

"There are more pics coming through. Look."

The entire team gathered around the monitor, watching in awe as Fisher's captures of the Babylon Phoenix came into view. Lambert didn't waste any time running back to his office. He picked up the phone on Bruford's desk and ordered, "Get me the president."

37

NASIR Tarighian wiped the sweat from his brow and looked at his watch. The sun had completely risen, and he felt that time was running out. If the American had contacted his people during the night, it was only a matter of hours—maybe minutes—before the forces arrived to stop his plan to punish Iraq.

His advisers had been telling him for months that the plan was folly. Albert Mertens and his team were against targeting Baghdad, and his committee heads strongly protested the choosing of Iraq. Tarighian knew fully well that he might be sacrificing the Shadows as an entity to satisfy his lust for revenge. He didn't care. His most trusted colleague, Ahmed Mohammed, had said that this was a plan of "madness." But Tarighian knew he wasn't mad, at least not in the "crazy" sense. He was simply intent on allowing his wife and children to rest peacefully. If it meant that he had to die a martyr, then so be it. Many others had done the same.

He looked out the control room window and up at the

magnificent creature that was his to command. The Baby-lon Phoenix was primed and ready, calibrated to fire the MOAB at Baghdad. He was awaiting last-minute prepara-tions that Mertens assured him would take no longer than a half hour. That was forty minutes ago.

"Mertens!" he called across the room. "What the hell is going on?"

Mertens exchanged glances with Eisler, and Tarighian didn't like it. He had seen too many furtive looks between those two.

"Yes, sir?" Mertens asked calmly.

"Are we ready yet?"

"Not quite. There seems to be a problem in the engine room. I would like you to come with me to check it out. I want you to see with your own eyes the problems we are having. This rushing to fire the weapon on such short no-tice is having a domino effect."

"What kind of problem is it?"

"I'm not sure. The engineers want us down there in person. I suggest that you come with me."

"Damn," Tarighian muttered. "All right, lead the way." Farid started for the door and Tarighian said, "Yes, Farid, you come with us." The mute strongman grunted and held the door open. Once again Mertens and Eisler exchanged looks, and both men rose to head out of the control room. They followed Tarighian and Farid down the short flight of steps and walked across the platform to the bloated hy-draulics base that was supporting the Babylon Phoenix on ground level. Several of Tarighian's more loyal armed sol-diers stood nearby. They watched as Mertens opened the heavy iron door that led to the bowels of the mechanism, which were enclosed deep within.

Mertens gestured inside. "After you, sir."

Tarighian ducked his head and clambered down the steel steps into the engine room. Although illuminated by work lights, the place was darker than other areas of the compound. The monstrous engines that manipulated the hydraulics dominated the room, which pounded noisily with life. Several men were busy at control panels while two worked feverishly on one of the hydraulics.

Once the four men had entered the room and shut the door, another man wearing a *jeballa* and turban turned from the control panel and faced Tarighian.

"Ahmed!" Tarighian said. "What are you doing here?"

Ahmed Mohammed gave Tarighian a slight bow. "I have been in the complex since last night. You were too busy to notice."

"Why, I'm sorry. You should have—"

"I was concerned about your plans, Nasir. That's why I am here."

Tarighian put an arm around his Political Committee head and said, "I am happy that you are. You are just in time! This morning we shall fire the Babylon Phoenix and finally show the West that Islam will not let America and its allies control Iraq or the Middle East. In a few minutes there will no longer be a Baghdad. What do you think of that, Ahmed?"

Mohammed shook his head. "Nasir, my friend, I must tell you that we all feel you have strayed too far from the path. This insane notion you have of destroying Baghdad is nonsense. Baghdad is a Muslim city. Iraq is a Muslim country. You are blinded by your thirst for revenge. Your goals are misplaced and inappropriate. The decision has been made to relieve you of your leadership."

Tarighian blinked. He wasn't sure he had heard the

man correctly. "What did you say? I don't think you understand, Ahmed. We are ready to fire the gun *now*. We will soon be the masters of the Middle East, and we will kick out the Western dogs."

"No, Nasir, it is *you* who does not understand. You were once a great warrior and leader. You brought the Shadows to unprecedented glory. But you veered from the path of true Islamic spirituality. You live like a Westerner. You do business with Westerners. You have friends that are Westerners. You constantly seek publicity and you crave money. In the eyes of Allah you have sinned a great deal."

Tarighian took a step back. "What are you saying? You can't take the Shadows away from me! You can't take *me* away from the Shadows!"

Mohammed had a sad, cold expression on his face. "Yes, Nasir, we can."

Tarighian didn't expect Albert Mertens to lift a Glock, suddenly point it at the side of Tarighian's head, and squeeze the trigger. Nasir Tarighian's skull exploded, spraying a mass of blood and gray matter onto the wall beside them. His body collapsed to the floor.

This was Eisler's cue to act. In a swift, unexpected maneuver, Eisler drew his Swamp Monster knife, grabbed Farid's hair through the turban, pulled the man's head back, and sliced the exposed throat from ear to ear. Farid's reflexes were abrupt and forceful—he swung around and slammed his free arm into Eisler, knocking him back onto a desk. The big man wanted his assailant's hide, but it was too late. Blood gushed from the open wound below his chin as if it was a spigot. Farid's grunts became gurgles as he clutched his neck in a helpless attempt to close the lesion. Then, in a rage, he tried to grab hold of Eisler's leg

but clumsily knocked over a computer monitor instead.
Eisler scrambled to the floor on the other side of the desk
and backed away from the man-monster bellowing in
front of him.

Farid threw himself forward, trying to go around the
desk, but he stumbled and fell to the floor. Emitting a sickening, choking noise, Tarighian's bodyguard thrashed violently for nearly a minute until he began to lose steam.
Finally, after what seemed to be an eternity, Farid lay
dead.

The others in the room stared at the carnage in disbe-
lief but looked up at Ahmed Mohammed, Albert Mertens,
and Heinrich Eisler with newfound respect.

Mohammed looked at Mertens and said, "As leader of
the Shadows, I now give you the authority to recalibrate
the Babylon Phoenix and point it at the target we spoke
about."

Mertens put away his gun and nodded. "Thank you, sir.
This is really the best decision." He turned to the workers
and said, "Take these bodies and put them inside the engine." Four of the men came forward, picked up
Tarighian's corpse, opened the engine doors, and shoved
the lifeless form inside. There the hydraulics would mash
it to a pulp. Then they did the same with Farid.

Mertens, Eisler, and Mohammed left the engine room
and stood against the closed door. Tarighian's armed men
watched them with curiosity. Where was their leader?

Before anyone could register what was happening, two
dozen men leaned over the circular balcony rail and fired
AK-47s on Tarighian's loyalists. The sudden burst of
noise reverberated through the complex, frightening the
rest of the workers to a standstill. It was as if hell had
rained down from the heavens, chopping up any living

thing that dared to be in the way of the ammunition. The loyalists never had a chance to aim their weapons for a return volley. After twenty seconds Tarighian's loyalists lay in pools of their own blood. The men faithful to Mohammed ran down the ramp from the upper balcony and stood at attention, awaiting further orders.

Ahmed Mohammed shouted to everyone. "Sons of Allah! Hear me!" Every worker in the complex turned to look at him. "Nasir Tarighian is dead! I will be assuming leadership of the Shadows from now on. Continue your good work and Allah will reward you."

Some of the workers cheered. Others were confused. Only a few were disappointed.

Mertens looked at Mohammed and explained, "As you can hear, Tarighian's objectives were not very popular."

"No, they weren't," Mohammed said.

As they returned to the control room, Mertens asked Eisler, "Are you all right?"

"I am fine." He wiped his knife clean on his trouser leg and sheathed it.

Mertens nodded and said, "Recalibrate the weapon for a new target."

"Yes, sir," Eisler said. "And what is the new target?"

"Jerusalem."

38

THE two armed goons march me up the ramp and onto the perimeter balcony. As we head for the double doors, I notice several guys with AK-47s crouched below the rail as if they're waiting for something. The one closest to us nods at my two guards, and they give him a silent acknowledgment. What the hell's going on? If I didn't know better I'd say there's going to be some kind of rebellious action happening soon. Do I smell an uprising in the air? Is that something I can use to my advantage?

I've lost track of how much time is left on the frag grenades. It *has* to be nearly forty-five minutes since I set them and was caught. I suspect that there's less than five or ten minutes left to go. I really don't want to be on this balcony when they go off—it's liable to collapse.

"Sam?" It's Lambert. The tiny voice in my ear. "Sam? Are you there?"

Shit. I can't respond.

One of my captors uses his keycard to open the double doors and we walk through. I don't particularly relish being marched to my death, so I need to think of something quickly. The guy with the keycard has my stuff. They didn't remove the OPSAT, but it's not going to do me much good with my hands tied behind my back.

Lambert speaks again. "Sam? If you can hear me, get the hell out of that shopping mall. The UN forces will be there in about ten minutes, maybe sooner! If you can read me, get the hell out, *now*!"

I'd like to do just that, Colonel.

We walk through the empty department store, and we're now level with the upper half of the supergun barrel, which is poking through the opening in the middle of the shopping mall complex. They haven't opened the domed ceiling or raised the supergun to its maximum height yet. My fascination with machinery and weapons makes me want to stay and watch them shoot the thing, but I know I can't do that. I don't want to be caught inside this place when the cavalry arrives.

They take me around the supergun into one of the three storefront wings. A steel door marked "Maintenance" in Turkish and in English appears to be our destination. Abbott takes a set of keys from his pocket while Costello sticks his AK-47 in my lower back. Abbott unlocks the door and holds it open for his pal and me. Once we're inside, I see why Tarighian called this the "incinerator room"—there's one dominating the far wall. I figure they throw their garbage into it. The room is also full of hardware and tools, a table saw, and a few of those three-wheelie carts.

There's also a video camera sitting on a tripod in the middle of the room. A couple of floodlights on stands point to an area of the floor near the incinerator. I wonder how many executions they've put on tape or if I'm their debut production.

Abbott opens the incinerator's grilled door. The flames

inside cast a golden glow over the room. I figure they think this makes their home movies more aesthetically pleasing. Abbott then turns on the floodlights and checks the video camera. He looks through the viewfinder, makes sure it's pointed in the proper place, and then says "Put him in place" in Arabic. These guys aren't Turkish.

Costello jabs his gun into my back again, pushing me over to the "stage." Abbott presses the Record button, the camera's red light turns on, and then he moves to join us in front of the lens.

We're standing in a line with me in the middle—Abbott on my right, Costello on my left—facing the camera. Abbott announces to the audience in Arabic, "This is American spy Sam Fisher. He is to die today for waging war against Islam."

Suddenly we hear the sound of gunfire in the distance. It's intense, too, as if an entire platoon is firing machine guns at enemy forces. Abbott and Costello look at each other and smile. "We have a new leader," Costello says.

Now's my chance. I hip-check Abbott—I ram my hip-bone as hard as I can into his, knocking him sideways. At the same time I lodge my right boot on the inside of his left leg, causing him to fall to the floor. Before Costello can react, I raise my left boot, run it down his right shin, and stomp hard on his foot. I take a step to my right, turn, and then kick the ever-loving *shit* out of his right knee. I hear the bones snap as he screams and falls to the ground.

By now Abbott is scrambling to his feet and trying to level his AK-47 at me. I turn to him and kick him hard in the face with my right boot. He falls onto his back, dropping the rifle.

Part of my training included perfecting a maneuver that allows me to roll my legs through my tied arms—like jumping rope backwards. You have to be *really* limber to do it, and I spent weeks getting to where I could just manage it. It's possible to execute the move while doing a forward roll—you just have to throw your arms around your body in the opposite direction from the way legs are going. Scrunching yourself up into a ball beforehand makes it easier. So, very quickly, I squat, form my body into a ball, and perform that forward roll, bringing my arms over and around my body. Perfect. I jump to my feet and now my tied hands are in front of me.

Abbott is on his knees now, trying to get up for a second time. Another kick to the face sends him to Neverland. For good measure I scoot the AK-47 across the floor out of his reach. I then turn my attention to Costello, who's writhing in agony on the floor. I raise my left boot above his head and bring it down as hard as I can. No more pain for him.

All this occurred in five point four seconds.

I glance at my OPSAT, check the timer, and see that two minutes are left before the frag grenades go off. I go back to Abbott and empty his pockets, retrieving my knife, Five-seveN, goggles, and other equipment. He left my SC-20K over by the incinerator, and I'll pick that up on my way out. But first I have to cut the rope around my hands. I move to the table saw, switch it on, and carefully hold my wrists over the spinning blade. I nick the rope just enough for me to unravel it and I'm free.

I gather all my stuff and get the hell out of there. I open the door carefully, peer outside to make sure no one is around, and step into the corridor. I run to the edge of the central area just in time to witness the domed ceiling parting. Simultaneously the supergun's huge barrel begins to rise vertically as the hydraulics lift the entire weapon flush with the ground floor. For a moment I have to stand and watch the thing, it's so goddamned awesome. Eventually the tip of the barrel protrudes through the domed opening. The machinery inside the massive breech then begins to rumble, and I see the barrel tilt and point in a southeasterly direction.

Then—*wham-wham-wham*! I hear my frag grenades go off in a succession of explosions. I'm not sure what kind of damage they'll do, but I hope it will delay firing the weapon for a bit. I run around the supergun to the wing where I originally entered and head for the glass doors I smashed earlier. The floor beneath me shakes, and I hear what sounds like an earthquake. Hoorah!—the perimeter balcony must have collapsed as I had hoped. That will surely cause some confusion.

I make it outside into the sunlight. No one is around. The electrical company van is gone, so I'm going to have to hoof it.

At that moment I hear the sound of aircraft. I look northward and see a squadron of six planes heading this way. Time to move!

I run as fast as I can out of the parking lot and toward the front gate. Two guards are there, weapons in hand. I have no time to argue with these guys, so I draw my Five-seveN, stop, assume a firing stance, and pop them—*one*, *two*—before they have a chance to ask me for my "papers." I resume speed and hurdle over the gate.

Once I'm out of the compound, I breathe a little easier but I keep moving. I climb the hill overlooking the site, the one I had used early this morning, and figure this is as good a place to watch the main attraction as any.

I press the implant in my throat. "Colonel?"

"Sam? My God, where have you been?"

"Uh, a little tied up. But I'm out now. I can see the planes."

"Thank goodness. You had me worried. Get to the Famagusta docks. Captain Martin will meet you there in his patrol boat and take you back to Dhekelia. We have transportation to Israel all lined up for you."

"Thanks, Colonel. Any news on Sarah?"

"Not yet, Sam. But get going."

I sign off but linger a few moments to watch. I recognize two F/A-18E Super Hornets leading the formation—leave it to the U.S. to do so—followed by two British Sea Harrier F/A Mk 2s. It takes me a moment to identify the other two planes and then realize they're F-16s from the Turkish air force! I'm happy to see the Turks getting involved, which must have been a major diplomatic coup for Lambert.

The Super Hornets let loose a couple of Maverick ASMs, which score direct hits on the supergun. The explosions are immense, and I feel the heat wave all the way up here. The Harriers drop an array of bombs I don't recognize, but they produce magnificent blasts all over the complex. The Turks follow with another spread of bombs, but the smoke is way too thick for me to see what they are.

By now the entire shopping mall is engulfed in smoke and fire. The only thing I can see is the supergun's barrel poking out of the dark cloud. The six fighters circle around, bank, and head for the complex for another round of strikes.

Suddenly there's a huge *boom* and the entire earth around me shakes. It's like a sonic blast only it's right in front of me. My first thought is that I'm in the middle of a ten-point Richter-scale earthquake, but my second thought is even worse.

They've managed to fire the Babylon Phoenix!

I find I'm lying on my back, a bit stunned and squinting into the sky. Then I witness something I'll never forget as long as I live.

The supergun's payload is shooting up into the sky, soaring high above the fighters at a tremendous speed. *My God*, I think, *it's all over*. The bad guys win after all. But then I see the two Super Hornets veer off their courses and head up and in pursuit of the MOAB. I'm able to think to reach into my Osprey, grab my portable binoculars, and watch the drama unfold in the blue sky.

The MOAB is over the sea now, disappearing from view, and the two American fighters become tiny dots following it. Then I see two air-to-air missiles—no, *four* AAMs—leave the fighters. They're probably AIM-120 AMRAAM Slammers, supersonic fire-and-forget missiles.

Holy shit! The sky over the sea bursts into a bright orange-and-red fireball, one that certainly engulfs the two fighters. I'm aware that I'm not breathing for a moment as I watch the flaming horror fall in slow motion to the Mediterranean. All I can think of is what heroes those men in the fighters are. They sacrificed themselves to take out the MOAB and succeeded against tremendous odds.

I get to my feet and watch the debris hit the water.

"Sam? What's happened? Talk to me!" Lambert calls.

I press the implant. "We lost our two fighters, but the guys are heroes. They shot the MOAB right out of the sky. It fell into the sea."

"Christ. What about Tarighian's complex?"

I turned back to look at the inferno below me. The remaining fighters had apparently suspended their attacks after the supergun fired. Now they swing back around and continue to bomb the shopping mall to smithereens. In fact, the supergun's barrel is no longer in view. It must have collapsed while my back was turned.

"You don't have to worry about it, Colonel," I say. "All gone."

I can see Lambert rubbing the top of his head and sighing with relief. The rest of the Third Echelon team is most likely pulling out the champagne.

"How did you get the Turks to cooperate?" I ask.

"Carly created a slideshow file that presented all the photos you took, backed with all the written evidence, and we sent it to the Turkish government. Needless to say, she did a convincing job."

"Of course she did."

"What about you? Are you all right?"

"I'm fine, Colonel. But now I have to get to the docks and catch a ride to save my daughter."

"Go for it, Sam."

39

I arrive in Tel Aviv that afternoon and have another twenty-four hours to acknowledge to Sarah's captors that I'm in Israel. Before making the call, though, I have a conversation with Captain Abraham Weiss of the Israel Security Forces in the back of an unmarked black Lexus. Captain Weiss met me at Ben-Gurion Airport, where I was whisked away as a government VIP without the rigmarole of Israel's tight security and Immigration checks.

"I've been in contact with your people," Weiss says as the car rolls out of the airport. "And we've been working around the clock to locate your daughter. I'm happy to say we know where she is. At least we think we do."

My heart nearly leaps out of my chest, for I was really sweating it out in the short plane ride from Cyprus. "Where?" I ask.

"We're nearly one hundred percent certain she's in an abandoned warehouse very near the small airport north of Jerusalem." Weiss speaks confident English with a heavy Israeli accent. I have a good feeling about him and did so from the moment we met. I have great respect for the Israelis' security personnel. They live day in and day out with the threat of constant danger. The pressure must be immense.

"We got lucky when we raided the Russian-Israeli Bank this morning," he continues. "At first it seemed as if the bank was completely legitimate and we'd hit a dead end until we began to examine real estate transactions. Most of them were perfectly reasonable, but then one of our analysts questioned the validity of a couple of buildings because of where they are located. One is this warehouse. The Russian-Israeli Bank owns it. However, our analyst happens to have performed some work in another building not far from this location, and he remembered that it's on a street full of derelict buildings. They're all due for demolition sometime next year. We made a leap of faith and posted a hidden surveillance team outside the warehouse. Within an hour Eli Horowitz was seen leaving the building. He returned almost an hour later. The surveillance team is certain there are others in the building with him, but it's not clear how many."

"I don't care how many assholes are in there," I say. "I'm going to wipe them clean."

Captain Weiss shrugged, not getting the poor attempt at humor. "I've been told by my superiors that this is really the U.S.'s show, although we'll be supplying you with a backup team. In other words, you're in charge. We'd like to arrest the men responsible for your daughter's kidnapping and for the murder of Rivka Cohen, but should an accident befall any of them, there would be no questions asked by our government."

That's his way of saying I'm free to do whatever the hell I want with the kidnappers. I probably have Lambert to thank for that.

"I want to go in tonight. Alone," I say.

"I assumed you would say that," Weiss says. "Let's meet your backup team first."

After a forty-minute drive we reach the northern out-skirts of Jerusalem and stop at a staging point in front of an auto parts factory. We're in an industrial area, and the captain says the warehouse is two miles away. A team of ten Shin Bet Special Ops soldiers are here, equipped and ready to go. Shin Bet, or Shabak, is a branch of the ISF responsible for internal security. They spend a lot of time protecting government officials, preventing violent insurrection, gathering intelligence, pinpointing terrorist cells and dealing with them. Shin Bet's activities are always classified. Their job is a lot like mine, so I feel as if I'm with family.

They appear well equipped, too. I really like their replacement for the Uzi, the Tavor "Bull Pup" Assault Rifle, made by Israel Military Industries. It comes in a few different designs, each one suited for specific needs. One of the men shows me his weapon and says it's the Micro T.A.R., which is uniquely configured for security forces and special missions. They use a 30-round magazine of standard NATO 5.56mm ammunition.

Captain Weiss hands me a cell phone and tells me to call the kidnappers' number. He says the phone is untraceable just in case they try to figure out where I'm calling from. I bring up the stored number on my OPSAT and dial. I get a recorded message from a man with a heavy Russian accent.

"Mr. Fisher, if you are in Jerusalem, please indicate so at the sound of the beep, and we will be in touch with you shortly."

When I hear the tone I say, "This is Sam Fisher. I'm not in Israel yet but will be tomorrow morning. I'm traveling from a great distance. I will call again before noon and will await your instructions. Please keep my daughter safe." I disconnect, look at the captain, and ask, "Now what?"

"We wait until nightfall. The team will deploy around the warehouse, out of sight," he says. "I understand you have a subdermal implant for communicating with your superiors in Washington?"

My, my, nothing's sacred in the intelligence community. "That's right," I say.

"We will have your people configure the transmissions so the team can hear you. I've already spoken to your colonel about this. That way, you can call the shots should you be required to lead the assault team into the building."

"That's mighty accommodating of you."

Someone provides kosher turkey sandwiches for us, and we spend a few hours in the captain's Lexus. We talk about the security situation in his country and the different plans of attack for combating terrorism. Mid-evening I take the opportunity to grab two hours of sleep. When I wake I find it's just after ten o'clock. In the meantime, Carly St. John has provided me with the warehouse blueprints via my OPSAT. I now have a complete map of the building, showing entrances and exits, corridors, and rooms. I'm itching to get going, but I decide to wait two more hours, hoping to catch them in their pajamas. Finally, at midnight, I tell the captain it's time to move.

"You know they're probably setting a trap for you," the captain says.

I shrug. "Trap, Shmap. Let's go."

"You ready?"

"Absolutely."

He gives the order and we move out in separate unmarked civilian cars toward the site. A minute later we arrive at a crossroad. The captain points to the new road and says, "It's that way about a mile. We'll get out here and go the rest of the way on foot."

The drivers park the cars behind various empty buildings, and we proceed to hike through undeveloped terrain off-road. There's not a lot of trees and natural cover here. Israel is an arid country and it's hot and dry at this time of year. For a Mediterranean destination, I've never found Israel to be particularly pretty. I guess it is if you like sand and rocks. The land is fertile enough, although I can't imagine why it was once considered the "Promised Land."

I separate from the Shin Bet as we get closer to the warehouse. I want to make the first approach on my own.

"Mr. Fisher?" It's the captain's voice in my ear. "Do you read me?"

"Loud and clear," I say, pressing the implant.

"There are three cars parked in the back of the warehouse, under a tarp. A Ferrari, a Jaguar, and a Chevy Cavalier."

"Then there's probably not too many men inside."

"That's what I'm thinking, too."

I can now see the warehouse, but I'm well hidden behind some rocks, fifty feet away. I know the Shin Bet have surrounded the building, but I see no signs of them. These guys are good.

The building looks as if it hasn't seen a human being in thirty years. It consists of a large space that takes up most of the structure. From Carly's blueprints I understand there's a second floor with a window. This second floor is more of a "loft" that hangs over a third of the first floor space with a stand-alone staircase connecting the two. Along two sides of the building are corridors with rooms—old offices, I imagine.

"How do you want to handle it?" the captain asks.

"I'm going to find a way in, probably from the second

floor. Stand down until I give the order. Then storm the place with everything you've got. Until I find Sarah and make sure she's all right, I don't want them to have any indication that you're out here."

"Understood," he replies.

I emerge from my hiding place but stick to the shadows. There are no lights on around the building so that's a plus. The first thing I do is a quick recon around the warehouse. The front door is a rusty steel job with faded paint and lettering. The few windows are painted over. In the back I find the three cars covered by a tarp and another steel door. Up high I see another window, one that's not painted over. That's my target.

I take my cigar holder and rope and fashion a grappling hook. I sling the thing around and toss it, catching it onto the roof on the first try. I give it a tug and then climb up the side of the building. When I reach the window I peer inside.

I see the loft; it's full of junk and extends maybe thirty feet. A lone lantern burns on the floor next to an empty bedroll. I can't discern anything beyond the edge of the loft, mainly because of the junk piles. The main thing is that no one is there. Good. I wrap the rope around my waist so I can use both hands as I hang by the window. I draw my Five-seveN, flip on the T.A.K. laser microphone with my thumb, and point the barrel at the glass. The square in the center of the camera screen doesn't turn red—it's not picking up any sound. Excellent. I switch off the T.A.K. and holster the pistol, then try to raise the window. It doesn't budge. The decades-old paint has hardened, but the window itself doesn't appear to be locked. I draw my combat knife and chisel away on the window edges, finally getting to where I can stick the blade through the slits. I sheath the knife and try the window again. This time it moves a little. I rearrange myself so I can put my weight into the very center of the top windowsill and push it up with a forceful thrust. The window gives way and slides open, a bit too noisily for my comfort. But it's enough for me to snake through. I unwrap the rope from my waist and go through the window, feet first.

Once I'm inside, I carefully move to the edge of the loft and look down. It's a wide-open, empty warehouse except for a lot of junk stacked along the sides of the room—mostly old appliances like refrigerators and stoves. I see a couple of doors leading to other parts of the building.

There's no one around.

A set of unsupported wooden stairs leads down from the loft. I start to take them, but they creak loudly. Instead I leap off the steps and land on all fours with a quiet thud. One single noise is better than a series of horrible creaks.

I focus on the door I know leads to a series of rooms in a corridor. Once again I take the Five-seveN and flip on the T.A.K. I aim it at the door and this time the screen turns red. Somebody is talking behind the door. I creep to the wall, flatten myself, and listen.

The voices are muffled, but they're speaking in Russian, that much I can tell. I consider storming through the door and blasting the hell out of them, but before I can act, I hear footsteps approaching.

The door swings open, hiding me behind it. Two men emerge and walk toward the middle of the warehouse. They've got AK-47s around their shoulders.

"Turn on the lights, Yuri," one says in Russian. "I can't see a fucking thing."

The one called Yuri walks toward the front of the building. Shit. They're going to hit the lights and here I am standing behind the door. So what do I do? I slip around the door without being seen and go into the corridor, just as the lights come on.

The corridor is well lit, but there's no one else here. I see three rooms. The doors to two rooms are open, probably the Russians' quarters—I see cots and signs of day-to-day living. One door is closed. I flip on the thermal vision in my goggles and see an indication that there's a warm body lying horizontally inside the room. Could it be Sarah? I decide to give it a try.

The door is locked, of course. With one ear trained to the open door at the end of the corridor—I can hear the Russians talking in the warehouse—I carefully take my lock picks and try them. After three attempts, I have it open.

Sarah is inside, lying on a cot.

40

"SARAH!" I whisper. She looks up, startled. Her eyes widen when she sees me. Of course, I look like an alien from outer space in my uniform and goggles. I raise the goggles so she can see my face.

"It's me," I say.

"Dad!" She lunges and grabs hold of me as if I'm the last man on earth.

"Shhh!" I whisper. "You've got to be quiet. I'm gonna get you out of here."

"Oh, Dad, I knew you'd come!" She starts to cry and I stroke her dark hair.

"Are you all right? Did they hurt you?"

"A little. I'm . . . I'm a little weak."

"Can you walk?"

"I'll try."

She gets to her feet, but I can see she's very unsteady. I'll have to carry her. I let her lean against the wall as I peer out the door to the corridor. It's still clear.

"Honey, wait here, I'll be back for you," I say.

"Don't leave me!" She almost panics.

"Sarah, the bad guys are right in there. I have to take care of them first. I promise I'll be back for you."

She takes a deep breath and wipes her face. "Okay."

"That's my girl. Don't make a sound."

I leave and close the door behind me, unlocked. I take the Five-seveN, attach the suppressor, and shoot out the two overhead lights in the corridor. I'm plunged into darkness, so I lower my goggles and turn on the night vision.

I peer through the door to the warehouse and see that the two Russians have stepped outside through the front. The place is empty. I quickly enter the space, drop to one knee, and aim the Five-seveN at the work lights. I shoot out all six of them. Now the only illumination in the place comes from the open front door, and it's not much.

I run and find the steps leading to the loft. I quickly ascend the stairs and make it to the second floor just as the two men return. I quietly swing the SC-20K off my shoulder and ready it.

"Hey, did you turn off the lights?" one of them asks the other.

"No." I see the one called Yuri go back to the light switches and flick them. "What the hell?"

"Did we lose power?"

"I . . . I don't think so. Vlad, quickly!" They start for the front door, picking up on the possibility that I may have arrived earlier than expected. I rise, aim the rifle at the door and prepare to pick them off—when I feel the muzzle of a gun at the back of my head.

"Don't move!" shouts a voice. "Drop the weapon! Yuri! Vlad! I have him!"

The two Russians stop and look to the loft. "Eli? Is that you?"

"Yes. Drop it!" I let the rifle fall. "Raise your hands!" I do so.

Eli. Eli Horowitz, the one who betrayed my daughter. He's standing behind me with a gun to my head. The nearby lantern casts a dim glow over us, and now the Russians can surely see me.

"Bring him down!" one of them shouts.

"Get moving," Horowitz says. "To the stairs."

I slowly walk toward the stairs as Horowitz follows, the gun in one hand and the lantern in the other. A bright light flicks on below. Apparently one of the Russians found a floodlight that isn't connected to the main work lights switch. Now the room is dimly illuminated.

"You're early, Mr. Fisher!" the one called Yuri says. "We had a surprise party prepared for you, but it's not ready yet."

"Yeah, come back in the morning," Vlad says, laughing.

When I'm at the top of the steps, I abruptly step back into Horowitz, grab his gun arm, easily pull the weapon out of his hand, and then throw his body over my shoulder onto the stairs. He lands in the middle, on his back, and the entire staircase collapses from age and his weight. Horowitz yelps in pain as he falls to the floor amidst the debris.

Before I can do much besides leap for cover, both Russians let loose with their AK-47s. The bullets rattle everything in the loft as I crouch behind an old stove.

"Mr. Fisher?" I hear Captain Weiss in my ear. "What's happening?"

"Bring in the men, Captain!" I order, pressing my implant. "I'm up in the loft, there's three of them on the ground floor!"

More bullets whiz at me as I dart from behind the

stove. I feel the heat of a round snapping at my right boot, too close for comfort. I make it to a more strategic position behind a large refrigerator, though, and take a moment to catch my breath. I turn off the night vision and see that the two Russians have taken cover behind the appliances on opposite sides of the floor. Shit, they'll be able to pick off the Shin Bet as they come through the door.

"Captain!" I say. "Don't come through the front do—"

But it's too late. The front door bursts open and three men rush inside. The two Russians are surprised but have the presence of mind to draw their fire toward the intruders. The three Shin Bet are hit and fall to the floor.

I reach into the Osprey and pull out two smoke grenades. I activate them to explode on contact and then throw them into the middle of the space. They burst loudly, quickly enveloping the room with thick, black smoke.

The Russians below me fire blindly into the middle of the room and up in my direction. I take the risk of jumping off the loft, landing hard on the floor. I hear windows breaking in other parts of the building—probably in the back rooms—as more men penetrate the hideout by other means. I run for cover as the Russians continue to fire in all directions. There are shouts and bursts of gunfire in the back of the building—were there other kidnappers inside? In the cover of the smoke I rush across the floor and return to the dark corridor. I burst into Sarah's room and find her lying by the cot. I pick her up in my arms and carry her out. When I reach the warehouse again, more Shin Bet have entered and taken cover, shooting in the direction of the hidden Russians. The noise is intense, and I feel my daughter shaking against me. I can't go that way, so I run through the corridor to the back door of the building.

More Shin Bet have broken it down and are rushing inside. I let them through, and then Sarah and I leave the building, out into the fresh air. I run a good thirty yards from the warehouse before I stop and place her on the ground.

"Sarah, honey, talk to me!"

"Dad!" She isn't letting go.

I raise my goggles and finally get a good look at her. She has some bruises on her arms and around her face.

"What did those bastards do to you?"

"They hurt me with pliers," she sobs. "I didn't want to give them your secret number, but I couldn't take it, Dad. I couldn't take it."

I hold her close and stroke her head. "It's all right, Sarah. You did the right thing. No one can handle that. But you're going to be all right now."

Captain Weiss and another soldier appear behind me. "Mr. Fisher? Is she okay?" Weiss asks.

I nod, but she's not about to let go of me.

"Sergeant Marcus here will take her to safety," Weiss says.

I pick up Sarah again. "Sarah, honey, this soldier will take you away from here."

"Don't go!" she cries.

"Sarah, I promise I'll be right back to be with you and take you home. But first I have to go in there and play angry father. They can't do what they've done to my little girl!"

She smiles but still clings to me. I turn to the sergeant and he takes her into his own arms. Sarah doesn't protest. The sergeant runs with her down the road as Captain Weiss hands me a Tavor Micro Assault Weapon.

"Would you like this?"

"You bet."

I take it, lower my goggles, and rush for the back door.

The inside of the warehouse is a firestorm. I take cover behind more junk on the side and see that the two Russians are perched behind strong cover, firing at us with impunity. Another dead Shin Bet lies on the floor, and the rest of the team is firing from behind whatever protection they can find. I take aim with the Tavor and shoot, but the two targets are very well protected. The one mistake they made, though, is that they have no way to escape. Eventually they're going to run out of ammo.

Then one of the Shin Bet throws a grenade at the wall where a Russian is holed up. When it explodes, I hear the man cry out in pain. The Russian, obviously wounded, makes a last ditch attempt to kill some of us. He stands— it's the one called Vlad—then steps from behind a refrigerator and wildly fires his AK-47. The Shin Bet easily pick him off, and the man falls, hitting the floor with a *splat*.

The smoke from my grenade has begun to clear, and the other kidnapper continues to shoot at us. This time I take one of my own frag grenades, set it to explode on contact, and toss it toward him. When it goes off, the Russian's gunfire ends abruptly. All is quiet for a moment. I hear the captain give an order, and two Shin Bet run to inspect the damage. They rummage around and eventually pull Yuri's limp body from the junk. They drag him to the clear area and toss him to the floor. Another *splat*.

I move to the dead kidnappers and look at their faces. I don't recognize them.

"Search the rest of the building," the captain orders his men. He approaches me and asks if I know them.

"I've never seen them before," I answer. "They called each other Vlad and Yuri."

"We'll be able to identify them soon enough."

I turn back to the rubble of the fallen staircase and realize that someone is missing. "Where did—? There was another one here earlier," I say.

"My sergeant tells me they got one of them in the back. Shot him when they came through the windows."

I move toward the back rooms and find the body of the kidnapper in question. He's a young man, shot several times in the chest, but he's not Eli Horowitz. One of the Shin Bet is going through his wallet and papers.

"You have an ID on him yet?" I ask.

"Yes, sir. His name is Noel Brooks. Lived in East Jerusalem."

I join the search through the rest of the building but stop momentarily to consult Carly's blueprint.

"Hey, there's a trapdoor to a basement in this place," I tell the men. I point and lead them in the direction where I believe it to be. Sure enough, I find it near the back entrance. One of the soldiers opens the large trap, revealing a set of stairs descending to a dark basement. I follow two men down and switch on my night vision.

The place is moldy and dusty. It's full of scrap metal and pieces of broken bathroom fixtures—sinks and bathtubs. The air is foul and I can't imagine anyone being down here for more than ten minutes. The Shin Bet soldiers shine flashlights around the room and look behind some of the junk.

"Nothing here, sir," one of them says.

"Yeah," I say. "Carry on, I'll stay and take a closer look."

The men ascend the stairs and disappear. I stand in the center of the basement and slowly circle in place. Just for grins I switch my goggles to thermal vision in the hopes that I'll catch a breathing body. Nothing. However, just before I switch back to night vision, I notice some heat signatures on the floor. I bend to examine them more closely and realize they're not heat signatures at all but rather footprints left on the dusty floor. I switch to fluorescent mode and pick up more indications of disturbance in the dust. I can now trace an imaginary line along the footprints that leads to a corner of the room where more dilapidated kitchen appliances are piled. There's a lot of junk in-between so I shove stuff out of the way, making a clear path to the area. Eventually I have to climb over a pile of rubble to get there.

I see three old refrigerators, several sinks, two stoves . . . all of it appears to be from the sixties or seventies. I open each of the refrigerators and find them empty. I try the stoves next and there's nothing inside them. I'm about to give up when I notice that a bathtub is leaning sideways against the wall, tub-side in. I reach over and pull the thing down.

Inside is Eli Horowitz, cowering in fright. My Tavor is in his face faster than he can blink.

"Don't shoot!" he cries.

"Get the fuck out of there and keep your hands where I can see them."

The young man scrambles out of the tub and raises his arms. With one hand I frisk him. I don't find anything, but I'm intentionally rough on his groin. He winces but stays silent.

Once I'm satisfied that he's unarmed, I grab him by the shirt collar and lift him off the ground. His eyes widen with fright as I growl, "I ought to kill you right here. I ought to snap your neck in two and leave you to rot, you filthy little shit." I swear I'm about to do just that, too, but the look of fear in the kid's face stops me. He may be twenty-three years old, but right now he looks thirteen.

I let go of his shirt and he falls to the floor. He grovels in front of me, muttering, "I'm sorry, I'm sorry."

"Get up, asshole." I pull him to his feet and shake him. "Pull yourself together." He sniffs, wipes his nose, and nods.

I bring Eli Horowitz upstairs and take him outside. The Shin Bet's vehicles have been brought to the warehouse, and I see Sarah sitting in the back of one. I lead Horowitz to Captain Weiss and say, "Here's a live one for you. I think you'll find he's willing to tell you everything."

Horowitz's eyes move to the car where Sarah sits.

"Please, sir," he says to me. "I'd like to tell her I'm sorry."

"I don't think so," I answer. "You're lucky I didn't cut your balls off when I found you."

But Sarah calls out, "Eli!"

She opens the car door but remains sitting, a blanket around her, and gestures for us to come over there. What the hell, I think. I take the boy to her but keep a firm grip on his neck.

"Sarah," he says. "I'm really sorry . . . for everything. I didn't . . . I really didn't think . . ."

My daughter manages to find the strength to stand and face him. Before he can finish his meandering thought, she spits at him.

"Screw you, Eli," she says. Then she falls back into the seat and wraps the blanket around her.

"I'll take him from here, sir," one of the Shin Bet says. Horowitz is handcuffed and led away.

AFTER an overnight stay in Tel Aviv, I pick up Sarah at a military hospital located at Ben-Gurion Airport. The doctor tells me that she's undernourished and very weak but otherwise in pretty good shape, all things considered. Sarah had undertaken a hunger strike for nearly a week but wisely kept drinking fluids. If she hadn't done so, she'd have been severely dehydrated and very ill. With a few days of rest and a slow buildup of food intake, she should be back to health in no time.

The psychological effects, however, might take years to overcome. The two Russians, who were identified quickly by the Mossad, apparently tortured her to get my contact information. I won't detail what they did, but suffice it to say it involved pliers and a hammer. Thank goodness nothing is broken or maimed—just a lot of bruises that will eventually heal.

Eli Horowitz spilled his guts as soon as the Shin Bet had him in custody. He revealed that he worked for the Shop and there had been a standing order to find me and eliminate me. The only way to do so was through Sarah. I made a full report to Lambert, who is now making arrangements to keep a permanent bodyguard on duty for my daughter, no matter where she is. I realize the odds of this happening again are small, but I'll certainly rest easier.

As for the Shop, the Swiss-Russian International Mercantile Banks in Zurich and Baku were cleaned out, and everyone associated with them has been interrogated and/or arrested. Unfortunately, the top thugs of the organization, including mastermind Andrei Zdrok, have escaped. No one knows where they are, but I'm sure we'll hear from them sooner or later. A major concern for all of us is how our security might have been breached. The Shop had a hit list of Splinter Cells—how did they get it? I'm sure this will be a priority for me in the near future.

The Shadows is a crippled organization. Nothing was left of the shopping mall complex—or the Babylon

Phoenix—and over a hundred of the men working there were killed. It's unclear if the terrorists have the capacity to regroup and elect a new leader, but one thing is for sure—they'll have a much harder time obtaining funding. The Turkish came out of the situation with egg on their faces, but in the end they owned up to the mistakes made with regard to Namik Basaran, aka Nasir Tarighian. The Iranian government sent the Turks a congratulatory note, thanking them for uprooting Tarighian and doing the job of getting rid of him. It saved Iran the trouble. Ironically, though, they didn't send the U.S. a thank-you card.

Later in the morning Sarah and I board a military jet to take us to Washington. A couple of young U.S. Marines push her in a wheelchair and lavish her with a lot of attention, which she loves. She's beginning to eat and, more important, starting to smile and laugh again. She's tough, like her old man, so I expect her to bounce back relatively quickly.

We settle into our seats and wait the obligatory twenty minutes before the plane is ready to lift off. Sarah takes my hand and rests her head against my shoulder. She yawns and then sighs heavily.

"I'm glad you're okay," I say. "If anything had happened to you . . ."

"Shhh," she whispers.

I chuckle and say, "All right, I won't make a big deal out of it. At least not until we get home."

As the plane lifts off, she says, quietly, "I love you, Dad."

I answer, "I love you, too, kid," but she's already asleep.

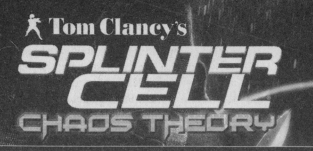

Tom Clancy's SPLINTER CELL CHAOS THEORY

Coming to All Next-Gen Consoles and PC

www.splintercell.com